SOLOMON'S DREAMS
THE HUNTING AT HUNTINGTON

ERIC SUDDOTH

RISING SMOKE PUBLISHING

Unless otherwise indicated, Scripture quotations are from:
Holy Bible, New International Version®, NIV©
1973, 1978, 1984, 2011 by Biblica, Inc. ®
Used by permission. All rights reserved worldwide.

Rising Smoke Publishing
ISBN 978-1-949869-01-9

Then Solomon awoke –
and he realized it had been a dream.
1 Kings 3:15

Monday

CHAPTER 1

The yellow-line subway of the Washington Metropolitan Area Transit Authority slid its way from the bustling touristy areas of the Smithsonian museums and Archives to its routine stops of Pentagon and Crystal City. The nighttime crowd had dwindled, and all that remained on the chilly moonlit October night at the King Street station were the typical residents of Alexandria and a few night owl tourists trying to catch the photogenic sights of Lincoln Memorial beneath the stars.

Burt and Pam Hamilton, an older couple in their mid-sixties, sat wide-eyed, clutching their MetroCards and tattered map as they quickly took a snapshot of the George Washington Masonic Memorial before the Metro proceeded to the next to last stop. "So, what do you want to do tomorrow?" Pam asked as Burt tucked his camera into his fanny pack and pulled out a notepad of his must-sees of D.C.

"We haven't gone to Ford's Theater yet," he answered, making a note for the next day's agenda.

"Sounds good to me," she responded, scanning the subway car for a friendly face and catching sight of a couple in surgical masks three rows ahead. A surge of emotion rose when she caught a glimpse of the gentleman, who was also wearing an oxygen mask with tubes traveling over his ears down to the tank resting between his feet.

"You're going to love Ford's Theater," the blonde woman cordially replied behind the mask. "Dad wanted to go there himself but didn't have the energy to make it today." She patted the leather-gloved hand of the pale bald gentleman beside her. "He's always wanted to come to D.C. and see the sights, and he wasn't going to let his cancer keep him from it."

"Right on," Pam smiled. "That's the perfect attitude. I mean, you never know what can happen."

"No, you don't." She looked over at her father and squeezed his hand tighter as he continued to doze. "So, where are you from?"

"Carbondale, Illinois," Burt gruffly answered pulling his car keys from his fanny pack as the subway car came to a halt at the Eisenhower Avenue station, allowing a couple of other passengers to disembark.

"Well, I hope you enjoy the rest of your visit," she kindly replied as she nudged her father awake. "Dad, the next stop is ours. You need to start waking up." She looked over at Burt and Pam, a hidden smile behind her mask. Her brain was going through the outline they had been plotting for months. Find some older tourists. Check. Become friendly with the tourists. Check. Note if they drove to the station. Check. She loved older tourists because they were so easy to spot and so easy to sway.

"Last stop, Yellow Line, Huntington Station," the subway conductor announced over the staticky intercom system as the train slid into the concrete structure built in the 1980s. The cold and unwelcome exterior of hard geometric lines and circles was reminiscent of other buildings erected during this time period. All it needed was graffiti, and it could have passed for what was left of the Berlin Wall.

As the train screeched to a halt, the few remaining passengers quickly jumped up and headed to the sliding doors, gripping the metal poles with one hand and their iPhones with the other. They exited when the doors parted, leaving the four to follow slowly behind.

The sickly father stood shakily, rolling his oxygen tank behind him while his daughter helped him exit the train. "Enjoy your day tomorrow," the daughter said, waving to her new acquaintances who returned the wave and headed to the stairs with their MetroCards ready.

"We've got to catch up to them," the not-so-ailing father whispered, eyeing Burt and Pam who were quickly disappearing down to the lower level.

"It's okay; we will catch up with them," she calmly answered with the objects of her cat and mouse game in sight. They proceeded down the stairs and found their soon-to-be victims having issues with the MetroCard exit. "See, I told you," she remarked as he eyed her suspiciously. "Tourists."

Pam quietly snickered at Burt, who mumbled a few choice words under his breath before finally figuring out the complexities of his MetroCard. "He never listens to me," Pam giggled towards the father and daughter duo as they routinely slid their paid with cash cards through the exit.

3

The four proceeded down the brightly lit sidewalk between the two car garage structures and turned right to enter the larger multileveled garage built into a hill beside the connecting station. Burt laughed about his aging legs and the daily travels on his sore feet as they journeyed up the stairs, reaching the first level in the garage.

"I can't make it up anymore," the father mumbled as he gripped the stairway handle. "I'm too weak and tired."

"Okay, wait here and I'll go and get the car," she said as she had rehearsed many times.

Pam turned around as Burt proceeded to walk towards their 2011 Ford Explorer. "Where'd you park, hon?"

"I'm not sure, but it was further up," she answered as she turned to her father. "Will you be okay while I go get the car?"

The father coughed out a few words that resembled, "I'm not sure." The daughter moved closer to her father, easing him down until he was seated on a step.

"Burt, let's give them a ride up," Pam said.

The father squeezed his daughter's hand, cocking his eyes sideways in her direction. "No, we couldn't put you out. You've already had such a busy day," the daughter replied sympathetically as the father squeezed tighter as if trying to control the reins on a stubborn horse. "Here, Dad, take a sip of your orange juice. Maybe your blood sugar has dropped," she said, releasing her hand from his deadly grip and taking his juice carton from her purse.

"No bother at all. You wait here, and we'll get the car. You two can hop in and we'll take you the rest of the way up."

Pam walked to her vehicle, getting into the backseat as Burt pulled away to pick up their new acquaintances.

As she watched their victims grow closer, the daughter leaned toward her father. "Are you ready for this?" Her father slowly nodded, taking in a deep breath.

"It's now or never."

CHAPTER 2

"Thank you so much for this," the daughter gushed as she buckled herself into the vehicle. "You okay up there, Dad? Are you drinking your juice?"

He grunted and nodded.

Burt slowly proceeded up the circular garage ramp, allowing them time to look around the garage for their vehicle. "Do you see it?" Burt asked looking around, unsure of what he was looking for. "What do you drive?"

"No, I don't see it," the daughter answered maneuvering her head around Pam. "I remember that we parked near a corner. We got here late, and that was one of the last spots we found."

"Burt never gets anywhere late," Pam laughed warmly. "I tried to sleep late this morning, but Burt never sleeps past 6:30. It's his biological clock."

"After waking up at six every morning for thirty years, it's just in my bones to wake up early," he answered defensively.

"Oh, simmer down, Burt. I'm only teasing you," Pam replied, patting his shoulder. "Men. Sometimes you just have to rub them and tell them everything is going to be okay." She winked to the daughter who was sitting directly behind her father.

"I have to do that with my father as well."

Burt's vehicle continued to slowly climb to the next level, giving her ample time to search for the car.

"Oh, dear," the father moaned. "Honey, I spilled some of my juice; can you give me a wipe?"

"Yes, Dad." She quickly pulled out his black container of handy wipes, popping open the lid and pulling on one of the cloth napkins. "I am so sorry about this. I hope it didn't get on your car seat."

"I've spilled much worse than juice up there," Pam sympathetically remarked. "Don't worry your pretty little head about anything."

"Dad, do you see the car?" she asked. As she was about to pass him the napkin, she noticed a spot open beside a black Honda Accord in the corner of the garage. "There it is; the black Honda."

Burt headed in that direction, stopping his vehicle behind the aging compact car. "Oh, can you park real quick? It might take a minute to clean up my dad's mess, and I don't want to stop other cars leaving the garage this late at night. My dad hates to cause a ruckus."

"Burt, park the car," Pam agreed.

Burt let out a defeated huff, backed up the car, and parked it beside the Honda.

"Dad, here's your wipe; clean up, and I will help you get out."

The father leaned back, grabbing the wipe and started mumbling, "I can't see anything in this dark garage."

Burt reached up and touched a few buttons on the car roof, trying to find the interior lighting when suddenly the father and daughter started to move swiftly. The father removed his oxygen mask and hit a button on the tank, causing a new flow of air to enter the mask. His cloth-covered hand quickly went to Burt's face, causing Burt to breathe in the chloroform fumes before he had any idea of the surprise attack. Burt's arms started flailing around trying to fight off the attack, but he was no match for the muscles of a younger man. In seconds, the oxygen mask was covering Burt's face, causing pure chloroform to pump into his aging lungs.

At the same moment, terror filled Pam's eyes as the daughter lunged putting another cloth over Pam's nose and mouth. She let out two screams, but the stifled yells for help were quickly subdued as she inhaled the fumes. "I need the mask!" the fraudulent daughter yelled as the man pretending to be her father removed the device from Burt's face and helped her secure it over Pam's porcelain features.

He continued to hold the napkin over Burt's airway passages as he raised the motionless hand up and let it go, watching it fall into the sleeping man's lap. "He's gone."

"Good. I think she is too," she replied as she raised Pam's arm and watched it fall limply to her side.

"Round two," he coolly remarked, leaning over, unbuckling, and reclining Burt's chair. "We can do this."

"We've got to do it fast. The next train is going to be here in a few minutes."

CHAPTER 3

They wrestled Burt's body on top of Pam's contorted torso in the backseat. It took a few tries, because no matter how many times they had practiced, this was the first time they moved actual people. "I think I hear the next train coming," she said, shimmying her way to the passenger seat as her partner situated himself in the driver's seat of the Ford Explorer.

He backed out of the parking spot and started to roll down the ramp, catching a glimpse of a few heads entering the garage from the rearview mirror while his accomplice rummaged through Burt's fanny pack, looking for their hotel room key cards.

"Do you have the prepaid credit card?" she asked when they got near the garage's exit gate.

"Yes," he answered coolly.

"And when you purchased it, you paid for it with cash, so they can't track you, right?"

"Yes."

"And you didn't buy it around here, right?"

He nodded his head as the electric window started to roll down so the microphone couldn't pick up either of their voices. He slid in the credit card and waited for the authorization to be completed. The gate rose and they were one step closer to their completed task. Rolling up the window, he turned to his partner without a word. His eyes spoke the words that he wanted to say, and she understood the infuriated tone of his unyielding gaze.

He circled the surrounding streets, looking for a homeless person to whom he could give the hotel room key cards and cellular phones. Someone might as well enjoy the older couple's hotel room for the night and help lead the police on a little goose chase. He slowed down when he saw a grungy-looking gentleman in his late forties wearing a worn-out sock hat and a baggy sweater and jeans, carrying a tattered makeshift satchel. The homeless man was reluctant to accept the free night, but after she mentioned that he could have whatever he found in the room, he took the deal. "You just have to be out of the room by breakfast," she said, handing him the key cards and phones and looking down to see the room number written on the envelope. "Room 124. Out by breakfast. Got it?"

After he sped off and headed north toward Interstate 395, she broke the tension-filled silence. "I just wanted to make sure," she said, folding her arms to her chest. "That's what big sisters do."

"I'm not a child," he sulked, keeping his eyes on the road as he drove through Lady Bird Johnson Park and saw the Arlington Bridge come into view. "You don't have to question everything I do."

"I know," she said resignedly staring out the window, counting the columns on the Lincoln Memorial like she did when she was a child. "You know..." she started, unsure if she should finish her thought.

"I know what?" he grumbled, entering the Rock Creek and Potomac Parkway.

She looked over at him and then in the backseat at the unconscious. "If only Dad could see us," she stopped and wiped a falling tear. "He would be so proud."

"Yeah," he said as he looked over at his older sister and smiled. It was moments like this that he enjoyed. The closeness and affection they had for one another. Even if their childhood had been destroyed, one of them overcame the statistics of a foster care system, and the other hit its bullseye. But together, they were a force to be reckoned with.

They journeyed beside Rock Creek making the final leg of their first expedition. They passed beside Montrose Park and drove through the Smithsonian National Zoological Park. They entered the desolate Rock Creek Park, which closed at sundown, thankful that the restricted areas of the park were easy to overlook in the late evening hours.

They drove the winding path until they came to a small, shaded parking lot unnoticed by most travelers. It was far from the limelight of the visitor center, golf course, and Carter Barron Amphitheater.

The parking lamp overhead had burned out months earlier, and the park service had yet to replace the old bulb, leaving the area nice and dark. Turning off the car, they got out and quickly worked together to move Burt and Pam to the front seat. She checked their airways and noticed that they were both still breathing, but they wouldn't be for much longer.

"Give me the hose and tape," he said as she dug into her bag, pulling out a twenty-five-foot garden hose and industrial strength duct tape. "I'll do this as you clean up the scene." He straightened the hose on the ground, duct taping one end to the muffler exhaust.

"There's not much to clean up since we wore our winter gloves," she said as she searched through Burt's fanny pack and Pam's purse for their MetroCards and any other evidence that the cops could use to track them down. She loved that older tourists carried cash; she grabbed $600 but left a little under $100 so the cops wouldn't suspect a robbery. "Almost done?" she asked, getting out of the car and making sure that no traces of them were left inside. No fingerprints would be found by the police. No strands of hair would be lost since she was wearing a wig and he was wearing a bald man's cap. No blood, bodily fluids, or DNA would likely be located. They were as careful as could be.

"Done," he announced standing up behind the Explorer. He leaned over Burt on the driver's side and turned the ignition, cracking the window slightly to snake the hose into the vehicle.

"How do you feel?" she asked as they stepped away from the vehicle and headed toward the black forest.

"Feel?" he asked as he stopped and turned around to watch the windows fog with the rising carbon monoxide. "I feel good," he said removing his gloves, surgical mask, and bald man's cap before combing his brownish locks with steady fingers.

"That's good. I got a little something for you," she said, hugging his shoulder and handing him the wad of dollar bills. "This will help with your rent."

"I didn't think we were going to steal," he said with a childlike innocence as if making sure it was okay.

"I didn't take it all," she said. "They won't suspect anything." She turned him around so they could start their moonlit hike to where they had stashed their bikes earlier in the evening. "My adrenalin is pumping!"

"Mine too," he said taking a step into the woods. He could walk these trails blindfolded, which was about as well as he could currently see. "I put our bikes a little ways up." He continued to walk deeper into the darkness, as the moon had disappeared behind the clouds and tree limbs. He listened intently for his sister's footsteps behind him. With each twig she stepped on, it was music to his ears. She was the best sister he could have ever wanted. "Thanks, sis."

Tuesday

CHAPTER 4

A computerized voice resounded over the flight intercom system in the blackness. "Attention, attention passengers of Flight 854 from Chicago to Washington, D.C., we are approximately 30,000 feet in the air, and we are experiencing some extreme turbulence. Please return to your seats and fasten your safety belts. Attention, attention passengers of Flight 854 from Chicago to Washington, D.C., we are approximately 25,000 feet in the air and are experiencing some extreme turbulence. Please return to your seats and fasten your safety belts. Attention, attention passengers of Flight 854 from Chicago to Washington, D.C., we are now in a nosedive. Assume safety positions for a crash landing. Attention, attention passengers of Flight 854 from Chicago to Washington, D.C., we have stabilized, but we are making an emergency landing in Pittsburgh due to the turbulence. Please prepare for a landing. Attention, attention passengers, welcome to Pittsburgh."

In an instant, the voice silenced, but a clicking sound and a sudden flash of an old Polaroid camera filled the void, causing a black and white photograph to materialize. It was a picture of a gentleman in his mid-50's dressed in a tuxedo with a much younger gorgeous blonde woman in a tight-fitting silver sequin evening gown. Suddenly, another click and a flash brought a new image. She was laughing, and he was

14

smiling as they walked down a long hallway with many doors. Once again, with a click and a flash, a new picture was taken. A door opened, revealing a large king-size bed. The pictures kept coming and coming, as if telling a story. They kissed. He unzipped her gown. She unzipped his pants. He stood in his boxers. She stood in her lingerie and whispered in his ear. He pointed to his wallet as she retrieved it. He pulled out cash and she kissed him. He sat down on the bed while she went toward the door. Looking terrified and exposed, he quickly tried to cover himself when she returned with a badge and other officers. Click and flash -- he walked with his hands behind his back in his boxers toward the door with a headline blazing in neon red letters: "Family Values Senator from Mississippi Caught in Prostitution Raid". The last image dissolved from the forefront, just like his political career.

Seconds went by and the torrid scandal was but a memory while a new story took the limelight in a scroll tape of typewriter ribbon. "Burt and Pam Hamilton, ages sixty-eight and sixty-five of Carbondale, Illinois, were found dead in Rock Creek Park in their 2011 Blue Ford Explorer early this morning by a female jogger. 'I came here for my morning jog like I do almost every morning and noticed a hose was duct taped to the muffler with it going into the driver's side window. I quickly went over and looked through the glass and saw the old couple sitting in their seats. I hoped that they weren't dead, but I was pretty sure that they were. I could still smell the exhaust fumes when I walked up to the car door.' The police are investigating this incident as either a murder or suicide. More details to follow."

The typewritten words ended their steady stream as a cheesy meteorologist in front of a green screen filled the video camera lens. "This just in, Tropical Storm Irina, which was supposed to follow the path of the jet stream and stay safely in the middle of the Atlantic, has some devious plans of her own. The Weather Center just sent a warning a few minutes ago forecasting that it will reach landfall in Southern Georgia tomorrow evening where it will become a Category 3 hurricane. It will run its course up along the Eastern Seaboard through South and North Carolina before it juts away from land and heads back out to the Atlantic Ocean. This is a significant redirection with very little preparation time for the residents of these states. None of the forecasting models believed that Irina would hit the United States, let alone become a Category 3 hurricane. No one could have predicted this. No one."

"No one?" she thought as she woke from her sound sleep, stretching and rolling over in her comfortable bed, gradually opening her right eye to turn on her lamp. She found her journal and pen on her nightstand and flipped it open to the first empty page to begin writing. *October 19th*... After she had completed her synopsis of each of her dreams, she flipped back to the prior days and saw a checkmark beside each one. Her dreams always came true. Always.

CHAPTER 5

The digital Timex I got 17 years ago when I was in the eighth grade told me that I was just twelve minutes late to Wint's birthday party. Officer Wint Cooper, or Winston, as his wife Veronica corrected me each time, had been my best friend ever since the fourth grade when we both discovered the same hiding spot, a tiny crawling passageway under the football bleachers at school.

I was hiding from Gertrude Westerton, who claimed I was her boyfriend and would sucker punch me like her brothers taught her if the kick to the groin didn't buckle my knees. She was a piece of work just because I wouldn't give her my measly cookie or whatever snack I had at lunch. Looking back, those school cookies were not worth a kick to the jewels.

Wint, on the other hand, was hiding from the bully of all bullies, Chuck "Piggy" Hodgens. If I didn't already have Gertrude to run from, Piggy would have been the other reason. He got the name Piggy for obvious reasons and used his weight to his advantage by sitting on skinny kids until he squeezed their lunch money and dignity from their trembling hands. It was no wonder I didn't weigh much as a kid. Between the two of them, I never got dessert, even if I had money for it.

Wint had outsmarted Piggy with a grand scheme for a fourth grader, a type of Robin Hood Ponzi scheme. He designed a deal to help Piggy get money from his victims without torture and then Wint would deposit the money into Piggy's lunch account at school so he could eat all he wanted.

Fortunately, Wint told all us kids on the first day of their deal to give him a dollar. He wanted to show Piggy the money he got from us so Piggy wouldn't squash us anymore. I didn't know if I could trust Wint, since I only knew him as the kid who sat on the other side of the cafeteria during lunch, but it was only one dollar. Instead of putting the money into Piggy's lunch account, Wint put the wad of ones in his locker. Each day, Wint would show Piggy the cash like it was a fresh batch and tell him that he was going to make the deposit. In reality, they were the same dollars from day one. After a week, I noticed more kids than ever on the playground because no one was afraid of the wrath of Piggy.

Unfortunately, all schemes must come to an end. I remember the shock I felt as I crawled under the bleachers to escape Gertrude's kick and found a new buddy watching the playground from a safe distance. "Why are you here?" I asked, hoping he wasn't here to get another dollar.

"Piggy," he answered with a hint of fear in his tone, his eyes darting back to the swing sets and slide.

"Why?"

He gulped but didn't lose focus on his target who was storming across the yard like a hound trying to catch the scent of a fox. "His mom must not have put any money into his lunch account for this week. I heard the lunch lady tell him that he didn't have enough money to get extra today. That's when he threw his tray across the cafeteria."

"No!" I gasped. "He didn't!"

Wint turned to face me deadly serious. "He did. Macaroni landed on Mr. Landing's glasses, but he didn't do anything because it hit the lens of his glass eye."

"He has a glass eye?" I asked surprised. "I thought he was just cross-eyed."

"His eyes are two different colors," he replied in disbelief. "Didn't you notice that?"

"Well, I had a dog like that. I just thought…"

"He was like your dog?" he smiled with a light chuckle as he continued watching the grassy field as if landmines were hidden around the monkey bars.

We sat in silence for a few minutes. I was unsure what to say since this was only the second time I had ever spoken with him.

"He's looking for me. He's already gotten to Max and Avery. They didn't even see it coming." He turned to me, I guess to distract himself from the war zone of Piggy beyond the bleachers. "What's your name?"

"Solomon Davis."

He stuck his hand out and we shook. "Solomon, that's a funny name. I've never met anyone called that. I'm Winston, but you can call me Wint; all my friends do. Got a nickname?"

"Nope."

"Well, Solomon… Solomon… Solomon…" he kept repeating it over and over with various speeds and enunciations until he found it. "Got it. I'll call you

Solo. Everyone's gotta have a nickname. Even Piggy."
I stared in amazement at Wint. It was like his fear left
him. He was smiling and telling stories like there was
nothing to be afraid of. Either that or he was replaying
his life like a wake for a funeral.

We eventually crawled away from the bleachers to
go back to class. I got kicked, Wint got punched, and
we both got sat on. I wouldn't say we were blood
brothers, but on that day, after I finally regained
consciousness, our blood mixed for the first time
when Wint reached down to help me up.

I guessed it was true what people said, that
tragedies would either tear people apart or weld them
closer together. We'd been best friends since.

CHAPTER 6

I walked up the driveway of Wint's home in the Spring Valley neighborhood – one of the richest and most prestigious of the District of Columbia, with Lexuses, Mercedes, Hummers, Porsches, and other luxury vehicles lining the winding entrance. It was like entering a gala for a dignitary, a diplomat, or a high-priced fundraising dinner for the latest endangered animal. I would have only been invited to one of these events as a mere waiter. Wint's police officer salary would never have been able to afford such a posh estate, but his father-in-law was a managing partner at the law firm of Manfield & Hyde; like father, like daughter, Veronica Hyde-Cooper was rising fast on his coattails.

My gold Honda Civic looked like a cheetah with rust patches for spots. Animal prints were great for a throw or coat, but on an automobile, it just radiated poverty. It was fitting for mine to be parked at the end of the line to make a quick getaway, or even be easily towed should someone call to complain about a junked-up car blocking their exit.

My car was so out of place that I could almost hear it cry in humiliation, but that was just the engine quieting down after I stepped away from the vehicle with keys in hand. Most people at the party would have been concerned if their cars continued to sputter after they turned it off, but for me, it was just proof that the car still had some life in it. I would have been scared if I'd turned it off and it instantly stopped.

I'd never really felt that self conscious about my car before because earthly treasures never shone bright on my radar screen, but walking past all these expensive cars that were worth more than I made in a year, well, it just put a little perspective in my humble pie. I wasn't ashamed of my life, but it kind of made my car stand out like pee in snow. I could go out and splurge on something nice thanks to the life insurance money I received a few years ago, but using that money for myself just seemed a little too selfish for me. Over the last few years, I had just been living mainly on the interest it was accruing each month and wedding photography jobs.

When I rang the doorbell, the chimes sang in my head like opera singers announcing, "Château de Cooper." The extremely opulent and formal sound warranted the need for a butler or a voluptuous maid, but the only one who came for my greeting was Veronica. I would have preferred Lurch.

"Verny!" I shouted with exuberance. I never knew what she hated more, being called Verny or the simple presence of my company.

"My name is Veronica," she smugly corrected. "You're late, Solomon. The celebration commenced at seven."

"Oh, sorry," I boomed without a hint of sincerity. "And I'm Solo. Only my mom calls me Solomon."

"Not only," she replied with a roll of her eyes. "Where's your camera?"

"My camera?" I shook my head in confusion. Why would I need my camera? Yes, I used to be the photographer for the *Washington Post*, and I currently freelanced at weddings and other gatherings, but do surgeons always carry their scalpel? Do barbers always carry a pair of clippers? Do mob bosses always carry a cement block? "Why my camera?"

"To take pictures," she answered with an air of superiority. "You didn't bring it? That's why you were invited. To be the photographer. We're not going to pay you for eating the hors d'oeuvres."

"Oh, and I thought I was here because it's Wint's birthday, and we have been friends since we both wore Superman underwear."

"Thankfully, Winston grew out of that phase years ago. There's hope for you yet." She hissed Winston's name like a venomous snake showing her fangs before an attack.

If it weren't for Wint's birthday, I would have turned around and mooned her, but I didn't want to impress her with my grown man's underwear. "My camera's in my car. I will go and…" but before I could finish, she had already shut the door. I did the mature thing and flipped her off. Not with just one hand, but the double bird. Fly away birds. Fly away from this evil Verny. If she were a man, I would have decked her years ago. Whatever Wint saw in her must have been something great because all I saw was a witch (replaced with a b if I were being completely honest) in desperate need of a hug as my mother would say. Heck, she needed medication.

With the camera dangling around my neck, I entered the home that oozed prestige and wealth like an open wound begging for gangrene. Every time I visited their home, which lately had mostly been on occasions when Verny was away, I would look around the décor to see markings of Verny everywhere, but seldom did I see the fingerprints of Wint. People may have pitied me for being single, but I pitied him for not having his own identity.

I picked up my camera and started taking a few snapshots around the foyer, or as Verny would say it in her fake French, "foi-ey." Women were dressed in evening gowns with jewelry that sparkled like twinkling stars in the Cassiopeia constellation. Men were dapper in their custom-made suits and tailored tuxedos that would give any red carpet a run for its money. I wanted to ask who was getting married, but in this crowd, the joke would have been useless or better yet, ignored.

With each photograph I took, it looked less like a birthday party and more like a Calvin Klein photo shoot. There were the beautiful size zero model types holding onto their ultra handsome playboy husbands. There were older men with their graying hair and strong jawbone structure holding their brandy while talking about their yachts. No hairs were out of place, every smile was perfect and dazzling; everyone was exquisite, even the few kids that were running around looked like the kids in the advertisements of J. Crew with their joyful laughter and bow ties.

Not to be vain, but I considered myself a nice-looking man, six-foot-one with a lean build and decent facial features, but in there I felt like the red-headed stepchild that was beaten with the ugly stick and locked away in his room when guests came over. I looked down at my khaki pants with a ketchup stain and my penny loafers; even if I had a $100 bill poking out instead of a penny, they would still not be worthy to such a crowd. It was sickening.

I continued to click away at the assembly as I lurked around the walls of the room. No one noticed my flashing lights. It was as if they'd been taught for years to never look at the help or photographer; they were there to capture moments, not befriend or be part of the memories. I suddenly knew how homeless people felt when I pulled up to a corner and stared ahead at the red light, praying for it to turn green. I knew my powers of telepathy were absent, but I would still fixate on that blazing bulb for the chance, just the slightest chance of it working. I had known he was holding a sign, and he knew that I knew he was holding a sign. It was a strange relationship we had always had with one another. I had never been the one holding the sign before, and today, the sign had been replaced by a camera.

Shaking away my depressing self diagnosis, I moved to another room, thick with the same type of people. I mentally screamed, Where are my people? as if I were an alien in a new land. I continued to take brilliant shots, but with this group, it was child's play. There were no photo bombs to worry about or even the possibility to spice up the stiff atmosphere. I even bumped into a waiter serving champagne, which caused a few goblets to clank together, but no one looked in my direction, except for Wint.

"Solo!" he shouted, so unashamed of my attire or economic status. Dressed in a classy tuxedo, Wint broke away from his huddle of comrades and almost sprinted in my direction. I didn't know what I appreciated more, the look of excitement in my best friend's eyes or the look of disgust in Verny's. I'd call it a tie.

"Hey, man, thanks for coming. It wouldn't have been a good birthday without you." He patted my shoulder like we were in middle school again. "You brought your camera? Do you ever take that thing off?"

It was then that I realized I wasn't invited to work. I was invited as a friend. It was just another power play for Verny, who was currently across the room with a group of her ritzy girlfriends, snickering. "You know me. Never know when I'll need it."

Wint leaned into my ear, "I'm really glad you're here. Veronica said that the rest of the gang couldn't make it, so we are stuck with this group." He frowned slightly. "Most of these people are ones that Veronica works with one way or another, or people we have met in the last few years. She's gotta make a good appearance, you know. But this is a good group of people. Just different."

"That's what they'll say about me," I laughed. "Any of your cop friends here?" I asked, noticing that no one looked like they were on a police officer's salary.

"Only a few: the captain, the chief, and a couple of higher ranks who know Veronica's father." He lowered his voice. "You know me. This isn't my type of party, but Veronica wanted to throw it, so, you know."

"Yeah, I know. Sorry about the way I look. I didn't know I needed to rent a tux to come here tonight."

"Don't worry about it. I only wore this because she made me. I would rather be wearing jeans and a t-shirt." He scanned the room and noticed Verny beckoning him. "Well, I see I'm being summoned." He turned and walked away as I picked up my camera to take another shot of a couple across the room. I felt a tug on my elbow. "Come on, you're coming with me."

We entered the family room with Verny chatting with a couple of ladies about the drapery while the men were practicing their golf swing. I saw Verny's eyes shoot in my direction like fiery arrows. She didn't need to look twice; I felt it with the first look. "Look who showed up!" Wint announced. "Everyone, this is one of my oldest and best friends, Solomon Davis, but you can call him Solo."

The conversation was a little awkward, but Wint never left me hanging for a moment. Baseball talk was quickly replaced with the stock market insurgence; *The Book of Mormon* was mentioned, not the religious text, but the musical; and the only celebrity name uttered was the politician that was arrested in an upscale hotel with an escort.

The main thing I took from the conversation was an hour before Wint's next party I would need to review the news headlines or try to stay up to date on current events. That is, if I was invited again.

CHAPTER 7

I walked away from the center ring of the rich and famous circus to collect my thoughts and center myself. In the four years that Wint had lived in Spring Valley, I had only been to his house a handful of times, for his birthdays or brief visits. I roamed around the maze-like corridors, examining the mediocre family photos strategically placed by some interior designer Verny found in *Home and Country*. Even though Verny and I mixed like ice and gasoline, I couldn't help but see that in every picture Wint smiled like he actually loved her. I approved of their marriage because that was what true friends did; even if they didn't like the choice, they respected it.

Another turn down the hall led to a darkened room with a barely lit fire in a lake-cabin styled fireplace. I quietly walked into the room and found that it had all of Wint's sporting trophies and ribbons scattered around the bookcases and walls. It didn't have the air of royalty or French designs, but rather unpretentious Wint with handsome dark wood moldings and rustic earthy tones. He was always the star athlete, but he never let his speed or agility out-shadow his integrity and character.

I turned around to find a light switch, feeling around the walls beside the door when a voice within the room chimed, "Hey, Timex, a little higher."

Slightly taken aback, I flipped the switch to see a modestly dressed woman in her mid-twenties sipping champagne in one of the leather chairs beside the fire. "I didn't know anyone was in here."

"Yeah, I kind of noticed that," she remarked casually, yet aloof, remaining seated with her legs crossed as she set her goblet down. "Sneak around much?"

I nervously laughed and took a step away from the door to examine more of the room. "I wouldn't say sneak per se, but just..." My mind went blank searching for an explanation, but why did I even care? It looked like she was hiding as well. "What about you?"

"What about me?" she questioned in defense. "I'm not the one patting the room down like a lonely down-on-his-luck security guard trying to cop a cheap feel."

I continued to study the history of Wint, seeing old photographs of him and his family. "Oh, calm down, I was just trying to get away from the party."

"Hmm," she huffed. "I could see that, and by the way you are dressed..."

"Yes, you got me. I wasn't aware that it was black tie," I interrupted proudly showing off my glow-in-the-dark Timex watch. I didn't understand rich people. They either looked down on others because they weren't rich or they pitied them. "I would hate to be a bother, so I'll just leave." As I turned to leave, a picture caught my eye, causing me to freeze and smile, forgetting my earlier discomfort. It was a picture I hadn't seen since middle school.

"You don't have to leave," she groaned as she stood up from her chair and made her way over to where I was standing. "What are you looking at anyway?"

"Me," I laughed, pointing to a picture of me and Wint, arms around each other's shoulders with dirt on our faces and two pairs of bloody knees.

She leaned forward to get a better view of the picture and then squinted up at my face. "You haven't changed much, Solo. Just a little fatter in the cheeks."

I looked at my reflection in the glass and noticed the same quizzical smile. "No, I guess not. How do you know my name?"

"Oh, I've heard stories about you," she smiled and moved on to the next photo of Wint in his high school baseball uniform. "Are they all true?"

"If it's Wint telling them, then they're true," I chuckled following my fellow party dodger to the next picture. "Wint was always the honest one."

"Honest one? Aren't you a theology student? Isn't being honest one of your core values or something? Don't you have to say some kind of pledge to not lie or be stripped of your get-into-Heaven pass?"

"I'm a work in process," I said. "And it's a motto branded to my chest during my initiation."

"Was that before or after the cookies and Kool-Aid?"

"Who are you?" I asked, puzzled at how this stranger knew so much about me without me knowing anything about her.

"I'm Elizabeth," she sighed. "Elizabeth Hyde." She said her name as if I would have had an aha moment, but it was more like an uh-oh moment as she added, "Veronica's sister."

"That's right," I kindly and awkwardly replied. "Verny's, I mean, Veronica's sister." Suddenly my mind started racing. *Oh, I've heard stories about you. Are they all true?* "So, you said you heard stories about me?"

She continued to walk along the wall, examining the room like it was the first time that she, too, had entered it. "Yes, many, many stories," she said coolly.

Oh well, I thought. Another one of the Hyde family members didn't like me. It wasn't like we would see each other any time soon, just next year on Wint's birthday if she showed up.

"Funny, I don't remember ever seeing you before," I commented, treading in uncomfortable water.

"Yeah, the doctor thought it would be good to get me out of the ward for the evening and have interactions with non-crazies, as he calls them. Good old sis picked me up for Wint's party. Just a warning, keep sharp objects away from me as I have a tendency to stab things. Poor Perry." She spoke rationally and calmly, but her eyes bugged out at the word stab, and I didn't want to know anything else about poor Perry.

We stood in silence for a few minutes. I felt uncomfortable about leaving and really uncomfortable about staying. She finally cut through the awkwardness. "I'm only kidding. God, you're gullible."

I laughed awkwardly, not fully certain what was the truth and what was the lie. She pointed to another picture of me; this time Wint and I were about fifteen, jumping up from the couch in our underwear. "So, what about this picture?"

"I cannot believe he kept that picture, let alone framed it," I smirked, recalling the good memories of our childhood. "We were doing some yard work and wanted to come in to rest, so his mom made us strip at the door so we wouldn't get dirt and grass in the house. We sat down and then his little sister had a crazy idea to take our picture when we weren't paying attention. We jumped up to get her, but it was too late. You know little sisters."

"I am one, so yes, I do know." She leaned closer to the photo as if trying to see something in our white briefs.

"Stop that," I jokingly pushed her away. "You can't see anything."

"Are you sure? I thought I caught a look at something," she winked.

I was desperate to change the subject from my near nakedness. "So you know all about me, and probably a little too much from Veronica, but I don't know anything about you."

"After this picture, I know even more about you," she wickedly smiled as she raunchily looked me up and down like I was a tasty hunk of meat dangling on a hook in a butcher shop. "Oh, the stories I heard weren't from *Verny*. Is that what you call her? Wint told me. Me and *Verny*..." she enunciated the name like it was going to be her new favorite word. "Well, we aren't that close."

"Not that close?" I questioned shockingly. "I mean, who couldn't get close to the warm and likeable Veronica?"

"Well, since you don't know much about me, that just proves that our relationship isn't one that Hallmark glamorizes or that *Verny* prioritizes," she commented, reclaiming her seat on her leather chair.

"Well, as you can tell, Verny and I are not the closest either," I said following suit, trying to relax in another chair while scanning the room for letter openers or anything else that resembled a weapon.

"I guess we're just the black sheep of this party," she said raising her goblet. "To the black sheep. May we stay hidden until we die," she announced with a wicked laugh before downing her remaining drink.

"To the black sheep," I echoed with an imaginary glass in my hand, taken off guard by her twisted sense of humor.

"You gotta lighten up, Solo. No wonder *Verny* doesn't like you."

"Me lighten up?" I replied shocked. "Have you met your sister?"

"I've been looking for both of you," Wint said as he entered his room. "Come on to the party. Dinner is about to begin."

"Wint, I didn't know that was your name," Elizabeth stood up giving him a kiss on his cheek. "Can I call you Wint as well?"

"Sure," he said with a smile that would welcome even the most distant of strangers.

"Just not in front of Verny," I remarked, slowly getting up from my comfortable state.

"Especially in front of *Verny*," she laughed as she strutted down the hall. "Coming, boys?"

"Is she…" I stopped not knowing how to phrase the remainder of my sentence, "you know, sane?"

"Oh, Solo," Wint answered with a broad smile as he started to follow Elizabeth out of the room, flipping the light switch off as he passed.

"Wint, that's not an answer," I shouted from the darkened room. "You still didn't answer me, Wint. Wint?"

"And just a little warning," he stopped to let me catch up to him as he leaned and whispered in my ear, "She's packing."

"Packing what?"

"You know," he laughed, walking down the hall leaving me shocked and confused.

"No, packing what?"

CHAPTER 8

Are we on for tonight? he texted on his disposable phone as he sat on one of the bottom steps of the Lincoln Memorial, watching the awestruck tourists bask in the dazzling sight of the Greek-like temple lit up in the early fall evening. He scanned the Reflecting Pool as if the tranquil waters would reflect the horrors of the night before. He hadn't slept in the last 24 hours and knew that he would eventually crash from the high he was feeling, but he wasn't ready to succumb to that temptation.

He glanced down at the phone in his hands and had a chilling thought that he'd just sent a text with the same pair of hands that took a life the night before. He wondered if he would once again feel the rush of adrenaline that medicine couldn't fully explain. He yearned for the feeling.

Last night, as glorious as it was, was like a groom losing his virginity. It was planned, choreographed, and rehearsed, with no room for inspiration, but it was just the first time. He had an entire lifetime to awaken that untapped spirit and wondered if his sister would be willing to stray from the script for some added excitement.

A few minutes passed, but he still had no response to his text. He squeezed the phone, hoping it would vibrate with a simple yes, but he knew that he would just have to sit and wait a little while longer. Breathing in the cool autumn air, he could almost smell the sweet Japanese honeysuckle from the Glover Archbold Park, a mere three miles away, the scene of their next attack.

He replayed his movements from the day. He had filled his oxygen tank with chloroform to ensure it wouldn't accidentally go empty. He had hidden his bike under some tree limbs and leaves in the park near the residential neighborhood for an easy escape through the backyards. His sister was more into kayaking, so he'd hidden her kayak under a cluster of trees and bushes near the Potomac River with an electronic sensor so her tracking device could find it. Their plan was to never be seen together after a kill.

Are we on for tonight? he texted once again. He leaned back and reclined on his elbows, staring past the Reflecting Pool and watching the lights and fountains dance at the World War II Memorial. This was always his favorite spot his dad had taken him to as a kid before he and his sister were separated into a ruthless foster system. From this one spot he could see some of the most iconic sites of Washington aligned perfectly. He tilted his head and saw the peak of the Washington Memorial, recalling the time that he had counted each and every step with his best friend, his sister, as their dad coughed and complained from ten feet behind. At least, that is the story his sister had told him.

"Why did we decide to do this on the hottest day in July?" his dad had growled as he and his sister kept moving upwards with their childish smiling faces.

Lastly, he saw the beautiful Capitol, a building that he had dreamed of working in since the age of four, but life didn't always live up to one's plans. He shook his head, shifting the tragedy of broken dreams out of his mind. He had lost his family once, but not anymore.

He scanned the surrounding area full of unknowing visitors, and smiled. They didn't know there was a killer in their midst. They didn't know any one of them could be the next victim. They didn't know…

He stopped his train of thought as he felt a slight vibration in his hand. He closed his eyes and took a deep breath, as if the news were going to make or break him. He opened his hand and read his text; a wicked smile emerged.

Yes.

CHAPTER 9

Wint's dining room was decked out with the finest china, the most elegant crystal, the freshest long-stemmed roses, and the costliest wine. It reeked of Verny in every way. Even the meal that was supposedly a feast of Wint's favorites, grilled salmon and scallops served with garlic dipped asparagus with mushroom and goat cheese risotto, smelled strangely of Verny. They could have at least had a bowl of his momma's macaroni and cheese for the birthday boy. The only sign of this being Wint's birthday was his name on the four-tiered cake sitting between two angelic ice sculptures. Nothing said masculinity like chubby naked baby-men draped in togas with harps and lyres in their hands.

The long table had 32 strategically assigned seats, 15 on each side and one on each end. The guests consisted of rising political stars, aging diplomats, brilliant legal minds, published scholars, and me. If this table was one of royalty with Queen Veronica and Wint at one end, then I was but the feeble court jester with failed attempts at jokes at the other end. Despite the proverbial glass wall between me and the majority of the guests, the few I sat beside were cordial and pleasant company.

Dr. Jeremiah Huffington, PhD was a 40-year-old professor of anthropology at the American University who'd received tenure four years ago and published his first bestseller at about the same time. He looked like a stereotypical professor with a brown tweed jacket, a burgundy sweater, and a pair of thick black framed glasses that contoured his lean face. Despite all his achievements and credentials, he was sitting on the loser end of the table with a former mediocre newspaper photographer. In order to get a closer seat to Wint, it had to benefit Veronica, and sadly, Dr. Huffington didn't need any legal services at the moment.

Beside Dr. Huffington was Jennifer Ascot, who preferred to be called Jenny. She was an attractive brunette with her hair in a bun, wearing a blue pantsuit that showcased her slim and athletic figure. She had been childhood friends with Verny, the sister she'd never had since she was an only child. She currently worked with her at Manfield & Hyde, but unlike Verny, she was working herself up from the bottom floor. She started her legal career wanting to change the world by working as public defender, but in the past year, she had desired to be rewarded financially instead of with pats on the back from felons she had just helped by manipulating the legal system.

Last but not least at this end of the table was the possibly psychotic Elizabeth Hyde.

"So, you single, Solo?" Elizabeth calmly questioned, catching me slightly off guard as she nodded to where I was rubbing the place where my wedding ring used to be.

"You been on any hot dates lately yourself?" I retorted, placing my hands in my lap like a schoolboy.

Elizabeth pursed her lips, squinted her eyes and nodded her head as if to say touché. "So, Dr. Huffington," Elizabeth began, drawing the attention away from herself, "any new books?"

Dr. Huffington wiped his mouth with his white linen napkin. "As a matter of fact, there is," he smiled, hoping someone would beg for a little detail of his upcoming story.

"Well, can you tell us anything about it, or is it hush-hush?" I asked, ready to take a bite of the bait for the sake of keeping the conversation going. Elizabeth winked at me in appreciation, and I didn't know what was more confusing, her flip-flopping personas or her relation to Verny.

"I don't want to bore you with my studies," he resigned, taking a sip of his water.

"If I didn't want to hear you speak, I wouldn't have asked you in the first place," Elizabeth snarled like they were old friends.

"But I thought I already told you," he said.

"Oh, Jeremiah, for heaven's sake, just tell it to me again. You know I don't listen to you half the time anyway," Elizabeth sighed with a dramatic eye roll, and I couldn't help but bust out laughing at her frank demeanor.

"Yes, come on, Dr. Huffington," Jenny respectfully chimed in with a slight giggle as she placed her napkin on her plate, casually looking at the time on her Tiffany watch. Her new gig paid substantially more compared to her measly salary as a public defender.

"Well, I have always been intrigued with tribes and cultures that hold positions of diviners or prophets in as high regard they do warriors and kings. The belief that people can crush some tea leaves and forewarn of imminent tragedy or glance up at the stars and regale of unlikely great fortune. The belief that some mere mortals can be that connected with the gods to see what others do not see just fascinates me."

"I'm not trying to pry, but I thought you were an atheist. Do you really believe in that?" Jenny questioned shyly.

"Oh, dear me. I hate that term 'atheist'. It sounds so condescending as if I am above the simple-minded faithful followers of some deity from afar. And you don't have to believe in something to consider it fascinating. Look at all the blockbuster science fiction movies. Those are almost as far from reality as you can get."

"And yet you still sleep with a robot nightlight," Elizabeth scoffed.

"C-3PO is an android," Jeremiah corrected.

"Whatever. He's more like a man in a Lady Gaga costume to me," Elizabeth remarked, contorting her upper body while starting to sing "Paparazzi".

"Anyway," I said, grimacing like I was a judge on *America's Got Talent* interrupting her fatally flawed impromptu karaoke rendition, "what would you prefer to be called?"

"A human. Or a man. Or a son. Or a brother." He stopped and looked at the three of us as if the rest of the table were a world away. "Labels are what divides us. If we strip away our manmade nametags and see one another for what we are, the world would be a much better place."

"Here, here!" Elizabeth exclaimed, waving off her sister's sideways glance from the other end of the table, causing each of us to laugh and Wint to smirk. "Don't mind us, *Verny*," she announced, as if speaking to the head of state. "Keep talking with, with, with…" she repeated trying to come up with the name of the gentleman she clearly didn't know. Instead of continuing her showcase with Veronica, she turned around and continued her conversation with us. "Interesting take, Jeremiah."

From the expression on Veronica's face, she was livid with her little sister's flamboyant charade. I did what any other gentleman would do in this situation, I gave a congratulatory thumbs-up. "Anyway," I started until Elizabeth unashamedly interrupted with a flare of superiority.

"Do you start every sentence you say with, 'Anyway'?"

"Only when I'm trying to steer us back on topic from your split personality dialogues," I kidded. "Anyway…" I purposely started as everyone erupted in a hearty laugh. "Now, with all seriousness," I started as Elizabeth once again took the limelight.

"Yes, let's premise this next topic with the seriousness disclosure. Hey, Jenny, it's going to get serious. You ready for that?"

"Oh, Elizabeth, you are too much," Jenny chuckled.

"The table is all yours, Solo," Elizabeth stopped and waved her hand allowing me to continue. "Anyway."

"Yes, as you said," I started, pointing to Elizabeth. "Do you really think the world would be better like that?" I leaned onto the table with an attentive ear.

"Jeremiah, Solo here is going to become a preacher man," Elizabeth commented as she stood up and gulped her merlot, throwing her hands in the air. "Hallelujah!"

"A preacher?" Dr. Huffington asked with a higher tone in his voice. "So, you're one of the simple-minded followers? Are you afraid of the dark as well?" he smugly laughed, quickly stopping as the rest of us struggled to catch his joke. "I am only kidding, Solo, is it?"

"Yes, and I'm not going to become a preacher," I replied leaning back into my chair with folded arms, as if making a shield for his elitist philosophical arrows. It was all fun and games until that moment. I felt the undercurrent and I didn't want to get swept in the degrading undertow.

"Why not? Why are you going to, um, where are you going?" Elizabeth asked as she returned with four pieces of chocolate cake.

"I'm going to Wesley Theological Seminary," I started saying before being quickly sidelined as Elizabeth handed us each a piece.

"Lovely school. We are practically neighbors. Do you know Dr. Wright?" Jeremiah asked, taking a bite of cake.

"I've heard of him, but I haven't had him yet."

"Well, he is an old friend of mine. We played neighborhood ball as kids. I would go to Sunday school with him, and he would read Nietzsche with me on Mondays. He always tried to convert me; still does as a matter of fact, but that is what friends do. They want the best for each other. He thinks that is the best for me, and since he is such a good friend, I let him try. As he makes a good point on his belief, it only makes me think harder and wiser about my own. We don't let our differences hinder each other."

"That's really interesting," I said, tasting the cake and slightly gagging, wondering if they forgot the sugar. This definitely wasn't Wint's choice. Verny won out on this as well.

"You have to wash it down with something, or it will stick to the roof of your mouth," Elizabeth said sliding in and savoring the conversation. "A good glass of wine will wash away all your problems."

"So said the alcoholic," Jeremiah replied.

"Oh, Jeremiah, you made a joke," Elizabeth snidely gushed, reminiscent of a proud momma as she topped off her wine. "Anyway, why preacher school then?"

"I don't know. I just felt like I needed to go there."

"Kinda expensive for just a feeling. Did you have some kind of revelation?" Elizabeth smirked, winking to Jeremiah from across the table. "Some kind of vision?"

"Oh no, nothing quite as superficial as that," I answered honestly. Deep down I wish I knew what made me want to study theology, but I hadn't uncovered it yet. I just knew in my bones it was something I had to do.

"Superficial?" Elizabeth huffed under her breath as she stood up. "Anyone need another glass of wine?"

"No, thank you," Jenny stood up as well. "I really need to be going. I have an early deposition tomorrow morning."

Jeremiah and I gallantly followed suit and rose for Jenny's exit as Elizabeth walked away to get another glass of wine.

"Might as well get an unopened bottle," Jeremiah smiled, as I gave him a nice job thumbs-up sign as well. "It will last longer for you," he snickered as she gave a mocking expression. "Oh, what am I talking about it? No it won't. You'll finish that like it was a glass of water."

CHAPTER 10

The three of us continued our conversation. Well, mostly Jeremiah and I discussed various topics while Elizabeth occasionally nodded. The population of the rest of the table started to dwindle, and from the look in Verny's eyes, she wanted my side of the table to leave as well.

I looked down at my watch noting it was a quarter to ten. It wasn't late by my standards, but I knew that Verny and I could only be in the same room for so long before we would both break, and being a gracious guest, I didn't want Verny to go all fire-breathing dragon on the remaining few guests.

"I think I'll head out," I said, standing up and bidding my dining partners a good evening. "It was a pleasure meeting both of you."

"You too, Solo," Dr. Huffington said, rising to shake my hand. "This has been a nice evening for making new friends. We three should do this again sometime."

"Sure thing," Elizabeth agreed giddily, but deep down, I thought there was a hint of sarcasm in her tone. After gaining an understanding of her personality, I realized she was friendly for most of the evening, but then her mood shifted. I didn't dwell too long on the change. We had been talking for a couple of hours and she might have grown tired of the idle chit-chat. She was Verny's sister, so irrational blindsided moodiness could be in her DNA.

We exchanged numbers and promised to be in contact, knowing that was something people said they would do, but seldom followed through. I walked down to the other end of the table where Wint was talking to an elderly gentleman. I patted him on the shoulder, and he turned around, quickly jumping to his feet.

"I didn't mean to disturb you," I apologized, mainly to his guest and not to Verny.

"Oh, man," he hugged me like a brother. "Thank you for coming. It really means a lot to see you."

"You too, Wint. Thank you for inviting me, Veronica," I commented facetiously leaning down to give her a friendly goodbye kiss on the cheek. She quickly turned away from it as if my lips would cause damage to her flawless complexion. I wanted to rub her head like an annoying uncle and say *later gator*, but I didn't. I let her proverbial backhand slide because I really didn't want to kiss her anyway. Vaccinations for snobbishness and elitism were hard to find. I turned back to Wint and said, "Good night, bud."

I walked across the dining room, looking around before I grabbed another piece of cake to take home and eat later. Even though it tasted stale, it was better than nothing. I roamed the halls, trying to find my way out as Elizabeth stood by the door putting on her light coat.

"It was really nice meeting you," I said as I surprised her by helping her with her coat. "You really do have the best brother-in-law anyone could ask for."

"Did you mean what you said when you said 'superficial'?" she asked, ignoring the pleasantries of my last statement.

"I'm not sure I know what you are talking about," I said, putting my hands in my pockets to find my car keys.

"You said, and I quote, 'No, nothing quite as superficial as that,' when I asked if you'd had a revelation." When she spoke, I finally saw the resemblance between her and Verny.

"I don't quite believe in revelations," I said.

"Isn't your Bible filled with revelations?" she asked defiantly.

"Well, it's not just my Bible," I said with a smirk, hoping to bring a lightheartedness to the tirade. It didn't work. "I just have a hard time believing when people say God spoke to them. How does one know the difference between God speaking and their self-conscience?"

"Where's your faith?" she demanded throwing her hood on, opening the front door, and walking away. "That's why people think you all are hypocrites."

"Really? Elizabeth, stop. Come on, stop. There must be something else than just my thoughts. What's really wrong?"

She stopped but didn't turn around. She stood as if frozen under the crescent moon. "It's just that sometimes people say things to people not knowing they are talking about them right in front of their face, and it just pisses me off."

I didn't know what to do. Should I stay still? Should I walk up to her? I couldn't understand how my choice of the word *superficial* could have this much of an effect. "You are going to have to explain yourself a little better than that if you want me to understand. I'm not a mind reader or…"

"Or what?" she asked, turning around coldly.

I didn't respond. I knew I had struck a nerve again, but for the life of me, I still didn't get the connection.

"Or what?" she asked again, bringing back visions of Gertrude on the playground. I subconsciously placed my hands in front of my delicate area, expecting a kick soon.

"Tell me what's going on. Why is it that when I said I don't believe in something you are ready to tear into me like a momma bear smelling Oreos for the first time, but when Dr. Huffington flat out said he didn't believe, you just smiled and laughed him off like a school girl."

"School girl? You male chauvinist ego-testicle pig!" she barked.

"Did you say ego-testicle? Or do you mean egotistical?" I laughed.

"Really, Solo? That's all you got out of that? Yeah, ego-testicle, because all you men are the same! You think that just because you have a pair, no matter how small they may be, you can talk down to us women!"

"You know I didn't mean it that way!" I yelled before counting to five to calm down. But with dealing with her, I needed to count to twenty before I said anything else. "You know you are treating me and

51

Jeremiah differently." I stopped for a moment to ease away from the tension and started to laugh, "And ego-testicle? Who are you?"

A small tide of calm seemed to wash over her. "It's just that you have faith, and he doesn't," she said as she leaned against a Lexus. "He's set in his ways and can't see beyond what he sees, but someone with faith should be more open-minded."

"More open-minded? I'm still not following." I gradually moved beside her trying not to make a sudden move in case it freaked her out.

"Really? Are you just that blind, or are you just trying to annoy me?"

"Well, if you were Verny, I would annoy you for sport, but since you're not, I guess I'm just a man."

"See, men are so clueless sometimes."

"That we are." I shrugged my shoulders in surrender.

"Okay, so you believe all the stories in the Bible. no matter how crazy they sound. I'm not a real religious person, but I know that there are some really crazy drunk-off-your..."

"Yeah, yeah, I know," I intercepted before she could finish her statement. "I believe them. There are just as many odd things that happen today, and people believe those. They may try to find an explanation for why it happened, but they can't deny that it did."

"So, what if I tell you..." She stopped and slammed her fist onto the car hood, causing the alarm to go off. "Nope, I'm not going to do it."

"What are you doing?" I jumped away spooked by the alarm blaring as she dug into her purse and clicked it off.

"Don't worry. It's mine," she smiled, dangling the keys. "No cops are going to come after you out here tonight unless I want them to. All I have to do is shout and three of them would come running out of the house."

"But would they be running to help you or running to get away from Verny? This evening probably took a toll on those hard-working police officers who usually only deal with thugs and murderers. One night with Verny may seem like inhumane torture."

"True."

"Anyway, where were we?" I asked before realizing that I did say 'anyway' quite often. I shook off the overuse in my vocabulary and delicately slid beside her once again, making sure my weight didn't sound the alarm. "What are you not going to do?"

"I don't know why I'm talking to you."

"To be honest, neither do I," I kidded as she looked at me annoyed. "Ah, there it is."

"What?"

"I finally see it. I saw Verny in you just then."

"Shut up," she smiled, slightly agitated that she and Veronica did share similar characteristics. "You just seem…" She stopped and stared overhead.

"Dreamy? I've been told that a lot. I have to swat the ladies off with a stick."

"It must be a short stick," she laughed. "But dreamy isn't the word I would use to describe you," she sighed as she lowered her coat hood from her head.

"Incredible. Fine. Sexy. Devilishly handsome. Irresistible," I continued as she rolled her eyes with each adjective. "I can go on all night, *Verny*," I said, pointing at her facial expression.

"I bet you can, and your delusions are, well, hilarious, but there's just something about you that just says, talk to me."

"Oh," I moaned with an eye roll.

"What?"

"That's what every guy likes to be told. 'You're a good listener,'" I laughed. "News flash, don't tell a guy that."

"Well, I'm not trying to pick you up."

"That's good because you're my arch nemesis' kid sister, which would make for some awkward conversation." I stopped for a second. "But it would drive her bat-eyed crazy, which does have its benefits." I once again stopped as I continued to debate myself, shaking my head no at the notion. "Nope, strike that thought, it wouldn't work."

"Now that you have straightened that out all by yourself, I haven't told very many people this. I think only a few people know from when I was a kid, and they probably don't remember or even care anymore." She stopped and took a deep breath.

"And...?"

"I have visions."

I looked at her, unsure of how to respond. It wasn't meant to be a condescending look, but I couldn't guarantee that wasn't how it appeared.

"I do, and they always come true."

I let the words sink in for a few seconds before I responded. "So, you see visions."

"You don't have to say it like that," she frowned. "I didn't ask for it."

"No, I'm just. I'm just trying to understand."

"What's there to understand? I go to sleep, a dream comes to me, and sometime during the next day, it happens."

"I'm not calling you a liar, but…" I said as I stood up to pace.

She grunted. "By saying you're not calling me a liar, you are implying it."

"Why does it affect you so much what I do and don't think? It's not like we're friends."

"See, this is why I was telling myself that I shouldn't say anything."

"Well, you did, and you can't take it back. Why does my opinion matter so much? We just met a few hours ago, and since we never met before, you probably won't have the luxury of another evening with me for a few years. Unless you're lucky."

"I need boots to get through a night with you."

"I need waders for you."

"Back to my point," she said, corralling the conversation to where we began. "If you, a man of faith, don't believe me… I don't know, I just would like to know that someone does."

"I bet there are some people out there who would believe you."

She once again rolled her eyes in annoyance. "Do you meaning crazies in a mental ward when you say 'some people'? Or people who call the 1-900-PSYCHIC hotline? I'm not a psychic. It's not something I do for money or to amuse my friends at the bar."

"I can't just go by you saying that you have dreams. I need some proof. Tell me a dream you had."

"So, a man of faith needs proof? Ironic." She rolled her eyes in disgust.

"Aren't you too old to roll your eyes like a 13-year-old?"

"Aren't you too old for that watch?"

"Anyway. Why do you keep saying 'man of faith' like that? As if it's a putdown?"

"Because if your faith requires proof, where's the faith in that?"

"My faith doesn't depend on you," I said staring up at the stars through the semi-cloudy sky as if they could feel the weight of this conversation and decided to hang a little lower tonight. "I don't have faith in you."

"Fine." She closed her eyes and recounted her dreams of the previous night. "There was an older couple found dead in a park by a jogger."

"Yes, I saw that on the news today."

"Also, there was a plane from, where was it from, Chicago to Washington that had an emergency landing somewhere in Pennsylvania. I have it written down at home. No one has ever quizzed me before."

"Planes have emergency landings. That isn't anything new."

"The flight number is 854."

I stood motionless. These so-called predictions were nothing spectacular. Any self-proclaimed psychic could make similar claims. 'Someone whose first name begins with an L says that they love you and that they are proud of you.' If the spirit is right there, why didn't they just say their full name and relation? Did they forget it after they died? It would be easy to research flight numbers earlier in the day and keep up with the news.

"So, you're still not buying it?"

"I don't mean to be coming off that way, but I just have a hard time with things like this."

"Fine. The tropical storm off the coast of Florida will become a Category 3 hurricane by tomorrow evening, making landfall in Southern Georgia and moving up the coast to North Carolina before it juts off the land back to the Atlantic Ocean," she spit out in one long breath. "None of the news stations are saying this. But tonight at 11, they will."

"Sure," I said, quickly pulling out my phone to do a search for the storm as she watched.

"Search for Irina, Tropical Storm path."

"I'm getting there," I said as the forecasted map sprang to life, showing the trajectory of the tropical storm hundreds of miles from the Georgia coast and nowhere near the strength of a massive Category 3 hurricane.

"You still don't believe me," she shook her head in disbelief. "That's fine. That is perfectly fine. I know what I know. I just don't know *why* I know what I know, but I wish to God that you would see what I see and then you would know."

"I'm sorry, Elizabeth. I don't think you're crazy, but..." I stopped as she jumped up from the hood to get into her car.

"Once again, saying that you don't think I am crazy is saying I'm crazy in an undertone." She slammed her car door, started the engine, and drove away in a mad dash.

"Fine, you're right, you're crazy," I muttered under my breath, watching the rear lights disappear as she turned down a neighboring street, squealing her tires. "Freakin' crazy."

CHAPTER 11

Separately, they each made their way through the shadows near the International Spy Museum and entered the Gallery Place Chinatown Yellow Line Metro Station near the Verizon Center. They met, snuck into a nearby hidden tunnel to transform themselves from young, fit twenty-somethings into a cancer-stricken father and his feeble caretaker daughter.

"Ready for round two?" he asked from behind the medical mask as they waited for the next train to arrive, clutching the chloroform tank with one hand and her arm with the other.

She nodded in agreement, but it wasn't needed. He could read the anticipation in her eyes. The train entered the station with a surging gust of wind, causing some Marilyn Monroe dress moments for a few unsuspecting passengers. "Come on, Dad," she said beneath the medical mask, channeling her alter ego. She helped the decrepit old man to a middle seat so they could people watch for the next 30 minutes. They scanned the crowd for possible hits but knew that it was still too early to pick a worthy target.

"I've been thinking," he whispered, leaning his head down to appear to be falling asleep.

"About what?" she asked, casually scanning her eyes around the cabin for the unsuspecting souls.

"What if we changed the script?"

"Change?" she quietly gasped. "We only did it once and it was perfect. What would you change?"

"Well, maybe we could throw a little twist in there for some added excitement." He grinned to himself.

"A twist?" she asked. "We didn't plan on twists. If we don't go by the plan there could be problems," she said in a snarl, wrapping her arms around him and causing his head to slide onto her shoulder.

"But it could be more fun."

"Do you not remember what Dad taught us before he left?" She rubbed his bald head as if petting her favorite pet. "Always be prepared."

"Yeah," he sadly relented.

"If we change something now, are we going to be prepared?"

"No," he answered like he was five years old again. "You're right."

She tenderly grabbed his face so their eyes could meet. "It's not about whose right or wrong. We are in this together. We are a team. Together til the end, and I'm not ready for it to end just yet."

"Me either."

"Most of all, we are doing this for Dad," she said endearingly. "Remember?"

"Let's do it as planned."

The subway car traveled over the Potomac River, allowing her to catch sight of the Jefferson Memorial at night. She pressed her head against the window, catching sight of the massive standing statue of one of the founding fathers. Having her brother by her side almost made her want to wave to the statue like when she was young, sitting on her father's lap.

"We're doing this for you, Papa," she whispered to herself, recalling the tender moment of her childhood before it was stolen. "This is all for you."

The memorial left her sight as the train moved back on dry land, entering the Pentagon Station. The doors opened, allowing a few military men and women to vacate the train and a couple of possible new prospects to join their journey to their final destination. She looked around the train and saw three older couples that fit the tourist mold. Only a few more stations until they discovered their lucky playmates.

CHAPTER 12

The flamboyant mansion where Wint resided greatly overshadowed the rundown studio apartment I called my own. The sink of dirty dishes was calling my name, but not as loudly as the couch that snagged my attention with the cozy worn afghan beside the television remote control. I turned on ESPN to watch the day's highlights of the extremely athletic, but my favorite portion was the recap of the daily bloopers. One can never get enough of overly cocky running backs, slamming the football down for a touchdown on the three-yard line. Imbeciles.

So, what did you think of Jenny? my phone chimed with a text from Wint.

She was friendly, but quiet, I replied, connecting the dots of why Verny's lifelong friend was seated at the section of misfits.

She is quiet. Anything else?

I stared at the phone wondering how to respond. Married people always tried to bring their single friends into their ranks. They acted like marriage was an exclusive club and we needed a personal invitation to enter the elite social circle. Where was my Member's Only jacket when I needed one?

You there?

Yeah, I'm here, I sent. *So, it was a setup tonight? Could have given me a little warning.*

Last time I gave you a head's up, you weren't yourself.

That was a year ago, and I told you I wasn't ready.

I waited for the phone to chime, but it didn't. That was also what single people did. They perceived a well-intentioned married friend as one who had a plan in helping the less fortunate, treating singleness like a disease and matchmaking like a lifesaving antibiotic. When in reality, what they were doing was just showing they cared in the only way they knew how.

Thanks anyway, I slowly typed, waving the white flag and swallowing the barbed wire pill of pride. *She was cute.*

I thought she was your type, he replied, quickly followed by another message. *So, wanna do a double date sometime? It can be like old times.*

Sure.

Cool. I'll get Verny to talk to her tomorrow. Night bud.

Night. I laid the phone down, picked up the remote, and flipped through the channels hoping something would catch my interest. I wasn't that fond of home improvement shows because it was sickening to see how the rich lived when I was living in the police-infused ghetto. At least if I ever got shot in a mugging gone wrong, the police would be by my side in three minutes.

I could only watch so many episodes of *Friends* or *How I Met Your Mother* before I realized that even the poorest members of those shows still lived in a better apartment than I did. It wasn't that I salivated at the notion of seven-figure salaries, but sometimes television was so far from reality no matter where the real housewives lived.

If you're not ready yet, I won't force you. I just know that she would want you to move on and be happy.

I read the text, and I knew he was right. Quite a few years had passed, and I hadn't had a successful relationship since. Not that I tried too hard. I always felt a twinge of guilt for moving on, as if seeking someone new would push her memory away. I knew it was just me. All our friends had told me to take a chance on someone new. Even her family tried to set me up once, which was a little too awkward to carry through.

My phone chimed once more. *Love ya bro.*

I was never one to reply with such words. Wint knew how I felt. It was like an unwritten law. Wint would say it, and I would just silently agree, but tonight felt different. *Back atcha.*

I unconsciously changed the channels until I saw Rock Harrison, the awkwardly orange spray-tanned meteorologist on Channel 9. My mom had always told me not to trust pretty people, so I watched Channel 9 News for that reason. He might have been attractive in his prime, but too many cosmetic improvements can hinder more than it can improve.

"Thanks Amanda. I wish I could say that the next few days would be perfect weather for picking out some pumpkins or indulging in some pumpkin spice lattes in the park as I said a few hours ago, but everything has changed from today's earlier forecast. The Tropical Storm Irina, which was supposed to follow the path of the jet stream, missing land and staying at a safe distance in the middle of the Atlantic, has some devious plans of her own. Just minutes ago, The Weather Center sent a warning forecasting that the storm will make landfall in Southern Georgia tomorrow evening where it will become a Category 3 hurricane. It will run its destructive course along the Eastern Seaboard through South and North Carolina before it juts away from the land and heads back out to the Atlantic Ocean. This is a major change with very little preparation time for the residents of those states. None of the forecasting models believed that Irina would hit the United States, let alone become a Category 3 hurricane. No one could have predicted this. No one. Back to you, Amanda."

"She's good," I laughed, shaking my head. I reached for my phone to send her a text to congratulate her on her ruse but decided not to. Being the little sister of Verny, she'd probably had a long life of telling tales to gain attention. This was just another one of her fraudulent dramatizations.

"Sad. Just sad."

CHAPTER 13

It was a lonely walk home from Cleveland Park Metro Station to her apartment on Ordway Street. The sidewalks were empty, except for a few employees closing their shops and restaurants for the night. A couple of them smiled as they passed. She looked them in the eyes but didn't return the gesture, forgetting that she had already taken off her medical mask and was now fully exposed. She enjoyed the medical mask more than she originally realized.

An hour earlier, she was surging with the anticipation of another kill, but how her plans had quickly been tarnished. She and her brother found a couple of targets on their last ride to the Huntington Station. She had done her pre-check flawlessly in combination with idle chit-chat with the tourists. She was warm and friendly, and they welcomed her ideas for the Capitol Building Tour. Charlie and Janet, a retired couple from Maine, were starting their journey south for the winter by stopping at various cities before taking up residence in Fort Myers until April.

The two huntsmen followed the happy travelers to the parking garage, just as they had with Burt and Pam the night before. The only problem with their plan was they didn't foresee that Charlie and Janet were not the mini-van type. They were motorcyclists instead.

Their hearts sank into their stomachs as they saw Charlie and Janet straddle their Harley, put on their helmets, and wave a friendly goodbye before puttering down the ramp into the crisp night air. They had planned for every type of scenario, but they had never envisioned this.

They sat on the garage stairs for a few minutes, waiting for all the passengers from the last train to depart before they journeyed back to the station. "Wanna do another round?" he asked, clearly disappointed with the events of the night.

"Do you?" she asked, looking at her watch. "It's almost midnight and the garage is getting pretty empty."

"Yeah, you're right, we'd better call it a night," he said resigning himself to these new circumstances. He then stood up, with her help, still playing the part of the helpless old man.

They entered the Metro car for their trip back into town, exiting at the Metro Center Station where they snuck into a darkened hallway. There, they removed their costumes and parted company like strangers.

"Tomorrow," she said, giving him a wink before leaving their hideaway. She walked toward the Red Line, and he waited seven minutes before leaving the hallway for the Silver Line.

Wednesday

CHAPTER 14

"Please help me," said a little girl about seven years old. She trembled with tears running down her frightened face, causing her blonde locks to stick to the wetness. Her white blouse and blue and green plaid tie were partially hidden from her tucked khaki knees to her chest as she rocked in the corner. "Let me go home," she squalled as the overhead light flickered like a sleazy hotel vacancy sign.

"It's going to be okay," a gruff voice said behind the door. "You'll be home as soon as we get what we want."

"Please!" she screamed, jumping up and running to the locked door, beating on it with her fists. "I want my mommy," she sobbed, "and daddy."

"Soon enough," the voice answered as the room went dark. "Soon enough."

The darkness vanished like a candle in the night, illuminating the scene and spreading its light to the entire area. Wesley Theological Seminary came into focus as a few of the last autumn leaves chased one another on the grounds of the campus. Traffic on Massachusetts Avenue had a steady stream of vehicles, until a weaving Metrobus crossed the centerline, missing traffic and hopping the curb before it crashed into the modern styled building of the American University Music Library.

"Help! Help!" a female passenger screamed running toward the driver. She noticed that his eyes were open, but he wasn't breathing. "He's not breathing!"

"Is there a doctor?" another man shouted as he unbuckled the driver's seatbelt. "Someone get his feet! We need to get him out of here!" Two young men carried him out of the bus and laid him on the barely green grass.

"He's still not breathing," one of the men shouted as a pedestrian ran over saying that he was a doctor.

He quickly felt for a pulse and started CPR, pressing on his chest and breathing into his purpling lips, "One, two, three, four…"

The counting faded along with the scene as another image slowly appeared in the form of text messages from a cell phone.

So, you want to meet for a double date? the text appeared on the screen as a chime sounded.

Hello? You there? I've tried calling you, but it goes straight to voicemail, another message appeared with a smiley face emoji.

Well, if you're interested let me know. We are all free tomorrow night, so it's in your court, man. Let me know soon.

It appeared that the text messages ended when one came through more slowly. *Learn something today*, which stayed on the phone until it went to sleep a few minutes after it was received. The darkness once again filled the scene as muffled voices could barely be heard.

"It's time, Dad," a young woman's voice announced.

"Ready?" a man's voice whispered anxiously.

"Very," the female voice replied as a beeping sound entered from afar followed by the sound of a car door shutting. "Thanks for giving us a lift. You really shouldn't have, but we greatly appreciate it. Don't we, Dad?"

"Uh huh," the dad's voice answered.

"I know how it is," another woman's voice said, older than the first. "I was sick a few years ago, and the littlest things would tire me out. Good thing I had Sam by my side the whole time. He's a keeper."

"Good ol' Sam," the young woman answered. "You doing okay up there, Dad?"

"Uh huh," the man answered.

"What level did you park on?" another man's voice asked, much older than the first.

"I, I, I don't remember," the young woman frantically laughed. "But I will know it when I see it."

"Just like Marge," the older man's voice grunted.

"See, it's not just me," the older woman commented. "Sam always makes fun of me for forgetting where I park at the grocery."

"Oh, there it is. The green Kia in the back corner," the younger woman exclaimed.

"Oh rats. Can you give me a wipe? I spilled some juice," the dad said, slurring his speech.

Suddenly, frightened screams filled the darkness ending the pleasant conversation from the four people.

Bolting up from bed, I felt my forehead dripping in sweat. I hadn't had so many dreams and in such vivid detail in quite some time. I looked toward the alarm clock, and the neon red numbers caused my heart rate to subside as I realized I had four more blissful hours of sleep before it would scream me awake at 6 a.m. for my morning jog. Falling back, I was fast asleep before my head hit the pillow.

CHAPTER 15

The morning alarm came earlier than I wished, but there were some things that one had to do, even when they didn't feel like it. I jogged my typical three miles in Eakin Community Park, nestled in the small community of Mantua, Virginia, where I called home. It was far enough from the busy life of D.C., but it only took 30 minutes to get there when I wanted a little action in my mundane existence.

After cleaning up after the jog, I grabbed a health-conscious breakfast, a piece of the leftover cake, and dashed out to school. Wednesdays were my busiest days for classes. I had Old Testament Exegesis: Isaiah at 9 a.m., then Pop Culture and Christian Formation at 11:15, then time for a quick lunch, followed by Evangelism and Emerging Generations at 1:30, and Sociology of Religion at 3:45.

Dr. Paul Whitcome, an elderly gentleman, probably near 80 years old, taught my Isaiah class with the same boredom with which it was probably taught to him in the 1950s. It wasn't that the book of Isaiah wasn't interesting, but some theology classes tended to lose the intrigue of the story by focusing on what was underneath. I was for discovering something new and exciting, but not when it caused me to desire a cup of caffeinated coffee when I wasn't even a coffee drinker.

In the middle of Dr. Whitcome's nasally and well-rehearsed speech that he likely wrote in 1981, I felt my phone vibrate in my pocket. I looked to see who was calling. It was just Wint, so I hit ignore, even though I desperately wanted to talk to him in the hopes his conversation would spur me awake. Out of common courtesy, I declined the call. Teach on, Dr. Whitcome, I thought. Teach on.

I laid the phone on the desk, hoping to focus on the time ticking by rather than the back of my own eyelids, when the phone vibrated again – this time with a text.

So, you want to meet for a double date? the text from Wint read.

I stared at the phone, thinking the message was familiar, but dismissed the notion. It must have been from the texts the night before. I clicked on the phone to cause it to sleep, but it suddenly lit up again with a vibration.

Hello? You there? I've tried calling you, but it goes straight to voicemail, he texted again with a smiley face emoji. This caused me to chuckle to myself, but a little too loudly from the looks on the faces of my neighbors. Luckily, Mr. Whitcome's hearing aid didn't pick up on the sound because he continued his speech as if everyone's attention was on him.

Since Mr. Whitcome wasn't watching me, I decided to respond and started typing when another message from Wint came through. *Well, if you're interested let me know. We are all free tomorrow night, so it's in your court, man. Let me know soon.*

Sure, I replied. I didn't know how I felt about this double date, but it was too early to get hopes up or walls built. I laid my phone down to give Dr.

Whitcome my undivided attention for the rest of the class. That was when his last sentence perked an interest in my ear.

"Call them what you will: dreams, prophecies, visions, but when God speaks, listen up. There's a reason why He's revealing Himself."

My phone lit up with another text from Wint, *Learn something today.*

I stared at my phone and then up at Dr. Whitcome and then back at the phone, immediately brushing it off as a mere coincidence. I mean, that was what it had to be, just a coincidence. Déjà vu, per se.

CHAPTER 16

Metal steel tables lined the sterilized room like desks in a classroom, but unlike a classroom, no one wanted to end up here. Dr. Raul Santiago, a 42-year-old chief medical examiner for Washington, D.C., welcomed a couple of police officers into his sanctuary. He covered the nude corpse on the table with a thin sheet that left nothing to the imagination. He lowered his surgical mask and inhaled the chemical smells that he had grown accustomed to while exposing a scar on his right cheek from a hostage situation gone awry in this very room a decade earlier when he was working under the former chief medical examiner. He'd quickly learned the hard lesson of not trusting anyone in the room. Because once a person lowered his guard, the scalpel used to answer deathly questions could quickly lead to deadly consequences.

"Please come in," he said, allowing his rich Hispanic accent to flow like a mariachi band as he stowed the medical equipment he'd been using on Burt and Pam Hamilton. One could never be too safe. His dark skin, jet black hair, and youthful good looks caused the women on the floor to admire him from a distance. What made him even more desirable was his love for his wife of 16 years and his darling six-year-old twin daughters. "I would have done their autopsies yesterday, but someone labeled their deaths as a suicide, so it was moved to the bottom of my priorities."

"So, was this a suicide or homicide?" asked 25-year veteran Captain Bradley Johnson as he held his stenographer's notepad in his rough, strong, black hands, ready to take any and all details that Dr. Santiago could give. He was a bit older than Dr. Santiago, but there was a mutual respect between the two in their respective areas of expertise.

"There were no signs of a violent crime on either of the bodies. No bruising, cuts, stabs, or anything were found anywhere on the bodies. Preliminary tests showed the couple died of carbon monoxide poisoning, which is understandable based on how you found the deceased. This would make you assume suicide, but after further testing, I found large traces of chloroform on their faces and in their lungs. There was small amount on their hands, which would make this appear to be a homicide."

"Are you sure about this?" asked Detective Smith Young, a 32-year-old newly promoted detective. Detective Young, who was trying to get a foot in the door and a name for himself, was first at the scene the day before and immediately tagged these deaths as a suicide in his report.

"I'm pretty sure," Dr. Santiago answered, giving Captain Johnson a look that required no words. "You did not find any chloroform rags or containers at the scene, correct?"

"No, we did not," Detective Young answered. "But..."

"Well," Dr. Santiago quickly interrupted, "if this couple drugged themselves, there would have been some remnants of the chloroform in the vehicle. Also, given the amount of chloroform in their nasal passages, if they were using a rag on themselves, there would have been a large amount of chloroform on their hands. With the small amount found on their hands, it appears that they could have been fighting off their attackers."

"Did you find any other DNA under their nails perhaps?" Captain Johnson asked, trying to steer Dr. Santiago away from the arrogant and nearly deflated Detective Young.

"No. I didn't find any other DNA. The person who perpetrated this crime was thorough."

"If you find anything else, Raul, let me know," Captain Johnson said as he stepped away. "Detective Young?"

"Yes?" Young followed him out the doors and into some fresh air.

"I need you to go back to the scene of the crime and see what we missed. If this was a murder, there has to be something."

"Yes, sir," Young said, frowning as he walked down the hall, realizing that once again his gut instinct had been wrong.

"Young, no one is right all the time. That's why we have Raul. He helps us see the things that we can't see," he said in an encouraging tone that he despised, especially when speaking to Young. "Now find something we can use to catch this guy."

"Yes, sir."

"And Young, quit being so cocky. None of us like it."

CHAPTER 17

My mom always said that I was Elvis reincarnated because there were two things that Elvis and I had in common – our love of peanut butter and banana sandwiches and crisp strips of bacon. The sandwich was my go-to when I was in a hurry, and typically, that was my Wednesday staple -- a light lunch and a short walk up Massachusetts Avenue. After a morning of lectures, sunlight and fresh air were dearly needed to make it through the rest of the afternoon. On rainy days, the drops of rain on my face were an added bonus refreshment. It was hard to fall asleep in class when I was drenched. Luckily today, the storm of Irina was still south of us and the rays of sunshine were beating warmly down my back like a heavenly massage.

I fumbled in my pocket, trying to get my phone out hoping to send another text to Wint. I wished to get more details about the setup. Then something happened. An odd feeling came over me. I could not explain it; it was as if the world continued its normal speed, yet I was locked in slow motion watching from the outside looking in. I looked down at my phone, but I couldn't move my fingers to type. My body seemed to want me to do something totally different, but what?

I slowly looked up, and everything else around me appeared normal. I went to text, but I felt something lightly tap my foot behind me. I turned my head around noticing that someone had thrown their trash to a receptacle, but missed, hitting my foot instead.

"Sorry, man," the college student said as he quickly stooped down to pick up the McDonald's bag.

"No problem," I answered as a familiar image came into view. A swerving Metrobus, barely missing the other vehicles on the street, came barreling up the road as my heart rate slowed in disbelief. The slow motion I felt earlier reappeared. I turned my head and saw that I was across the street from the American University Music Library. "This can't be happening," I said as the young man looked up at me with his McDonald's bag in hand.

"I said I was sorry, man. Chill. It's only a bag."

"No. Not you. That bus is about to crash," I said as the two of us watched the events unfold like a movie we had seen a million times. The weaving bus quickly turned from our direction and crossed the adjacent two lanes of traffic. Horns blared from the quickly stopping Mercedes and Honda CRV as the bus proceeded to jump the curb, slowing down only slightly before crashing into the large white building.

"Dude! How'd you do that?" he yelled as I quickly ran across the street to help in any way I could.

"Help! Help!" a female passenger screamed from somewhere inside the bus. "He's not breathing!"

"Is there a doctor?" another man shouted from within the bus as the door flew open. "Someone get his feet! We need to get him out of here!" Two young men struggled to carry the overweight individual down the steps, laying him on the grass.

"He's still not breathing!" one of the men shouted, rising from leaning over the 50-year-old man in a Metro uniform with Frank embroidered in blue thread on his shirt.

"I can help," someone announced, running over and throwing his satchel on the grass as he leaned over feeling for a pulse. He started administering CPR, pressing on his chest and breathing into his purpling lips. "One, two, three, four..."

"Jeremiah?" I gasped, watching as he kept breathing life-giving air into Frank's lungs. Stepping back to give him some room to work, I watched as someone jumped into the bus to shut it off as smoke from the crumbled hood rose into the sky. The rest of the bus passengers exited shakily. Some of the elderly were being helped by some of the younger passengers.

"Did anyone call for help?" a woman asked as she leaned against the sturdy library wall, panting and fanning herself. She watched Jeremiah try to save the lifeless bus driver.

"Yes," a gentleman with a briefcase answered with his ear still pressed to his phone. "They are just a few blocks away."

Everyone who was standing looked up and down Massachusetts Avenue, listening for the sirens as they became audible and breathed a little easier knowing help was nearby. I continued to watch as Jeremiah unrelentingly counted and pressed Frank's chest to no avail. Beads of sweat were forming as Frank's purplish color started to spread out from his lips.

"They're here!" a woman by the curb shouted as she directed the medics to Jeremiah and Frank.

"I've tried CPR," Jeremiah calmly stated. "I tried."

"We've got it," one of the EMTs said as they quickly moved Frank's body from the ground onto their gurney and raced him to their ambulance. In a flash, the ambulance was out of sight, heading to the nearest hospital.

More ambulances arrived to care for the needs of the other passengers. No one was seriously injured, but many were badly shaken. A couple of young overly dramatic college girls had even fainted, either from the excitement or the need for attention.

"You did try," I said walking over, trying to console Jeremiah. I didn't know what else to say. 'You did your best,' didn't sound appropriate. 'Good job,' sounded disrespectful in Frank's current state. 'My condolences,' seemed impersonal.

"Nothing more we could do," he said, shrugging off my statement. He picked up his satchel. "Want to grab a coffee?"

CHAPTER 18

I gingerly sipped my passion fruit tea, waiting for the boiling temperature to cool to something more pleasant than scalding. I was bewildered by the carefree attitude Jeremiah was displaying when only minutes earlier he had been trying to save a man's life.

"You okay?" I asked, trying to be both sensitive and respectful without prying too much into his feelings.

"I'm fine, why?" he asked, seemingly confused as he stirred his green tea with two packets of sugar.

"Frank?"

"Who?" he asked taking a sip of his drink. "Oh, you mean the bus driver? It's nothing to take personally. I didn't know him. I just tried to help. Maybe I did and maybe I didn't, but that's all I could do."

"Aren't you a little shaken?" I asked noticing that my hands were still trembling from the excitement as I held my swaying cup of tea.

"Solomon, I mean, Solo, people die. It's a fact. Do you feel remorse for every obituary you read in the paper?"

"No, but I didn't try to save a man's life either."

"I would probably feel remorse if I had just stood and watched him die knowing that I knew CPR. But since I did something, I have no remorse."

"Not even a little?" I asked, grimacing at how well he compartmentalized his feelings.

"Not even a little," he answered, noticing my baffled expression. "Does that make me a bad person?"

I looked around the coffee shop, watching the barista hand out coffee after coffee for sleep-deprived college students as they channeled their newfound caffeinated energy on their midterm papers. "I wouldn't say bad."

"Well, what would you say?" he prodded.

Darting my eyes around the room, I tried to find something new to talk about since this conversation was starting to feel a little intense, but I couldn't find anything in my arsenal of knowledge. "So, any classes this afternoon?"

"Come on, don't change the subject. What am I? Does your teaching say I am not a moral person for not feeling some sadness for a loss of life?"

"It's not a Christian teaching. It's just a human thing. Seeing someone injured and not knowing if the person is going to make it should stir something inside you. Shouldn't it?"

"There are some cultures that believe death is a beautiful experience. There are others that show no emotions at all. Then there are some that grieve with tears and wailing. Which of these is moral?"

"I see what you are getting at," I said, smiling and taking a gulp of my warm and comforting tea. "But in our culture, seeing a dead man in front of your eyes isn't a common occurrence. Most people would feel some sense of grief."

"What about a mortician, or a scientist in a lab, or a homicide detective? They see dead bodies and probably never feel any sadness for the deceased. Are they outcasts in our society?"

"I don't know how to respond to you," I laughed. "I feel like I am in a philosophical debate, and no matter what I say, you will turn it around into another question. Like a never-ending rabbit hole. What do you think about me?" I turned his questioning around on him.

"I think you are a man who thinks he sees the world in millions of colors, but really only sees black and white."

"I don't get it."

"Okay, how about this. Would you feel strange eating a cheeseburger right now?"

"I'm not hungry," I grinned.

"Fine. Say you are hungry. Would you feel strange eating a cheeseburger right now?"

"No."

"Okay. What if I was a starving man? Would you feel strange eating it in front of me?"

"I would give you some."

"So, you would feel strange!" he exclaimed. "Because by giving me some of it, you are trying to change the situation."

"But that doesn't mean that I feel strange. I am just feeling compassion toward you," I rebutted.

"Is it really compassion out of your goodness, or is it out of selfishness to eat without me staring?"

"I don't get the color analogy."

"How about if you were in India? Would you eat a cheeseburger in front of a Hindu that reveres cows as sacred?"

"No, that would be rude," I answered. "Me not eating a cheeseburger isn't out of selfishness, or pride, or self-centeredness at all. It is just me being a kind person and respecting someone else's beliefs. It is just being nice."

"Funny how your answer changes in each scenario, but you can defend each one perfectly, like it is the right answer. Because to you, it is the right answer. You are so black and white."

I looked down at my watch and noticed I had missed my class after lunch, and my last class for the day was going to begin in twenty minutes. "I need to be heading back to school."

"Can I tell you something before you go?" he asked as I stood up to put on my backpack. "I'm black and white too."

"Huh?" I asked, lowering myself back to my chair, realizing that I was looking like a stubborn child trying to run away at the first sign of someone disagreeing with me.

"Solo, we all make daily decisions, and we always believe that the decisions we are making are the right ones. We never make decisions to purposely make the wrong one. If we do not go with what our mind is telling us is the right decision, there is ultimately a reason for not making that decision. This, in turn, causes us to think that it is the right decision. Every decision I make, I think I am right. Just as you always think you are right. Every decision I do not make, I subconsciously think is not the best one." He stopped to sip his tea. "See? Black and white."

"I understand your concept, but I still don't see how you don't feel anything for Frank. Concepts are theories, but not all theories work in life."

"Why are you going to theology school? If you want to study history and civilizations, you should study anthropology."

"Why are you changing the subject?"

"Because some theories are purely theoretical and not applicable, but that doesn't mean that I am saying you are right." He snickered as he looked down at his phone. "Good meeting up with you, Solo. Want to meet up here next Wednesday to discuss my failing morality?"

"This is actually during one of my classes. How about lunch here next week?"

"Preacher man skipping class?" he laughed as he put on his satchel.

"I'll just tell the professor there was a death," I remarked as we headed toward the door.

"Doesn't God frown on stretching the truth?"

"Let's just say I'm playing in the gray area of your color analogy."

"You have no gray area, Solo," he laughed. "Just as I don't either."

CHAPTER 19

The screen on Detective Young's computer in the squad room was plastered with photographs from the Hamiltons' crime scene. Yellow caution tape marked the vehicle, while its contents were strewn on the blacktop, much like a rummage sale gone wrong. Burt and Pam were pictured as if posing for a morbid family portrait. Sadly, this was the last one they would take together.

"What am I missing?" he asked himself, looking at each picture with careful scrutiny.

"Cooper, come over here!" Detective Young shouted from across the room as Wint Cooper sat behind his computer, trying to connect the dots in the increase in drug trafficking in D.C. Officer Cooper's partner had retired a few weeks earlier, and he was in a transition period while the department found him a permanent partner. Until that time, he was on desk duty.

"What do you need, detective?" Cooper asked, walking away from his case to help his senior. There was some added tension between these two that could be detected by anyone after just two minutes of watching them. Cooper held a grudge that he was passed over for a promotion by Detective Young. The story behind Detective Young's quick rise in prominence was his parents' substantial political contribution to the current mayor's campaign. Without the large donation, Detective Young would most likely still be on the streets writing parking tickets or serving as a private school crossing guard.

"I have looked at these pictures all afternoon, and I can't see any clues."

"Scoot over," Cooper said, moving his chair behind the computer to examine the various forms of evidence. "Where's the list of items at the crime scene?"

Detective Young found the list under the loose sheets of paper that haphazardly covered his desk. Cooper gave it a quick look over. "Huh."

"Huh?"

"Yeah, you thought this was a suicide?"

"Why not?" Young's temper skyrocketed in defense.

"They came from Illinois to kill themselves?" Cooper quizzed doubtingly.

"I've heard of stranger things before. Haven't you?"

Cooper didn't respond but continued to look at the listing on the sheet. "Where's their luggage?"

"Luggage?"

"Yes, if they drove from Illinois to here, they would have brought some luggage. Did you find a hotel room key?"

Young peered over Cooper's shoulder to look at the list. "We had a purse and wallet with their IDs and credit cards, and a little cash, but no hotel key. If they were murdered, why didn't the killer steal their cash?"

"Well, the medical examiner said they were murdered, so we can quit trying to convince ourselves that we were right." Young flinched at the verbal attack. "Isn't that a little odd?" Cooper questioned adamantly. "If they didn't have any luggage, most likely they had already dropped it off at their hotel. Have you looked through their bank and credit card statements to see their recent activity?"

"I got it here but haven't looked at it yet."

"Well, maybe you should," Cooper said, rolling his eyes, annoyed that Young made detective when he couldn't see beyond the scene to the evidence. Unless there was a bloody knife at the scene, Young was oblivious. "You look through those statements for purchases at any hotels around here, and I will keep looking at the photos."

"Hey, Smith," Dakota Peterson said cheerfully as she walked through the squad room with a coffee cup in hand. Her tailor-made police uniform accented her five-foot-three petite frame. Dakota was a 28-year-old dispatch operator who took every opportunity she could throughout the day to have a conversation with Detective Young. She was the type of woman who would go to medical school with only the intention of finding a doctor husband. She wasn't smart enough for medical school, so she was going to have to settle for a policeman groom. "What you working on?" she asked interestedly, stretching her head around at his desk to see the pictures. "Oh. Hi, Cooper," she casually said to be polite, but not meaning it.

"We are working on the new murder case," Young answered, enjoying the attention from Dakota.

"So, any leads yet?" she asked, smiling like the cheerleader flirting with the quarterback in high school, causing Cooper's breakfast to toss around in his stomach.

"So Young, what did you and Caroline do last night?" Cooper asked, bringing up Young's reporter girlfriend as Dakota grimaced in anger. He didn't care about Young's relationship with the crooked television reporter girlfriend who would do anything for a story, but he knew it would cause coals to burn on both of their heads at the mention of her name.

"Cooper, what are you doing?" Chief Grant Randolph asked as he snuck up behind the three of them.

"Bye, Smith," Dakota said, moving away like a child caught with her hand in the cookie jar.

"I was just showing him the proper way to look for evidence," Detective Young answered quickly with a tone of self-righteousness.

"Don't you have your own case to work?" Chief Randolph bellowed towering over Cooper like a concrete statue. They were both gloomily gray in complexion with carved wrinkles and hollowed out eyes. They each gave off just as much warmth and encouragement. Lastly, the only way that the chief was going to step down from his position was to be toppled over and broken to pieces with no hope of recovery. The chief was an old-school cop that worked himself up the ranks by rubbing shoulders and backs with a chosen few until he got where he wanted -- the very top.

"Yes, sir. Yes...yes, I do," Cooper said, heading to his desk as he gave Young an evil eye as if warning him to watch his back.

"Chief, it looks like the couple was staying at the Red Roof Inn in Alexandria, Virginia off of Richmond Highway," Detective Young interjected, quickly finding a charge on their credit card statement. "Since their key card wasn't found at the scene of their death, what if the killer took it and went back there?"

"It's a stretch, but look into it," the chief said stomping away. He stopped suddenly. "Good work on that, Young. Good work. Oh, and since that isn't in our jurisdiction, you need to contact Alexandria's police to help with the investigation."

"Thank you, sir," Young said, basking in the glory of the chief's compliments. He looked over at Cooper who didn't acknowledge his menacing gaze but stared at his computer, picking up where he had left off. Drugs, drugs, and more drugs.

CHAPTER 20

After throwing my keys on the coffee table, I grabbed the television remote and quickly discovered the local evening news was just beginning.

"Top story tonight," read Brock Michaels, the senior news anchor with his perfect bravado voice that soothed and informed the nightly viewers. I held my breath, waiting to hear about the kidnapping or the death of the older couple. I had already had two of my dreams strangely come true with frightening detail, and I couldn't help but wonder if it was some cosmic coincidence -- a million to one chance that all my dreams actually occurred. I kept watch of the news on my phone during my last class, but nothing was ever mentioned of the mysterious little girl or grizzly murder.

"Hurricane Irina is pounding the Carolinas as we brace for the possible flash flooding. Tell us, Rock, how did this happen and what is in store for us?" Brock asked as the tangerine-colored meteorologist walked over to his weather map, pointing out the storm's path.

I scrolled through a couple of texts that I'd received, rereading the ones from Wint. Did my dream really happen? Did I really see those texts, or have I known Wint for so long that we had a brotherly bond that knew each other's conversations before they were ever said.

The commercials ended, and the news continued as they mentioned a drug bust in Georgetown; the continuation of the prostitution sting on some very influential citizens in the D.C. area; a bomb scare at a local grocery store that turned out to be a diaper bag accidentally left behind; and the bus driver that had a stroke, ultimately crashing into American University. No sign of the two news stories I desperately wanted to see.

Another car commercial came on the screen as I darted to the kitchen to grab some supper, but I found nothing quick and easy in the refrigerator, so a few carrot sticks were going to have to tide me over until I could scrounge something up. I chomped away at the vegetables, hoping that the beta carotene would improve my aging eyesight.

The station announced some local football news followed by predictions for the upcoming basketball season and then back to the weather forecast. The news concluded with a few other minor stories, but nothing was ever mentioned about my other two dreams. There were no snippets of a missing child or an Amber Alert. There was no excerpt on a couple found dead. Nothing was said of upcoming stories that they were working on for the nighttime newscast.

Flipping off the television, I felt the need to relax. It was a hectic day full of confusion, but luckily some of the confusion was drifting away like a message in a bottle. After a few minutes of resting my eyelids, that mysterious bottle's message was out of sight and out of mind. People had dreams all the time, and sometimes they came true and sometimes they didn't. It didn't mean anything one way or the other. Today wasn't any more special than yesterday. Tomorrow would not be any more special than today.

It was just happenstance.

CHAPTER 21

"Do they have video cameras in the rooms?" Captain Johnson asked as he walked around Room 124 of the Red Roof Inn in Alexandria. He examined the ceilings and corners as a couple of police officers from Alexandria's police force questioned any hotel tenants who would talk to them.

"I'm not sure, sir, but I wouldn't think so. There are probably some kinky things that go on in these rooms," Detective Young answered as he quit looking through the Hamiltons' belongings with his latex-gloved hands. "I'll go ask."

Johnson shook his head in amazement as Young left before walking over to the phone and dialing the front desk. "Hello, this is Captain Johnson. Detective Young is on his way to ask about security cameras on the premise. Can you get us video of the last 24 hours from inside the room and then all the hallways and grounds of the hotel? Thank you."

He slammed the phone down. In a way, he was glad Young had left because he needed a few minutes of silence from his quick and baseless theories. Cops need to follow leads and develop theories in order to find criminals, but one could not jump on every thought like the case would be solved instantaneously. Johnson knew he needed to teach and have patience, but every passing day of having to partner with the know-it-all kid who couldn't tell the difference between a homicide and a suicide made retirement look better and better.

His mentor always told him, "Don't look for the smoking gun; look for the gun cleaner." For crimes committed in the heat of passion, evidence could be everywhere. For crimes that were planned, once again, evidence could be everywhere. The difference was it wasn't as obvious to tell the evidence from the mundane. Bloody knives and guns were thrown in dumpsters from people fleeing the scene, but when someone had planned every detail of their scheme, they were not going to leave an easy trail. One person may have thought they found a trail, but it could be a red herring.

He opened their suitcases and found Mrs. Hamilton had many outfits for all types of weather and occasions, but he found that Mr. Hamilton only had his trousers. "That's strange," he said to himself. "Where are all of your clothes?"

As he walked around the room to get a different vantage point, he felt something was off but couldn't place his finger on it. Something told him that someone came back to the room last night. If someone was here, then their DNA could be here as well. He walked into the bathroom, but the trashcan was empty. He looked around the sink and found each of the Hamiltons' toiletry bags. A can of men's deodorant and shaving cream, a mouthwash bottle, one toothbrush, and a razor were neatly placed on the counter.

He traced his steps back into the room to find the refrigerator full of hotel amenities beside the empty trash can. After pacing around the room with his eyes closed for about half a minute, he opened them and rescanned the area with a fresh pair of eyes. Nothing alarming stood out to him in the bedroom area. It looked like a typical hotel room with shabby curtains and stained bed sheets. Stepping into the bathroom, he examined the shower tub and noted a masculine-scented shower gel and shampoo. All the towels were fresh and unused. He turned to leave the bathroom as a few pieces started to click into place. He turned to look at the counter and then back at the shower and saw one common thread.

"A man stayed here last night."

CHAPTER 22

It felt like a boulder-sized weight had been lifted from my back when the nagging question of the unfulfilled dreams was resolved. I looked around in the kitchen for a bite to eat, but nothing stood out. It was still early, so I decided to have a night on the town.

I parked at the Orange Line Metro Station of Vienna/Fairfax GMA and hopped on the subway to take me to the heart of D.C. with my umbrella in hand. I wasn't really into people watching on the subways, so I basically stalked my friends' Facebook statuses or Twitter feeds for the 30-minute ride into town.

Federal Triangle Metro Station was ideal for a quick bite, a casual evening of free entertainment at one of the Smithsonians, and a stroll beside the National Mall. That was usually my security blanket of a night out alone. Usually.

"Solo!" I heard a man's voice from across Constitution Avenue. I looked quickly and found the voice, seeing a man frantically waving his hands between the passing cars.

I cautiously waved, still not able to clearly see the couple thanks to the sprinkling rain and blinding traffic lights. The well-dressed man clutched onto a beautifully attired woman's hand and played a very realistic game of Frogger in order to join me on the same side of the street.

"Dr. Huffington," I shook his hand and then stood shocked to see who accompanied him. "Elizabeth, how are you two doing?"

"Just about to go eat. We have reservations nearby," he answered warmly, huddling with her under their umbrella. In his evening wear, he looked fit for a night at the opera as did she in a stunning red evening gown with a large diamond pendant draped around her neck. "Nice night," he laughed, sticking his hand out under the falling rain.

"Could be worse," she answered a bit awkwardly, not making any eye contact with me. She did, however, clutch her purse as if I were going to mug her for it.

"Interesting day, today, wasn't it, Solo?" Jeremiah bantered, trying to keep the conversation rolling. It was obvious that Elizabeth would not have minded if the next phrase was 'goodbye'.

"Very," I commented, wondering if the events of the day were more interesting than catching the two of them on a date. "Not something you see every day."

"Hopefully not," he said looking down at his watch. "I would hate to get the Jessica Fletcher complex," he snickered. Elizabeth rolled her eyes at the 1980's television reference which Jeremiah caught like a playful jab. "She's always telling me that I'm too young to be so old."

I cordially laughed as Elizabeth looked in every direction but mine. "Well, you two have a good evening. You have your reservations to get to," I said as I, too, looked down to examine the time on my watch.

"Yes, yes we do," Elizabeth said coolly. "Good seeing you again," she uttered, obviously lying, before she casually snickered as she looked in my direction for the second time tonight.

"What? What's so funny?" I asked.

"Oh, just a grown man with a fifth grader's watch," she giggled. "It just gets me every time."

"So, where are you heading off to?" Jeremiah asked, either not catching the derogatory slap in my face or being too polite to rebuff her cosmopolitan arrogance.

"Oh, nowhere spectacular. I was thinking about going to the Museum of Natural History."

"What do you say?" Jeremiah asked Elizabeth.

"What do I say about what?" she asked, apparently confused as if she'd missed something in this riveting conversation.

"About joining Solo at the museum?" he beamed. "We can go to Sonoma another time. How often do we run into one of your friends out on the street?"

I wanted to correct him by saying that we were not friends, but something stopped me. "Oh, you two don't have to do that. Go on and enjoy your night," I remarked quickly, practically pushing Jeremiah away as Elizabeth's eyes silently filled with rage. "I just didn't feel like being at home tonight and thought about killing a few hours, but you two go. Go to Selma's."

"It's Sonoma," she hissed as if my greatest flaw tonight, out of the many, was mispronouncing the restaurant's name.

"No. It will be fun, won't it?" Jeremiah smiled, looking at Elizabeth as her fiery eyes glazed to an icy bath screaming "no" so loudly even a blind man could have seen it.

"Why not?" she smiled sarcastically. I caught the undertone, but Jeremiah remained clueless to her annoyance. For someone so intelligent in human studies, he must have missed the class on sarcasm and body language. Oh, well, if he remained with Elizabeth, he would quickly learn that overlooked art form of smug.

"I'm looking forward to exploring the museum like it's my first time," Jeremiah started. "I mean, I don't remember the last time I went to one of these museums. You would think that since I'm an anthropologist I would live at the museums on my free time, but just like any other resident here, I don't experience all the wonders of D.C."

"Sad, isn't it?" I remarked with a sympathetic shake of the head. "I come here all the time, but when I mention it to other people who live here, they hardly go."

"Probably because they go to other things – the theater, fine restaurants, weekend getaways to New York," Elizabeth said as we started to walk up the steps of the museum.

"But those things cost money. These museums are free," I smirked.

"Yes, that's probably why I don't come here," Elizabeth spit out harshly. "I have money."

CHAPTER 23

The windshield wipers rhythmically went back and forth sloshing the heavy downpour around like someone was casually throwing buckets upon buckets of water on the Dodge Caravan. They didn't say a word as they drove in circles, trying to miss all the traffic cameras because one could never be too cautious.

It was strangely soothing, he thought, as he continued to drive, making his way to Grover Park. He casually glanced in the rearview mirror, checking on the old saps Sam and Marge slumped over their captain's chairs, like he was a caring father looking after his sleeping children in their car seats. But things couldn't be more different.

It took them a little bit longer to coax a homeless individual to take the hotel room key and enjoy a dry night in a warm bed. Luckily, his sister was able to persuade him with an extra $50 and the cell phones as well. "It sure is raining heavy tonight," she said, looking out the passenger window and watching the street lights reflecting their reds and greens on the solid black river. She caught sight of her tilted midnight black wig and carefully readjusted it to its perfect position.

"Uh huh," he nodded as he continued to drive carefully, hoping to not skid on the flooding roads. He heard a slight rustling as he saw Marge's head move slightly. "We've got a mover," he said quietly, as if not to wake the sleeping guests.

She grabbed his chloroform tank, placed it over Marge's face, and doused her lungs with the sweet sleeping nectar. Marge didn't scream or moan, or even see the end coming. After about a minute she got back in the front seat and leaned back in her chair. "That should do her for a while."

"Uh huh," he nodded, smiling as he knew that she always hated it when he didn't speak. But that was what brothers did – got under the skin of their big sisters.

"I didn't think about it raining so much. Are you going to be okay getting home afterwards?"

"Uh huh."

"I don't want you to get sick, riding your bike all the way home in this type of weather. You can stay at my place tonight."

"No," he grunted. He knew she meant well, but that was a risk that he couldn't take. Even though in his picture-perfect world he would like nothing more than to spend the night in her home. It would be like a sleepover when they were kids. Pop some popcorn, lie on the living room floor and watch scary movies, and then sleep peacefully knowing that kin was just an arm's length away. He longed to see the place where she lived, from a perspective other than the sidewalk outside of her building. There had been many nights when he couldn't sleep and would walk the lonely streets, finding her building and wondering which window was hers.

She stretched in the minivan and agreed.

"Maybe another time," he smiled. "Are you going to be okay kayaking to your next stop? Your boat won't sink, will it?"

She stared out the window in a peaceful state. "I will be fine."

They made their way to Grover Park, snaking through the winding roads to a hidden parking lot. He parked the car and they both took a deep breath. They both knew it was going to be a long night ahead of them.

CHAPTER 24

"Don't leave good footprints," she kept telling herself as she walked through the woods holding her tracking device to find her hidden kayak. She'd decided through trial runs that if she pretended like she was skating and never lifted up her foot, there would not be a good muddy footprint to connect her to the crimes. She was also thankful that the rain would likely wash away her tracks.

She slithered her drenched legs into her kayak and paddled to freedom while the frigid rain pelted her face. If it had been any other night, she would have been freezing, but as it was, she needed a cool down. Her heart was beating. Her blood was pumping. She wanted to savor the memory, but she was also in need of some balancing calm. She closed her eyes and paddled slowly, taking a few deep breaths and finding her center.

Opening her eyes, she noticed that the moon was beginning to peek through the clouds for part of her journey across the Potomac River. She didn't need the moonlight to direct her path because she could see the lights from all directions, on the bridges, traffic, streetlamps, or the oncoming Coast Guard boat.

Coast Guard boat?

"Don't freak out," she muttered to herself as she watched the boat near her rocking kayak. She looked in all directions, trying to see how far she was from her starting point. She craned her neck and realized she was a little more than halfway across the river. What if they already found the bodies and they were looking for someone? she thought. What if they already had her brother?

"This is the U.S. Coast Guard. What are you doing out on the river tonight?" a speaker blared as she was blinded from the boat's powerful search light. When her vision came back, she saw three sailors behind the captain's glass. "It is dangerous for you to be out here."

"I'll be okay," she shouted, trying to wave them off. But she knew that it was no use as she saw two of the sailors leave their dry confines and lean over the boat's railing with a life preserver. He threw the circular floating device with pinpoint accuracy, landing on her kayak. "I will be okay!" she shouted at the two sailors. "I just needed some fresh air and decided to go for a trip."

"We have come to rescue you," one of the sailors shouted. "Just grab the ring and we will pull you up."

"I don't need rescuing! I'm just going across the river."

A voice thundered through the boat's speaker, "We got a call from someone saying they saw you and thought you were in trouble."

"No, I am fine. I am not in any trouble at all," she shouted back. "A little embarrassed now, but not troubled." She smiled, hoping they would listen to her and leave her to carry on. "Look, it's not raining anymore. I will be fine."

"One second," one of the sailors said as he turned to go talk to his captain. The sailor looked to be explaining, even pointing at the moon as he spoke. She kept nodding her head yes as if she were agreeing to every word he was saying.

"I'm sorry, but we have to pick you up," the captain calmly said into the speaker. Simultaneously, the other sailors left the captain's room to come to her rescue.

"I am fine!" she yelled as she started to paddle away from the boat. She knew that their boat was bigger, but her kayak was more agile and easier to maneuver.

"Stop! Stop! Stop!" the captain yelled into his speaker, but she didn't follow his orders. She saw the only chance she had, and she was going to take it. The other sailors ran around the sides, trying to decide whether to help or not. It had been proven to not save a drowning victim while they were fighting to survive, because they would take the rescuer under as well.

One of the sailors ran back into the captain's room as she made her way behind the boat, paddling to the plot of land she'd initially spotted. She looked over her shoulder to see the sailor arguing with the captain as a few were still awaiting commands.

"Fine!" the captain yelled into his speaker. "But I shouldn't let you do this! I should take you in, but someone else has called us!"

"Be safe," one of the sailors added as they pulled in their life preserver that had drifted away from her trail.

"Thank you," she said, waving and paddling away from the boat. She wanted to get a few good strokes away before they revved their engine. They flipped their siren and lights and started down the river, probably to a suicidal citizen on a bridge somewhere. She wanted to kiss that person on the lips for inadvertently helping her but thought she could possibly read the obituaries tomorrow and send a little donation in his or her tragic honor. She knew she would never follow through on that well-intentioned thought, but it still put a smile on her face. Good deeds should not go unknown, but murders should.

Laughing heartily to herself, she knew that she had just dodged the bullet of a lifetime. If they had picked her up, they would have asked hundreds of questions, including her identification. In one instant, everything could have ended. If only. She knew that since she had skidded past this incident unscathed, she probably had a long future with her brother. Look out, D.C., we're coming for you.

Thursday

CHAPTER 25

A neon green light shone through the dark, illuminating a glowing golden winged lion emblem on the white blouse of a little blonde girl about seven-years-old moaning softly as she lay on a burlap sack in the middle of a small dark room. "I want to go home," she said.

The room changed. There was a closed door, and the sound of footsteps echoed down a darkened narrow hallway lit by a singular fluorescent bulb dangling from a rusty chain. Instead of a forward view, the perspective changed to walking backwards. The hallway ended in a fairly empty living room. A worn recliner faced a scrambled television with a clumsy rabbit ear antenna on top and the volume at the max. The person quietly moved along the walls, stopping periodically as if looking for something.

A knock sounded, causing the room to spin as the person sped up, heading in an unknown direction. A turn of a deadbolt and the fumbling of a door chain were barely heard over the Fruity Pebbles commercial. A creaking door opened. "You're late," a gruff voice said.

"There was a line," another male voice commented as the sound of a paper bag crinkled.

"Call me if you have any problems," the first voice commented, exiting the room. There was a quick glimpse of the backside of the new guard, who stood tall and muscular, wearing a backwards Colorado Rockies baseball cap. The apartment door closed. 4G.

The tilted 4G floated away like a distant star until it vanished from sight. Suddenly, photographic images started developing, falling until they covered the floor. 11:03 a.m. was emblazoned with flashing red lights on each photo. One was of a group of preschool children playing duck-duck-goose. The children looked to be of all sizes and ethnicities. There was a cute girl with pigtails in a pink sweater and white pants being chased by a redheaded boy with a San Diego Padres baseball jersey. Subsequent pictures showed the two run around the circle as their teacher clapped her hands and the students got up and formed two lines. The kids held hands with their partners as they journeyed through the park toward Little Future President's Preschool.

Singing lightly rose from the silence. "One, two, three, four," they sang like a choir of joyful angels. "Five, six, seven," the singing continued before it grew more and more quiet as the song progressed.

The pictures scattered like leaves in autumn until they were gone. Suddenly, a blinding white light shone from the distance as a bell chimed twice. A crackly operator's voice filled the airwaves. "We have a robbery in progress at Bank of America on the corner of 13th and G Streets. Two suspects are believed to be armed and dangerous. Do you copy? Robbery in progress at Bank of America on the corner of 13th and G. Shots fired! Shots fired! Proceed with caution. Shots fired! Suspects are fleeing the scene in a rusty blue van, heading north on New York Avenue. Suspects are heading toward…" the radio reception died, and only static was heard until it to faded.

The blinding light dissipated as an advertisement for McDonald's appeared overhead. A head-bobbing hippie college student wearing a pair of Beats looked around his surroundings and took off his headphones. "Oh, man!" he shouted, looking down at his iPhone that showed 4:49 p.m. "Come on, this can't be happening. I got somewhere to be."

"We all have somewhere to be," a decorated military officer spoke as she stood holding onto the handrails and glancing down at her watch. "It should be back running soon."

"I hope so because I got to be somewhere," the student with the Bob Marley t-shirt said again, starting to fidget. Anxiously and awkwardly, he looked around, his black dreadlocks swinging. He was beginning to panic.

"Just stay calm," the military officer commanded.

"I can't! I got somewhere to be!" he shouted, jumping up and running to the door, using all his strength to pry the doors open.

"Sir, sir, stop that! Get away from the door!"

"Back off, chick!"

"He's got a gun!" a woman screamed from a few seats away as bullets flew through the air, hitting an elderly gentleman in his chest. "Help!"

I jerked awake, raising my damp head off my pillow to look around the darkened room as the alarm

113

clock blinked 3:35 a.m. I watched the numbers change until it said 4:09 before I drifted back to sleep.

CHAPTER 26

"So, get me up to speed, Young," Captain Johnson barked, climbing out of his black Tahoe that he'd parked beside a dozen other police vehicles. He held a cup of steaming coffee in one hand and an umbrella in the other, unavoidably splashing his black leather shoes in a growing puddle. Rolling his eyes, he looked down and felt the cold water seeping through to his nylon socks.

Young quickly found his notes on his iPhone and proceeded to give him a play-by-play of the events so far. "Samuel and Marjorie Dunn, both 66, died of apparent carbon monoxide poisoning. Identical to the deaths of Burt and Pamela Hamilton. Once again, these decedents were tourists," he said as Johnson interrupted.

"From where?" he asked.

"From, from, from..." Young stammered, looking through his notes not finding that bit of information.

"Barre City, Vermont," Johnson said with a disgusted groan. "Randolph already gave me some of the details. Do not overlook anything! You never know what is important, so get everything. Even if it doesn't seem important at the time." He stopped and watched the young pupil soak in some of the lecture but knew that next week, he would have to go over it again. "Continue."

"They didn't have any luggage or hotel room keys in their possession, just like Burt and Pamela," he said as he stopped and walked around the car. "They attached the hose with duct tape to the exhaust in a similar fashion as Burt and Pamela Hamilton, running the end to the driver's side window. They were found by Jolene Aderhall, a nearby resident taking her dog, Paco, for a morning walk." He looked up, hoping to see some signs of approval from Captain Johnson, but he rarely gave him a thumbs-up for a job well done.

"And the dog's name is important because...?" Captain Johnson asked annoyed, not waiting for an answer. "Where were the victims in the car?"

"Oh, right. Samuel was in the driver's seat and Marjorie was in the front passenger seat. Just like the Hamiltons."

"Were there any signs of an attack?"

"No, sir. No signs at all. Not that I can see. But the medical examiner might see something more. The victims look just like the Hamiltons."

Johnson finished his coffee, crushing the Styrofoam cup in his hand and quickly handing it off to another deputy to throw away. "You know what this means if your assessment is correct?"

Young had a frightened look in his eyes, as if it was pop quiz time. "Um...we uh...have a killer on the...on the loose?" he slowly and unconfidently answered.

"Bingo. What's your next step?"

Young started ticking off the general steps in crime solving: getting the bodies to the medical examiner; getting a warrant to look up their credit card history; notifying the closest kin; but Johnson had other things on his mind. He stood beside the car and spun around in place, looking at the crime scene in all directions. He started posing questions to himself. Why did the killer pick this spot? How did the killer get away? Was there just one killer, or was it a team?

"You got your plan," Johnson said, walking toward his vehicle, shaking his shoes like a wet dog as he got in. "Now let's move."

CHAPTER 27

Rolling over in bed, the blurry alarm clock read 8:57 a.m. I never slept this late, but after last night's dreams, my body wasn't ready for a morning jog. Grabbing my iPhone, I quickly opened the local news website to see if the weather was going to improve from the current dismal gray. That was when my day quickly went from gray to stormy.

"Breaking News," a news ticker scrolled across the top of the website. "The Carbon Monoxide Killer is on the loose, killing another couple. The latest victims were Samuel and Marjorie Dunn." My memory went scrolling back to the previous night's dream when the names Sam and Marge were mentioned.

"Oh God, oh God, oh God. Calm down, Solomon, just calm down," I told myself, taking a deep breath. There had to be a reasonable explanation. I must have overheard the news as I was falling asleep, I told myself rationally. Yes, that explained it. I must have fallen asleep when the news was on, and I subconsciously thought I was dreaming it when it was on the news. I started throwing punches in the air in excitement as if giving an imaginary friend high-fives. "That's it!" I said confidently.

My mind quickly scanned through the recent night's dream, trying to remember more of the details. There was the kidnapped girl dream again, two nights in a row. "That had to be on the news," I thought as I quickly did a search for a kidnapped blonde girl in

Washington D.C. Once again, I found nothing. "Huh," I moaned with confusion. "What is the deal?"

I got out of bed and walked around my apartment, trying to recall the details of the dreams. I closed my eyes and waited for clarity. Slowly the details began to surface. There was a bank robbery and a shooting on a subway. Those would definitely be newsworthy. I started clicking away on the phone, searching for events similar to those dreams in the Washington D.C. area. But once again, there was nothing. "Come on!" The high-fives subsided to more of a twitching fist of defeat.

I sat on the edge of the bed contemplating what to do. There was only one way to settle the issue of whether this was real or not. I needed to go into investigation mode. After a quick breakfast, I set out for the city. On the subway I prayed more than ever before. "Please let me not find anything today, Lord, please. Amen."

CHAPTER 28

The squad room was buzzing with the news of the latest killing. In the last few years, the city had tried its best to clean up the moral filth and lower the crime rate. So when there was a sign of two possibly related murders, it took precedence over a majority of the other cases.

Young went to the evidence board and started putting pictures and possible leads for everyone to see. "Cooper," Johnson said commandingly as he walked through the doors. "I want you off the drug case for now so you can help us with the four murders."

"Yes, sir," Cooper answered quickly, closing his computer with the drug trafficking evidence and heading toward Young.

"Young, did you release the names of the victims this morning to the local news?" Johnson roared.

"I, uh, I..." he stammered like a nervous schoolboy.

"Spit it out. Did you give them the names of the victims before you contacted the next of kin?"

"I, uh...I thought..." Young stuttered looking around the squad room while every set of eyes watched him. Every police officer knew to never release the identities of the deceased until the family had been contacted.

"You thought what?" Johnson said. "You thought what?"

"I thought..." Young mumbled with his head down.

"Did you give this tip to your girlfriend?" Johnson's anger rained down on him like asteroid-sized hail. "Did you compromise the integrity of this office to give your girlfriend a little tip to boost her career?"

"I...I wasn't thinking," Young said, whimpering like a hurt dog. "I was trying to help get the word out for possible future victims."

"How is telling the news that we have a supposed Carbon Monoxide Killer on the loose going to help? What if these killings are not related? What if one was a suicide? What if it's a copycat killer, and now by getting the news involved, we are opening up the city for more copycat killings or some unneeded terror?" Johnson shouted at Young's stupidity.

"I've been talking to the chief about you, and for some reason he doesn't want to fire you! So, you better thank your lucky stars that he has your back, because if it were up to me, I would have let you have it! You would be fired!"

"It won't happen again," Young responded ashamedly.

"You bet it won't! Cooper, come with me!"

"Yes sir," Cooper commented, smirking at Young for his emasculation.

"Walk with me," Johnson said, stomping down the linoleum floor. "I need you to work with me and Young on this case. I see something in you, Cooper, so don't let me down."

"I won't, sir," Cooper said casually. But on the inside he was beaming with joy.

"I need you to go back to Young, look over the evidence and solve this case. Because things could get worse," he grunted as he charged down the hall. "I'll be back as soon as my meeting with the chief is over."

CHAPTER 29

After exiting the Smithsonian Metro Station, I continued to walk down Independence Avenue, passing some of the various parks and sitting areas. There was one particular park I was searching for. I glanced down at my watch; it was 10:45 a.m. I walked a little further when I barely heard the repetitive words I'd been dreading. I turned my head and saw a group of laughing preschoolers in a circle.

"Duck, duck, duck," said a young boy who was wearing thin-framed glasses and patting the heads of his classmates. He suddenly chose a girl with blue jean overalls. "Goose!" he squealed! She giggled, jumped up, and tried to catch the small boy with skinny but speedy legs.

I watched their innocence and smiled at their laughter as the little boy slid safely to the spot that she'd just relinquished. She stomped her feet in friendly frustration as a smile stretched across her face. She then took the reins and began the process of choosing. "Duck, duck, duck." She circled the group, carefully picking out just the right person.

I entered the park and took a seat on a drying bench. I prayed silently that something would happen, and my dream wouldn't come to fruition. I just kept praying fervently until I noticed my watch said 11:02 a.m. I took a deep breath and looked ahead as my heart stopped.

"You can't get me," an adorable girl said mockingly, her black pigtails swaying over her pink sweater. The little boy wearing the San Diego Padres jersey tried with all his might to tag the girl. She kept running around the circle, passing the free space, allowing her lead to diminish. The redheaded boy stretched his hands ahead of him to tag the giggling girl. He just needed a few more inches to clinch his victory.

"Kids, kids," the preschool teacher announced, clapping her hands, "it's time to get in line." Instantly, the students stood up and formed two lines. Then they began marching their way out of the park. "What do you want to sing?" the teacher asked.

"The number song," one of the kids shouted.

"Okay, will someone start us off?" the teacher asked.

Instantly, my heart started pumping faster as the melody was one that I had heard before in my dream. "One, two three, four," I started to sing along as I slowly stood up and followed them. They continued to sing as they entered the doors of Little Future President's Preschool.

I stood on the sidewalk, trying to appear like a random citizen and not a child predator lurking in the bushes. My knees were shaking at the eeriness of the events and how perfectly they were in unison with my dream. I walked on wobbly legs to the nearest bench and sat down, needing to regain my composure.

I sat in silence, watching the pedestrians dangle their umbrellas, anticipating the next spotty shower, when a school bell awoke me from my near meditative state. I turned around and saw St. Mark's Elementary School. My heart rate intensified at the thought of the possibility. St. Mark's?

The winged lion.

CHAPTER 30

Oh God! Oh God! Oh God! What do I do? What do I do? What do I do? I prayed, hoping the perfect answer would drop out of the sky at my feet. I was sickened with the thought that my dream with the preschool students with their laughter and singing was real. That would mean the ruthless kidnappers must be real. And the crying, terror-stricken kidnapped girl must be real too.

Doubts filled my head. Could a person see visions like the prophets in Biblical days? Then the realization set in that the bus crash and the dead couple in the woods really did happen. This internal struggle caused a tornado of anxiety in my stomach. If the bus crash happened, and if my dreams were coming true, that also meant that someone was going to rob a bank later today and get shot on the subway.

My world was spinning. The smiling pedestrians were oblivious to my dilemma. All they were worried about was if their stock portfolio was going to be higher before the ring of the bell on Wall Street or what they were going to have for lunch. The notion that they would be sleeping peacefully at night with quiet dreams revolted me to the core. Meanwhile, I kept hearing the static operator's voice informing the police of the robbery.

Leaning my head between my knees, I braced myself in case I passed out. But all I could think was 'what if?' What if I'd had these fortune-telling dreams five years ago? I took a deep breath and subconsciously circled my fingers around my ring finger, recalling the smooth texture of the gold metal band. What if I could have warned her not to go out on that assignment? I could almost smell her perfume that used to annoy my sensitive nose. Looking back, I would suffer a lifetime of runny and reddened noses for a second chance. What I wouldn't give just for a chance to ask Chelsea to please stay in bed with me that day and go back to work the next day. A single tear fell, sliding down my nose that had been crooked since one of Wint's boxer blows went haywire in high school.

"This is ridiculous!" I shouted, raising my head up and wiping by eyes. "This isn't happening. There is a perfectly reasonable explanation," I said to myself. I stood up and dialed the police station. If a child had been taken, the police would definitely be aware. Maybe they were following the kidnappers' orders by not leaking it to the press.

"911, what's your emergency?" a stoic man asked.

"Yes, can I speak to someone who handles kidnappings?" I asked, feeling strange at my casual tone. "I mean, not that I have kidnapped anyone. I just have some information, or am needing to get some information, I mean." I stopped and tried to collect my thoughts as the operator said he would connect me.

"Lieutenant Walker here," said a man with a surprisingly squeaky voice.

"Yes, this is going to sound odd," I started. He assured me that they get odd phone calls all the time. "Yes, well, I usually don't call, but has someone reported a kidnapping in the last couple of days? A blonde girl about seven years old? She goes to St. Mark's Elementary School?"

"One minute. Let me check my database," he said. He started typing on his keyboard, and I could hear each keystroke through the phone. "The system is running through some information. While it's searching, do you know of something that you would like to report?"

"I'm, I'm not sure. I just have a strange feeling," I buckled, quickly checking my surroundings as if a patrol car were going to stop me because of my phone call.

"What kind of strange feeling, sir?" he asked and started typing some more.

I quickly came up with a lie. "My son goes to St. Mark's Elementary School, and he was talking about one of his friends at school who has missed every day this week, and no one knows anything. I'm just concerned for my son."

"Have you contacted the girl's parents?" the police officer asked.

"I don't know them that well, and my son said he saw a strange guy following them the other day. I just want to try to calm his nerves and tell him that she is sick or something," I said, piling white lie on top of white lie. "If you can just tell me that there is no one that fits her description, I will sleep better tonight," I added. At least that wasn't a lie.

"Blonde, seven years old from St. Mark's Elementary School," he recited. "No, I do not see anything in our system with that description."

"Are you positive?" I asked.

"Yes. As soon as we get a kidnapping case, it immediately goes into our system, and we issue an Amber Alert. Nothing with that description has been issued in the last month. Tell your son that his friend is probably just sick. Maybe you two can take her a get-well package, and that way he can see for himself that she is fine."

"Thank you, officer," I said. A haunting feeling lingered as the officer's words seeped into my soul.

Well, I've already lied to the police today. Why not lie to a school as well? I said to myself as I walked up the sidewalk to St. Mark's Elementary School.

CHAPTER 31

Schools always needed volunteers to read with students, and what better excuse to get into the school's library than say I had come to help with their reading program? I had good credentials; I was a theology student for heaven's sake. After giving them my school identification and filling out contact information and references, I was given a volunteer's pass.

Following the directions, I quickly found the library, the place where they kept all their books, including all of the school's prior yearbooks. I showed the attentive librarian my volunteer's pass and proceeded to the yearbooks. It wasn't long before I found the newest edition and quickly flipped it open to the first grade section. I closed my eyes, visualizing the seven-year-old girl with her long blonde hair. I tried to look past the hair, since last year it could have been short, curly, up in a bun, or even a different color.

After scanning the pictures of smiling six-year-olds, my finger stopped on an image of a dimple-faced blonde with short bangs. Rachel Fiddelstein – the girl from my dream. She was the essence of innocence with lightheartedness in her sea blue eyes.

As I was leaving the library, my nose caught a whiff of tacos. I followed the alluring scent to the cafeteria where it looked like the entire school population was eating. "Hello, can you tell me where

Rachel Fiddelstein is?" I asked a table of girls, trying to trade their carrot and celery sticks for some potato chips from the boys at the table behind them.

"I don't know," one girl answered, rifling through her new bag of sour cream and onion potato chips.

I went to the next table and asked the same question. Once again, no one knew. "Do you know Rachel? Is she in your class?"

"She's in my class," said a brunette girl in between slurping her chocolate milk. "But she hasn't been in school this week."

"Oh, really?" Just then I felt a tap on my shoulder from behind.

"Excuse me, but what are you doing here?" asked Elizabeth, who was glaring at me with beady eyes that would rather hit me than listen to my explanation.

"I didn't know you worked here," I said, smiling in an attempt to ease the tension.

"Oh no, no, no, no," she laughed condescendingly. "I don't work here. I just come to volunteer a few hours a week. My father is one of the trustees here."

"Of course," I answered, remembering that with her family's wealth she didn't need to work here, or anywhere really.

"So, why are you here?"

"Strange that I see you here. I really need to talk to you about some things," I said, pulling her away from the students' listening ears as the table of snickering girls oohed like I was her boyfriend.

"What do you want to talk about because I don't have time right now," she said, swatting the girls' notions away like an annoying gnat.

I looked around the room, taking in all the precious children's faces. "We can't talk here."

"Is this about Jeremiah? Because that is none of your business," she snarled menacingly.

"Jeremiah? No!" I protested. "I don't care who you date." Her eyes blinked in shock at my quick response.

"Well, good," she growled as the school bell chimed signaling the end of lunch. "I've got to go."

"I still need to talk to you later," I shouted as she clapped her hands to lead a line of students out of the cafeteria.

CHAPTER 32

"What do these four murders have in common?" Cooper asked himself, staring at the white evidence board with pictures of the victims and their information written with a dry erase marker in an off-center slant.

"What did you say?" Young asked, walking up with two cups of coffee. He handed one to Cooper, catching him a little off guard with the act of kindness. After all, it was the first from Young in the six years they had worked on the force together.

Cooper took a sip and stepped back to get another perspective of the evidence. "Just trying to see the correlation between these murders. Has the medical examiner's report come back yet for the latest victims?"

"Not yet. But he said that he would have it by this afternoon. When I spoke with him earlier, he said that these victims had traces of chloroform in them, just like the Hamiltons."

"Can you hand me the pictures from the hotel rooms?" Cooper positioned the pictures of both rooms looking for any similarities. Unfortunately, the cleaning staff had already cleaned up the room of Samuel and Marjorie Dunn. There was nothing to see in either room. "Have you gotten the security video from the Dunns' hotel to see if the same person stayed there as in the Hamiltons' hotel room? The picture of the man who stayed at the Hamiltons' room isn't very good. Can they work on getting a clearer image?"

"Someone in IT is looking over the newest videos now. They are working on getting it."

"Um, Young?" Cooper said with an epiphany. "Did you find any cell phones from the victims?"

Young quickly looked through the list of contents and noticed that none of the victims had a cell phone.

"Don't you think that's a little odd? Almost everyone has a cell phone these days, and we found four victims without one."

"I guess that is strange," Young agreed, starting to see the significance. "Do you think that could be the killer's target?"

"No," Cooper said, somewhat annoyed that even with the trail of breadcrumbs, Young still couldn't find the connection on his own. Cooper wondered if Young couldn't see the obvious, what else he was blissfully ignorant of. "It's a possibility that the killer took them."

"Oh, I see," Young said in a way that made Cooper wonder if he truly did.

"If we can find who has the phones, we may find the killer, or someone who knows the killer," Cooper said, picking up the grainy image of the man who had stayed in the Hamiltons' hotel room. "Let's see if we can get a warrant to have the phone company ping their phones. It would help to find out where they are right now."

"Got it."

Cooper was amazed at Young's lack of knowledge. At any other time, he would have savored the moment, but his celebratory dance would have to wait until after they caught the killer. This was his first murder investigation, and he wanted to prove to Johnson that he was ready, willing, and able.

He looked through the crime scene photos from various angles, searching for anything that jumped off the paper. There were multiple sets of fingerprints in each of the vehicles. Now they had to wait to see if any of the sets appeared in both vehicles or in their criminal database.

"Cooper, what do you know?" Johnson barked as he walked into the squad room. Young quickly hung up the phone and bounced into action.

"I just..." Young started to say, when Johnson shut him up with one fierce look.

"I'm talking to Cooper."

CHAPTER 33

She ate a garden salad and half a chicken salad sandwich before she commenced her lunchtime walk. The clouds were starting to dissipate as the sun's fragile rays tried to break through. She popped in her ear buds and let the music of Chopin take her away from the daily routine and into her murderous daydreaming world.

She stopped to take her pulse, knowing that after the last few nights of excitement, her heart would barely be beating from just a casual stroll. People said that when they ran, they could break that ceiling of pain and reach a high that only marathoners could appreciate. She wondered if their metabolic high could even come close to hers during her murderous rampage.

Letting her mind drift, she wondered what her brother was doing that day. She was hoping that he was resting, because after last night's hunt, they had decided to take a night off. Even though their adrenaline could force them to go out tonight, she decided it would be best to slow down, reevaluate, and rejoin tomorrow evening. Also, today would give him some time to enjoy the extra spending money that the Hamiltons and Dunns so graciously provided through a violent and unwilling last will and testament. One could say that her brother was bequeathed a part of their estates, knowing full well that would be the only estate he would get.

Somehow in the game of life, when they were separated into the foster system, she was dealt a royal flush, and he just got five duds. She was adopted and became a member of a stable family that adored her and treated her like she was one of their own. He was bounced around various orphanages and foster homes until he reached the age of 18 and was kicked out of their often abusive and dysfunctional child welfare system.

After that, he decided to move to New York. Because, as the saying went, if he could make it there, he could make it anywhere. Sadly, he didn't. And so began the slow, winding trek back to Virginia. He learned that he had to provide for himself because no one else was going to give him any handouts. So, if that meant stealing to have his belly full, he stole. If that meant selling drugs to have a roof over his head for a few nights, that is what he did. Morals went out the window when someone didn't even have a window of his own.

In contrast, she grew up in the suburb of Bethesda, Maryland where she was allowed to ride her 10-speed bike carefree through their predominately middle-class neighborhood as her cocker spaniel Buttercup would trot beside her. She was given every chance to better herself, and she didn't fail at any of them. She trumped the foster care system and didn't let her secret past hold her back. That is, until that fateful day when she saw her brother for the first time in 15 years.

They stared at one another for a few minutes – she tried to remember why he looked so familiar, while he knew exactly why. It took a little deprogramming for her to remember the events of a childhood that she'd locked away through years of therapy. It took a little time for him to trust her.

Because she was his big sister, it took a while for him to get over the notion that she hadn't come looking for him. That was why they did what they did. It was a sort of family bonding way to reconnect -- a way for the big sister to protect her little brother again. A way to get back at the older generation who hadn't wanted to adopt her little brother in the first place. A way to show society that their wrong deeds would not go unpunished.

CHAPTER 34

On the walk from St. Mark's Elementary School up 12th Street I bumped into multiple bystanders like I'd had too much vodka before lunch. Rachel Fiddelstein's picture was all I could see; everything else was invisible. After a few minutes of Facebook stalking, I discovered that Rachel's parents were Isaac and Amanda – a well-to-do family in the area. Isaac was a senior partner of an investment brokerage office, and Amanda was a former model and UNICEF spokeswoman.

Turning left onto G Street, I glanced down at my watch: 1:45. I hopped into Au Bon Pain next door to Bank of America for a quick sandwich while I waited for the robbery to occur in the next fifteen minutes.

A few bites was all my stomach could handle, like I was on death row waiting for the infamous dead man walking scenario to begin. I wished that the robbery wouldn't happen. That no gunfire would erupt. That it was all just an elaborate dream from watching too many violent movies.

My lunch jumped into my throat as a rusty blue Ford van passed by the window before slowing down to turn left onto 13th Street. Taking a deep breath, I tossed the remaining two-thirds of my sandwich away and headed toward the bank. With each step, I felt in my gut that for the first time in my life, I had total confidence that something was going to happen, and I didn't like the feeling.

Two men in ski masks sprinted from the shady van and entered the bank. A third remained behind in the driver's seat keeping the van running with a slight sputter. I snuck behind the bank's concrete pillars, getting closer so I could hear the commotion inside.

Suddenly, two gunshots went off and screams filled the once quiet vestibule. "If you do what I say, no one is going to get hurt!" one of the robbers yelled in an off-kilter British accent.

"Empty your drawers, ladies!" another voice commanded in a thick Aussie tone. "You too, mate."

After no more than two minutes, the robbers had come in and left, but not before firing a few more bullets for some added confusion.

"And you all have a good day!" they yelled in unison as they fled the scene, storming across the traffic to get into the waiting van. I stepped away from my safe confines, watching the robbers jump into the van when one caught notice of me.

"You, down!" he yelled, pointing the gun in my direction. My knees collapsed without haste. "Good boy!" he laughed as the van revved its engine, taking off in their planned escape route.

"You okay?" a well-dressed man shouted from across the street. He stepped from behind the construction truck where he'd taken shelter. "I thought they were going to get ya!"

"I'm fine. I'm fine," I said, slowly rising, looking behind into the bank and noticing that everyone appeared safe.

"You were lucky," he said, helping me to my feet and brushing off my back.

"Stupid me, trying to get a better look," I scoffed, shaking my head in self-disgust as sirens screamed. A pair of police cars was in pursuit as another two units stopped to check on the bank.

"Did you see anything?" one of the police officers asked. The others entered the bank with their guns in hand to secure the scene and take employees' and customers' statements.

"More than I wish," I said. "More than I wish."

CHAPTER 35

Per Johnson's advice, Cooper placed some Vick's VapoRub under his nose before entering Dr. Santiago's exam room. "Once you get a foul smell, you can never stop smelling it," the older detective warned. Johnson had the reputation of being brutal to new officers, but Cooper had somehow found some favor in his eyes early on.

"Thanks," Cooper whispered to Johnson as Dr. Santiago revealed the Dunns' cold bodies under the strong light of the exam room.

"So, Doc, what did you find?" Johnson asked as Young and Cooper stood ready to take detailed notes.

"It looks like we have a problem," Dr. Santiago said, frowning. "These deaths appear to be connected."

"That's what I was afraid of," Young commented with a cocky head bob.

"Once again, there was no sign of a struggle on the victims. These two were apparently knocked unconscious with chloroform. They then inhaled a deadly dose of carbon monoxide."

"Could this be a copycat of the first deaths?" Cooper asked.

"Could be, but not likely," Dr. Santiago commented. "The chemical composition is an exact match to the chloroform inhaled by the Hamiltons. There are multiple companies that make chloroform, or a similar substance can be made at home, so unless the copycat got the exact same brand, it is unlikely."

"I don't believe that it was reported to the news that they were chloroformed first, was it?" Cooper questioned.

"I, uh, I don't believe so," Young stammered.

"Have you looked at the hotel footage yet?" Johnson asked, picking up Dr. Santiago's written report.

"They are supposed to be sending it to me as we speak," Cooper answered looking at his phone. "Hopefully, we can see if it is the same person from the first hotel. Okay, I just got the new image." As he opened his email and downloaded the photograph, the three men huddled behind, holding their breath.

"That's not the same guy," Young announced as they looked at him, fully aware of that conclusion.

"I got something else coming," Cooper said watching another email being received. "The warrants came through and it looks like someone is using their cell phones," he said, showing them a map with four blinking dots clustered within a five-block radius in Alexandria.

"Let's go find 'em," Johnson said, smiling as he shook Dr. Santiago's hand and exited the swinging doors, quickly followed by Cooper and Young.

CHAPTER 36

The afternoon spent with the police, who were determined to get every detail I'd witnessed about the robbery, was exhausting. It might have also been the whole emotional roller coaster taking its toll as well. Collapsing on the couch for a thirty-minute nap was not enough to fully refresh me.

I turned on the news and saw the lead story was the Bank of America robbery. The three suspects finally surrendered after a two-hour chase through parts of Maryland and Delaware. The next story was the subway slaying, just as my dream had predicted. "We have exclusive video of the Blue Metro Line Subway killing taken by Joel Beck," news anchor Brock Michaels stated in his most sincere tone. "Warning, the images you are about to see are disturbing."

The hidden camera phone was strategically placed, giving full view of the subway passengers. The events quickly spun out of control, just as they did in the frightening dream. "Major Bridget Richmond jumped into action, tackling the gunman before he was able to fire any more shots. Sadly, George Kiesel, age eight-four, died this evening from a gunshot wound to the chest. Now, tell us Rock, can we expect to see any sunshine tomorrow?"

Silence was beckoning, so I turned off the television. I desperately needed to have a moment of quiet. After a few minutes, I knew it was time to start getting ready for my double date. I wasn't sure how I was feeling about it, since I was still numb from the newscast, but I promised Wint I would join them, and a promise was a promise.

After taking a somewhat relaxing shower and splashing on some decent cologne, I dressed in a pair of tan slacks, an evergreen shirt, and a corduroy blazer. I was not a suit and tie kind of guy, but if she was Verny's friend, she was probably used to an upper-class gentleman. I preferred places like Subway, and she probably would frown or turn her nose up at the notion of a six-inch meatball sandwich.

I looked down at my phone and saw I had a few minutes before I had to leave for the Metro station. I held the phone and debated whether or not to text, but if anyone knew how I was feeling, she possibly would.

I really need to talk to you tonight, I texted to Elizabeth, watching the phone in shock as her response instantly appeared.

What now?

Can we meet somewhere tonight?

Why should I?

I read the text and wondered why she should meet with me. It wasn't like we were friends or even had a friendly moment at the museum or at the school. I had basically called her a liar. I wondered if she would believe me or if it would appear like I was being condescending.

I just need to talk to you, Elizabeth. I stopped before I hit send, holding the phone uncertainly in my hands.

In just a few days, my life had flipped. Sadly, I didn't know which way was right-side-up. *I believe you.*

LIAR!

No. I really do, I pleaded. But all she could see were those eleven letters as a smack in her face.

I don't believe you, came her reply.

I was tired of communicating via text messaging. It was so easy to misconstrue the meaning of texts, so I called her.

"Really?" she snarled as she answered the phone.

"I knew you wouldn't believe me, but you gotta trust me, Elizabeth. I really do," I stated sincerely, grabbing my keys to walk out the door.

"So what? You believe me. What do you want? Want to quiz me about tomorrow's events? Want me to give you the winning lottery numbers? Want me to tell you how your date is going to go? What do you want from me?"

I stopped in the stairwell and leaned against the wall. I was in a state of disbelief regarding what I was about to say. "I just want to know how you get through the day when you know something terrible is going to happen."

"Why does that affect you?" she asked in a slightly calmer tone.

"Because...it's happening to me now."

CHAPTER 37

Verny was standing in the waiting area of the restaurant. Actually, her posture revealed barely suppressed agitation. In fact, she was twitching. Probably at the thought of sitting through an entire dinner with me. At Wint's birthday party we didn't have to talk since we sat at opposite ends of the table. But tonight, she would always be within arm's reach.

"Veronica," I said kindly. Her eyes squinted at my cordial but insincere greeting. "Jenny, good to see you again."

"Nice seeing you again too," Jenny warmly greeted me offering a friendly smile. Verny nodded dismissively.

"You two look exceptionally lovely tonight," I said. Jenny thanked me, but Verny couldn't take the compliment.

"I didn't have time to freshen up. I had to leave a client's office and rush down here to make it on time," she said, enunciating the 'on time' with ferocious tenacity.

"I'm on time," I said with a wink while looking at my watch; in fact, I still had a few minutes to spare.

"Yes, but barely," she scolded.

"Where's Wint? Heading here now?" I turned to Jenny and in a slight whisper said, "Hope he doesn't get here late, or he will be toast."

She freely snickered as Verny's eyes again squinted unappreciatively at me. "What did I do? Just stating

147

the obvious," I said raising my hands in surrender as Verny looked down at her phone.

"Well, this is just great," she said, wincing before stuffing her phone back into her Gucci purse.

"What's great?" I asked.

"Winston," she said, making his name sound even more prestigious than it should ever be. "He's not going to make it. He's working a case tonight."

"Bummer."

"Yes, too bad," Jenny agreed.

"Well, there's no need in us staying for a double date. We can reschedule for another night when Winston isn't too preoccupied," Verny announced as if she'd made the rules for the night.

"Well, since we're here, Jenny would you still like to have dinner with me?" I asked politely with my hands in my pockets.

"I would love to."

"Well, Jennifer, you enjoy, or try to," Verny said, turning to head out the door after delivering her final insult of the night.

"See you tomorrow, Veronica," Jenny said warmly.

"Yeah, see you later, Verny," I shouted, watching her shiver at the sound of her informal name. She flung her hand in the air like a backhanded good riddance. "Well, that was something."

"She doesn't care for you much, does she?" Jenny remarked, scrunching her nose and pursing her lips.

"What? Veronica doesn't like me?" I laughed. "I never noticed."

We dined casually, telling each other our selective childhood history. We didn't want to release too many horror stories on the first date. She spoke of her tight-knit family and being an only child. She also spoke of how Veronica was like a sister to her in high school.

"And you're still friends with her after all this time?"

"Yeah. I could tell that you two are not the best of friends. Why is that?"

I sat there for a moment and tried to think of the birth of our enmity for each other. "I really can't remember. Breaking a vase? Wearing white after Labor Day? Begging Wint not to marry her? If you ask Verny, I mean, Veronica, she will probably remember."

"Oh, I bet. She never forgets anything."

"Except my birthday," I frowned theatrically. "She and Wint seem to always have something going on the night of my birthday."

"Poor you," she consoled, sympathetically playing along. "You and Winston are pretty close friends, aren't you?"

"The best."

"Did you really beg him not to marry her?" she asked, lowering her voice as if discussing the Manhattan Project in broad daylight.

"Well, I was the best man, and it was my duty to protect him from making a lifelong mistake."

"So you did beg him."

"Every best man makes sure that the groom is happy. Wint did it for me first." As soon as I said the

149

last words, I knew I had made a mistake. First dates were not the place to talk about previous marriages. I didn't think fifth dates were either.

"So, white after Labor Day?" she asked, graciously changing the subject.

"I know. Who knew that was a fashion faux pas?"

"I'm more surprised that you said 'faux pas.'"

CHAPTER 38

The date went exceptionally well. Maybe a little too well for my standards. She was smart, funny, and attractive, but there was one flaw. I couldn't see how someone like that could be friends with someone like Verny. Then again, my best friend fell head over heels in love with Verny, so there must have been something that allured people to her. Maybe she just picked and chose to whom she was pleasant and let the rest of the world feast on her elitist scraps.

"So, how was your date?" Elizabeth asked facetiously when I found her sitting in the corner of her favorite bookstore sipping a cup of pumpkin chai espresso.

"You know, it wasn't half bad," I said, stopping to rephrase. I plopped down on the most comfortable chair I had ever sat on. "No, not half bad. It was pretty good."

"Solo met a girl. Ooh," she teased like a middle school girl. "So, when are you two going out again?"

"I don't know. This was just a first date," I said, smiling while wiggling around in my new love. I was afraid I would drift off to sleep if I sat still long enough. The chair fit me like a custom suit, finding places on my body that I didn't know needed a little loving.

"Nice, isn't it?" she asked, grinning wickedly.

"I want to take it home with me. I'll name it Honey because it's just so sweet. Is there a price tag on it?" I laughed, snuggling deeper into the cushion. "Especially after the last couple of nights I've been having."

"So, tell me, Solo, and be honest because I can read people better than the CIA. If you start to lie to me, I will walk out of here and get Veronica to make your life miserable. She's good at it. Trust me; it's a gift of hers. Some people can bake or sing, but she can find that one button that will send you off the deep end and keep pushing it for the fun of it as she smiles."

"Oh, I know," I said, quickly running through my memory bank of cringe-worthy moments that were single-handedly spearheaded by the lovely Verny.

"So, tell me why I am here," Elizabeth said.

I started my story with the first night we met and how I doubted her ability. Even when the weatherman mentioned the hurricane, I thought she was pulling my chain. "I mean, you are Verny's sister, and I assumed that the saying 'birds of a feather…' may apply to you as well."

She nodded in reserved agreement, "Okay, I can see that."

"I mean, you were in top form at the beginning of the other evening. I even asked Wint if you were loco."

"Yeah, he told me. He gave me $20 to keep it up for the night," she laughed.

"Really?"

"No. Come on. Get on with it," she said, snapping her fingers to have me carry on with my story.

I continued with the first night of dreams and how the next day I witnessed the bus crash and the text messages, and how all the details aligned. Then there were a couple of other dreams that didn't happen. She sat there and listened, letting my words seep into her like the espresso she was sipping, probably realizing how crazy I sounded.

My story continued with the next night and more dreams. I told her about waking up to find that one of my dreams had occurred with the murders in the park.

"You dreamed that?" she asked apprehensively. I could see her move closer to the edge of the cliff of belief, although still hesitant.

I continued describing the dream of the preschool kids and how I'd been having a dream of a kidnapped girl who, it turned out, hadn't been at school all week.

"Wait a minute! That's why you went to the school?" she erupted in shock. She looked around, noticing that no one else was there to tell her to shut up. "Stalker."

"I had to know. I called the police," I said as she interrupted.

"You called the police, too?" she ignited in combustible laughter. "Solo, you sound like one of those freaks you hear about going to the cops and telling them that they saw the murder suspect in their Frosted Flakes."

"Elizabeth," I said shaking and slumping my head in defeat. "If there is a girl out there, kidnapped, and I know something that can help her but do nothing, I don't know if I can live with that."

She leaned back in her chair, set her espresso down on the column of books, and stared inquisitively at me for about a minute. "I believe you."

"Thanks. I believe you too now. So tell me," I started with the main purpose of this whole meeting. "How do you deal with the dreams?"

"I keep a journal," she answered nonchalantly as she picked up her espresso. "I'm going to get another," she said, standing up. "Want anything?"

I shook my head no and thought, a journal? That is how she handled this? With a dear diary moment?

"Don't you love fall?" she asked as she inhaled her giant cup of coffee that had nutmeg spice infused with the coffee beans.

"A journal?" I remarked, ignoring her musings about autumn, coffee, and sweater weather. "What do you do with the journal?"

"Well, when I wake up, I write down the dreams. As they occur, I mark them off. Kinda like a check list. I'm still batting a thousand," she said unconvincingly rolling her eyes with angst. "So, I'm pretty good."

"A list? That's all you do? Make a list and see if it happens?" I said in disbelief.

"Well, what do you suggest?"

I didn't know what I was expecting from Elizabeth. A quick fix. A simple technique to ignore the dreams or even some concoction of pills to forget them. Keeping a journal and waiting to see if the dreams came true wasn't something I was keen on.

"Do something."

CHAPTER 39

"We have found three people with the victims' cell phones sir, but none of them know anything about the murders," Young explained to Johnson.

"Did you give them some milk and cookies too while you asked them?" Johnson snarled angrily. "Not very many murderers admit to knowing anything. That's why you keep asking them questions until you know that they don't know anything. Sometimes they slip and say things they didn't mean to say."

"Um, sir, one of them is drunk. Another, I think, is high. Then the third is just enjoying being off the streets for the night."

"Cooper!" Johnson shouted from across the room. "Did you get anything out of them?"

Cooper walked over with his notepad and started reading him information like a walking encyclopedia. "Billy Thorngood, known as Skeet on the street. He was stopped the night of the first killings and given the cell phones and the hotel room key. He said that he stayed in the room overnight, but the woman was adamant about him leaving by breakfast. He traded one cell phone for a bottle of Jack and kept the other for himself. He couldn't remember what the woman looked like, but he remembered seeing a man in the driver's seat."

"So, it's a pair?" Johnson said thoughtfully. "Go on."

"We picked up Romeo Iglasia, known as Roro. He was the guy who traded his bottle of Jack Daniel's for the phone. He swears that he didn't have anything to do with anything except the phone. Sadly, he is the one that Young was saying is happy about being questioned. He's also the one who doesn't seem to know anything. Billy backed up Romeo's story.

"Lastly, we have Porter Rockwell. Nickname is Rocks due to his apparent drug use. He was stopped last night by a woman who gave him money, the hotel key, and cell phones. He hid one phone, get this, in the dumpster behind IHOP, in case he lost the phone he was using. But once again, he couldn't remember any details about the two people in the vehicle except that he thought it was a white woman. He couldn't see the guy, since it was dark and rainy."

"So, to sum it up, we have nothing," Johnson grunted, shaking his head in aggravation. "We have four deaths, two people who might have seen the killers but who were either too drunk or high to remember, and that's about it?"

"We do have one thing, sir," Young interrupted, trying to make a good impression on Johnson. "The three men are homeless, so they can't travel too far quickly. Both Skeet and Rocks were stopped by the murderers in Alexandria. What if that is where they are finding their victims? They attack them in Alexandria and then move them to D.C.?"

"It could be something, but we need more than an entire town," Johnson stated. "Did you look through the victims' bank and credit card records? Is there anything that stands out?"

"On the last day of activity, they both ate at restaurants in D.C. and took a bus tour or other touristy activities in D.C.," Young stated, looking over Cooper's shoulder.

"But there is something missing," Cooper said. "Most of the city parking lots or garages in D.C. use credit or debit cards. It's rare to find an attendant to pay cash to anymore. If they were driving around D.C., and they did these things, they would have had to pay for parking somewhere. Did you find any parking receipts or vouchers in either of their cars?"

Young scrambled to his desk, flipping through his notes and frantically looking at the crime scene pictures. "No, I don't see anything like that."

"What if…" Cooper started, but then stopped and looked at his watch that said a quarter til eleven. "I don't know what I'm saying. It could still be anyone: a cab driver, a hotel worker, a transit employee," he stammered, stomping away to his desk. "I thought I was onto something, but then it just left me."

"It happens, but I like the way you were thinking," Johnson said encouragingly. "Outside the box."

CHAPTER 40

"Solo, are you sure about this?" Elizabeth asked as we sat in her idling car under a flickering streetlamp. "What are you going to say?"

Collecting my thoughts and planning my dialogue on the ride didn't work out as planned since the house was only a ten-minute drive from the bookstore. "I don't know. I guess I'm just going to wing it," I said letting out a heavy breath.

"Wing it? You're going to go to some strange girl's parents at almost midnight and 'wing it'?" She laughed hysterically. "You are a piece of work!"

"Why, because I want to do something?" I blurted out looking through the passenger-side window at the colonial-style two-story home, which was pitch black except for the front porch light.

She shut off the engine and turned to face me with a pair of compassion-filled eyes. "What are you going to get out of this?" she asked calmly, lowering the radio volume to give me her undivided attention.

"I don't know," I said resignedly. "I just don't know." Looking at her I felt a strange sense of peace that I hadn't felt during the last two days. I felt a connection of unknowing. Even though I was on the beach of the sea of uneasiness, I knew with all my heart I couldn't keep walking on the sand while someone in the abyss was screaming for help. "I just can't do nothing."

"That's a double negative," she said smiling, lightening the mood.

"Really?" I laughed. "That's your takeaway?"

"Sorry. I was an English major," she kidded. "So, you still want to do this?"

"I'm here," I said, putting my trembling hand on the door handle.

"Well, here. Take this to be safe." She reached down to get her purse.

"Wint wasn't lying? You've got a gun?" I stammered, startled by the notion of a debutant carrying a pistol in her bag like it was 1849 in the wild west.

"It's a dangerous world," she answered, pulling out her Smith & Wesson Airweight revolver. "A girl's got to be safe."

"I'm not sure the world is a safer place with you having that," I said, slightly freaking out with all the possible scenarios of accidental shootings. Also, I hadn't totally nixed the idea of her being bat-eyed crazy. "Put that up! I'm not taking a gun."

"Fine. Have it your way," she remarked with an attitude as she hid her weapon. "But when this blows up in your face, don't say I didn't warn you."

"If it blows up in my face, tell it at my funeral."

"Deal," she said, nodding in agreement. "Well, do you want me to wait for you?" she asked as I opened the car door to get out.

"If you want to you can, but I'm not going to ask you to stay."

"Oh jeez," she said with a moan, hitting the lever to recline her seat. "Now I can't leave. Especially since I wonder if I caused this whole mess for you in the first place."

"You did what?" I asked confusedly, holding the door open as the interior light shone down on her closing eyelids.

"I'll tell you later," she remarked carelessly as I stood dumbfounded. "Can you shut the door? The light is in my eyes."

"Thanks for the pep talk," I said sarcastically.

"Oh, good luck," she winced before I quietly shut the door.

I walked up the narrow cobble-stone pathway from the sidewalk to the front door practicing my opening greeting. "Good evening Mr. and Mrs. Fiddelstein. My name is Solomon. I have some news about your daughter. Good evening Mr. and Mrs. Fiddelstein. My name is Solomon Davis. I believe I know something about your daughter. Good evening Mr. and Mrs. Fiddelstein. My name is Solo. I have something I need to tell you about your daughter," I whispered over and over, changing the opening line each time as if I was recording the perfect voicemail message.

As I reached the front door, I inhaled deeply and then released. I pressed the doorbell, still reciting the fumbling introduction as a light inside the house turned on. I heard the deadbolt turn and the door cracked open. "Good evening Mr. Fiddelstein. My name is Solomon Davis. I know something about your daughter."

CHAPTER 41

"Who's at the door?" Amanda asked apprehensively, walking up behind her husband who was still standing motionless with the front door wide open. Even though the house was dark, and it was close to midnight, neither was dressed for bed.

"My name is Solomon Davis. This is going to sound crazy, but I know something about your daughter," I said, my voice trembling, petrified of their reaction.

"We don't have the money yet. Please give us more time," Isaac pleaded hopelessly as he stood between me and his emotionally distraught wife. "We just need another day."

"Oh, God!" Amanda cried from behind.

"No, no, no," I quickly waved my arms in the air, watching Amanda strain her neck for a better view around her husband. "I don't have your daughter, and I'm not connected to her either. I just have some information."

"We haven't called the cops, just like they told us. How do you know anything if you are not connected to the kidnappers?" Isaac asked instinctively.

"I promise, I am not crazy. You've got to believe that," I said, reinforcing my words with a sincere tone. "But I had a dream."

The expression on Isaac's face was not one of relief or even doubt, but of uncontrolled rage. "Get off our property now before I call the cops!" he shouted, gripping the door to slam it in my face.

"Mr. Fiddelstein, I swear to you, I am only here to help," I said pleadingly, taking my stance in case the door pushed me out.

"You come here, to my house, at this hour of the night and say that you are only here to help?" he erupted. "Honey, get the gun," he whispered to his wife as her lips trembled in fear. My heart started to beat faster.

A gun? I didn't expect this! "I'm not here to hurt you. I promise," I said, raising my hands in surrender. I turned around and lifted up my shirt so he could tell that I was not packing any weapons. "I don't know why I dreamed about your daughter two nights ago, but I did."

"Two nights ago?" he inquired in a gentler voice.

"Yes. That's when it all started for me. Two nights ago."

"How dare you? How dare you? You are sick!"

"No! No, I'm not! I'm really here to help."

"No one ever comes to just help. They always have an ulterior motive. If you are out to get some money, we don't have any for you," he barked as his wife returned, shaking, with the shiny handgun pointed in my direction.

"I don't want your money! I don't want anything! I promise! I just want your daughter to come home safely. That is all I want. Nothing else. I promise. I just want to help you get your daughter home!" I spewed my words as if this were my last moment on earth. But

I wasn't leaving. I wasn't going to give up on Rachel that easily.

"Amanda, give me the gun," Isaac said, taking the gun from her trembling hand and aiming it at my face. "Just tell me. Is our daughter alive?"

I looked down the barrel of the gun, following the frigid path up his arms to his cold, calculating eyes. Amanda stood behind him, her fragile face showing that at any second a flood of tears would begin. I nodded my head yes. Isaac gritted his teeth. "Get off my property!"

I shook my head in disappointment and turned away walking slowly back to the car. I thought about looking back to see if he had lowered the gun, but something told me that his finger was still on the trigger.

As I walked back to the car under a blackened sky, a few holes in the clouds let a glimmer of moonlight through. I turned before getting in the car. I saw the two silhouettes standing in the shadows of their foyer with the moon's light reflecting off the metallic gun still pointed in my direction. I wanted to say something, but I knew that it wouldn't be received. This didn't go at all as I had hoped.

"How'd it go?" Elizabeth asked as she started the engine to leave the quiet suburb. "I couldn't see much going on. Good thing for your watch."

I looked back. As we pulled away, I saw Isaac and Amanda leave the shadow of their home to stand in the middle of the deserted road. They watched us depart the usually secure neighborhood. Isaac clutched onto Amanda, and I could picture both of them sobbing uncontrollably in the street. It was as though they would crumble like a house of cards if they let go of one another. I closed my eyes and said an audible prayer, "Please God, help me to have another dream tonight about Rachel."

CHAPTER 42

"You've got to tell me how to make sure a dream comes to me tonight," I begged as Elizabeth hummed along with the radio, tuning out the awkward silence in the car.

"I don't know. It doesn't work that way," she answered truthfully. After all, there wasn't a science to her dreams. "I told you, I didn't ask for this. Do you ever listen?"

"Well, do you have a guess? What if I listen to relaxing music or picture Rachel and what she is doing now? What if I drink some warm milk?"

"Solo, you are in a new arena all by yourself," she replied coolly. "If I could pick and choose which dreams I had, I would pretty much stay away from deaths of any kind. But it doesn't work that way."

"You must have some kind of tip, though," I remarked hopefully. "I mean, how long has this been happening to you?"

She continued to drive, not really sure where she was heading. "I really can't remember a time I didn't dream. When I was five I had a dream about getting a dog, and then the next day we got Biscuit."

"You're telling me that you have been having these dreams since you were five?" I scoffed in a mixture of horror and dismay. "I thought this was a fluke and would pass."

"It's not a cold," she said snickering. "Orange juice and some Vitamin C aren't going to cure this."

I had a million and one questions for her. Since she was still being cordial, I decided to start my first round of twenty questions. "Do a lot of people know about you?"

"About me?" She rolled her eyes. "I'm not a freak show performer."

"That's not what I meant, and you know that," I said with a smirk.

"I know. Anyhow, no. Not very many," she responded hesitantly. "And fewer believe."

"Does Verny know?"

"Heavens no," she chuckled. "She would have locked me up in a mental ward for sure. She tried to send me to a private school somewhere in Europe when I was in middle school because I ruined one of her sweaters. So if she knew about this, she would definitely have a hay-day."

"Does Wint know?"

"No, but I believe if I ever did tell him, I could trust him," she said, turning into a busier section of town. "Where am I taking you?"

"You can drop me off near any station, and I can find my way home."

"No bother. I don't have a busy day tomorrow, so I can just take you home."

"You don't have to do that," I commented. "I feel like I have already ruined most of your night."

"It's okay," she said smiling. "Good company is nice sometimes."

"Good company, huh?" I laughed. "Earlier today you wouldn't have picked me up if I was about to get mugged. Now you are driving me home out of the kindness of your own heart?"

"Is that what you think of me? Do I come across as heartless?"

"Some people would use another word for you than heartless, but I'll be nice."

"I would make you blush if I told you all the names I have been called this week alone," she said, continuing to drive the dark, lonely street, as I nodded in agreement. It was so dark I couldn't see her swinging palm until it connected with my face.

"Hey, I was just agreeing with you," I laughed, rubbing my stinging cheek.

"I know, but you didn't have to. You could have said, 'What? Who would say something like that about you?'"

"What, and lie?" I asked snickering.

She burst out laughing. "You didn't have a problem lying to get into the school, but when it comes to me, heaven forbid. I would hate for a scarlet L to show up on one of your ratty old t-shirts you picked up at the Goodwill." I leaned my head on the headrest and closed my eyes. "You are something, you know that?" she continued. "Anyhow, I have another reason to be nice to you. So what's another question you have for the all-knowing 'Lizbeth?'"

Friday

CHAPTER 43

A neon green light filled the room as Rachel sat in the corner drinking a small bottle of Coca-Cola and dipping her McNuggets into mustard. "Need anything else?" a friendly voice asked.

"No thank you," Rachel said with a slight smile.

"I will be back later to check on you, okay," he whispered as she continued to lick the mustard off her chicken nuggets.

The door closed on a darkened narrow hallway with a light bulb swaying at the end of the chain. The hallway ended at an empty living room with only a worn recliner facing a television. The watcher paced around the room, passing by a window that looked out over a small park in the middle of the city. When he walked past the window, a clear reflection appeared of a tall, skinny man wearing a Colorado Rockies hat. A knock on the door caused him to quickly sprint to it, showing a small kitchen and eating area.

"Hey Billy," the friendly voice said.

"Shut up, man. Don't ever use my real name. That brat is probably listening," the other man scolded. The black dog tattoo on his muscular right bicep even looked like it was growling in anger.

"Sorry, sorry," he shrunk back. "I'll be back later."

"Whatever," he responded, pouring himself a bowl of Fruity Pebbles. "Be back by three. The boss said the drop is going down at four at Union Station."

"I still don't understand why we get to split it fifty-fifty. What is he getting out of it?"

"Don't you know anything? Quit asking questions!"

The friendlier man left as a clear image appeared of the second man at the bar, slurping his cereal. He looked to be in his early thirties, balding with a graying goatee. He had a visible scar on his left cheek that ran from his mouth to his ear.

The door closed and 4G glowed in the darkened hallway. He proceeded through the hall and then down the four flights of stairs. As he neared the bottom, the music of a steel drum and hands clapping became barely audible. His heavy footsteps joined in unison with the clapping and a cloud of darkness surrounded him. The clapping continued but started to fade as the sound of fingers typing on a keyboard began to overtake it.

"Dad, you okay up there?"

"Yes, yes, I'm fine. Just tired."

"You're going to sleep good tonight. I know Frank is going to sleep good tonight."

"Yes, yes, I am."

"Cancer is such a sad thing. It seems like everyday I find out someone new has it."

"I know. Terribly sad, but Dad is doing pretty good. The doctors are giving him a good chance of beating it."

"Yes, yes."

"Do you mind if I pray for you?"

"You don't have to."

"Oh, I don't mind. Dear Lord, it's me Margaret. Please take care of this family and help them to grow stronger in health and in love. Be with the doctors. Give them the skill and knowledge to beat this awful sickness. Be with, oh, I'm sorry dear, what did you say your name was?"

"Oh, it's, well, there's our car there. Can you pull beside it so we don't hold up any traffic?"

"Oh, where was I? Bless them, Lord. Bless us all. Help us to love as you love us. Amen."

"Dad, you feeling okay enough to get out?"

"Can you hand me a wipe? I just spilled some juice."

"Here you go."

"So, what are you two going to be doing tomo…."

Scream.

"I never thought Margaret was going to shut up."

The typing subsided as photos from a digital camera began to fill the scene, one after the other. The first showed an image of a computer at 3:30 p.m. Another image of the computer gave a glimpse of a dialogue box that read, "Username: Partner1" and "Password: L3HC4R$." The next picture of the computer was timestamped 3:31 p.m. and showed a list of names with large dollar amounts beside each. Quickly, the picture changed. A screen appeared showing a view of where the funds were being transferred to an offshore bank account in the Grand Caymans. Another picture of the computer was timestamped 3:41 p.m., showing that the balances were $0 by each name. The next picture zoomed in on one of the names on the computer screen, "Isaac Fiddelstein." The final picture was of the Fiddelstein family being held in a pair of hands.

"Thanks, boss," a male voice said with a chuckle. "I quit."

CHAPTER 44

As I opened my eyelids, I breathed a sigh of relief at the newfound knowledge I had received in my dreams. I had originally scoffed at the notion of keeping a journal, but it did have its benefits when some of the dreams had specific details that could easily get jumbled.

After turning on my lamp, I grabbed a pen and pad from my nightstand and quickly wrote all the details I could remember. The descriptions of the kidnappers; the details of the apartments; even part of the dialogue that I could remember. Then I moved to the next dream which was just an odd play-like conversation. I had no clue who was saying what and to whom, but I was pretty sure it ended abruptly for a reason.

Lastly, I scribbled descriptions of the pictures of the computer that appeared to be someone stealing funds from a bank or other type of financial institution. Oddly enough it had Isaac Fiddelstein's name on the screen.

Why? I thought to myself, staring at the ceiling as the alarm clock read 3:48 a.m. Are these events connected? If so, how?

My racing mind was not slowing as it tried to connect the moving dots like asteroids. I visualized the additional clues or snippets of data that I might have missed in my first write-up of the dreams. I read and reread the three dreams. Each time I thought I had a new detail, a chill of doubt engulfed my body. Dreams were so easy to misinterpret because they were just unconscious memories. And memories could be easily distorted.

I thought I needed to try to get a few more hours of sleep. Based on the dream, it may turn out to be a busy day. But no matter how hard I tried, sleep was as elusive as the understanding I needed.

Grabbing my phone, I quickly texted Elizabeth to let her know I had another dream. I waited impatiently for a response that never came. During my many failed attempts to fall asleep, my alarm clock had quickly shifted from 3:48 a.m. to 5:12 a.m.

"No use just sitting here," I thought as I rolled out of bed to take a refreshing shower. As my heart rate gradually slowed to a reasonable pace, I haphazardly planned my day. "They might not have listened to me last night, but I have to try again this morning," I thought while the soapsuds vanished down the drain. "I have to give it another try."

CHAPTER 45

"Winston, come back to bed," Veronica moaned as she fluffed her goose-down pillow. Her head pressed into the softness, yearning for a couple more hours of sleep.

"I just can't sleep," he said, lying on the floor doing crunches.

"You're not going to be of any help falling asleep on the job," she said mothering him.

"There is a pair of serial killers out there killing random people. It's on my shoulders to figure it out," he said after another round of twenty quick sit-ups.

"It is not all on your shoulders, Winston," she said, rolling over and hanging her head off the bed to see his rolling eyes.

"This is the break that I've been needing," he said, continuing with another round of bicycle crunches. "And I need to prove to them I can do it."

"Oh, I have no doubt that you can do it."

"You're just saying that because you married me," he smiled, leaning up to give her a gentle kiss.

"Yes, pretty much," she answered coldly as she rolled back to her spot. "You've already figured out that they are getting their victims from Virginia. That's a step. Then tomorrow morning you will figure something else out because I married a smart, capable, detective."

"I'm not a detective yet," he corrected her as he rolled onto his stomach to do a few sets of push-ups. "Not yet."

"But you will be," she responded drowsily. "I'll get my father to make a call to the mayor."

"No!" he shouted, punching his fists into the floor, causing the bed to shake Veronica.

"I'm only trying to help!" she replied arrogantly with a hint of annoyance.

"I don't need your father's help! If I can't do it myself, then I shouldn't get it."

"I didn't marry a quitter."

"You didn't marry a cheater either," he barked.

"A cheater? Is that how you see me?" she snapped, jumping out of bed and stomping away on the hardwood floor down the hall.

He knew that he should chase after her and do his husbandly duty, but at the moment, that was the furthest thing from his mind. He was tired of hearing that her father was the answer to every question. If he was the only answer, he didn't want to be right.

CHAPTER 46

My old Honda Civic moaned and sputtered down the palatial suburb street as if it felt the bullying headlights of the other luxury automobiles housed in their three-car garages. I parked my car as it coughed and gyrated to a halt like an old man hacking up some phlegm.

Last night, the Fiddelstein's home looked cold and dark, like all the life had left it. This morning, the grand estate caused my knees to tremble at its opulence. Yet it still had a frigid feel of doom and despair.

As I walked up the footpath, I tried to gain some composure and a morsel of backbone. Even one vertebrae of steel would be better than none.

"What are you doing here?" Isaac Fiddelstein shouted at me, clutching his new best friend, the gun, with his right hand. I stood awkwardly in the middle of the footpath about ten feet away from the door. I never got the chance to take a deep breath before I could ring the doorbell. He must have heard my car.

"I just came to check on you two this morning," I responded politely with a sincere smile.

"I don't care!" he berated, waving his pistol-bearing hands like he was holding a pom-pom instead of a deadly weapon. "Get off my property! If you come back, I'm going to call the police."

"Yes, yes, please do, call the police!" I pleaded. "They know how to handle kidnappings. You don't. For the sake of Rachel, call the police!"

"Shut up!" he whispered angrily as he stomped in my direction and grabbed my arm to pull me in their house. I didn't see that coming. He slammed the door with brutal force and pushed me onto the couch in their adjoining family room.

"Honey, what's wrong?" Amanda shouted hysterically as she ran down the stairs. She stepped into the family room to find me sitting on the couch with my arms folded neatly in my lap, trying to appear cordial and respectful. "What's he doing here?" she cried, taking a step closer into the family room.

"Just go back upstairs. I'm going to handle this," Isaac ordered, pacing around the couch like a lion in a cage.

"Why'd you come back here? Tell me why!" she shouted.

"I had another dream last night about Rachel," I stated, rubbing my forehead to help relieve some of the tension.

"Stop lying!" Isaac barked just inches from my face. "Just stop your lying!"

"I'm not lying," I answered respectfully, looking him in his quickly aging and lifeless eyes. They were bloodshot from the tears and sleepless nights. "I had a dream," I said as I pulled out my journal and gave them the play by play.

"Where is my little girl?" Amanda shouted, running into the room and slapping me in the face. "Where is Rachel, you con?"

"I promise! I don't want anything," I said, blocking her fists with my palms. "I just want to help get your daughter home safe."

"If you want to help," Isaac said emotionless, raising his gun to my forehead. "Get out of my house and never return."

CHAPTER 47

"How are the three witnesses doing this morning?" Johnson asked as he towered beside Cooper's desk, looking over his shoulder to see what he was doing.

"Well, Skeet and Rocks have somewhat sobered up, but they still don't know anything except that there were two people in the vehicle when they were given the hotel room key cards," Cooper answered, looking over the evidence. "Last night, I thought I had something, but then it didn't seem right. But I still can't get it out of my mind."

"What was it?" Young asked, strutting in and hanging his coat on the back of his chair.

"I still have a feeling that there is something to the victims not having any garage charges on their cards."

"Yeah, like what?"

"Well, no offense," Cooper said looking at Johnson who was graying around his ears. "But many older people who live in smaller cities don't like traffic. So what if these victims purposely got a hotel outside of the city and then commuted in?"

"Go on," Johnson said with a grimacing look. Cooper couldn't tell if it was from interest or anger.

"Well, if they commuted in, what if the killers picked them out on the subway as well? What if that's their M.O.? They follow older tourists and then get them when they are not expecting it."

"Really?" Young scoffed. "There are security cameras all over the Metro stations. For heaven's sake!

There are even security guards at some of the stations."

"Yes, but there are not usually any guards in the garages," Johnson commented. "They usually linger together around the ticket counters. If you ask them, they probably couldn't tell you anything that happened those nights."

"I will call the Metro to get the video recordings of all the stations for the nights that the murders happened," Young said, quickly picking up the phone and dialing.

"I wouldn't bother with all the stations. Just the stations around Alexandria," Cooper remarked. "If they were attacked in the garage, it would most likely be the Metro stations closest to their hotels."

"Okay," Young said with a grunt, knowing he had been proven wrong again.

"This could be your lucky break," Johnson said, smiling and patting Cooper on his back. "Good work, Cooper."

"Thank you, sir."

"Thank you, sir," Young mocked quietly, but Cooper caught a whiff of his tone. The homicide telephone line started to ring, but everyone in the department was busy or on the phone. "Hey, Cooper, get that for me, will you?"

"Homicide. Officer Cooper here."

CHAPTER 48

My Honda Civic was purring like a newborn kitten once I left the ritzy neighborhood. I headed toward school for the one class I had that day. The dialogue between me and the Fiddelsteins didn't go as planned once again, but that wasn't going to stop me from searching. Something was going to happen that day, and I needed to find out soon where she was located.

Flipping to the second page of my dream journal, I saw the mysterious dialogue that seemed strangely familiar to the conversation in a previous dream – the dream where individuals were murdered by the supposed Carbon Monoxide Killer. The police were always saying that if anyone had any information related to any case, they should call. I decided to do my civic duty. I pulled my car over when I finally saw a very rare, almost extinct species – a telephone booth.

"911, what's your emergency?" a female operator asked calmly.

"I have some information about a homicide."

"Please hold. I will connect you."

The phone rang a few times. "Homicide. Officer Cooper here."

"Cooper," I said with shock in my normal voice. Coughing, I tried to quickly disguise my voice. "Officer Cooper, I mean."

"Yes, how can I help you?"

"Yes, I, uh, I have some information about those Carbon Monoxide Killers."

"Yes, sir, I am listening. What do you have?" he asked as his tone piqued with interest. "Did you say killer or killers?"

"Killers," I repeated. "There are two of them."

"How do you know that, sir?"

"Because I heard them talking about it," I said, which wasn't technically a lie since both of my dreams about them had been purely dialogue.

"Where did you see them? What other type of information can you tell me about them?"

"It's a man and a woman," I answered. "A father and a daughter."

"Go on! What else do you have? Do you know how they get their victims?"

"They pick them up in some type of parking lot somewhere, but I am not sure where."

"Good, good, very good, sir. Do you know anything else?"

"Yes! They are going to kill again tonight," I said, quickly hanging up the phone. I jumped into my car wondering if I made the right decision.

CHAPTER 49

The lecture today by guest professor Dr. Wright was on the different approaches of evangelism in the Middle East. Sadly, it didn't draw enough interest for me to follow along with the discussion. It also might have been the lingering feeling of Rachel crying in some possibly nearby apartment that caused my mind to drift away from the topic.

As the majority of the class was taking notes and adding insights on the growing demand of spreading the gospel, I was doodling in my dream journal. I was still trying to see how the dots connected, as if it would form some directional constellation pointing me toward the right path.

"One method doesn't fit every scenario," Dr. Wright said continuing with his lecture. "There are some people for whom it will take a lifelong friendship to allow them to hear any mention of the name Jesus. Then there are others that will only be willing to listen during a hardship or crisis. Some may be more ready to sit down and discuss the differences between faiths. Then there are some exceptions of people who have been waiting for someone to talk to them, as if they were given a vision of hope."

Hearing the word vision caught my attention and my scribbling ceased. "What do you mean by a vision of hope?" one student asked from a few rows behind me.

"There have been reports and stories of people in third world countries embracing the notion of Jesus Christ just because they experienced a dream or vision the night before. It is sad to say, but people in America may doubt these types of interactions because they do not happen as often nor are they as openly discussed here as they are in other countries. I like to call it the Faith Effect. When you rely on faith as a necessity for life, you tend to see more faithful things. Whereas, if you rely on sight as a way of life, you tend to see only what you can tangibly see. It's kind of a spiraling circle. The less faith you need, the less faith you will get. God bless the United States of America," he said smiling as he continued answering other questions.

As the lecture ended and everyone was packing up to leave, I heard someone call my name from across the lecture hall, "Solo," the familiar voice said. I turned to see it was Dr. Jeremiah Huffington coming my way. "Good seeing you here today."

"Likewise," I said, smiling as I stuffed my belongings into my backpack.

"Nice lecture today, wasn't it?" Dr. Huffington commented, watching the lecturer interact with students.

"Parts of it were," I said truthfully. Yet as I said the words, I felt I had misspoken. "My mind was elsewhere today."

"Oh, it's all good. Eugene often puts me to sleep when he leads his lectures. I am pretty certain I have seen him nod off a few times during some of mine," he said with a laugh as he waved Dr. Wright over to join the conversation.

"Dr. Eugene Wright, this is my new friend Solomon "Solo" Davis. Solo, this is my oldest and best friend Eugene," Jeremiah introduced.

"Solo, glad you could make it," Dr. Wright greeted as we shook hands.

"It was indeed very interesting," I remarked kindly, looking at Jeremiah to take the lead on the conversation. I hoped he wouldn't tell his friend my true feelings.

"I could tell that I riveted you by your drawing," Dr. Wright said laughing, which caused my face to quickly redden. "It's okay. Everyone has different passions. That is what makes the world go round."

"Very true," Jeremiah nodded. "True indeed. I especially liked it when you mentioned the dreams and visions."

"Well, it went with the topic," Dr. Wright said, smiling warmly. "And I knew that you were coming and wanted to try to give you some additional information for your upcoming book."

"You've already told me your thoughts and beliefs on the Middle Eastern culture with visions," Jeremiah said, snickering as he comfortably swayed on his heels. "Always trying to convert me, aren't you?"

"Just as I said earlier, no one method will ever fit every scenario," Dr. Wright commented kindly. "I'm not giving up hope yet."

"So, have either of you had any personal experiences with visions or dreams?" I asked casually, wondering if Jeremiah knew about Elizabeth's abilities or if there were many people in the world dealing with what I had come to know as truth.

"I've heard accounts and met people while I was studying and traveling abroad who presumably have the ability. I am still hesitant on their genuineness," Jeremiah answered, locking eyes with Dr. Wright as if there was a constant battle between faithful and skeptic.

"Well, I have traveled to many places and have seen first-hand a few incidents that I could not explain if I didn't have faith," Dr. Wright said grinning, his eyes fixed on Jeremiah as I watched their apparent staring contest.

"Have either of you met anyone here that has these gifts?" I asked again, bringing an end to their standoff as they each exchanged friendly smirks and laughs.

"Not personally. I don't doubt that it can happen here, but like I said, in America, faith is different than it is elsewhere. Look at the medicines and hospitals we have. Yet in Africa, where those items are scarce, they rely heavily on prayer for healing. I have seen miraculous healings that sprung the near-dead back to life through prayer and anointment of oils in Tanzania. Whereas, I have seen the same result here when a pill is popped or surgery performed. I believe God works in a million different ways, and maybe there are traces of God's mercy in our technology of blood pressure medicines and chemotherapy just as he shows the same mercy to a mother praying over her child in Cambodia who suffered a snakebite wound. Who knows? All I know, Dr. Huffington, is you can never limit God," Dr. Wright concluded.

"Just fake psychics preying on the weak and easily swayed for me," Jeremiah snidely commented as the three of us started to leave the lecture hall.

As I was walking, I couldn't get one of Dr. Wright's final comments out of my head. I wasn't giving up hope yet on Rachel either. I just had to find the right method for talking with the Fiddelsteins.

CHAPTER 50

"What are you so giddy about?" Young asked belittlingly as he entered the squad room. He was just returning from IT where they were getting the videos from the Metro garages.

"A tip was just phoned in. This guy said he heard a father and a daughter talking about killing someone. He assumed they were the so-called Carbon Monoxide Killers," Cooper explained, reading him the rest of the short conversation which ended abruptly.

"So, you don't know who this mystery man is that called?" Young scoffed. "Don't you know that 99% of tips are from people who just want to feel important?"

"Yes, but it was interesting that what this man was telling me agreed with what the other three eyewitnesses were telling us. How did he know that there were two killers, and that there was a male and a female? The majority of serial killers don't work in pairs, and an even smaller percentage work with a member of the opposite sex."

"Could just be a lucky guess," Young remarked, plopping down at his desk as if defeated that Officer Cooper had taken the call and not him.

"Yes, but he warned that there is going to be another killing tonight," Cooper said, jumping up to start scribbling the various puzzle pieces onto the evidence board. "We can stop these killers if we figure out where they are going to be. Has IT gotten the videos of the Metro garages yet?"

"They're loading them now. I should have it soon," Young said.

"Can you believe it? This may be the break that we need!" Cooper yelled, positive adrenaline coursing through his veins. "Even if we can't figure out which garage they are going to tonight for sure, we can tell the guards to be on a lookout for a father and daughter," Cooper said as Young interrupted him.

"That could be anyone, Cooper. Come on, we need something more than that," he moaned pessimistically.

"Something more than what?" Dakota asked as she swayed into the squad room with her hair meticulously fixed to impress Young.

"Cooper here thinks he is on to the Carbon Monoxide Killers. I keep telling him that he has nothing," Young scoffed, turning his back to Cooper to focus more on Dakota's smile and her other God-given gifts.

"Come on, Smithy, be nice," she giggled, patting his arms, getting a feel of his flexed bicep. "Really, what do you have?" she asked, leaning over Cooper's desk, allowing her uniform to reveal her red bra to anyone who looked.

Cooper noticed the accented cleavage but turned away like a gentleman, while Young leaned in to get a better look at her show. Cooper went through his story again, not to please Dakota, but to see if there was anything he was missing. He prayed and hoped that Young wasn't right.

"Oh, that's all you got?" she remarked snidely, standing up and straightening her uniform with a little wink to Young.

"Just like I was saying, we need something more than that," Young commented as he charmed Dakota with his good looks by returning a smoldering wink.

"What do you have?" Johnson asked as he stomped into the squad room. Dakota skirted away, rubbing Young's backside as she passed. Cooper started giving Johnson a play-by-play of the morning events. Oddly enough, Young jumped in to tell a few tidbits of information when he noticed Johnson's furrowed brow ease with signs of relief.

"Good work, Young," Chief Randolph said beaming, appearing out of nowhere. "You can learn something from him," he commented to Cooper, patting Young on the back before preparing to leave. "Keep me posted on this Johnson. I want this case solved quick."

"That's what we're trying to do, Chief," Johnson said, grimacing as he watched the chief leave the room. He rolled his eyes as his brow furrowed tighter than it had been moments before. "Talk to the three eyewitnesses one more time, and then let them go, Young."

"Yes sir," he said smiling, putting on his designer jacket. He straightened his silk tie and strutted out of the room.

"Now that he's gone, we can get to work," Johnson said agitatedly. "We probably have an hour or so to look through all the evidence again. Look at every piece of information from a different angle. We're missing something. I'll call IT to send the videos to me, and hopefully we will have some of the footage before he gets back."

CHAPTER 51

The drive to the Fiddelstein's was a schizophrenic good-cop/bad-cop dialogue, with me trying to pinpoint the most forceful and demanding opener. I had tried being polite. I had tried being caring. I had tried being the good Samaritan. But those were not working. It was time to get real, jab them low and then hit them high! I didn't want to harm or confuse them, but I needed to show them that I meant business.

I quickly walked up to the door, pounding my fist against the wood and altogether ignoring their classy doorbell chimes. "Get away from us!" Isaac shouted from behind the closed door, peering out from the glass windows aligning the mahogany craftsmanship.

"I am not leaving!" I shouted as I kept pounding away on the door. I started wondering if my pinky finger would soon feel the effects and if my blood would become embedded in the wood.

"I'll go get my gun if you don't get off my property!"

"Fine! Get your gun. Try to shoot me, but I will have already called the cops and told them that your little girl has been kidnapped. What do you think the kidnappers will do then?"

Click. The deadbolt of the door quickly turned as Isaac opened the door with trembling hands. "Please, no. Don't, don't do that."

"I need to come in now, because if you don't let me in, I will go to the cops."

"Stop that," he said in a more conversational tone. "Stop yelling and come in," he said, resigning himself to my demand. He pulled me into the house, looking around at the neighbors to see if anyone witnessed the commotion before shutting the door.

"Why do you keep bothering us?" Amanda asked as she walked over from the sitting area in the family room.

"Because someone has to do something," I answered forcefully, without any reservation or hesitation. I had come to battle, and I wasn't going to walk away wounded or defeated.

"They are supposed to call me today," Isaac started to tell me before I quickly interrupted.

"Yes. I know. They are going to tell you to bring the money to a drop-off point at Union Station around four this afternoon," I said, giving them the details while they looked shocked at my straightforwardness.

"How do you know what they are going to do?" Amanda asked, squeezing her husband's hand for support and strength.

"I keep telling you. I dreamed about Rachel." I spit out the words quickly, telling them the details of the dream before they could say another word.

"You said that she was eating chicken nuggets and drinking a pop?" Amanda asked, her voice cracking in fragility. "Was she dipping them in anything?"

I closed my eyes, trying to look back at the vivid dream. Even though it was very detailed, it was also so short. "She was dipping it in something bright yellow,"

I said, my eyes squeezed shut. "I would think honey mustard, but it looks like regular mustard. Yes. I remember seeing the mustard packets. Why?"

"She dips everything in mustard. Most kids eat ketchup, but she only uses mustard," she answered, a smile enveloping her face as she wiped away a few running tears. "And she knows that she's not allowed to have soda," she said with a laugh as more tears were flowing down her face. They were different tears, though. Tears that I hadn't seen in a while. They were tears of joy.

"Honey, it will be okay this one time," Isaac said laughing as his eyes, too, began to fill with tears. "She can drink all the soda she wants."

CHAPTER 52

"Okay, okay, okay," Isaac said, pacing around the living room as Amanda and I sat watching him.

"So, do we need to call the police or not?" Amanda asked, looking at me with a longing for answers.

"No. We can't call the cops," Isaac said, standing his ground. "We've waited this long, and Solomon said that she's okay. If we get the cops in it now, it may cause the kidnappers to do something drastic."

"Drastic? Drastic? They kidnapped our little girl! That seems pretty drastic to me."

"Honey," Isaac consoled, rushing to his wife's side and looking at me for a second opinion.

"I think we should listen to Isaac since he's the one who actually talked with the kidnappers, right?" I asked, trying to get my facts straight.

"Yes. They always call my cell phone, and each time they tell me not to call the police."

"Well, in any other circumstance, I would say to call the police. But if we work together, I think we can figure this out."

"Really?" Amanda said, looking at me with some renewed hope. "She's been gone for three days, and all we've had are a few phone calls."

"The kidnappers are not going to hurt Rachel. I know that. So if we keep doing as they say, we should get her back safe and sound."

"You okay with this, sweetheart?" Isaac asked, holding her hands in her lap. "We have to be together on this."

"Do you trust me?" I asked, reaching out my hand to give their hands a strong squeeze.

She didn't know how to respond. I could see the look in her eyes that trust wasn't something she was willing to give right then. In a world where backstabbers could turn out to be a close friend, how could one truly trust a complete stranger who seemed delusional?

"Scratch that. I don't know if I would even trust me right now if I were in your shoes. But," I stopped and looked at Isaac and then back at Amanda unsure if words from my heart would do any good, "I just want you to know that if we do not work as a team, I will be working by myself to get your daughter home. That I can promise you with nothing in return."

"It just seems so unbelievable," Isaac responded, shaking his head, mentally weighing the pros and cons of accepting my help.

"Unbelievable? Unbelievable? The last few days have been unbelievable, Isaac," Amanda stuttered as a lone tear trickled down her cheek. "What more do we have to lose? Our baby is gone! You won't go to the cops!" she squealed, burying her head into the cleft of his arm. "If he's a fraud, I just don't care anymore. A little hope is better than none."

"A liar would tell you to trust him. And I have no proof to give you to trust me except for my word, which as I just said, sounds like something a crook

196

would say," I said muttering to myself to collect my thoughts that were jumbled like scrambled eggs. "I'm sorry. I'm new to all of this. I've never been one to communicate my thoughts very well. I'm not here to tell you a story of fluff. That's not me. I just want to help you guys. Even as absurd as that sounds, that is all I want. Just to help."

"Okay," Amanda rose from her husband's protective clutches and wiping her face dry. "I have a question for you."

"Shoot," I answered like an open book, hoping that I could recollect the details of the dreams that I had had over the last few nights.

"If you could have dinner with one person, alive or dead, who would it be?

I sat shocked in disbelief. "Are you serious?"

"Very. Who would you have dinner with?"

My heart sank with the idea of having dinner one more time with her. My life had been in shambles once, and it seemed like some days were easier than others. The memory of her could bring such joy and happiness, but also a punch of despair and pain. I swallowed my emotions that were billowing from inside and choked out my reply. "My wife."

"Why her?"

I sat frozen, recalling the month that I took away from life to a nice retreat at an institution with daily rounds of group therapy and healthy doses of medications. Some may have seen that period in my life as a moment of weakness, having to seek help from someone other than myself or my faith. That I wasn't man enough to carry on with life and the daily struggles that any other widower faced. But the truth was, I wasn't. I debated ending it all multiple times, and I still had the mental scar tissue as a reminder. But I learned that though no one is guaranteed an easy life, we are guaranteed that we will never walk alone. "She was killed five years ago. So, if I could have dinner with anyone, it would be her. Hands down."

"Okay," she responded in a matter-of-fact tone. She squeezed her husband's hand, looking into his protective eyes and nodded as if signaling she was good to continue.

"So, tell us what you saw in the dream again and do not leave out anything," Isaac said as their grandfather clock chimed twelve times. I began to retell the events of the dream.

"Oh, oh, oh," Amanda wiggled in her seat, trying to get the words out, but unable to formulate a proper sentence.

"Breathe," Isaac said, humming compassionately. "Just take a deep breath and then say it."

"Remember a few weeks ago, I was talking about the Foundation having a diversity parade. One of the groups was a Jamaican steel drum troop. What if the parade is today and that is what you were hearing when you heard steel drums? What if the parade is passing by where Rachel is?"

"What street is the parade on?" I asked before Isaac could ask the same question.

"I don't know, but it should be on the news or website or somewhere."

"Do you have a computer?" I asked as Amanda speedily opened a drawer in the built-in cabinets. She pulled out a sleek laptop just as Isaac's phone rang.

"Hello, Tom," he answered in a sickly tone as he got up from the couch. "Yes, the surgery went fine. I hope to be back next week," he said nodding his head as if hoping to end the conversation quickly. "Yes, yes, she is taking good care of me." He stopped to listen to Tom fill him in on the details he had missed at work. "Well, I need to get off here. I need to take another pill. See you next week, Tom. Thanks for calling."

"Tom again?" Amanda asked as Isaac sat on the couch beside her. "Such a good friend he is to always watch after you." She smiled as she booted up the computer noticing that there wasn't a Wi-Fi connection. "The Wi-Fi isn't working," she shouted in Isaac's ear not realizing that he had sat down.

"Ouch!" he gasped, rubbing his ear to stop it from ringing. "You have to put in the password."

"What is it again?" she asked, waiting to type.

"It's Rachel backwards with a 3 and a 4 for the vowels," Isaac answered as Amanda carefully typed, saying each letter and number as her fingers pressed the keys.

"That worked," she said, quickly searching for a diversity parade in Washington, D.C.

"Did you just say your password is L3HC4R?" I asked, flipping through my journal of dreams and seeing a similar password.

"Yes, it's Rachel with a 4 for the A and a 3 for the E, but backwards," Isaac confirmed.

"Do you use this password at your work?" I asked, watching some of the puzzle pieces moving closer together.

"It's similar. Why?"

"I think I know why the drop is going to happen at four today."

CHAPTER 53

Johnson and Cooper huddled around the grainy, black and white video of the Huntington garage, looking for images of the first set of victims. "There. Slow down," Cooper said as Johnson slowed the video. They watched a couple, similar to Burt and Pam Hamilton, walk toward their Ford Explorer. "That looks like the Hamiltons, and isn't that an Explorer? Can you read the license plate?"

"No, but do you see there?" Johnson said pointing to the right side of the screen. "Pam appears to be talking to a couple that looks like a man and a woman wearing surgical masks."

They watched the video like it was a horror movie as the Hamiltons picked up the unknown couple and started driving up the levels of the garage. "Why are they driving up?" Cooper asked, trying to find another garage camera to follow the vehicle's journey. "There! There's the vehicle. Why are they stopping?"

They watched as the SUV stopped and then parked beside another car. Cooper quickly looked through the remaining camera videos, but there wasn't a garage camera that could see anything except the rear end of the vehicle. "That's where it must have happened. That's where they were attacked," Johnson remarked coldly as they watched the frozen image, waiting for any movement.

After a couple of minutes, the vehicle backed up and proceeded down the ramp to exit the garage.

"That's not Burt driving the car anymore," Cooper shuddered as a chill ran down his spine. "Can we freeze the image and print it out, so we can distribute it to garage security?"

"The picture isn't very good," Johnson commented, moving closer to the computer screen to get a better view of the blurry image. "I wouldn't have figured out that was Burt and Pam if we hadn't known what to look for."

"Maybe we can get a better image of the killers from another camera or maybe IT can clean up the image so it's crisper."

"Computer nerds can do a lot," Johnson said, nodding with some hope. "Give 'em a call and see what they can do."

"What are you two looking at?" Young asked, sliding between them to watch the video.

"The killers."

CHAPTER 54

"Explain it to me again," Isaac said. He stood by the window as Amanda continued to look for the diversity parade information.

"Someone is going to use that password to hack into one of your computers to steal a lot of money this afternoon, including your money. That's why they don't want to hurt Rachel. They are using the ransom money as a distraction because they have something bigger brewing," I explained. I watched the little shred of life that remained drain from his eyes as I mentioned his money. It quickly reappeared when he heard that Rachel would be spared. He processed it as his fists slowly tightened in a shaking rage.

"Are you double-crossing them?" he yelled from across the room. "Are they cutting you out of the deal, so now you are playing with us? Grasping for any last hopes for a payday?"

"Isaac!" Amanda commanded as she looked up at her husband. Then she quickly looked back at me. I saw the doubt wash over her like a new layer of makeup had just been applied.

"No! You've got to believe me," I pleaded. "I'm not connected to them at all. If I was, and if I was going to double cross them, I would have already told you where they were to try to get some kind of reward out of you. You are desperate, and I am pretty certain you would pay me whatever I wanted to get your daughter back."

"But what if you're just playing us? What if we are just some pawn in your sick game? What do you have to lose? Your wife is already dead!"

"Isaac!" Amanda erupted in disgust. Isaac left the room and headed toward the kitchen. "How dare you bring that up as a reason for him helping us!" she yelled, looking at me with a horrific expression of guilt and remorse. "I'm so--" she started to say.

"No. It's okay," I said quickly so she didn't have to finish. "He's stressed. He's upset. He's in a downward spiral and here I come, a complete stranger, telling you that I know something about your daughter. If he didn't have some doubts about me, he would be the most gullible man alive."

I heard a cabinet door open and the kitchen faucet turn on. I went to the kitchen to try to ease a little of the tension and found Isaac gulping a glass of water and holding the counter for support. "I just, I just..." he started to say quietly as he began to release a few of the tears that were being held in by a dam of masculinity and strength. "I don't know what to do," he said letting out a fragile stifled cry. He continued to hold himself up as he watched for Amanda, hoping that she didn't hear his emotional crumbling.

I watched from a slight distance. I didn't know if I needed to move closer to catch him in case his knees went weak or to stay away in case he lunged at me in vengeance. "I know."

"I'm supposed to take care of my family. The one day that I was supposed to pick her up from school someone kidnapped her because I was late."

"You didn't cause this," I said, quickly defending him. I began to see that it wasn't just the fear of having his daughter missing. It was also the guilt of not being a good father. "You're a good father. You are. If you didn't care for her, you wouldn't have such dread right now, and Amanda knows that."

"If I just hadn't taken that stupid, stupid phone call. If I had only told Michael to take a message and I would call them back. If I had only left to pick up my little girl when I was supposed to, we would not be in this spot!"

"It's not your fault, Isaac," I reassured him as Amanda came running into the room.

"What? You were late?" she bellowed. "You caused this? You got my baby kidnapped? You did this? You made this mess?" she wailed like a wounded animal caught in a trap. She ran to him with fists ready for pounding. He didn't try to stop her; he took each and every punch like a numb man.

"I'm sorry. I'm so, so, sorry," he cried, almost hysterically as his eyes gushed tears. "It's all my fault! It's all my fault! I'm such a horrible father! I'm the worst husband! Oh God! Oh God! It's all my fault! I don't deserve to live!"

"How could you? Rachel, my baby!" As she cried, her punches became weaker and feebler. "You stupid, stupid idiot!"

"I know! I know! Tell me something I don't know!" he wailed at the top of his lungs. His emotional pain was so intense, the major blood vessels in his neck were bulging from the strain.

"You did this," she mouthed, her voice barely audible. "You did all this yourself."

"I'm sorry," he whimpered, wrapping his shaking arms around his wife.

"No!" she screamed, pushing away his embrace with such torrid force that his back collided with the counter.

"Stop that!" I screamed, rushing to their aid when I saw him look at the butcher knives in their wooden block. I put myself between him and the deadly weapons. "Rachel is going to be home this afternoon. She is going to be fine."

"Why should we believe that?" Isaac shouted in my face. His words sprayed me with his salty tears.

"Because it's the truth. If it's the last thing I do, I will find Rachel and bring her home to you! But before that happens, I need you both to calm down so we can figure this out!"

"But..." Isaac started as I snapped my fingers as if commanding a dog to sit.

"Did you say that you got a phone call right when you were about to leave?"

"Yes, why?"

"Who was it that called?" I asked.

"Yes, who was it?" Amanda joined in angrily. "I hope it was worth it!"

"It was a possible new client...um, Scott...Scott something."

Suddenly, another wave of clarity splashed up on our shaky sand. "There is no new client. That was just a hoax to get you to stay so they could get your daughter. You have a traitor working for you. Is there anyone you can think of that would do this?"

"Well, no, not that I'm aware of. But I don't know everyone at the firm. We have new employees every month, and HR handles the hiring and firings. Sad to say, but I don't mingle much with those who work for me. There's Tom, who's been an advisor with me for years; Cathy who handles all of my PR and marketing; my assistant, Michael; and Scott, who is my financial analyst. These are the ones in my inner circle."

"Well, someone knows you and doesn't like you much."

"That could be anyone," Amanda remarked snidely. "You sideline anyone who doesn't bow to you."

"I'm sorry," he crumbled once again.

"Amanda, you love him. I saw it in your eyes earlier. You don't mean that. And Isaac, she's right! It could be anyone. Remember what I said before, they are not out to hurt Rachel. They are out to hurt you. Who would you rather have them hurt, you or Rachel?"

"Me! Me! I would let them have all of this if they would just give me back my little girl."

"Well, a loving father wouldn't have said that, would he?" I asked, looking at Amanda for some support, but she was slow to respond.

"You know I love you," she whispered in his ear. "I just feel so helpless."

"Me too."

"They tricked you. They knew that you would take the call, and they dragged it out to get you stuck in this place."

"Yes, yes, I kept telling him that I had to leave," he said, trying to find some support and forgiveness from his wife and himself. "But he kept asking more questions about possible investments. I didn't want to talk to him. I thought it was just going to be a quick call, and then I would have plenty of time to get her. I was just a few minutes late," he defended, not only to his wife, but also to himself.

"If they didn't succeed in getting her then, they would have gotten her eventually. It's no one's fault but the kidnappers'."

Closing my eyes to regain my center, I prayed for the tension and conflict to ease. Suddenly, a vision of the various computer images from my dream sprang up from my memory bank. The last image revealed itself with a pair of hands holding their framed family portrait, similar to one that people had on their desk. "He's going to do it on your computer around 3:30 this afternoon."

"My computer? But who?"

"I don't know, but he called you 'boss'."

"Oh, and I found where the diversity parade is today. It's at one o'clock on Georgia Avenue," Amanda added.

"Georgia Avenue. That's around Howard University, isn't it?" I asked, trying to see how everything was connected.

"Yes, they are the ones holding the event," Amanda answered, wiping away a few tears. "You think you know where our little girl is?" she asked me.

I didn't want to be wrong. "Let's look at a map. Is there a park along that street? I remember seeing a park."

We quickly went back to the family room, conducted a search on the laptop, and found a small park. "Maury Wills Field is on the parade route." She hovered over the laptop screen as a smiled radiated from her face. She lifted her head to look at her husband. "There's a McDonald's too."

"We have to leave now!" Isaac shouted, grabbing for his keys and wallet. "It's gonna start in thirty minutes."

"What about the ransom drop and your employee stealing your money?" I asked, trailing behind the speedy pair.

"I don't care about that. I want my daughter now!" Isaac spurned as he and Amanda jetted back to the kitchen. "Aren't you coming?"

"Well, yeah," I stammered, jogging with them to their Mercedes parked in the garage. "The thing is, the guy who has your daughter now seems like a rough dude. The other guy coming at three seems like someone we can take easily."

"I don't care how big this guy is! He's mine!"

Sitting in the backseat, I braced myself as Isaac sped through the city, running through stop signs and red lights. Despite this, I couldn't get past what was going to happen later. "If we get your daughter now, what if the guy behind all this stops what he was going to do and makes another plan, but this time, he doesn't care about your daughter or anyone that he attacks?"

"So, what do you suggest?" Amanda asked, gripping her arm rest and praying that they didn't have a wreck before getting to Georgia Avenue.

"Sorry, but I don't care what you say," Isaac retorted. "I'm getting my daughter back now!"

CHAPTER 55

Isaac was determined that no matter what I said, it wasn't going to change his outlook. I didn't know what to say. I felt Amanda staring at me through her sun visor mirror. I closed my eyes, needing a minute to think through the situation. I needed time to process a few possible scenarios and decide which one would lead to the best outcome. I took a few deep breaths, twirling my fingers anxiously, playing with my ring finger where my wedding band used to be. I could see her smile, which always made me feel like I could handle anything that was thrown my way. I slowly felt the weight of the world lift off my shoulders.

"Are you sure about this?" a voice asked, quietly running up a few flights of stairs.

"Yes, I am certain. We have to do this now," another man's voice huffed.

"Okay. Got a plan?"

"No," he stated calmly, followed closely by the sound of a pounding fist on a door. "We know you're in there, just give me back my daughter!"

"Come and get her!" a new voice shouted, muffled behind the door.

"One, two, three, ahhh!" a voice yelled. The sound of wood cracking resounded as they barged through the door.

"You okay, Isaac?"

"Yes, where is she?"

A little girl's scream was heard from the distance, "Rachel!" A pair of running feet stomped over the wooden floors, coming to a sudden halt. "Put the gun down!"

"Never! You know who I am now, so there is no way out of this!" he shouted.

"Just put the gun down! Just give me back my daughter, and we will pretend like this didn't happen."

"Oh, but it did happen!" he hissed as a bullet was fired.

"Isaac!"

"Daddy!" the little girl whimpered as a loud thump hit the floor.

"Now, who are you?"

"Solomon," the voice quivered. "Just let the girl go."

"Nice meeting you, Solomon," he mocked, and another bullet whizzed through the air, followed by another thump to the ground.

"Nothing personal, little girl, but I can't take you with me," he growled. She screamed and the last bullet was fired as a lighter thump filled the silence. A single pair of footsteps gradually walked out of hearing.

"Solomon! Solomon!" Isaac shouted from the front seat. "Wake up! The kidnappers just called, and they want us both with the money at the drop at Union Station at 3:50, just like you said. I need your help!"

Waking up from my sudden narcoleptic sleep, I looked around. I noticed that we were parked on a side street off Georgia Avenue. The McDonald's golden arches were within view. "We can't go now!"

"Why not?" Isaac growled. His eyes burned like coals of fire.

"Because I don't want to die today. Do you?"

CHAPTER 56

The blurred gray photo didn't provide any facial details that would help with the case. "It's as if they knew where all the cameras in the garage were located," Cooper said, noticing any time they drove near a camera, they would both turn their heads away. Even the camera at the payment kiosk hadn't captured a good image.

"Much good that did us," Young commented snidely throwing down the printed images on Cooper's desk.

"Like you could do any better?" Cooper scolded defensively. He rose quickly from his chair, looking Young in the face. "Why don't you call your dad and see if he can solve the case for you? He's done everything else in your short career."

"What was that, *Officer* Cooper?" Young scoffed arrogantly in a demeaning tone, taking a step closer to Cooper.

"You heard me!" Cooper spit out, not stepping back or cowering from intimidation. "Everyone knows how you got the promotion, and everyone is waiting for you to prove yourself as a failure."

"Why you little…" Young growled, reaching back with his clenched fist only to be stopped by Johnson's lineman arms.

"What are you two doing?" Johnson shouted as he broke up the possible fight. "I just leave you two for a few minutes and you start this!"

"He said…" Young started as Johnson quickly shut him up with a stern look.

"I don't care what anyone said or what anyone did!" he exploded at Young and Cooper. "We have a case to solve! If you can't work together, you can be moved back to the drug unit, Cooper, and you can go back to patrolling, Young. You got me?"

"Yes, sir," they chanted in coerced unison.

"I'm too old to be dealing with childish things like this," he groaned, picking up the gray pictures. "This was the best they could do?" he mumbled loudly in aggravation as Young walked back to his desk.

"Yes, that was as clear as they could get it," Cooper answered, trying to shake off his frustration and get a handle on his rage.

"We need something better than this to give out, but it's a start," Johnson said, shaking his head in irritation. "I'll be back."

"Good one," Young shot back to Cooper as soon as Johnson was out of earshot. "And don't you ever talk to me like that again."

"Oh, don't say the truth to you? Fine. Then you're doing a great job on this case."

CHAPTER 57

Isaac and Amanda sat numb in the front seat after hearing the details of my short dream. His anger-ridden desire to hijack the situation quickly derailed with the notion of the bloody demise of his innocent child. "So, which one has Rachel?" Amanda asked as she looked past the parade, peering her head toward the various apartment buildings overlooking the small park.

"I'm not sure," I said pessimistically as her eyes felt my loss of joy. "But we will find it. We will."

"Let's start looking," Isaac said getting out of the car.

"It was looking over the park. So it has to be along this part of the street," I said, pointing along the section of the street with various apartment buildings. "It's just trying to find the right one."

"Well, you said that she was on the fourth floor, right?" Amanda remarked, looking around, noticing that a few of the buildings didn't have four floors. "We can cross off some of the buildings."

We walked up and down the street across from the park, bumping into parade viewers while groups of various ethnicities marched down Georgia Avenue, playing their culture's music and throwing candy from that region. "Does anything look familiar?" Isaac asked, but I told them that I never saw the outside of the building, just the park.

"Do you remember anything else?" Amanda pleaded with me. "I just want to start shouting for Rachel, but I know that's not going to do her any good."

Closing my eyes, I went back to my dream. I slowly tried to reexamine each room, looking to see if anything had been missed. "Where are the steel drums? Isaac asked frantically. "You said you heard steel drums! What if this isn't even the right place? What if you are just playing us?"

"Stop that!" Amanda commanded, but her demand wasn't met.

"What? I'm just being reasonable. We only met this guy last night, and we are trusting him with our daughter's life. How do we know for sure that we can trust him?"

"You don't," I stated bluntly. I watched Amanda's eyes fill with disillusionment. "You don't know for sure. Just as I don't know for sure if I should be trusting you. Ever thought of that? Maybe you're the mastermind trying to steal from all your partners. Sounds like a good plan to pretend to have a kidnapped daughter somewhere to confuse your wife. I don't know for sure why this is happening to me. But I do know that it is happening. And you just have to trust me blindly."

"No, Isaac, you're not behind all of this," Amanda said somewhat confidently. "You're not, are you?"

"Really?" Isaac asked, his face drooping from seeing his wife's questioning gaze. "You know me better than that. I would never do this. And you know that."

Standing awkwardly, Isaac watched the smiling faces of the parade-goers pass by him as Amanda wiped a tear away. She continued to look around at the apartment buildings from the safe confines of the sidewalk. "Didn't you say that there was a green light in Rachel's room?" Amanda asked as she looked away from the parade, causing Isaac to turn his back to the crowd also.

"Yes. Why?" I asked, turning to look in her direction and patting Isaac on his back. "I know you didn't do this," I whispered in his ear.

Isaac nodded in understanding.

Her arms raised up to point at a bar and grill restaurant that sat on the corner across from a five-story building. McCarthy's Irish Pub.

"Could that be what you were seeing?" she asked pointing at a large neon green shamrock sign just about four stories off the ground.

"There's a good chance it is."

CHAPTER 58

We rushed over to the apartment building but found the front door to be locked. "Rats!" Isaac shouted, slamming his fist into the door.

"Stop that! Stop that!" Amanda whispered. "Do you hear that?"

"Hear what?" Isaac asked bewildered. "All I hear is the parade."

"Exactly," she smiled. "Wait for it. Wait for it."

Instantly, a wave of a tropical breeze brushed past me and I could almost smell the sweetness of a coconut fragrance. "The steel drums are here," she sighed gratefully as the drumming became louder and louder when the Jamaican procession became center stage of the parade.

"Quick! Get away from the door," I shouted, pushing the two of them down the stairs toward the crowd as I witnessed a tall skinny gentleman walking down the stairs. I quickly hurried back up the stairs to catch the door as it opened. "Good afternoon," I said calmly, looking into the eyes of the friendly kidnapper. He was so young looking, with a mild case of acne on his forehead.

"You too," he squeaked as he skipped down the stairs to get lost in the crowd. His teeth looked like straight white picket fences, as if his braces had been taken off just a few weeks prior.

I stepped inside, waiting for the kidnapper's baseball cap to be out of my view. "Come on," I whistled, signaling Isaac and Amanda, who hurried up the steps while I finagled the handle to keep it from locking us out later.

Amanda's bronze complexion quickly faded to white. "Honey, sit down. You don't look good," Isaac begged, helping her to the stairwell. "Are you okay?"

She looked up into my eyes and all I could do was nod in agreement. I knew what she'd just figured out. She had just passed one of her daughter's kidnappers.

"You mean, that guy is one of them?" Isaac fumed. His body tensed, and I watched his muscles ripple underneath his shirt.

"Calm down! That just means that we are in the right spot. Do not do anything crazy!" I commanded, recalling my untimely death in my last dream. "I am going to walk up the stairs and see if the door of apartment 4G looks like it did in my dream. Then we can come up with a plan for what to do later."

"You're not going up there by yourself," Isaac barked out angrily. "For all we know, this could be a trap to get us in here together and kill us all at once."

"Really?" I moaned, rolling my eyes with his lack of confidence. "Fine, come up with me."

"What? You could have known I would say that, and this could be a trap," Isaac rebutted again.

"Really, Isaac? You really think that I am two steps ahead of you this whole time? Thanks for the compliment, but I'm really not that smart."

"I'm just…" he started to say, but I stopped him from finishing.

"I know. I know," I said, patting him on the shoulder encouragingly. "You have to trust me. You can stay down here, or you can come up with me. Either way is fine, but we have to be really quiet. The other kidnapper might know what you two look like, so we have to make sure we don't make any sounds that would cause him to look out the door."

"Good point," Amanda commented, feeling her strength come back and her ghostly white skin return to a golden tan as she stood up a bit wobbly.

"Fine! You lead the way," Isaac demanded, pushing my back to start heading up the stairs. He clutched Amanda's hand with a tight grip as if telling her that they were in this together.

"Okay, okay," I responded with his incessant pokes between my shoulder blades. "Can you stop that?"

"Just keep moving," he remarked as they followed closely behind. When we finally reached the fourth floor, we quietly walked up to 4G. It looked just like it had in my dream.

"My baby," Amanda sniffled, a little too audibly.

"Back! Back! Get back now!" I commanded quietly, as I heard a pair of heavy footsteps coming from behind the door. "Quick!" I hurried down to the third floor, making it just as I heard the squeak of 4G open. "I told you two to be quiet," I scolded, but there was no use. I felt their pain as well. Isaac was trying his best to console his wife who was on the verge of a waterfall of tears.

"If we're not going to do this now, we need to get her out of here now," Isaac pleaded with me as we each got on one side of her and helped her down the remaining three flights of stairs.

"My baby. My baby," was all she could say with each step. "My baby."

CHAPTER 59

"I know. I know. But I have to work late again tonight on these serial killer cases," Cooper said, talking to Veronica on his cell phone.

"What am I going to tell Father? He was expecting you there tonight so he could introduce you to some of his golf buddies who have some important connections," Veronica commented, trying to hide her disdain for his lack of initiative.

"Tell him that I am working on a case. I would think that would show my dedication to my job. He can tell them that if he wants," he said sarcastically. She felt the icy tone in his voice.

"Fine. I will," she replied coldly in return. "I mean, someone has to look out for your future."

"Veronica, I am just fine," he remarked confidently and securely. "I like what I do, and I like how I got here."

"Well, I just need you to move up faster because I can't be married to a cop for the rest of my life," she hissed, shooting flaming arrows at his heart.

"Is that all you think I am?" he asked, feeling the daggers in his back. "Just a cop?"

"You know what I mean," she sneered trying to belittle her comment like it could be swept under her oriental rug. "I just know you deserve much more than they give you credit for. I'm just trying to help you reach your goals."

"My first and foremost goal is to make you proud of me, and it seems like lately that has almost become impossible," he said. When she didn't respond to that comment, he stated simply, "I've got to go. I got to get back to work."

"But…" she tried to say as he hung up the phone.

"Trouble in paradise?" Young asked mockingly as he and Dakota walked past carrying some Chinese takeout.

"None of your business," Cooper countered, giving them a vicious look before getting up to head out to get some lunch from the nearby food truck.

"Come on, Cooper. We are here for you," Dakota consoled compassionately.

"Whatever. You're so out of your league with a woman like that," Young said, adding salt to Cooper's wounds like the soy sauce he was dribbling on his rice. Dakota stared at Young annoyed.

"And what do you mean by that?" Cooper remarked, stepping closer to Young instead of the exit.

"Yeah, what do you mean?" Dakota interjected with her hands on her hips.

"All I mean is when you marry out of your economic status, there are bound to be problems," he snickered like a prep boy making fun of a homeless man.

"You better shut up before I stab you with one of your chopsticks."

"I would like to see you try," Young said throwing down his utensils and splattering hot and sour soup on his desk as he stood up, taking an aggressive pose.

"Boys! Boys! Stop that!" Dakota buffered between them, mentally taking note of Young's egotistical behavior that she'd always overlooked in the past.

Cooper decided to be the bigger man and turned to leave. "Just let it go," he told himself as he walked away.

Young mumbled under his breath, "That's what I thought."

"Shut up, Smith," Dakota jabbed, smacking the back of his head as she passed by, "before I stab you myself."

"What did I do?" Young laughed, taking a bite of his food as Dakota stomped out of the squad room away from ear shot. "You'll be back."

CHAPTER 60

The time passed quickly on my cheap Timex watch showing it was 2:34 p.m. as we sat in McCarthy's sipping our drinks. The parade had wound down and the crowds dispersed back to where they came from. The next phase of the plan was about to commence.

"What's he doing here?" Isaac asked suspiciously, indicating the attractive golden blond man standing on the sidewalk right beyond the glass window. He was wearing a pair of designer sunglasses and a black Nike backpack.

"Who?" I asked confused as Amanda quickly turned around to see.

"It's Tom. Why is Tom here?"

"Tom, the guy who called you earlier? *That* Tom? The Tom you work with?" I asked, my eyes widening with an unsettling feeling in my stomach.

"Yes, the Tom I hired fifteen years ago," he spewed pushing back his chair and ramming it into the table behind him.

"Isaac, stop! What if he…" she started.

"Is the kidnapper?" he growled with unreserved fury. "Well, he's about to be a dead one."

"Do something," she said pushing me out of my chair to stop him before he could ruin everything.

I jumped up as he threw open the door and greeted Tom with a friendly right hook to his jaw. "Why are you doing this to us?" Isaac shouted, rearing his arm back to throw another punch at Tom's well-defined cheekbone.

"Isaac, what was that for?" he shouted back as he bobbed and weaved, avoiding the second punch. He quickly grabbed Isaac from behind to pin him against the wall.

"Where's my daughter? Where's Rachel?"

"Rachel?" he asked baffled, quickly letting go and taking a stance to guard himself from me.

I immediately raised my hands to show I was not going to do him any harm. He kept his knees bent, ready to disengage the next attack.

"Come off it! I know you have her!" Isaac screamed. "You've got to have her. Just tell me you have her and that she's safe. Just tell me that she's safe!"

"I don't know what you're talking about! I thought you had surgery! You lost Rachel?"

"Stop playing me, Tom! You can take all my money! Go ahead and wipe my bank account clean. Just give me back my little girl!" he bellowed as he launched himself from the wall like an aging torpedo. Tom quickly sidestepped and twirled Isaac back against the wall, apologizing to the pedestrians for the scene they were making.

"Quit being so polite. Just do it. Just do it!"

"You have to calm down," Tom said calmly looking at me for some help.

"His daughter was kidnapped the other day," I said as I tried to help hold Isaac back.

"No!" Tom responded in disbelief. "What are the cops doing? I haven't heard anything about this. No one has mentioned this at work; they just said you were out for a surgery."

"I lied," he hissed. "Just like you. You liar!"

"You know me. I wouldn't do that to you or Amanda. Amanda," he jumped back as she stumbled out of the restaurant. "I don't have your daughter, I promise."

"Why are you here?" she yelled, jabbing her finger into his chest. "Why are you here and not at work?"

"Really? That's why you think I have your daughter because I'm at the parade?" he scoffed at the logic, looking at each of us. "My brother, Johann, was in the parade because as you know, we are Norwegian, and this is a multicultural parade. I also came as a representative of the firm. I had a table over there," he pointed two blocks away where various booths were located. "I was trying to tell people that I work at a great place that accepts everyone, but I guess I spoke too soon," he said, pulling off his backpack to show various pamphlets and brochures about their investment firm.

"So, you're not the kidnapper?" I stuttered since his explanation seemed reasonable. "Where's your brother?"

"He's getting us some lunch at one of the food trucks."

"It's not him," Amanda cried, hugging her husband who leaned tiredly into the wall. "It's not him. Someone else has her."

"I promise. It's not me."

"Oh, Tom...I'm..." Isaac started as he hung his head low in embarrassment.

"Never mind that. What about Rachel?"

"She's in one of these apartments," I answered as Isaac and Amanda tried to regain their shattered dignity.

"Well, let's go find her."

"We already know where she is," Amanda answered. "It's a long story, and we are just waiting for the changing of the guards."

"The changing of the guards? Are you serious?" he asked shocked and bewildered. "You know where she is, yet you're out here having lunch?"

"It's not that easy," I interjected.

"Why not?"

"Come on. Let's go inside before someone sees us and gets suspicious," I said, opening the door to go back into the pub. We took our seats as Tom called his brother to tell him he had a change of plans and that he would see him later. I gave a summarized version of our story, leaving out the part of the mysterious dreams. I wasn't ready to reveal my secret to just anyone.

"Oh, man, I'm really sorry about all of this," Tom said as he clenched Isaac's shoulder and reached across the table to squeeze Amanda's tiny hand. "So, are you sure about all of this?"

"No," Isaac said negatively. "Not at all."

"Well, I say screw just waiting around here and go get her!" Tom huffed like a quarterback in the state final.

"No! That's a death sentence," I squirmed.

"Who says? I can take care of myself."

"They have guns," I refuted, like I was back in high school trying to convince the school jock that there was more to life than the big game Friday night.

"We can take them, can't we?" he banged his fist on the table to Isaac, trying to rally his team with a pep talk that would have worked in the locker room.

"I want to, but I think we better stick to the plan we've come up with." Isaac sunk back into his chair, looking at me with a clear warning that the plan better work, or I would have blood on my hands.

We sat in awkward silence for ten minutes as Tom whistled a few bars of the Norwegian national anthem. I wanted to trust this Tom character, but there was something about him that seemed devious and suspicious still. I couldn't tell if Isaac and Amanda felt the same way, or if they were just living in a hypnotic state of denial.

"So, are you all set?" I asked, gulping the last bit of my sweet tea and slamming my glass into the wood as if I had taken a hard shot of whiskey.

"As ready as I'll ever be," Amanda said exhaling and stretching her arms and neck, trying to relieve the tension in her shoulders. "Just ready for this to be over."

"What about you?" I asked, watching Isaac fidget on his bar stool.

"More than ready! Let's get them!" Isaac shouted, causing Tom to clap his hands in enthusiasm, which escaped the notice of a bartender who was trying to pick up a college-age brunette. Isaac looked at me and noticed that I was playing nervously with my fingers, "Are you ready?"

"Oh, uh…" I stuttered, looking at him and Amanda while a strange sense of peace wrapped around me. It could have been like the adage to keep one's enemies close because right then, I wasn't sure if Tom was a friend or a villain. Or it could have been that I felt Isaac and Amanda trusting him so I knew I should trust him too, but I couldn't. I looked down and noticed Amanda's iPhone in her open purse. I swiped my arm across the table flinging my spoon towards the ground. As I reached down to pick it up, I quickly grabbed her cell phone.

"Oh yeah," I grinned as I had an unexplainable feeling that by dinner this broken family was going to be united again. "I just have one request." I carefully dropped my napkin in Tom's direction and slipped Amanda's cell phone in his open backpack. I needed to watch this guy.

Amanda and Isaac's hearts plummeted to their stomachs as I rose back up as if I had pulled the rug from under their feet. My words shot shrapnel to their hearts as if I were going to make my last-ditch sales plea for a reward for my services. Noticing their apprehension, I stammered incoherently, "No, no, nothing like that. Stupid me, stupid, stupid," trying to regain their trust as Tom looked around with a mixture of confusion and blank stare. "I was going to tell you to let Rachel have another pop tonight," I said smiling awkwardly. "I was just trying to lighten the mood. It just seemed so dark and heavy, and I'm not used to this. I'm so sorry with my failed attempt of a joke."

"What's wrong with you, man? Are you sure you want to trust this guy?" Tom questioned them.

Isaac stared at me in confusion as if trying to figure me out. All he could say was, "You are a rare breed, Solomon."

"My friends call me Solo," I said smiling hospitably and optimistically. "All my true friends call me Solo."

"Okay, Solo," Amanda responded with a heartfelt hug. "Solo, it is."

"Solo," Tom laughed. "Never heard of that name before."

"Yeah, funny," I politely commented trying not to roll my eyes in annoyance.

Tom glanced down at his Apple Watch and twitched his face in an afterthought. "Oh, man, I have to be somewhere in a little while. I forgot all about it, but it's really important and there is no rescheduling. Do you think you got this without me?"

I sat shocked. This family had their daughter kidnapped and he had something more important to do than help them? I wanted to sucker punch him in his other jaw as I watched Isaac's shoulders sink a little lower. Times like these tell us who are our true friends...or enemies.

CHAPTER 61

"Calm down, calm down," she repeated to herself from inside a stall in the ladies' bathroom. "You got this. You planned for this. You can do it."

Her mind was frantically spinning like an adrenaline-infused hamster wheel. "We can do this. The plan is still good. There are always going to be some hiccups, but we can still do this."

She looked down at her black flats and desperately wanted the next two hours to slip by without any glitches. She needed to get ready. She needed to be prepared. She needed to stick to the plan.

As she sat on the toilet, she heard the door open as someone else came into the bathroom. She didn't want anyone to know that she was hiding, so she quietly raised her legs. She held her position like she was doing some yoga. She controlled her movements just as well as she controlled her breathing.

The other lady quickly washed up and left, allowing her to relax and whisper to herself. "So what if they know some things about us? They don't know everything. And they'll never know everything."

Some people would feel the world caving in around their feet and crumble, but not her. She relished in this feeling. She had overcome so many obstacles in the last year and she wasn't going to let this bit of information deter her evening activities. She vaguely understood the body's reaction to a bullet or a stab wound. Some people would keel over and die at the sight of their own blood. Others just went harder and stronger, as if the bullet were a shot of adrenaline administered by a doctor. This latest information wasn't going to be the nail in her coffin. It was just going to be a driving force for her to be better and smarter than anyone else.

Leaving the stall, she looked in the mirror and gave herself a wink, telling herself that everything was going to be alright. "They can have Huntington Station tonight. There are plenty of other stations available on the other end of town. My little brother wanted to add a little excitement to our plan, and a little excitement is what he is going to get."

"Bring it."

CHAPTER 62

"So, that Tom, he's an interesting character. How long have you known him?" I asked as we sat on the park bench near the apartment building that housed Rachel.

"He was one of Isaac's first hires a while back," Amanda answered as if she knew what I was implying. "He couldn't be a part of this. I would bet my life on it. He would never do this to us."

"Never say never."

"Why not? He's just a good guy who has been with Isaac for over a decade."

"People change," I commented sadly. "Or they just play people really well."

"Not Tom. Just wait and see. It's not Tom."

"Let's see where he is," I said as I pulled out my cell phone and opened a device tracking app.

"What are you doing?"

"I am about to find out where he is," I grinned. "What's your number?"

"My number? Why do you want my number?" she asked, eyeing me suspiciously as she opened her purse to find her phone gone. "You really don't trust him, do you?"

"If he's so trusting, you'll get your phone back. Your number, please." I quickly typed in the number and waited for the satellite tracking device to find the location of her phone. "And, no, I don't trust him."

"Well, where is he?" she asked, straining her neck to see the blue dot on the map.

"Aw, really?" I shook in a surge of rage at the lack of people's concern for others and their own entitled selfishness.

"What? Tell me!"

"Looks like your friend had something really important to take care of. A massage," I said with a grimace handing her my phone.

"You're lying," she said, jerking the phone from my hand. She found the dot at Utopia's Spa and Relaxation. "Jerk!"

"Wisest thing I have heard in a while," I laughed as I watched her fume. She handed back the phone without looking at me. "I'm really sorry. I wish I never did that now."

"No, it's all right. At least we know he's not one of the kidnappers."

We sat for a few minutes in silence. I didn't know what to say. Her daughter was kidnapped, and she found out a supposed trustworthy friend wasn't so reliable. This had not been the best week for the Fiddelsteins. "So, what are you going to fix Rachel for supper tonight? What's her favorite meal?"

"The biggest bowl of mac and cheese," she smiled. "The absolute biggest bowl. And some ice cream for dessert."

"Sounds like my type of dinner," I said, timidly giving her a side hug. I quickly released my embrace after just a few seconds. I thought she needed it and thought I was doing something friendly, but it just felt uneasy and strange. "Well, that was a little awkward," I laughed as she joined in, nodding in agreement.

"You meant well."

"Yes, let's keep it at that. I meant well," I said as a familiar face came walking toward us. "Here he comes." I tapped Amanda on her shoulder, pointing out the young kidnapper sipping his Starbucks iced coffee and strolling a few feet away from us. He looked to be a hundred and twenty pounds soaking wet.

My fists clenched at the notion of tripping him as he passed, and the expression on Amanda's face mirrored mine. I glanced down at my watch as the blue screen lit up, telling me that it was 2:57 p.m. "Right on time."

I was prepping myself for the events about to happen. I got my phone out as Amanda tried to calm herself down. "I can't do this. I can't do this," she shook as her brain started filling with horrific failures. "What if he..." she stopped to wipe away a few tears. "What if he..."

"He's not," I answered confidently. "He is not going to hurt Rachel."

"But how do you know?"

"I just know," was all I could utter as we sat in the sunshine, waiting for the next step in the plan.

"So, how long have you and Isaac been married?" I asked, trying to swerve the conversation to one that she could easily handle.

"Last year was our twelfth anniversary," she grinned beneath her Gucci sunglasses.

"Wow! Twelve years! That is an accomplishment these days."

"Yes. Yes, it is," she replied quietly. "It hasn't been all good times," she laughed under the current circumstances. "But it's been a good run."

"That is really good."

"What about you? How long were you married?" When I hesitated, she said, "You really miss her, don't you? I notice you rubbing your ring finger often."

I didn't know how deep to get into my history because I didn't want us to get sidetracked from our ultimate purpose. "She was the strong, brave one. So I guess, subconsciously, any time I feel insecure I reach for a tangible memory of her. The only thing I can consistently remember was the feeling of the wedding band on my finger." I started to chuckle at the thought of the day we picked out the bands. "She wanted something unique and unconventional for our bands, so a plain gold band wouldn't do."

"You seem pretty plain to me," she commented before she realized that could be misconstrued as an insult.

"It's okay. I know what you mean. I told you she was the brave one."

"Well, you're being brave today," she smiled, patting my hand like an encouraging sister. "We were about to shoot you last night, and you came back this morning. That's pretty brave."

"She would say stubborn," I said, chuckling at the memory of her always telling me how hard-headed I was. "But we were both really happy."

"What happened?"

It wasn't the question that took my breath away as much as seeing the other kidnapper stomp down the front stairs. I quickly got my phone's camera out and snapped an unsuspecting selfie picture over my shoulder. "There he is," I said as she quickly turned her head. "No, don't look," I gasped as their eyes locked onto one another.

Hitching up his pants, he snarled at her menacingly.

Amanda quickly looked away as her trembling hand found mine.

"Are you going to call now?" she asked.

"I'm going to wait a few more minutes just to make sure he's gone." We sat petrified, and I knew that we couldn't be like this right before we made our move. "Why did you ask me about dinner this morning?"

She turned her attention away from the imaginary dot she was fixating on and turned to me. "It was something I was told one time. I don't remember who said it, but they said that if you want to find the true character of someone really quickly, ask a question that cuts to the core of that person. So, after you left last night, I looked you up. Gotta love the internet and how everything is out there. I read up on your history a little. Isaac didn't know, but I was hoping you weren't crazy. I wanted you to be our saving grace.

"So when I read a story about you and your wife, I knew that if you answered my question with a superficial answer like Abraham Lincoln or Michael

239

Jordan, you were not going to be the light that I needed. When you said your wife, I knew. I knew we could trust you. Call it intuition. Call it a gut instinct. But for some reason, I knew you were going to help us."

CHAPTER 63

"911, what's your emergency?"

"I have some information about a kidnapping ransom drop," I calmly stated as the operator connected me with the proper investigation division.

"Lieutenant Walker here," a familiar voice sounded over the phone. I recalled the voice from the day before.

"Hello, Lieutenant Walker, I have a kidnapping I would like to report, and one of the kidnappers is on his way to Union Station at Gate B to pick up the ransom. I also have a picture of this kidnapper I can send to you."

"Yes, yes, send it my way!" he shouted as he gave his phone number and email address. I quickly attached the picture to a text and his email and sent them on their way.

"Okay. I just sent it. Did you get it?"

"It's coming," he responded as I heard him clicking away on his computer. "Okay, I have it open. I am forwarding this information to local police units around Union Station. How did you come to know about this information?"

"My friend's daughter is the one that was kidnapped, and we have tracked them down," I answered in a matter-of-fact tone. I gave him the address of the apartment and told him we were waiting outside. I also gave him some details of the connecting investment heist of millions of dollars, and I could hear him typing the information on his computer.

"We have units on their way to Union Station and Georgia Avenue now. Why didn't they contact us sooner? That could have been a big mistake not coming to authorities sooner."

"I know. I know. But the kidnappers told them not to call the police." I heard more typing before he asked me to stay on the line with him as we waited for the cops to arrive.

I glanced down the road and my heart plummeted when I saw a large burly man walking quickly with his muscular arms swinging like a gorilla. "Amanda! Amanda! Is that the other kidnapper?" I asked as I saw her remove her sunglasses. Her eyes answered my question. "Oh God. He's back. The other guy is coming back! We need the cops here now!"

"What, what is that?" Walker asked urgently on the other end of the line with nothing to do but sit and listen. "They are on their way. Stay calm and someone will be there shortly. Just please remain on the phone."

Amanda started to moan as I continued to watch the criminal get closer and closer. "You've got to get the cops here quick. It looks like the other kidnapper is about three blocks away. If the cops don't come in the next few seconds, we are going to go up there ourselves."

"No! Stop! Someone will be there any minute," he demanded. "We know what we are doing."

"We don't have minutes!" I said jumping up from the park bench, raking my fingers through my hair, and pacing in distress. "The kidnapper upstairs right now is a skinny kid, so it shouldn't be that much of a problem to get her," I remarked. "I mean, I am pretty fit and he looked like a toothpick, but the other one, well, that's another story."

"Desperate people will do desperate things when they get cornered. Do they know that you are on to them?"

"No. Well, I don't think so, but the other bad dude is watching me. I think he may be on to me. He's walking faster. Tell the cops to get here now!"

"Rachel!" Amanda let out a blood-curdling scream that froze my inner core.

I turned around in time to see the young kidnapper walking down the steps with Rachel holding his hand. I looked to my side and saw the other, tattooed kidnapper starting to run up the sidewalk.

"Oh crap!" I bellowed while the chaos began to unfold.

"You little! You little!" the bigger kidnapper shouted as he ran up the sidewalk as fast as he could, huffing and puffing with all his might to make it back in time. "Trying to undermine me?"

"Mommy!" Rachel cried as the younger kidnapper grabbed Rachel's arm, threw her back into the apartment building, and darted inside.

"What's going on? What's going on?" Walker asked, but it was too late to answer.

CHAPTER 64

"Rachel! Rachel!" Amanda screamed hysterically, running up the steps. "Bite him! Kick him, Rachel!"

I swung the door open, almost tearing it off the hinges as I heard the kidnapper dragging Rachel by the arm. "Let her go, you little twerp! Lock the door, Amanda! He's coming! Lock the door and block it!"

"I can't, I can't now!" the skinny kidnapper yelled from a floor up as Rachel whimpered and called for her mommy.

"Rachel, fall!" I yelled as I ran up the stairs, taking three at a time, quickly catching up to the struggling kidnapper.

"Help!" Amanda screamed, as she put all her body weight in front of the apartment building's door, praying that the deadbolt could handle the two hundred-fifty-pound giant on the other side.

"Kid, you better not lose her!" the bigger kidnapper hollered as he rammed his shoulder into the hard wood, causing it to bounce. The door stayed locked as Amanda sat on the ground and braced the door with all her weight. The thin stained glass decorative windows aligning the door were instantly smashed by his fists which were bloodied in the process. The shattered glass clinked against the ground in a haunting sound as I continued to race toward Rachel. The tattooed kidnapper reached his massive trunk of an arm through the jagged glass window, trying to grab any part of Amanda.

Fear was in the younger kidnapper's eyes when he saw that I was just a few stairs away. Letting go of his grip of the child, he scurried up the rest of the winding stairway clutching the gun that was tucked into the back of his pants.

"Stay back! Stay back or I'll shoot!" he screamed as he quickly walked backwards up the stairs.

"No! Don't! Just drop your gun!" I shouted as I pushed Rachel behind me.

"You got the girl! Just leave!" he shrieked as his foot missed one of the steps, causing him to fall backwards before he caught himself by the railing. The sudden jolt caused his trigger finger to flinch. The gun fired. A bullet hit the ceiling and plaster rained down from overhead.

"You stupid moron!" I yelled wanting to run up the stairs and snap the little twerp like a twig for shooting his gun in front of Rachel. "Idiot!"

"Stop that! Just get away! Just get away from me!" he shouted in a frantic whimper. He scampered away on all fours to the apartment and quickly locked the door behind him.

"Rachel, you okay?" I asked picking up the frightened little girl and running down the stairs as fast as I could. Amanda screamed from the ground floor, dodging the swinging arms.

"My baby! My baby," she screamed with tears of joy when she saw that her little girl was alive and well. Fear quickly replaced her emotional high as she felt one of the kidnapper's hands grab onto a few strands of her hair.

"He's got me! Help! He's got me!" she screamed as he let out a villainous laugh that would have frightened even the bravest of men.

The kidnapper tightened his grip and started to swing his well-defined arm around. The tattooed dog on his bicep appeared to growl, causing Amanda's head to slam repeatedly into the painted white door, leaving a few red blotches.

"Momma!"

Amanda was scraping and clawing her fingernails into the arms of the kidnapper who just continued to laugh as if her tiny hands were only tickling him.

"You're messing with the wrong man," he yelled, doubling his strength, raising Amanda's body from the ground while she continued to try to release herself from his powerfully wicked hold. His raw power was too much for her yoga-toned body.

I jumped down the last few steps as I watched Amanda's arms fall and her eyes begin to roll back into her head like a lifeless corpse. I sprinted toward the door and saw a light reflect from the ground. It was coming from a large shard of glass. Picking up the blade, I gripped the edge as I felt the glass slice into my palm. "Ah!" I yelled as loud as I could, plunging the jagged blade into his wrist and digging it as painfully deep as I could to sever as many veins as possible with the thrashing slice.

He groaned in agony, cursing me through the door. He released his grip on Amanda who fell limply to the ground.

"Mommy!" Rachel screamed as she came running down the remaining stairs. I quickly grabbed Amanda before her head slammed into the hardwood floor.

"Amanda! Amanda!" I shouted as I hunkered down to guard the door with my weight. I tapped her cheeks as wounds from her head trickled blood onto my lap. "Rachel, stay there," I said, fearing the violence inflicted on her. I removed my arm that was cradling her head and saw that it was painted red. As I reached down to check her pulse, Amanda gradually awoke from her blackout state as a sudden burst of adrenalin kicked in.

"Got it?" she asked as she rolled off my lap, looking at the door behind her.

"I hope so," is all I could reply. I listened for the other kidnapper who was moaning and staggering on the other side of the door. I couldn't help but wish he would bleed to death on the porch.

"Stay back, Rachel," Amanda choked out as she slinked her body towards the stairs, watching overhead to make sure that the younger kidnapper didn't reappear from the fourth floor. Her daughter jumped to the ground and slid beside her mother. They hugged and kissed one another in joyful relief.

"Are you okay?" Amanda asked as Rachel brushed her mother's hair out of her eyes.

"I'm okay. Are you?"

"They're here!" I shouted as I continued to stand guard at the door. I poked my head out the window to see the cops encircle the bloody kidnapper who was begging them to take him to the hospital. I unlocked the door and sprinted up the stairs as Rachel started to follow.

"No! Stay back! Stay with your mom!" I shouted as I continued running up the stairs. I heard the younger kidnapper scream and cry two floors overhead. A few of the apartment residents poked their heads out of their doors as I passed, but many never even came to see what was going on. Not one came to help the screaming Amanda.

I knew that I couldn't let up, so I continued sprinting up the stairs and down the hall finding the door marked 4G. "I know you are in here!"

"Leave me alone!" he shouted from behind the door. "I have a gun!"

"It's over! The cops are here! They have your friend! They know all about the kidnapping!"

"Get back!" he ranted. "If you come in here, I will shoot you!"

"Come on! You don't have to kill anyone!" I pleaded, banging on the door. "You are not a killer!"

"I can't go to jail!" he cried and screamed louder. "Oh man, oh man, oh man!"

Four floors below, I heard a stampede of cops hurdling up the stairs, "We're up here on the fourth floor!" I shouted to let them know that I was safe. "He's locked in his room, and he's got a gun!"

A young-looking cop arrived first with his gun ready as two more cops quickly followed. "This is the police! Put your gun down!" one of the officers shouted as the other two took their stance, ready to enter. They motioned for me to get away and head to safety.

"I didn't hurt her! I promise I didn't hurt her!" he continued to cry as the cops shouted for him to drop the weapon and come out with his hands up. "I can't! I can't!"

As I started to walk down the stairs, I heard the cops warning the kidnapper that they were going to break down the door. The sound of a heavy boot smashing through the door overpowered my breathing. My heart pounded against my chest as I heard more chaotic shouting overhead.

"Drop your gun!" a cop shouted.

My body tensed. My heart stopped. Three bullets were fired followed by a lone, hard thump on the ground.

CHAPTER 65

She's safe was all the text said when he looked down at his phone at 3:29 p.m., waiting in the stairwell of his office building.

He didn't care about the money now that he had his daughter back safe and sound. He would have given everything to have her back, but he knew that he had to confront the leader of the kidnapping ring before they did it again. Seconds ticked by like hours as he watched his phone change to 3:30. He remembered what Solo had said: at 3:30, the thief would be in his office.

He stood in the lone stairwell, fuming at the thought of one of his employees doing this to his family. How dare they, he thought, putting them through all this turmoil and chaos for something as measly as money. If they wanted more money, they should have worked harder and asked for a raise, not kidnapped a defenseless child.

Holding his cell phone in his hand, he saw that it was 3:31 p.m. and knew it was time to go. He dialed his office number and asked the receptionist to connect him to Branch in the IT department, but it went to his voicemail.

Hitting redial he asked the receptionist to connect him with anyone in the IT department. "I'm sorry, but no one is picking up, sir. Want me to send it to their voicemail?" the receptionist asked as he hung up the phone. This wasn't a part of the plan, he thought.

Exiting the stairwell, he ran through the office. Everyone stopped what they were doing to watch one of the partners sprint in blue jeans and a sweatshirt. It definitely wasn't the normal attire for someone of his status.

"What's wrong?" a few asked each other from behind their cubicles. But no one knew.

"Branch!" Isaac shouted as he saw him coming out of the men's room.

"Yes sir! Why are you running? I thought you just had surg-" he asked as Isaac quickly shook off the question.

"I need you to shut everything down! Shut it all down now!"

"Now?" he hesitated.

"Do it!" Isaac demanded as Branch quickly ran down to his department. Isaac continued to run toward his corner office as he checked his watch and saw it was 3:35. He only had a few minutes to stop everything from transferring out.

When he arrived at his office, he found his door was locked. "Stop!" he shouted, fumbling with his keys to open his door. The keys shook like they were leaves in a tornado. Finally, he slid the key in the lock and heard it click as he threw it open. "Get a…" he stopped, walking into a darkened office with no sign of anyone on his computer or in his office.

"Huh?" he asked as a few of his fellow employees gathered from behind.

CHAPTER 66

The police ride from Georgia Avenue to the Fiddelstein's home was unnerving. Officer Hayden was friendly and chatting cordially, but he reminded Amanda that they were going to have to question Rachel soon.

"How's your head, ma'am?" Hayden asked.

"Oh, it's been better," Amanda replied, removing the towel from her head that she was using to stop the bleeding. "At least I didn't need stitches."

"You're going to feel that tomorrow," I said with a grimace.

"Yes, you will," Hayden groaned with a nod of his head.

"So, what do you call what I'm feeling now?"

"Lucky," I said, smiling as Rachel leaned forward to get a better look at me from the backseat. I could tell she was confused by my outlook.

When we pulled up to their home, the street was lined with police cars flashing blue and red lights as if it was an Independence Day parade. "Do you know whose car that is?" I asked, pointing at the black Acura in their driveway.

"I'm not a car person. A lot of people around here have that type of car," she answered.

Their front door was open as police officers filed in and out like it was a convenience store. "Want to wait for Isaac before you go inside?" I asked.

252

"No. I'm ready to get this over with," she said with steely determination, squeezing Rachel's hand. She told her to wait in the policeman's car and that they were going to be right back.

"Come on," she ordered. "You're going in too."

"I thought I could just stay here and keep Rachel company. Get to know her a little better. You know, I don't want to be a stranger danger."

"Who are you?" Rachel asked as she looked quizzically up my nose instead of in my eyes.

"Coming," I jumped up, walking beside Amanda as she linked her arm with mine.

"It was a good idea calling the police to come here. I wouldn't have thought about someone dialing in from his home computer to his work computer."

"When the ransom wanted both of you at the station for the drop off, I wondered if that was a way to get you out of the house as well," I said raising my shoulders like it wasn't just a lucky guess.

"I don't know how I am going to react," she whispered in my ear.

"React like anyone who was about to lose millions of dollars," I said, smiling. "I mean, you're going to have to figure that out yourself because the closest thing to a million dollars I have is..." I stopped to think, coming up short with anything of that value. "I can't think of anything."

"Stop making me laugh," she said, hitting my shoulder with a strong punch. "I need to be angry." When I stopped in my tracks, she looked confusedly at me. "What?"

"You need to be angry?"

"What about it?" she asked, not following my epiphany.

"Why do you need anger? Your daughter is safe. Your money is fine. And you all are going to be sleeping soundly tonight in each of your beds. If you're not angry after all of that, count it a blessing. Don't try to find it."

She stared at me in bewilderment. "My husband was right about you."

"Oh, he was?" I replied, feeling baffled.

"You are a rare breed," she smiled, tugging on my arm to take another step forward. When we walked into the house, three police officers were standing at the door, nodding their heads to say hello as they compared notes on their findings. The laptop with the frozen screen showing a listing of names and funds to be transferred to an offshore account sat open on the baby grand piano in the corner of the room. Beside the piano was a bay window overlooking a well-maintained backyard with high hedges serving as a privacy fence.

A blond man was sitting on the couch with his back to the door. Amanda walked around timidly to confront him, grabbing her chest in shock. "Michael?"

CHAPTER 67

"Michael! How? How could you do this to us?" she stuttered emphatically, clutching both the couch and my arm for balance. She was clearly bewildered at the mastermind behind this horrific scheme.

The twenty-four-year-old blond, who could pass for a Tommy Hilfiger model, didn't respond as he sat in his neatly pressed navy suit and red and white checkered tie. He didn't even blink at the sound of his name from a familiar voice. He just continued to stare straight ahead as if enjoying the view of the cardinal taking flight in their backyard.

"Ma'am," a police officer said from behind, startling Amanda. "Sorry, but it appears that he didn't break into your home since he had a key."

"Yes. He is my husband's *nephew* and assistant," she said, emphasizing the word like it was a slap in her face. "Well, used to be." She stopped talking to the police officer, returning to Michael with heart-stricken pain showing on her face. "I just...I just don't understand," she said, feeling betrayed. "He cared for you. He trusted you. He would have done anything for you. That is what family does." The cold shock vanished, quickly replaced by volcanic anger. She lunged at his throat, choking him with the deadly force of a boa constrictor wrapping around its prey. Yet he remained unfazed. He didn't try to stop her. He didn't even glance in her direction as his head jerked back and forth.

"Amanda!" I shouted using all my strength to unclench her fingers from his neck. I picked her up and whirled her away from the backstabbing relative as one of the cops dropped his paperwork to help handle the situation, albeit a few seconds too late. The only movement Michael made was to fix his disheveled hair.

I lowered Amanda back to the ground and unclasped my arms from around her waist. She promised she wouldn't attack him again. My stomach heaved when I realized the deceit that had been brewing a long time. Michael drove an Acura, so he wasn't a poor child that society had overshadowed. He was probably brought up in a privileged family with trust funds and private school tuition; definitely not the type of kid I played basketball with in the neighborhood.

He sat like a stone statue – angelic on the outside but sinister underneath. The man who plotted their child's kidnapping and schemed to leave them penniless wasn't just a jaded employee or a heartless opportunistic stranger. He was their flesh and blood. He was a Fiddelstein.

Amanda walked around the couch, finding the picture of their family that usually sat on one of the bookshelves. It had been thrown to the floor, and pieces of broken glass were now laying on the rug. "Why did you have to take my little girl?" she asked, pleading with him. She stooped to pick up the picture of the once happy family. "Why did you have to put her through this? Why didn't you just ask for a raise or a loan? Why didn't you just steal the money and run?"

"Ma'am, he hasn't said a word to any of us either. We were about to take him down to book him when you came in," the officer remarked.

"Just take him away," Amanda said, throwing her hands up in disgust. She placed the picture back on the shelf before walking out of the house. "I can't look at him one more second! I hope you get what you deserve!" she screamed from the front steps. "No! I don't think there is anything that bad. I hope you die! I want you dead! You are dead to me!"

"They got your friends too," I commented, causing the stone statue to crack as his eyes darted in my direction for a split second and then returned to staring straight ahead. "The big one, yeah, I stabbed him. And the small one, well, they shot him. So, count yourself lucky." I made my way out of the house, finding Isaac clutching a shaken Amanda in the front yard who continued to scream curses at Michael.

I could see the disbelief on Isaac's face as she kept saying, "It's Michael! I hope he gets it! I wish he was never born!" His fear was realized when they walked Michael, with his hands cuffed behind his back, out of the house. They passed within arm's reach of Amanda, who slapped him one more time before an officer restrained her.

"Ma'am, don't make me arrest you too."

"Come on, man. That kid almost ruined their lives," I said, appealing to him as another officer helped Michael into the backseat of a cruiser.

"I get it," the officer nodded. "But I still have a job to do."

"Why, Michael? Why?" Isaac cried as he clung to his wife for support. Michael still didn't respond, but sat motionless behind the glass window looking straight ahead at the passenger seat headrest.

"Where's cousin Michael going?" Rachel asked as she ran into her father's arms. "Is he coming back?"

CHAPTER 68

"I'm watching the news right now. Did you have a part in this?" Elizabeth asked over the phone as I drove home, ready for a relaxing night on the couch. "You did, didn't you?"

"Maybe," I replied sheepishly, grabbing a couple of fries from the paper bag that was settled in the passenger seat.

"Solo! You got three criminals today! That is crazy! No, *you* are crazy!" she laughed in shock. "And the girl? She's okay?"

"She was not harmed at all."

"Wow! I still think you are stupid though."

"I know."

"So, their nephew did all of this? Why?"

"Don't know. He wouldn't say a word," I answered, taking a bite out of a chicken nugget with mustard. It wasn't that great of a combination, so I quickly returned to the ever-faithful barbeque packet.

"Families," she said disparagingly.

"I know, right?"

"Well, good going, I guess. You did what you wanted to do."

"Yes. Yes, I did."

"Well, I got to go," she remarked, trying to end the call.

"Later. And thanks for talking with me last night."

"I didn't do anything. I thought you were crazy then, and I still think you're crazy now."

"But I saved the day," I said sarcastically.

"Well, don't get a big head with your saving-the-day antics. It could have backfired."

"But it didn't."

"But it could have," she snuck in before ending the call.

The rest of the way home was more peaceful. I tried to think of something else, but my spirit was blazing. It wasn't pride in my own behavior; it was just knowing that Rachel was going to be home with her family that night. That was the best reward. Even though Isaac did try to give me some of the cash from the ransom since he already had it ready, I kindly declined.

"Come on, take it," Isaac had begged, practically throwing the wrapped money in my face.

"I told you before and I will tell you again, I don't want your money," I said smiling as I got into my beat-up Honda. "I just wanted your daughter home with you tonight. That's all."

Coming to a stop light, I looked down at my phone. My earlier conversation with Amanda resounded in my head. I felt like I needed to take a chance, to be braver than I had been recently.

Want to meet for lunch tomorrow? I texted and sent quickly before I could change my mind.

Would love to, Jenny replied with a smiling emoji.

The light turned green, and I took off. It may not have been as brave as tracking down a kidnapper, but in terms of my relationship history during the last few

years, this was like taking my first step in climbing
Mount Everest.

CHAPTER 69

The squad room was buzzing over the upcoming events as Captain Johnson started going over the strategic plans for the evening. "We need three officers at each of the Metro stations around Alexandria; one person on the subway platform and two in the parking areas. We are looking for two individuals – a man who is presumed to be posing as a sick patient and a young woman," he said as Cooper started passing out the blurry picture to each of the officers.

"Be on the look out for anyone who matches this description. They are cunning, and based on the last two sets of victims, they will be seeking out a retirement-aged couple," he said, continuing to pace in front of the evidence board. "Be on your guard. It looks like they are well-prepared and know their surroundings better than the average person."

"Sir," Young interrupted as he stood beside the evidence board, gaining the attention of the entire room. "Do you think we only need three officers at each location?"

Johnson cocked his head at the notion of a subordinate questioning his superior, especially in front of so many other officers. "Three will be plenty," he answered frigidly. "There are over a dozen Metro stations in the Virginia area, and the remaining officers in this room not assigned to a station will be patrolling the surrounding area and other transit parking garages and areas."

"I just thought..." Young started boldly before Johnson put him in his place.

"I am in charge here, so if you cannot follow my orders and do as I say, you can turn in your badge," he barked as the room of officers watched the debacle of dueling egos. Young quietly shook his head and took a seat near the back of the room. "Good idea," Johnson noted. He then gave orders to each officer. "Young, you are with White and Knightly at King Street. Cooper, you will be with Franklin and Owens at Huntington."

"When are you going to learn?" Cooper whispered in Young's ear as he passed by to catch up with Franklin and Owens.

"Learn what?" Young spit back, watching Cooper move away. "To be a yes-man like you?"

Cooper laughed at the remark as he went to his partners for the night. "Yes, sir, that is all I am. Just a measly yes-man," he responded sarcastically, clasping Franklin's and Owens' shoulders. "Ready to catch the killers?"

"Sure thing," Franklin answered with a smile as Owens just nodded casually like it was just another night on the job.

CHAPTER 70

As I sat on my homey, comfortable couch, my appetite returned with a vengeance. I didn't have a real lunch. And although I picked up some fries and chicken nuggets when I left the Fiddelsteins, after a day like today, I needed something with a little more substance. I needed something more filling. I needed some delicious comfort food. Chinese.

Hey, want to grab some Chinese with me? I texted to Cooper. After a few minutes without a response, I assumed that he probably had a busy night with his cop duties.

I started going down my list of possible last-minute foodies, and it seemed that everyone in my contacts had either already eaten or had other plans. *Hey, wanna crab some Chinese food with me?* I texted to Elizabeth, quickly noticing that the auto-correct didn't do its job.

Can't tonight. Dinner with your Verny, she texted back quickly with a frowning emoji.

Jeremiah with you?

Nope. Why?

I'm hungry. Duh.

Whatever.

I stopped my conversation and started a new one with Jeremiah. *Hey, Jeremiah. This is Solo. Big plans tonight?*

I waited for his response with the same apprehension I had in middle school, waiting for Jennifer Loveless to respond to me on MSN

Messenger. New adult friendships were awkward at first.

Nothing too important. What about you? he responded.

Want to grab some Chinese? I replied, making sure to spell correctly this time.

Why not? Where?

I don't care. I am just starving.

I know of this place by school. Ming's. It's a hole-in-the-wall type of place, but really good.

Cool, send me the address, and I will meet you there.

I decided to drive to the local Metro station and have them take me into town. Friday night in Washington D.C. can be horrible with traffic, but the subway is always consistent. Jeremiah picked me up at the Tenleytown Metro Station and drove through the semi-heavy traffic to Ming's on New Mexico Avenue.

"So, why aren't you with Elizabeth tonight?" I asked after I gushed over his sporty Lexus convertible likely purchased with his book royalties.

"She had some soiree with her family tonight," he answered nonchalantly as he turned the tables on me. "What about you? Why didn't you have anything going on tonight?"

"Well, I had a date last night and didn't want to seem too desperate by calling her at the last minute. So, we're just going to lunch tomorrow instead."

"Lunch date. Interesting," he commented in a curious tone.

"Don't do that," I said with a laugh.

"Do what?"

"Try to psychoanalyze me. I know your type."

"My type?" he snickered. "And what is my type?"

"Well, you know, the 'there-is-always-some-hidden-meaning-behind-every-thing-you-do' type," I rambled like his passenger seat was a couch in my therapist's office.

"But don't you believe that everything has a meaning?" he asked. "Isn't that what your type believes?"

"Wow. Okay, I see how that sounded now. I didn't mean anything by it," I said, apologizing for my lack of tack.

"It's no bother. But since we are on that subject, don't you believe that everything has a meaning?" he asked again as the traffic moved like a snail.

"I like to think it does, but that's a double-edged sword."

"Why? Because if everything has a meaning, that would mean that the happy moments in life have just as much meaning and purpose as the darkest tragedies."

"Ding, ding, ding," I said like he took the words out of my own mouth. "With my faith, I don't mean to put God in your face," I said, apologizing as he shook his head as if it was no bother to him. "I believe God can use everything for a purpose. It's just what that purpose is makes me sometimes cringe."

"That would be cringe-worthy," he gasped. "So, since we are just talking theoretically, what is the cringe-worthy moment in your life, if you don't mind me asking?" he asked warmly, like a father figure asking his child about the school yard bully. "I will start. Mine has to be when I was seven and my dog Chase got run over by a speeding car right in front of me. I mean, if there is an all-powerful being, what was the purpose in that?"

"Yikes, you don't hold anything back, do you? You go straight for the jugular." I flinched, not only at the shock of the story, but at how calmly he said it. It was as if it were a piece of data from his lifelong research. No feelings, no attachment, no reservations – just a memory of a young Jeremiah and his dead dog.

"Nope! As I was told when I was young, go for the jugular in all you do. So, I said mine, what about you? What is your cringe-worthy moment?"

I flipped the proverbial coin in the air. Heads, I tell the truth; tails, I tell another truth, but not as cringe-worthy. As the coin twirled in the air, I saw his openness to his wound that had no explanation and felt comfortable enough to tell mine as well. Taking a deep breath, I inhaled some peace to expel some grief.

"My wife Chelsea and I used to work together. I used to be a photographer for the *Washington Tribune,*" I started. He commented that was a commendable newspaper, probably somewhat shocked that I used to work there. "Yes, well she was a great reporter who covered all the hard topics that most people didn't want to report. She wrote the award-winning articles and I took the mediocre photographs," I said as he commented that he didn't know that I was married.

"We were a great team. About five years ago, she got an outside tip about surging gang violence in the inner city and that the police weren't doing anything about it. She decided to interview people on the street where some gang violence had occurred. They wanted to gain some momentum in forming a neighborhood watch to protect their children. As she was interviewing a concerned mother, I took a picture of my wife and her interviewee. I unknowingly took the picture as my wife was shot in the head by a gang member driving by. I still can't get that picture out of my head or off my computer. It's the last one I took of her.

"Fast forward a few months. I had an emotional breakdown and went to, well, some say a spa or spiritual retreat, but let's be honest, it was a mental institution. I was there for about a month. I couldn't cope with seeing my wife getting murdered in front of me, and I had to get some help. That's my cringe-worthy tale." As I finished, I wondered if I'd said too much. Would he think I was still crazy?

"If you ever need to talk," he started as I was getting ready to jump out of the car, "go to a priest. They listen. They give advice. And they never look at you, so you don't feel the guilt. Oh, and they're free. It's a win-win."

"Did you just say to go to a priest?" I asked, laughing as the awkwardness of our wounded heart stories drifted away like forgotten messages in a bottle. "Why are you so, so…"

"Yeah, I get asked that all the time. No one can ever finish what I am."

"I bet Elizabeth can," I said, as we both laughed at the honesty of the statement.

CHAPTER 71

"See anything up there, Knightly?" Young asked, speaking into his two-way radio as he perused the parking lot for the perpetrators. He stopped to rest on a park bench under a streetlamp.

"Nothing here. What about you, White?" Knightly responded, pacing up and down the small King Street – Old Town Yellow Line subway platform. He watched closely as a couple of high school kids groped one another, remembering the good old days when he was the star quarterback in high school able to have any girl he wanted. Now he was a thirty-five-year-old has-been with a beer belly that stuck out further than his double chin and a once-attractive wife at home with their two bratty kids.

"All clear," White answered. He walked under the darkened subway line where the bike racks and panhandlers were stationed beside the main street of the old Alexandria town. This path led to eclectic quaint shops and tasteful fine-dining establishments while being stuffy neighbors to CVS and Chipotle.

The subway trains journeyed both directions, stopping at the platform every few minutes. Each train of cars was fairly empty as they neared the last stop at Huntington Station or headed to the city life of Washington, D.C. With each passing train, Knightly watched the exiting passengers and then hopped onto a few of the cars to look for the suspects. At the beginning of the evening, when each train stopped at the station, his heart would race with the belief that he was about to catch the infamous Carbon Monoxide Killers. But as the night went on, his enthusiasm deflated like helium in a three-day-old balloon.

In the shadows under the subway line, White watched the attractive ladies in their tight skirts and low-cut blouses more than he did possible criminals. He wondered if they were hookers but decided to let them enjoy their night rather than get harassed by a crooked cop that would drop the charges for a friendly gesture.

"Anything?" Young begged, propping his feet on the park bench. He was casually lying down as if he was a homeless man about to fall asleep. "Please tell me you got something. It's boring down here."

"Still think we needed more people at each station?" White mocked as Knightly chuckled to himself.

"Stuff it," Young barked out angrily. "I can't believe we are wasting our night playing lowly security guards just because that twerp, Cooper, got a call about a killing tonight!" Young sat up, wiping the flakes of crusty paint from his trousers. "I can't wait to see his face when nothing happens tonight."

Another subway train rolled into the station, coming to a screeching halt. Knightly watched suspiciously as a couple similar to the killers' description exited slowly from the train, taking their time down the cement steps. "I have two coming your way, White."

"Copy that," White answered, approaching the stairs to watch a young woman help a sickly-looking gentleman with the stairs. She was saying something into his ear while pointing at the parking lot, but White couldn't make out her words.

"What's going on? Tell me! Do you see them?" Young demanded, but the other two didn't respond.

"They are going to get the car for us, Dad. Okay?" the young woman said tenderly but loud enough for White to hear.

"I can make it," the older gentleman replied as he continued to walk toward the parking lot and away from White.

"Young! They are coming your way! A young woman in a pink sweater with her sick father! Do you see them?" White asked. "Oh, and don't ever blow my cover again, you got me?"

Young ignored the last part of the conversation. He strained his neck to see the two suspects walking in his direction. "I see them. They are heading my way." Young started towards them, weaving between the parked cars. He tried to be undetectable, which was pretty impossible, since the parking lot was half empty. "They are still coming my way. I am about thirty feet from them."

"I see them too," White answered, walking behind the couple towards the parking area.

Young watched as the two suspects slowly made their way further into the parking lot. A Honda CRV backed up to pick them up. "Back-up. I need back-up. They are getting picked up by the Honda CRV!"

Young shouted into his radio before taking off running in their direction.

"Freeze!" Young shouted to the two individuals getting into the backseat of the SUV. "Get out of the car!"

"My dad is sick," the young woman replied as she continued to help her father into the car.

"I said get out of the car!" Young shouted again, the gun in his hand pointed at the young woman.

"Okay, okay," the woman responded stepping away from the vehicle. Apparently, she wasn't fast enough for Young who made a mad dash towards her, tackling her to the ground.

"Help me!" the young woman screamed as she was slammed against the concrete like a flower being trampled by a linebacker. "Argh!"

"Susan!" the woman in the front passenger seat yelled as she watched the young woman lay sprawled on the ground, unable to move.

White ran up confused, seeing Young still holding down the young woman. "Put your hands up!" he shouted to the man in the back of the SUV. All of the vehicle's occupants placed their hands on the ceiling. "You in the front seats, get out of the car!"

"What's this about?" the man from the driver's seat shouted as he got out of the car. He was followed by the woman in the front passenger seat who was screaming hysterically.

"Susan! Susan!"

"Sir, Miss, please step away and let us do our job. These people are killers!" Young yelled as he

272

maneuvered his body to grab Susan's hands and handcuff her as she lay on the ground.

"Killers?" the woman screamed belligerently. "They are not killers. This is my little sister and father! We just picked them up from the airport thirty minutes ago!"

Young rolled off Susan, who had a bloody nose, a scuffed forehead, and had left a wet place on the pavement from her rushing tears. "Airport?"

"Dad? Dad? You okay back there?" the older sister asked rushing to her father's side. Her husband helped Susan off the ground, demanding that the officers take off the handcuffs.

"Really?" Susan's brother-in-law shouted in disgust. "You thought little Susan and my father-in-law, who had triple bypass four weeks ago, were killers? How messed up are you guys?"

CHAPTER 72

The two met at the Gallery Place Chinatown Metro Station and snuck into their hidden darkened corridor to change into their father and daughter outfits. "You want to mix it up tonight?" she asked as she put on her auburn curly-haired wig. She then helped him put on his bald man's cap, making sure it looked realistic.

"You want to?" His lips trembled with excitement at the idea of trying something new.

She warmly nodded in agreement, giving him a gigantic hug that radiated pure love for her younger brother. "Well, I think it's time we put a new spin on things. We don't want the cops to start catching on to us."

A wicked smiled stretched across his face at the notion of the cops getting close to their trail. It might have frightened some people, but it just caused his happiness to explode. "Let's give them something they aren't expecting."

"That's just what I was thinking," she said, grinning. She quickly removed her smile and got into character as the tender caretaker for her ailing father. "Ready to start something new?"

"Sure thing," he commented as he wheeled his squeaking oxygen tank behind him. "Like the squeak?" he asked as they stepped into the light. "It's just a little something that I worked on today."

"Very nice touch," she commented as they proceeded to their subway platform, passing the usual crowd of individuals dressed in their work attire, ready and willing to shed the drab clothes of a routine workweek for the exciting wardrobe of a mesmerizing Friday night. Dance clubs would be beckoning with their hypnotic techno beat and seizure-inducing strobe lighting or a chilled night at a soothing jazz bar with a sexy sound and even sexier atmosphere. But whatever their entertainment, it would not compare to the mad rush that the two of them would be feeling in the next few hours.

"Where you going?" he asked as she walked past their normal waiting area beside the ADHD medication advertisement.

"Come on, Dad," she answered as she locked her elbow with his. "Our subway is over there."

"Over there?" he asked confused as they continued to walk away from their normal subway car. His heart skipped a beat realizing that this was going to be the start of the shakeup. "Oh, over there," he coughed, melodramatically. "You know that these stations always confuse me, dear."

"I know, Dad. I know."

CHAPTER 73

"What happened?" Knightly shouted, running from the Metro station platform. He saw the young woman leaning her head back, trying to stop her bleeding nose.

"I thought..." Young mumbled before he was interrupted.

"He thought that my sick father and I were going to kill my sister and brother-in-law," Susan barked furiously, looking down at her skinned palms. "Can I see a mirror?"

"You're going to be okay," Young encouraged, watching his career go down the drain quicker than anyone in history.

"Here you go," said Susan's older sister, Becca, handing her a pocket mirror from her purse.

Susan carefully looked into the mirror and saw her bruising cheek start to swell. A few remaining drops of blood trickled down her slender nose from a hairline gash. "Do you always attack someone without stopping to think for a second that you could be wrong? Where was your evidence? A girl with a sick guy?"

"You fit the profile," Young answered defensively, looking around at Knightly and White for support. Yet, there was none to be found as sirens began to echo as they came closer.

"I guess we should be thankful that you didn't shoot her," the father quietly spoke up from the backseat of his daughter's vehicle. Becca's husband snidely agreed.

"Hope it's an ambulance coming," Becca remarked as Young's eyes widened.

"I'm sure that she will be fine. You didn't need to call an ambulance," Young said, envisioning his superiors taking away his gun and badge.

"I called the ambulance," White announced proudly. "You knocked the lady down pretty good, Young. She needs to be looked over for a concussion."

"Why don't you just step back, Young, and get some fresh air," Knightly said forcefully. "We have to get their statements on what just happened."

"I can tell you what happened," Young expressed angrily, pacing beside the Honda CRV. "I know what happened."

"Young! Step down!" Knightly demanded as White quickly backed him up.

"It's protocol to get the witnesses' reports of a police altercation."

"Altercation? I was just trying to do my job!" Young spit out childishly, moving closer to Knightly and White as if trying to intimidate them.

"Young!" White commanded. "Don't make me handcuff you! Just let us do our job."

Young limped away like an injured dog with its tail between its legs. Not only was his pride quickly deflating, but his shoulder was feeling the aftermath of his tackle to the parking lot concrete. He casually looked behind and watched each of the family members give their accounts of the event. They pointed and stared at Young, reenacting the tragic moment when the young detective hurled himself onto the five-foot-three Susan who could have easily been broken in half by a man his size.

He knew he'd messed up. He knew he hadn't followed the procedures on handling a possible hostage situation. Yet, even with all of his failures, he thought it was his fellow officers' jobs to stand up for him and side with him. He had never felt the knives of backstabbers before. Tonight, he thought he'd felt the first puncture wound from Brutus' blade.

The ambulance took Susan and her father away as Becca and her husband followed from behind in their Honda CRV. Knightly and White strolled over to the park bench where Young was sitting. "It's your turn now. Tell us your perspective of the events of tonight," Knightly said, getting out another page of the standard police report. "White gave me his account of what happened. So, tell me what you remember."

"What good is it going to do?" Young said, sulking like he had just lost an important football game. "You're out to get me. I know it."

"Out to get you? You've got to be kidding," White said lividly. "You're the one who tackled the poor girl, and you're playing the victim?"

"White, back off," Knightly said, trying to control the conversation. "Young, I really don't care what you think of me and White. But we have a job to do.

Either I can take your report, or I can write down what White and I know. It's your choice."

"Go ahead," Young rolled his eyes, leaving the park bench to get to his patrol car. "Write whatever you want."

CHAPTER 74

"So, where are we getting off?" he whispered into his sister's ear. They were riding the yellow line subway car, going in the opposite direction from Huntington Station.

"I don't know," she smiled warmly, clutching his hand. "Let's just play the evening by ear."

He looked forward to improvising the night. He knew that the main bullet points would remain the same, but there was going to be some wiggle room to spread their wings and take flight into an uncharted land. "They look interesting," he whispered, tapping her hand. He was indicating three seats ahead on the left where an older couple in their mid-sixties sat. She sat anxiously watching her wristwatch for the time as his head kept bobbing back pretending that he drifted to sleep. "I've been watching them for the last two stops."

"Well, we can give it a shot if you like, but they seem like an easy target," she remarked with a grimace as she had noticed them as well. "Sure you don't want anything more exciting?"

Eyeing her wickedly, his smile broadened, almost causing his eyes to squint from anticipation. They continued on their journey, watching and waiting for the perfect target. The subway train stopped at West Hyattsville Station, which was where their couple departed. "Rats," he whispered sadly.

As the doors were closing, another similarly aged couple entered. "Margaret, sit down, sit down," a man in his late fifties laughed as he motioned for his wife to quit gawking out the window.

"You're never any fun, Mark," she said loudly, laughing as she slowly made her way to her seat. She made sure everyone on the train heard her conversation. "I am tired, dead tired. You walked me too much today."

"Well, take a load off here for a few minutes," Mark commented as he stretched his arms.

She stretched her neck to look around the surroundings. "Where you from?" Margaret asked, taking the killers by surprise.

"Memphis," she answered in a southern drawl, curling her upper lip like Elvis would have done.

"Oh, honey, did you hear that? They're from Memphis," Margaret exclaimed with unfiltered jubilation. "Memphis!"

"Are you from around there?" she asked shocked since she hadn't heard a southern accent in Margaret's booming voice.

"Oh, dear me, no. We're from Spokane," she said, laughing hysterically. "Have you even been to Spokane, Washington?"

"No. I can't say that we have," she answered as her brother slightly snickered beneath his mask.

"Well, we like it. It's a good place to live, lots of good people," she said, leaning forward and noticing that there was a gentleman beside her talking partner. "Well, hello over there. Hope you are doing well."

He nodded his head slowly, closing his eyes as if thanking God for this little blessing. "I want them," he whispered. He knew that he didn't have to whisper too softly because Margaret was carrying on a new conversation with a bewildered teenage boy who was more interested in Snapchat than talking to her.

"Uh huh," his sister agreed. "I think they will do just nicely."

CHAPTER 75

The Yellow Line Metro subway train left the College Park Station, heading towards the final destination on its route, Greenbelt Station. Mark and Margaret continued to talk to anyone who was willing to listen. Sadly for them, that was only the young lady with her elderly father. The train conductor announced the final station; as the sick villain looked out the window, his heart rate started to pound.

"There's no garage," he frantically whispered. "What are we going to do? There's no garage."

"Calm down," she replied, glancing down at Mark's hand. She noticed that he was fidgeting with a keychain. "There is parking here. I checked before we left."

"See, Dad?" she said pointing over his shoulder at a parking lot below the train station a short walk away. "Remember? We parked down there."

"I...I...I don't know if I can make that long of a walk," he stuttered and coughed with his rehearsed line. "I don't know if I can make it."

"Oh, Dad," she sympathetically and loudly. "You have to come with me. I can't leave you here by yourself while I go and get the vehicle."

She casually glanced beside her at Mark and Margaret who were, for the first time, whispering to themselves and only themselves. She smiled kindly before turning her head back to her brother, continuing their charade. "Maybe you just need to sit and wait a few more minutes before we head out."

"I'm ready to go," he complained noisily. "I just want to go to sleep."

The train stopped smoothly at the Greenbelt station as all the remaining riders quickly exited the sliding doors, including Mark and Margaret. "Come on, Dad. We've got to get off now," she said with aggravation in her tone as she forcefully helped him to his shaky feet. "See, you can do it."

"I don't know," he said, as they stepped onto the station's platform, finding Mark and Margaret waiting for them by the stairs.

"It looks like you could use some help, so Mark will get on one side of him and help him down," Margaret shouted, as if the father were deaf instead of sick.

"Oh, thank you! Thank you!" she said, beaming with relief. "I didn't know how I was going to get him down these stairs because he is too stubborn to take the elevator."

"I understand," Margaret commiserated. "More than you know. My father was sick as well. There were many times I needed a helping hand, but everyone was just too busy to spare a moment. What is wrong with this world?"

"I do not know," she said with her lips pursed. "It is just so sad these days."

Mark gently grabbed the supposedly sick man's arm and placed it over his shoulder. He was basically carrying all of the feeble man's weight as they headed down the stairs. "See? We got this," Mark said huffing as he was two steps away from level ground. "We got this."

"Thank you, so, so, so, much," the sister said, hugging Mark and Margaret like it was Christmas. "Do you think you can make it to the parking lot, Dad?"

He squinted over at the parking lot as though it were miles away instead of just a few hundred feet. "I'm not sure."

"Dad, I can't leave you, so if you want to stop and rest, then we can try to make it over in a few minutes." She hoped she was dangling the worm enticingly enough for Mark or Margaret to grab the bait.

"Hon, I'm just tired," he groaned, taking a seat on the bench beside the stairs as his arms jittered by his side.

"You three stay here. I will go get the car and pick you all up," Mark said energetically before quickly heading over to the parking lot.

"You have a good one," she remarked to Margaret.

"I do, don't I?" Margaret replied, starting to talk about when she and Mark first met in biology class their freshman year in high school.

CHAPTER 76

The Nissan Altima Hertz rental car pulled up beside the three passengers, and Margaret continued to talk without catching a breath. Margaret and the devious sister got into the backseat while her accomplice rode shotgun. They circled the open parking lot, watching the passing cars on the road stream by just a few dozen yards away.

Margaret continued to chit-chat as the two killers kept watching one another, trying to pick up on one another's cues. They had always rehearsed this scene with the idea of being in an enclosed space such as a garage, but they had never had the nerve to do it in the open for any passing car to see their brutal act.

The brother glanced around the scene, noticing that the parking lot was void of people. There was no sign of an oncoming train, so if they were going to do anything, they were going to have to do it right then. He gave his sister a sinister wink, and suddenly their planned dialogue started like it had before.

Within three minutes, Mark had parked his car between two large SUVs. The evil siblings had chloroformed their victims and moved Mark to the backseat before they were ready to dispose of their victims in a park of their choosing.

"I never thought Margaret was going to shut up," she chuckled as she buckled herself into the passenger seat.

"That was awesome!" he squealed, reversing the car to leave the parking lot. "The feeling that any passing car could have seen us," he said giddily, shivering in excitement. "I have goose bumps."

"Well, calm down. We're not even halfway done."

"I know, but do you know how many cars passed by as we attacked them?" he asked as he pulled out of the parking lot. "Lucky thirteen!" he laughed heartily. "Thirteen times we darted getting caught! Oh, man! Oh, man! I am still shaking," he continued like he was a schoolboy being told that he was going to Disney World. "That was awesome!"

"Just try to drive reasonably without someone noticing us," she said, snickering like a proud sister. "It would be awful to get caught for speeding or reckless driving."

"Okay, okay. I got it."

The two drove on the side streets, trying to keep clear of any road cameras as they headed to Greenbelt Park. "Do you remember going camping at Greenbelt Park when we were young?" she asked, recalling the summer before they were separated when their father took them camping.

"No," he stated coolly. "We camped there?"

"It was only once, but Dad brought us, and we slept under the stars. He made a campfire, told us some stories, and then we fell fast asleep."

"I...uh...I," he shook his head distraught. "I don't remember that."

"Don't worry, we will do it again sometime," she said as they entered the darkened park surrounded by an orange forest, whose limbs were becoming bare.

"Do you remember where we camped?" he asked.

"Maybe if I saw it," she said.

He slowly traveled down the narrow park road and turned down the campground area. She maneuvered her neck, looking for any sign of a memory. "Do you see it?" he asked childishly as they crept through the dark where only a few campers had pitched their tents and were resting.

"There! There!" she pointed out his window causing him to stop. "I remember that tree where the trunk split and formed a V. Dad told us that was the tree of victory," she lied. She hadn't recalled where they'd stayed, but she didn't want to fail him. She wanted him to feel something, even if that something was a lie.

"Wow," he grinned, looking at the tree and then turning his head at his sister. "You're such a liar," he laughed as he softly pressed on the gas to continue on the circular park road around the campgrounds. "Don't you know that I can tell when you lie?"

"I've lied to you before and you never said anything," she commented, proving that her skills were not that bad.

"Oh, I knew. I just never wanted to say anything, sis."

They made their journey away from the campground and found a lonely parking lot away from all the commotion. There was nothing around except for a few hiking trails. They quickly arranged their guests like their victims before. He duct taped the hose as she went through their wallet and purse for phones, hotel key cards, MetroCards, and anything else that would give the police information about Mark and Margaret.

"Ready?" he asked, sliding the hose through the driver's side window.

"Ready," she answered as she closed Margaret's door. He started the engine to let the vehicle fill with the deadly poison. "Which trail are we taking?"

"We will go due east," he answered. "That is where my bike and your backpack is."

"Lead on, bro," she said as the two started on their way, getting about fifty feet away from the parking lot.

"You hear that?" he froze, listening for any slight sound.

"No, what?"

He turned, wanting to run back to the parking lot. He controlled himself and calmly walked back. "I hear a truck coming."

CHAPTER 77

"I got a tear in my beer cuz I'm cryin' for you dear," a young park ranger sang in his Ford pick-up. He came up on a lone running Nissan Altima. "Say what?" he asked himself as he pulled beside the car. "Teenagers."

He got his slender five-foot-eleven frame out of the tan truck, strolled over, and tapped on the foggy glass. "Come on, kids. This is not the place for this," he hollered, hoping to break up the teenagers making out. He waited for a sound to come from inside but heard nothing. Tapping on the windows again, he shouted louder, "Come on! You need to leave here!"

While he waited for the window to lower, he pulled out his flashlight from his utility belt and clicked it on, letting a powerful light cut through the darkness. He noticed that the windows weren't foggy, but smoky. He shone the light into the car, not expecting what he was about to find. "Oh God!" he yelled as he pulled on the door handle. It wouldn't open. He ran back to his truck for a weapon to break the glass as something else caught his attention.

"Help me! Help me!" a young woman moaned from the woods, crawling towards the parking lot. "Help me!"

He turned his attention away from the running car and sprinted to the young woman to check on her. "What's wrong? What happened?" he asked, shining the light onto her dirty face and seeing leaves tangled in her rustled hair.

"I was just raped!" she cried, reaching her trembling arms up to him. "I am so scared. Help me!" Her voice quivered with emotion.

"It's okay. It's going to be okay," he said stooping down. He didn't try to help her up; instead he was trying to bring some comfort while showing that he was in control of the scene. "You stay there! I will call it in, but first I have to save this couple!"

"Help me! Help me!" she screamed one more time, trying to keep his attention on her and not Mark and Margaret. "He may come back!"

"I will! I promise I will! But first..." He didn't have a chance to finish his sentence. He didn't hear the girl's brother sneak around the parked truck or see the hammer coming from behind to strike his head.

He hadn't planned on killing a victim with his bare hands, but this night was nothing like they had anticipated. It just kept getting better and better. He knocked the park ranger unconscious with his own hammer, continuing to slam it into his bloody head. The ranger's groans silenced, leaving only the sound of the wheezing and the blood.

"Do you want to try it?" he asked, grinning at his sister and wiping the blood off his forehead.

Standing up, she brushed off the dirt and leaves before confidently walking over to her brother. She grabbed the hammer from his gloved hand. "Don't mind if I do." She gripped the handle with her gloved hand and reared her hand back but stopped. "I can't. I can't do it."

"It's okay," her brother said as he patted her back compassionately. "You don't have to do anything you don't want to do."

"No. You don't understand. I can't do it like this," she barked, reaching toward the park ranger's hand. She picked up the flashlight instead. "Here, I need some light."

Her brother shone the light on the beaten and bloody face that looked like a raw piece of meat. "Better?"

"Much," she said, grinning as she raised her arm and slammed the hammer with full force. "Much better."

CHAPTER 78

Ming's was just as Jeremiah had said. It was a hole-in-the-wall type of restaurant usually overlooked by most people but loved and endeared by those who would take a chance on an unknown establishment.

The conversation bantered around from the Major League Baseball playoffs and frightening politicians to recent exotic travels and tragic loss of loves. The food was delicious, but the dialogue was tastier.

"So, since you are being so candid, do you mind me asking an off-topic question?" I posed, slurping some hot and sour soup.

"Nothing is taboo, Solo. With all of my studies of various cultures around the world, I doubt you can come up with such a scandalous question," he answered as he dipped his chicken and broccoli in more soy sauce.

"Why do you not believe?" I asked sincerely, glancing up at the cashier reading *The Hunger Games*. "I am not saying this to try to change your mind, but I have never met anyone whose beliefs differed from mine whom I felt comfortable enough to ask."

"It's all good," he said, smiling as he took a sip of his water as if about to start an eloquent soliloquy. "Do you want a long drawn-out lesson from my many years of studying different anthropological cultures with a detailed dissection of godless societies and peoples in the past, or my heartfelt answer?"

"Is there a difference?" I sat back, astonished with his response.

"At the core, there may not be a difference. But for layman's ears, there is definitely a difference," he answered as he took another bite from his quickly vanishing entrée.

"You just tell me what you want to tell me."

"My heartfelt answer is that I just don't believe. It's not because there is some scientific proof that there isn't a supreme being. It isn't because I was jilted as a young child and my anger caused my disbelief. There is not a moment in my history that I can pinpoint and say, 'This is why I do not believe.'"

I stared at him with a feeling of confusion. "So, you're telling me that you don't believe because you just don't believe?"

"Very simply put, but also very philosophical if you let it set for a while," he said, laughing as if he was Socrates and I was Aristotle.

"I am sorry," I said, shaking my head amazed at this lack of logic coming from such a brilliant thinker. "I can't wrap my head around that."

"What is there to wrap your head around? If there is no God, what is there to wrap your head around?" he asked, as if he was teaching a lesson and I was just one of his dimwitted students. "It's just like the notion of a blind man describing what a star looks like. He has never seen a star, and with his own personal vision he cannot expound on its beauty unless he was first told of its beauty. The blind man would not even know that there were stars overhead until someone told him that there was a grouping of stars forming the Little Dipper."

"So, are you saying that we are all born blind to God, and the only reason we believe is because someone else told us about God?" I asked, playing with my peanut chicken like it was a game on my plate.

"Very similarly," he nodded.

"I'm sorry, but I don't understand your reasoning with your blind man theory. I don't see how it relates to God. Someone who has seen a star can tell a blind man about a star, just as someone totally different can walk up to the same blind person and say, 'Yep, there are stars overhead.' The blind man can believe them or not, but that doesn't make the stars not real. So someone who has seen God, or let me rephrase, *believes* in God, can tell someone who has never heard about God that there is an all-powerful being. Then someone else walks up and says, "Yep, there's a God.' Once again, it comes down to that new person believing or not believing what they just heard. Maybe you are just a blind man when it comes to God."

"If there was a loving God who created all that we see, I cannot understand why he would be so silent."

"You say God is silent, but I see and hear Him all the time."

"Do you really see and hear Him? Or do you see and hear what you want to believe is Him? Have you ever heard of a self-fulfilling prophecy?"

"Yes, I have."

"Don't you think that faith is very similar to that?"

I didn't know how to respond. He was posing questions that I felt uncomfortable considering. Would questioning my faith be the start of going down a rabbit hole? Would posing theories cause my firm faith of steel to start to rust and dwindle under the pressure of diamond-like doubt? I slammed my fist onto the table, breaking open the sweet fortune cookie and reading the lackluster saying.

"What did it say?" he asked, probably seeing the fear in my eyes.

"'Some questions you ask may open wounds that will never heal,'" I said, shrugging my shoulders in faltering complacency.

"Solo, you asked my opinion," Jeremiah commented as he cracked open his fortune cookie, looking at it with a quizzical smile.

"I know, I know," I replied, trying to shake off my lingering doubts that sometimes weigh as much as my faith. "I really do appreciate you talking to me about this. I needed to hear it. It just saddens me a little."

"How so?" he asked.

I looked down at my fortune cookie and focused on the words 'wound' and 'heal' causing a stirring of emotions. "It's just that I want to take you outside and point up at the sky and show you all the stars and planets." I stopped and took a deep breath. "But if you are blind, no matter how much I point out the moon or Venus, all you can see is black. It just saddens me that you are missing out on what I can see."

Jeremiah nodded in agreement because he understood the analogy. "You should come to dinner with me and Eugene sometime. Just because people reside on different points on the spectrum, they are still found on the same line. We are more alike than we are different."

Something about what he just said resonated louder than anything else he'd said all night. "I'd like that," I said with a grin. "I would really like that." We got up to leave as he picked up his fortune and placed the tiny strip of paper in his wallet. "I forgot to ask what your fortune said."

He started to laugh as we walked out of Ming's and to his vehicle. "You really want to know?" he asked as if it would push me over the edge with the disbelief discussion. I nodded my head. "'It's better to be humble and learn, than to be proud and be wrong,'" he recited from memory like it was his life's motto. "Eugene always says that I am the proudest ignorant man. I thought he would get a kick out this," he said with a laugh. "And after tonight, maybe I should add blind to that saying. The proudest, ignorant, blind man."

CHAPTER 79

The hike through the woods was strangely peaceful after all the excitement. Mitch the park ranger hadn't expect to be bludgeoned to death on his last rounds of the night. If he had just ignored the running car or even skipped out early, he would be heading to the local sports bar for an entertaining Friday night with friends. Instead, he was curled up in the trunk of Mark and Margaret's vehicle with early onsets of rigor mortis, waiting to be found.

"Do you remember hiking these woods with Dad?" he asked as he let the moon's light lead them safely through the gravelly terrain.

"Not really," she conceded with sadness in her tone. "But I am pretty sure that if we ever camped here, we would have hiked through these same woods."

She looked up through the naked trees, catching a glimpse of a few stars, wondering if any of them formed any undiscovered constellations. She was always amazed that the early explorers used the celestial lights like a modern-day GPS since she constantly got lost using Google Maps to find the nearest Starbucks. If given a compass and a map, she would be wandering the woods for a lifetime.

"So, want to meet up again tomorrow night?" she asked, causing him to turn with a gleeful smile.

"Really? Tomorrow?"

"Yeah, I've been thinking that since it's the weekend, there may be some prime targets to pick off tomorrow night," she said as she smacked her brother's head to look forward. "Are you in?"

"Oh, I'm in!" he agreed, still feeling the last bits of adrenaline from the park ranger's death.

"I also think we need to make a few changes for tomorrow night."

"Really?" he asked, his voice piquing with interest. His night kept getting better and better. He had longed for the moments when they would improvise and go off script to see if they could do it. Tonight's first taste of change merely whetted his appetite. He was done snacking on the dollar menu. He was ready to sink his teeth into a filet mignon.

"Yes, because some changes need to be made if you want to continue this."

"I do, I do," he said, jumping like a schoolboy trying to get picked first for dodge ball. "I'm up for some changes."

With every step they took, she listened to the rustling leaves and crackling tree limbs. She let the soothing sounds of nature bring her to a Zen-like state of meditation. A calming sensation poured over her like a warm bath of goose feathers, causing her to lightly hum a sweet melody as if she were singing a lullaby to her baby brother. He listened to the heavenly tune before harmonizing a few octaves lower.

She stopped her humming and posed an interesting question. "How do you think I will look bald?"

CHAPTER 80

I didn't feel like going home even though my Timex warned me that it was a quarter past eleven and I had an early morning as a wedding photographer. My thoughts went through the day, and no matter how hard I tried, I couldn't get the Fiddelsteins out of my mind. Even though I had only spent half a day with them, I felt a strange connection. It wasn't like acquaintance or even Facebook friends that rarely saw each other in person, but there was a deeper bond.

My phone burned in my hands as if begging me to text Isaac or Amanda to check on Rachel. My courteous self warned me that it was too late to text. They'd had a stressful week, and they were probably sleeping peacefully knowing that once again, their entire family was under one roof. It was a feeling they didn't have just twenty-four hours earlier.

The subway was fairly lonely this Friday night. It was strangely quiet with just three passengers in my car, and one of them was fast asleep after an apparent hard day at work. After a few minutes on Facebook and Twitter, the lingering feeling of texting someone came surging back with a vengeance.

How was your night? I texted Elizabeth, hoping that she would break the boredom by responding. But after a few minutes of agonized waiting, I knew that she either had better things to do or she was just ignoring me. Neither option brought any comfort to me at this moment, but then again, Elizabeth wasn't the matronly type with compassion or selflessness.

How was your night? I texted to Wint, praying that he would reply. I was hoping that his response would break the monotony of passing through the empty stations. His lack of conversation was a signal to me that the entire world had something better to do than chat with me. I felt as though my own conscience was pointing out my shortcomings in life.

After losing hope in humanity and the dread of another fifteen-minute subway ride, a text appeared on the screen, stealing my breath. *Thank you again for your persistence. We owe you big time*, was all the text from Isaac read.

I read and reread the message before I nonchalantly replied, *No problem*, hoping not to come across as too needy, even though his text meant the world to me. It was as if for a moment, the world stood still, except for the subway train, which had quickly arrived at my stop. *Glad your family is safe and sound tonight.*

Me too, he replied quickly with a heartwarming picture of Rachel sleeping snug with her best friend, Violet the purple monkey, clenched in her tiny arms. They were lying beside the blissful Amanda. *Me too.*

I bowed my head in reverence as a lone tear trickled down my cheek. All I could mutter in my prayer was a rambling, "Thank you, Lord. Thank you, Lord. Thank you, Lord." Sometimes the shortest prayers were the ones I believed God treasured the most.

CHAPTER 81

Wint walked into the family room dimly lit by a crackling fire as Veronica lay curled on the couch with a velvet blanket, a glass of wine, and a biography on Eleanor Roosevelt. "How was your dinner?"

"Fine," she answered as she kept her nose in her book and a hand on her glass of Merlot.

"Was your dad upset?" he asked kindly, taking a seat in his leather chair and propping his feet on the ottoman.

"He understood," she remarked coldly, flipping a page in her book.

"I don't know what to say," he muttered under his breath, causing her to throw her book across the room, missing the fire by a few feet.

"Sorry! Sorry could be a start!" she yelled, gulping the last bit of wine out of her goblet.

"For what? Trying to catch a killer?" he argued, his shoulders broadening and chest puffing out.

"Well, did you catch him?" she asked belittlingly, cocking her head in superiority. "You didn't, did you?"

He knew that she would still be fuming even if they had caught the killers, so the answer didn't really matter much. "No," he answered remorsefully, pounding his fist into the arm of the leather chair. He was angrier with the notion of the killers walking free than Veronica's sideways glance.

"Why not?" she asked in her defense attorney tone. She was acting like she was questioning a crooked cop on the stand, ready to pounce and air out all of the skeletons she had found in her personal vendetta.

He didn't answer her. He turned his attention to the fire, watching the flames dance and swirl like they were passionate lovers. The only dancing he and Veronica did was strictly for appearances.

"I'm over here!" she bellowed, throwing her goblet above the fireplace, smashing it to fragments. The shards of crystals collided with the hardwood floor below.

Flinching from the sound of crashing glass, Wint stood up, grinding his boots into the shards and exited the room.

"Don't you leave me when I'm talking to you!" she screeched, jumping up from the couch and chasing him down the hall.

"Are you going to throw something at me now?" he snarled as he continued to walk down the hall toward their bedroom.

"Winston, I am talking to you! Look at me when I am talking to you!" she yelled from behind. But he didn't care. He just continued storming down the darkened hallway to their cold bedroom.

The spark they'd once had for one another had been extinguished about a year ago when Veronica started degrading his career in front of her friends and family. He had gone from being her heroic knight in shining armor to the court jester and the butt of her jokes. Slamming the bedroom door, he looked around the room and saw traces of Veronica in everything. The shimmering curtains, the antique armoire, the golden satin duvet that matched her decorative pillows. The room reeked of Veronica. He yanked open his chest of drawers to get his crimson silk pajamas. Not even his pajamas were his choice. In college, he'd slept in his boxers and a t-shirt. Now even when he slept, Veronica still had a hold on what he could and could not do.

Grabbing the pajamas, he ripped them down the middle, enjoying the sound of the splitting cloth. He caused them to look like tattered rags instead of expensive designer fashion. His blood was boiling as he did a quick spin around the room, seeing that nothing in the room said Wint. It oozed the fake persona of Winston and Veronica. He unbuckled his belt and unzipped his pants, letting them fall to the ground. He threw off his shirt and kicked everything into the bathroom hamper.

Returning to his bed, he grabbed his pillow and exited the room in his boxers and t-shirt, passing Veronica in the hall.

"Where are you going?" she asked disgusted as he passed her without stopping.

"I'm sleeping in my room tonight," he answered as calmly as he could. He made his way to the one and only room in the house that held his personal belongings. Flipping on the light switch, he saw family photographs and sports trophies from his childhood. He was tired from an exhausting day, but he wanted to see the happy memories that used to be his life. As he reclined on his couch, he looked around the room. He started smiling at the various moments in his past before falling asleep with the lights on.

Saturday

CHAPTER 82

"I don't think my parents are going to like this," said fifteen-year-old Sandy as she quivered beside Tyson, her boyfriend of two days. They were hiking the wooded trails of Greenbelt Park at 1:39 a.m. They had met as star-crossed lovers, each disgusted with their parents' ideas of camping in October. However, they soon decided it was fate that they had met under these chilly circumstances.

"Don't worry so much, babe," Tyson said, smiling as his braces reflected the moonlight into her swooning eyes. "No one is going to find out. We'll be back before anyone knows we're gone."

They walked hand in hand through the trails, each telling their life stories filled with jaded, tortuous middleclass angst of how their parents wouldn't buy them the newest iPhone or front row tickets to Taylor Swift's concert. They bonded in their mutual commiseration and deprivation.

"So, are you going to forget about me when you get back to Chicago?" Sandy asked timidly, her eyes twinkling like the stars in Orion's belt.

"Never. I will never forget you," he said sincerely, reciting the words he had uttered a dozen times at the various campgrounds this year. She was just another notch in his boyish escapades of seeing how far he could get in just a few days.

"But we're never going to see one another again after tomorrow," she said, starting to cry. He compassionately swooped in and embraced her tenderly as he felt around her back to find her bra straps for later.

"Babe," he moved her head from his chest to look into her eyes. "We can Facetime and text any time. This is just the beginning," he lied, knowing he'd give the same wrong number that he'd given to the other girls in the past. "But since this is our last night for now…" he leaned down to kiss her. "Let's make it one we will never forget."

She tilted her head, giving him the all-clear sign as their lips met for the first time. In the midst of their heavy breathing, they heard a strange coughing sound through the trees.

"What's that?" she asked, breaking away from his lips as he groaned in misery.

"Who cares?" he answered, pulling her back to him for another round of making out.

The chugging coughing sound started to get louder causing Sandy to break away from his grip once again as he was nearing the courage to try for second base. "What now?" he griped as she started to walk toward the unfamiliar sound.

"Something doesn't sound right," she said, walking further down the trail. "Something's not right."

"Fine!" he growled, slowly starting to walk behind her, feeling the night of pleasure slip between his sex-starved fingers.

The trees started to break, giving way to a parking lot with two vehicles. One was still running, but barely as it sputtered and coughed in the parking space. "That's weird," she commented. "What do you think is going on?"

"How would I know?" he hissed, showing his selfish and sleazy true colors. She quickly picked up on the chameleon act he had been putting on this whole time.

She looked at him in disgust then turned her attention back to the running vehicle. She thought she saw a silhouette of someone in the driver's seat. "I think someone is in the car."

"They are probably sleeping or making out, like we should be," he said with a smile, trying to recapture his charming charade.

"Maybe, but..." she commented, stepping out from the trees and moving closer to the parked car.

"Get back here," he said as quietly as he could from behind a prickly bush. "What if they tell your parents?"

"They are not going to tell my parents," she said mockingly, rolling her eyes. She started to see the illusion that she had been under the past two days a little more clearly, along with the sleeping man in the driver's seat. Stepping closer, she breathed in a pungent smell coming from the cracked window. "Gross!" she said, squirming as she covered her mouth and nose with her sweater. As she got closer, she knocked on the window, but no one woke up. She knocked again. Still no movement in the car.

"They're not waking," she said, turning to Tyson, who was finally stepping away from his woodsy protection.

"Maybe you're not beating on the glass hard enough," he commented. Suddenly he stopped. He had spotted the garden hose running from the exhaust pipe to the driver's side window. "Quick! Open the door!" he shouted, running up to the car trying to open the back seat.

"I can't! It's locked!" she shouted, continuing to beat on the glass. He quickly looked around the parking lot before running back toward the trail he just came from, leaving her alone.

"Tyson! Tyson!" she yelled, terrified and angry at his fleeing the scene. She grabbed her cell phone from her pocket and tried calling 911, but she couldn't get any reception. She walked around the parking lot, trying to get just one bar on her phone, when suddenly Tyson came barreling through with a large rock in his hands. "What are you going to do?" she asked as a bar suddenly became visible on her phone. She dialed.

"Break the window, duh," he huffed as he crashed the stone through the window and into the backseat. The glass shattered into a thousand pieces.

"Hello? Hello? We're at Greenbelt Park. There's a dead couple in the parking lot! We need help fast!" she screamed into the phone as the dispatcher tried to make Sandy calm down and give her more information. Sandy tried her best as she watched Tyson spring into action, opening the doors and shutting off the ignition. "Are they dead?" she screamed from across the parking lot, afraid that she would lose the signal if she moved an inch.

"I don't know!" he yelled as he smacked the couple on their faces, not sure how to check their pulse or their breathing. "They aren't waking up, and I can't tell if they are breathing or not!"

"Please hurry," she cried into the phone as the dispatcher assured her that someone was on their way and to stay on the phone until they arrived. "I don't know where we are, but it's a parking lot in the Greenbelt Park. We are camping here and went for a late night walk through the trails."

Tyson unbuckled each of the passengers and carefully tried to remove the man from the car, but his teenage strength couldn't handle the dead weight as he got the older man out of the driver's seat.

"Argh!" she screamed, watching the human domino as the older man face-planted onto the concrete like he was belly flopping into a frozen swimming pool. "They're dead. They have to be dead!"

CHAPTER 83

The first police officer arrived at the crime scene ten minutes after Sandy called. He assured the teenagers that they did the right thing by calling in this murder.

"Murder?" Sandy asked as her knees became weak. Tyson quickly caught her before she crashed onto the pavement.

"Just stay calm, dear," Officer Melton said as he quickly started gathering any evidence he could find. "Did either of you see anything?"

"No sir," Tyson answered as Sandy continued to rock back and forth with her knees up to her chest. "We only came up here because we heard the car sputtering."

"So you didn't see two individuals on the trail or leaving the scene?"

"They could have been out there?" Sandy asked squirming, realizing how close she came to being another fatality.

Tyson looked down at Sandy, who continued to sit and shake in a state of shock, before turning his attention to the parking lot. "No, we didn't see anyone."

"Okay. You two just stay here," he commanded. He gestured to the park ranger truck beside the car. "Did you see a park ranger come up here?"

"No. That was already here when we got here," Tyson answered as he sat down on the ground beside

Sandy, rubbing her back to give her some comfort. "It's going to be okay," he whispered in her ear.

"No, it's not. Now my folks are definitely going to know I snuck out," she cried selfishly, not caring about the dead couple a few feet away. "I'm going to get in so much trouble."

Tyson looked at her, shocked that she was more concerned with her punishment than the dead couple or even that a possible murderer was running loose in the woods. It surprised him that he cared about someone other than himself while she focused inwardly. He wondered if this night would be a pinnacle moment, causing a dynamic shift in his personality. After a minute of deep soul searching and reflection, he realized it probably wouldn't.

More police cars started to arrive as they began to block off the crime scene with yellow tape. Soon, the parking lot was full of cops and crime lab technicians trying to get any bit of information they could.

"Did anyone notice this?" an officer shouted as his flashlight illuminated a large red puddle between the two vehicles. He bent down and stuck his gloved hand in the liquid, quickly assuming that it was blood. "Has anyone checked the trunk yet?" he shouted. He popped open the trunk. "Oh, man! We got another one back here!" he leaned in to check the pulse of the bloody beaten man to find that it was useless. "He's dead too. Looks like he was beaten to death."

"Beaten to death?" another officer asked as he walked up to the trunk and shone his flashlight on the deceased park ranger. "Poor guy. They sure did a number on him."

"Hope he didn't suffer long," Officer Melton commented while a camera flashed capturing pictures of the crime scene.

"Hey, I think I found something!" a young female police officer shouted, pulling a hotel room key from the glove compartment. "It looks like they were staying at the Hilton Garden Inn on Walker Drive. Do you think they gave the other room key to a homeless person like the other times?"

"Could be," Officer Melton added, telling two officers to go check out the inn. "And if someone is there, question them until they give you something good."

"Yes, sir," Officer Cobalt and Meyers answered as they sped away in their patrol car.

"Has anyone found anything else?" Officer Melton yelled at the top of his lungs to the crowd of police officers roaming the crime scene almost aimlessly. Everyone stopped to look at Melton, then proceeded to do what they had been doing.

"I just can't believe they were murdered," Tyson said, standing up to peek at the body in the trunk.

"You aren't going to want to see that," one of the officers said stopping him. "Once you get an image like that in your head, it's almost impossible to get it out."

"Why, how bad could it be?"

"Ever see a bloody steak before it's cooked?" the agitated officer asked. Tyson nodded his head yes.

"Picture that as the poor bloke's head. Want to look now?"

CHAPTER 84

A black and white grainy video from a security camera showed a group of men huddled around a table eating lunch. Then a large muscular man stabbed a smaller blond male in the throat. A female voice broke the scratchy silence. "Michael Fiddelstein, twenty-four, died at 11:47 a.m. as he was being held in custody at the Washington D.C. Detention Center. He was awaiting trial for the alleged kidnapping of his seven-year-old niece and attempted fraud. The Washington D.C. Detention Center is currently investigating the death of Mr. Fiddelstein."

The image continued, showing the blond man twitching on the cement floor, clutching his throat as a lake of blood pooled around his body. Three guards tried to break up the commotion. One stooped down to apply pressure to the wounded man's throat. He knelt beside Michael Fiddelstein for a few seconds before shaking his head and standing up with blood on his hands and uniform.

The blurry video panned out, showing the entire cafeteria. A large muscular man with a bandaged right arm sat calmly at a corner table, enjoying the remainder of his lunch as if nothing happened. The footage stopped and froze on him chewing his sandwich as he looked up directly into the camera with a menacing smile.

The picture faded to black as a colorful set of photographs of a small sandwich shop's golden logo,

Henry's, emerged from the blackness. The photographs started to tell a story of a young mother enjoying her turkey and cheddar sandwich. Her three-year-old son munched on a plain hotdog. The mother turned her attention from her son to the latest post on Facebook, an unflattering selfie of her co-worker causing her to smile and quickly post a comment. Her son took another bite of his hotdog when suddenly fear filled his eyes. He grabbed his small throat. The child was kicking and trying to get his mother's attention who was scrolling on her Facebook feed, stopping to read an article on *Five Ways to Keep a Man.*

Finally, the mother saw the tragedy unfolding before her eyes. Her phone dropped out of her hands. As it flipped through the air, the phone showed 12:12 p.m. before crashing onto the floor. She jumped from her chair and screamed for help as tears flooded her eyes. The final picture showed two paramedics trying to resuscitate the young boy as the mother watched helplessly.

The pictures ended as harp music broke the silence. A collection of flickering ivory candles of varying sizes and shapes emerged. "What do you mean you can't find Jerry?" asked a concerned male's voice. "It's 4:30 and his wedding starts at five! Okay, we'll go look at his place. You go look! I don't know where to look," he stammered as the candles slowly started to extinguish themselves. "Have you tried calling his cell?"

A different man's voice came forth as the other decreased in volume, barely audible as the frantic conversation continued. "No! No! No! You can't be doing this to me on my wedding day!" he shouted as another candle went out. "Oh, man, I can't get any reception on my cell!" he continued to shout as he got out of his car, slamming the car door. "How is anyone going to find me out here in the middle of nowhere? I was supposed to be at the church at 4:30, that is all I was supposed to do was be there at 4:30 and here I am walking down…what road am I on? Powder Mill Road, I think. I just wanted to go somewhere and relax for this big day and look at me! No one knows I'm here! No one. I'm coming, Christy! Please forgive me!" he moaned as the last candle died out. The smoke drifted into the darkness as the harp was plucked a final time.

Suddenly, more random photographs: an empty subway car, a Huntington Station sign, an empty parking garage and various empty city roads. Then finally, a few pictures of a park entrance, a map of an unmarked trail path, and an empty darkened parking lot. Suddenly, the silence was filled with the sound of a vehicle's ignition. Then pictures of various items laid on the ground, including a garden hose and heavy-duty duct tape. Two weak coughs were heard before everything stopped.

I woke up with my head damp, so I reached over to my nightstand and found my so-called dream journal. As I turned on the lamp, I found the first blank page and started my new tradition of noting every detail of my dreams that I could remember.

317

After I finished, I reread my analysis and agreed with what I had written. I looked over at my alarm clock that radiated 4:06 a.m. in red lights and lowered my head onto my wet pillow to try to get a couple more hours of sleep before the busy Saturday ahead.

Just as I was about to fall back asleep, I sat up suddenly, wide-eyed. I shook my head in shock. "They're going to kill again!"

CHAPTER 85

Officers Cobalt and Meyers picked up a sleeping man in Mark and Margaret Hudson's room at the Hilton Garden Inn. They proceeded to interrogate him to get any information about the killers. "What is your name, sir?" Officer Cobalt asked as Meyers looked around the hotel room for any possible evidence or information.

"Charlie. Charlie Kitchens," he stumbled his name, petrified and startled as a pair of cops barged into the room he'd enjoyed for one night of comfort and luxury.

"Who gave you this room?" Cobalt continued to question as Charlie watched Meyers rifle through the belongings in the room.

"It was a man and woman," he answered. "They threw the room key card out of the car window and told me to enjoy a free night on them."

"Can you describe what they looked like?"

"I, uh, I didn't get a real good look at them," he replied as he nervously looked around the room. "They were both wearing those masks that you see doctors wear," he said, looking around the room.

"You searching for something?" Cobalt scolded as Charlie quickly returned his attention to the police officer.

"I, um…I…well, can I have a drink? My throat is dry."

"Fine," Cobalt answered, walking into the bathroom to get a cup of water where Meyers was looking for some type of clue. "Find anything of value?"

"Nope."

"Well, look again. They need us to find something," Cobalt stated as he watched the water fill the glass.

"You don't think I know that?" Meyers barked. "Have you gotten anything out of the kid?" he asked snidely, pointing out that they each had something to do.

"Not yet. Okay, Charlie here's your…" Cobalt said as he returned to the room, finding it empty and the door wide open. "Meyers, he's gone!"

"He's what?"

The two young officers fled the room, looking up and down the hall for any sign of Charlie. They noticed that the elevator was heading down, so they took off toward the stairwell where they could hear the running steps of Charlie a few flights below. "Charlie! Freeze! Charlie!" Cobalt shouted, but it didn't do any good as Charlie continued to round the stairs like a marathon runner.

Meyers warned the officers in their patrol cars that their witness, Charlie Kitchens, was heading toward the east exit. "Why do they always think they can outrun us?" Meyers laughed as they headed down the remaining flights of stairs.

They exited the building to find Charlie in the back of a patrol car. "Take him down to the station for questioning, and if he gives you any trouble, cuff him," Cobalt said. He motioned to Charlie to remain calm. "They are going to take you to the station. You are not under arrest. We just have some questions for you, that's all. You are not under arrest. Yet."

"So, did you have a blissful sleep?" one of the police officers asked Charlie as they exited the parking lot.

"A little," he frowned. "But I could have used a few more hours."

CHAPTER 86

After pacing my small apartment for an hour and tripping twice on the kitchen rug, the lagging clock finally struck six o'clock in the morning. I grabbed my phone. "Isaac! Isaac! I know it's early, and I am sorry for waking you, but this is important," I spit out in rambling gibberish, clearly unrecognizable or understandable by his lack of response. "Isaac, this is Solo. I am sorry for waking you, but this is very important," I enunciated, hoping he would wake up and understand me.

"Solo, what's wrong? Is this about Rachel?" he asked, quickly waking at my words.

"Rachel's okay. She's going to be okay," I assured him. I could hear him breathe a sigh of relief as I imagined him poking his head into his daughter's bedroom and seeing her sleeping peacefully beside her guards of stuffed animals. "It's Michael."

"Michael! What about Michael?" he answered confused.

"He's going to be killed in jail today during lunch." I stopped and grabbed a banana from the counter. I waited for Isaac to respond while I peeled the fruit, but he never did. He hung up on me.

I quickly called him back, but it went straight to voicemail. "Isaac, this is important. He's your family." I called him back, but once again it went straight to voicemail. I went through my contacts, finding Amanda's name and called her. I wondered if she ever got her phone back from Tom. That, too, went straight to voicemail. After trying each of their phones a few more times, there was only one option. Breakfast at the Fiddelsteins'. I tossed my half-eaten banana back on the counter, dressed in my wedding photography attire, grabbed all my supplies, and headed out.

After a quick stop at Dunkin Donuts, I was knocking on the Fiddelsteins' front door by a quarter to seven. "Solo, what are you doing?" Isaac stood in the doorway in his royal blue silk pajamas with his monogram embroidered on the cuffs.

"I brought breakfast," I said with a grin, opening the box to show the array of sugary goodness with sprinkles and icing.

"Solo, I do not care about Michael. As of right now, he is already dead to me," he growled, clenching his fist, trying to hold back more of the built-up anger inside.

"He's a messed-up kid that did a really messed-up thing, but even with all of our screw-ups, family are the ones that are supposed to watch each other's backs," I rallied, making the speech I had practiced in the car.

"Well, after your nephew kidnaps your kid and tries to steal all of your money, then you can talk to me about watching each other's back!" he shouted, slamming the door in my face.

"Isaac! Isaac!" I yelled through the door, knowing that he was just on the other side. "I don't know what I would do in your shoes," I said, lowering my voice to a more conversational tone. "I just hope that I would have a friend who would help me see both sides of the coin if that time ever comes."

I bent down to lay the box of donuts and muffins on the ground. I was retrieving one for myself as the door opened. "I was just leaving you breakfast," I grinned, popping the jelly-filled into my mouth and handing him the opened box.

"Solo, thanks for coming and bringing us breakfast. You really shouldn't have, but right now, I really cannot listen to you. Until you have been in my shoes...strike that. I hope you never have to experience what I have been through this week. But if you do, then you can come and talk to me about family and forgiveness."

"Well, your pair of shoes probably cost my monthly rent, but as a matter of fact, I do know a thing or two about this," I said, frowning and wiping the sugar off my face.

CHAPTER 87

"How's your shoulder feeling this morning?" Cooper asked as he walked with Young down the shabby hall in the police station. The walls reeked of a 1970s paint job that needed to be freshened up a bit, but no one cared about the décor when budgets were limited and bulletproof vests could actually save lives.

"Back off," Young remarked giving Cooper a grimacing gaze of pent-up rage, even showing a few of his bleached teeth in a tactic he probably learned from the neighbor's dog.

"I was just asking," Cooper laughed as they approached the examination room.

"Oh, how are you and your wife doing this morning? Make up last night?"

"Stuff it," Cooper hammered back as Young's icy expression faded to an evil smile. Both detectives entered the interrogation room.

"Hello, Charlie. I'm Detective Young and this is Officer Cooper. Do you need anything before we start asking you some questions?" Young asked politely as they took their seats on the opposite side of the metal table from the nervous-looking young man in a pair of flannel pajamas two sizes too large.

"Can I have some breakfast? I'm hungry."

"Sure," Cooper answered. "What would you like?"

"Can I have some biscuits and gravy?" he asked timidly as he twiddled his fingers.

"Sure thing," Cooper said and smiled as he looked over at the mirror.

"And some sausage," Charlie quickly added.

"Sausage too," Young spoke up before Cooper could, trying to play the good guy act as well.

"And get him some eggs and coffee while you are at it," Cooper said grinning at Young and then nodding to Charlie encouragingly. "So, now that we have that taken care of, tell us how you got the room at the inn last night."

Charlie continued to play with his fingers as he began to speak uncomfortably. "I was walking around Greenbelt Station, heading home for the night. Someone pulled up next to me and told me that it looked like I needed a nice warm room for the night and handed me the room key card with some money."

"You were heading home?" Young remarked, shocked. "Where do you live?"

"I live in a small apartment in Franklin Park on Springhill Drive."

"So you're not homeless?" Young prodded insensitively. Cooper noticed the derogatory tone.

"What Detective Young means is that most of the time when this couple gives a free night in a local hotel, they usually give it to someone who doesn't have a place to stay," he said, trying to smooth things over.

"Oh, no. I was getting off work and heading home when they stopped me," he commented. "I was shocked when they offered me some money and a nice place to stay. I mean, I have never stayed in a nice hotel before. And when I saw that it was a Hilton, I thought, why not? I've worked hard most of my life. I deserve a nice place to stay. Even if it was just for one night," he said smiling. Then a frown broke through the warmth. "Now I wish I'd just ignored them and gone back to my rundown apartment."

"Charlie, it's okay. You are doing fine," Cooper said, smiling. Young crossed his arms disapprovingly. "Can you tell us anything about the couple? What did they look like? Did you notice anything strange? Did they have an accent or say anything that could be of help?"

Charlie looked over at Young, who appeared as though he wanted to be anywhere but there. "I'm sorry. I don't know of anything. I couldn't see their faces because they had those surgical masks on. He was bald and had sunglasses on, which I thought was strange since it was nighttime. But I don't know much else."

Cooper nudged Young in his ribs, causing him to jerk in pain. "Thank you, Charlie, for your information. They should be bringing your breakfast any minute now."

As Young started to stand up, Cooper pulled out three grainy pictures from his binder on the table. "Can I show you some photographs and you tell me if these are the people that you saw?" He slid them over so Charlie could get a better look.

Charlie stared intently at the three pictures, looking closely and then leaning back to get a different view of the couple. "Maybe. I'm not sure. It looks similar to the people I saw, but I can't be certain."

"Thank you, Charlie," Cooper said taking the pictures. "Do you recall them saying anything as they drove away?"

Charlie closed his eyes and thought back in his memory. A smiled stretched across his face. He opened his eyes with a new fire in them. "She called him brother."

"Brother?" Cooper asked, quickly scribbling that down in his notes. He looked up, hoping that something else was going to come out. "Anything else?"

"He said something about camping, but I don't know what he meant," he responded looking downcast as his breakfast plate arrived.

"Here you go, champ," Young said, throwing it on the table as he got up to stretch. "Eat up and we'll be back in a few minutes," he said exiting the room.

"You are doing really good, Charlie. I will be right back," Cooper said following Young out the door. "What is your problem?"

"Problem?" Young asked, cocking his head in disbelief.

"Yes. You have a problem with me. You have a problem with Charlie. You seem to have a problem with everything," Cooper shot back sharply. He moved toward Young who was standing with a grizzly-bear stance. "I don't care what you think about me, but we have a witness who appears sober and coherent and was talking to the perps just a few hours ago! If we can get even just an ounce of information out of him, that is an ounce more than we had before! So, if you don't want to go back in there with me, you can just go wherever you want."

Cooper went back into the room as Charlie inhaled his breakfast, leaving only a few crumbs and drops of gravy on his plate. "Not bad food we have here, right?"

"Pretty tasty," Charlie agreed, wiping his face with his napkin and sitting like a completely changed individual. His fidgeting had calmed down and he was looking bright eyed and in control. "I think I have a little bit more information for you."

Cooper smiled and pulled out his tablet. "I'm ready when you are."

"As I was eating, I remembered a few more things," Charlie said as he once again started to tell his account of the evening.

CHAPTER 88

"I'm sorry to hear that," Isaac said, pouring a second cup of French vanilla coffee in each of our cups. I had just told him the story of Chelsea's death.

"Thank you. So you see, I have gone through something horrible too. DeShawn, the kid who shot my wife, may not have been a relative, but I had a decision to make on forgiveness. And sadly, looking back, I didn't make the right decision," I concluded, as I inhaled the sweet aroma loaded with sugar and creamer.

As we sat in the breakfast nook, Isaac stared at me with some confusion as the sun's rays started to streak through the window curtains, stretching past their dog's water dish on the floor. "What do you mean you didn't make the right decision? Who says which decision is the right one?"

"Well, each person decides that," I answered grabbing a blueberry donut from the shrinking dozen. "And I now see that I didn't do the right thing."

Isaac looked bewildered as he sipped his coffee. "You can do the right thing now if it weighs on you so heavily."

Licking the sugar off my fingers, I laid the donut on my saucer. "Actually, I can't."

"Why not?" he asked, shaking his head in disagreement. "It's not too late."

"Actually, it is," I said, stopping to take a sip and wash down the donut with the aftertaste of regret. "I wanted that kid to get what he deserved. I went to court every day. I pleaded for the jury to give him the harshest sentence. I begged them to not give him any leniency. I remember looking over at him as he stared down into his lap with his public defender by his side. I wanted to spit at him for not even looking at me when I spoke about him. He'd shot my wife in cold blood, and he was just a few feet from me sitting there without a care in the world. I wanted to snap his little neck like it was a wishbone at Thanksgiving.

"Well, he was sentenced to fifteen years, which I didn't think was long enough. I kept hoarding this grudge. I was even tempted to get a tattoo on my forearm as a way to always remember what he did. A few months passed and I heard that he was killed in prison. Apparently, one of the other gangs in the joint killed him."

"Vengeance," Isaac smiled casually. "He got what he deserved."

"That's how I felt. I was like, yes, my prayers have been answered. That gang banger got what he deserved. He got a knife to the gut and all was well in the world. But..." I continued as his eyes widened with that conjunction.

"But what?"

"But my anger never let up," I answered sincerely. "I tried therapy. I tried medication. I tried keeping busy. You would not believe how many hours I put in volunteering for various organizations. I was doing everything I could to not have a moment of silent solitude, because whenever I was alone, that tattooed ulcer in my stomach reminded me that even though he was dead, I was still alone."

"But you seem better now," Isaac remarked confidently. He crossed his arms as if that were his closing remark in the trial of disagreement.

"Oh, I am much better now. But it wasn't because of all of those things," I replied, crossing my arms as well. "The only reason I am somewhat better is because I forgave him. I never got to tell him that, but once I forgave him, that nagging weight of anger and vindication just went away."

"So, see, if I want to forgive him in ten years, I can. I can be just like you," he smiled as if finding the loophole on his own.

"But you didn't let me finish. I forgave him for killing Chelsea, but I still live with the regret of not letting him know that I forgave him."

"Solo, you've got to let that go," he consoled. "That hoodlum probably wouldn't have cared if you forgave him or not. He would probably do it again if given the chance."

"Maybe, but it hit me. If my faith lies in Christ forgiving me of my sins, then how can I not forgive someone when they have wronged me? How can I ask for forgiveness from God when He sees all the messed up things I have done in my life, yet not forgive a guy who did one really bad thing to me. It didn't balance."

"Solo, I'm Jewish. I'm glad that you have your faith in something, but that isn't my faith," he answered considerately. "Hear of an eye for an eye? That's my motto."

"I know. I know. But all I mean is that if your nephew dies today, you are no better than DeShawn, because you are aware of his possible death. You may not be the one to kill him, but you are allowing him to be killed."

He shook his head in disgust. "Why did you have to call me and tell me that this was going to happen, Solo? Why?"

"Because…Because I thought you should know." I got up from the table and finished my coffee after I glanced at my watch and realized it was a quarter till eight. "I have somewhere I have to be. Give Rachel and Amanda the remaining donuts."

Isaac got up without saying a word and followed me to the door. The sun was fully risen, signally the start of a brand new day.

"What happened yesterday is over, Isaac. I'm not saying you have to have a family portrait with Michael. All I'm saying is I don't want you to have any regrets. Whatever you choose, you have three hours to decide. It's your decision."

CHAPTER 89

After two and a half hours of asking the happy couple and their family and friends to say 'smile' and 'cheese', I was finally done with my wedding photography job. After a decade of doing these joyful ceremonies, one would think that I'd become calloused or despondent from the excitement and glee of the exchange of vows, but I wasn't. One can't help but smile when they are at a wedding, unless they are the stressed out members of the wedding party, counting down the moments until the wedded bliss comes to culmination.

As I walked through the parking lot of the quaint chapel, I had an added bounce in my step. I turned around and saw the black limousine with "Just Married" written with neon paint on the windows with the stereotypical tin cans and shoes trailing. I couldn't help but laugh. I took out the check that they paid me and did my ceremonial kiss on the face of it, knowing that I would make rent for at least another month.

I looked down at my blinking Timex telling me that my lunch date with Jenny was in about an hour. There was plenty of time to get to Henry's as traffic at 11:14 a.m. was typical, slightly gridlocked, but nothing that a little time couldn't handle. As I watched the minutes pass, I couldn't help but think about Michael and Isaac Fiddelstein. I couldn't get them out of my mind. I knew I said I was going to leave it to him to make the decision, but in my gut, I couldn't let a man die if there was something I could do to stop it.

When I came to the next stop light, I quickly found the telephone number for the police station that was holding Michael. "Hello, I'm not sure who I need to talk to, but I believe one of your inmates is in some immediate danger and needs to be put in solitary or whatever you call it when you separate them from the other prisoners."

"What is the inmate's name?" the woman on the other end of the line asked.

"Michael Fiddelstein," I said slowly, making sure to sound out every syllable.

"One minute, please." I heard her fingers typing away on a keyboard. My red light turned green, and I slowly proceeded through the intersection.

"Did you say Michael Fiddelstein? F-I-D-D-E-L-S-T-E-I-N?"

"Yes. Yes, that's him. He needs to be separated from one of his, well, I guess you could say partners in crime. I received word that someone was going to kill him today during lunch."

"Excuse me sir, but can you tell me your name?" she asked with an unconvinced tone in her voice.

"Robert Jones," I lied.

"Okay, Mr. Jones. I see that Michael Fiddelstein has already been removed from the general population earlier this morning."

"Oh, really?" I asked, shocked as my heart flipped with enthusiasm. "Is that easy to do?"

"Not usually, but there was a note in the system that this was a special situation," she commented coldly. "Is there anything else I can do for you?"

"No. That was all. Thank you." I threw my phone in the passenger's seat. The smile on my face grew three sizes at the thought of Isaac, much like the Grinch's heart did on Christmas Day. I wanted to call Isaac and give him an encouraging word, but at the same time, I didn't want him to know that I'd gone behind his back and called the jail. Some things were best left unsaid. He knew that he made the right decision. It may take time to forgive his nephew, but at least he would have the chance to try to reconcile when that time comes.

CHAPTER 90

The warm atmosphere and friendly staff at Henry's was what made it so delectable. The aging Henry Upton ran the old-time golden cash register. It rang up every order with plastic numbers springing up and the cha-ching sound of the cash drawer opening. His barbell mustache was a staple, just like D.C.'s cherry blossoms in the spring.

Gloria, his lovely wife of fifty-six years, greeted the customers with an enthusiastic smile, and for her favorite and frequent patrons, a hug. She could make the dullest lunchtime experience one that would beckon a customer to return later in the afternoon for a cup of coffee. Of course, the coffee would be accompanied by their classic homemade cherry cobbler, a recipe that had been handed down from Martha Washington herself, if the folklore of George and the infamous cherry tree was correct.

The rest of the staff were his children and grandchildren. Occasionally, his great-grand daughter would do a tap routine on the bar counter after she got home from school and before she headed in the back to complete her homework. For the most part, this type of establishment was a thing of the past. But not Henry's.

I met Jenny a few minutes before noon, still decked out in my all-black business attire. She was stunning in her casual Saturday skinny blue jeans and orange cashmere sweater. "Busy morning?" she asked putting away her phone as we headed into Henry's.

"Just a normal morning wedding. I prefer the morning weddings to the afternoon and evening ones because for some reason they tend to go by much faster." I grinned as I held the door open for her to enter and caught a whiff of her honeysuckle aroma.

"I was kind of surprised when you picked Henry's," she said, smiling as she lovingly hugged Gloria like she was her grandmother.

"And who might this be?" Gloria asked with a mischievous grin like a nosy beloved grandmother.

"Gloria, this is Solomon. Solomon, this is Gloria," she said as I stuck out my hand to shake hers. She shook her head no and spread her arms wide for a family style hug.

"No friend of Jenny's is going to get such a formal handshake," she said, laughing and patting my back like my mom used to do.

"Very nice meeting you, Gloria," I smiled, stepping back to let Jenny take the spotlight.

"How's Abigail doing?" Jenny asked sweetly, fixing Gloria's hair after the sudden gust of wind blew through the opened door.

"Oh, thank you! Abby is doing good, very good. Her studies are improving. Thank you again for tutoring her. I know she really appreciates it," Gloria commented as she noticed the next patron. "I'm sorry, one moment. Greetings," she said, smiling at the couple behind us.

"So, you're an attorney. You tutor. You're loved by everyone, apparently. What are you not good at?" I laughed as we walked over to a window seat. I looked around the room for the young mother and child and spotted them three tables away. The boy sipped his milk, waiting for his hotdog to be delivered.

"Well, I'm not that crafty," she remarked casually passing me a menu that was already on the table.

"I don't believe that," I replied in shock. "How hard can scrapbooking and sewing be?"

She glanced up from her menu with a devious smile, "Much harder than you think."

I looked down at my watch, which showed 12:07 p.m. I knew that the choking hazard hotdog was going to be in front of the child soon. I was bouncing my attention between Jenny and the child. "Only I can make a kindergartener's art project look like a Rembrandt next to my failed attempts."

"Come on, I don't believe that," I said, laughing as I watched the waiter bring a salad and a hotdog to the unsuspecting table. The mother didn't even look up to notice that anything was laid in front of her, but the young boy quickly reached for the hotdog.

Jumping up, I quickly walked over to the table. I grabbed the hotdog from the boy's hands as his mother stared at me cautiously. "I'm sorry, but hotdogs are very dangerous for young kids. Do you mind if I cut this into pieces for him? I promise I'm not a weirdo. Just trying to help."

She nodded for me to go ahead as she poured her salad dressing. I tried to chitchat with the young boy while slicing his hotdog meat into small, cubed pieces and sprinkling it back on his bun. "Want any ketchup or mustard, sir?" I asked like a maitre d'. He nodded enthusiastically, and I gave him a few lines of each. "Enjoy," I said with a smile. As I walked away, I heard the mother gasp, causing my heart to plummet.

"What's wrong?" I asked, quickly turning back to see her eyes looking on the ground.

"I just dropped my phone like a klutz," she said, laughing and bending down to pick it up. She quickly checked to see if the screen had any damage.

"Sorry about that," I apologized to Jenny as I returned to my seat. "Kids and food just scare the be-Jesus out of me."

"Me too," she said with a grin as she glanced down at the menu that she probably had memorized.

"Anyway, back to you," I started as my heart gave way to a little flurry of confusion when two emergency medical technicians strode through the doors, heading towards the young boy and his mother. What in the world? I thought, looking over at the boy chewing his minced hotdog while the mother continued to update her Instagram feed. I watched each of their movements as if watching a play in slow motion. The two EMTs stomped toward the child.

"Solomon, Solomon," Jenny said, snapping her fingers inches from my face. "What do you want to drink?" she asked as our waitress stood with a quizzical expression on her face.

"Oh, sorry. Water please," I answered trying to be cordial toward Jenny while watching the oncoming EMTs from the corner of my eyes.

"Just quit looking," she said, smiling as she touched my hand on the table, causing me to redirect my vision into her eyes instead. "That is what I always do," she commented as I became entranced by her intoxicating warmth. My tense body began to relax.

We continued our date at Henry's with good laughs, good food, and a very, very good time, while the EMTs ate their sandwiches just one table away.

CHAPTER 91

"Hey Veronica, are you and Winston better today?" Jenny asked over the phone as she parted from her date and headed to spend the afternoon running a few errands.

"I wouldn't say better," Veronica croaked angrily, flipping through a *Vogue* magazine on her bed, learning of the upcoming winter fashions to hit the United States from Europe.

"What happened?" Jenny asked considerately, stopping at the crosswalk of L and Fourteenth Street.

"He was so angry last night that he wouldn't even sleep in my bed. He slept on the couch," Veronica yelled, throwing the magazine on the floor beside her. "I mean, if anyone should be angry, it's me! He was the one who stood me up at dinner Thursday night, and then again last night with my family. I should have kicked him to the couch instead of him going there himself."

"Well, did he have a good reason for not meeting for dinner last night?" Jenny asked carefully, knowing that she was walking on a thinner line than the crosswalk.

"That stupid case he is working on. The one I told you about," she said with a groan as she wiggled around on her bed to fluff one of the many pillows propped at the headboard. "He's acting like he is the only cop in the world trying to catch these killers."

"Veronica, it's important to him. Just like when you are working on an important case. Nothing else matters except getting it done. That's probably what he's thinking of right now," she stated reasonably, knowing that rational thinking wasn't what Veronica wanted to hear.

"So you're siding with him then?" Veronica huffed, rolling her eyes in annoyance that no one was siding with her. "My father mentioned that last night too."

"Well, if your father wasn't upset that he missed the dinner party, I wouldn't give Winston such a hard time," she said. Veronica didn't respond. "Hello, are you still there?" Jenny asked.

"I'm here," she answered coldly. "I just don't like being second."

"Well, honey, coming from a friend, I'm sorry to tell you, but Winston is always second when it comes to you," Jenny stated, finally getting the courage to say what she had been thinking for years, as if a light switch of bravery had just been turned on.

"Jenny, how, how can you say that? I would do anything, and I mean anything, for Winston," Veronica stammered defensively, rising from her mountain of pillows and readjusting her position to sit cross-legged.

"You know that I have never said anything like this to you before. So, you know that it's not my intention to hurt you. I'm just telling you what I've seen," Jenny continued, strolling past a pet store. She stopped by the window to see some adorable golden retriever puppies chasing one another.

343

"As much as it hurts me to say it, you're right," Veronica breathed out in surrender. "I don't like this feeling."

"No one does, honey, No one does," Jenny responded as she continued to watch the wagging skinny tails and large brown eyes look into hers. Her heart melted like an ice cream cone in July. "So, tell Winston you're sorry."

"He's working again today. The entire force is doing all they can to catch these killers," she stated, falling backwards into her bed of pillows.

"So, do they know anything new? Should I be scared?"

CHAPTER 92

The date with Jenny went better than I could have hoped. There weren't any awkward silences; no clichéd jokes or stories; not even any 'emergency' phone calls for either of us to take in case the date was spiraling down in flames. I was starting to picture myself possibly wanting to see more of her. We left Henry's and decided that we each wanted to do this again soon. She headed north, and I tried to recall which parking garage I'd used.

As I walked toward the garage I assumed was the correct one, I called the police. "Yes, I have some information on the Carbon Monoxide Killers," I said, standing outside the garage as a few pedestrians passed by.

"Homicide. Detective Young here."

"Detective Young, I know where the Carbon Monoxide Killers are going to kill tonight. Huntington Station," I said calmly, staring up at the blue sky with only a few clouds passing overhead.

"Oh, really," the detective remarked snidely. "And do you have any other bit of information?"

I was confused. Didn't the police want tips from the public? "Yes, they are going to dispose of the body in a park that has some hiking trails in it."

"Oh, like Greenbelt Park?" he asked agitatedly.

"Well, yeah, similar I guess, but I am not sure which one, but I do know that they are going to pick someone up at Huntington Station tonight," I said calmly, hoping that Detective Young's unappreciative tone would quickly change to thankfulness.

"Sir, we get calls like this all day long. Yes, there is a reward for helping us catch these criminals, but making up information to get the reward, well, it doesn't work like that!"

"I don't," I started to say as I heard a dial tone. He had hung up on me. "That little punk!" I fumed as I flipped him the middle finger through the phone. I knew it wouldn't solve anything, but it felt good. I waited five minutes before I dialed again hoping to get someone else.

"I have some information on a murder," I spoke in a disguised voice. The same dispatcher picked up before she connected me to homicide.

"Detective Young," the same annoyed voice answered. I immediately ended my call with a few choice words that would have made my mother blush.

As I walked through the garage to my car, I considered calling Wint and giving him the information. But as the saying went, it's almost impossible to be a prophet in your hometown. Your friends will laugh and think you've gone crazy. They know your past and the lies that you have told in your childhood and would never believe that suddenly something as farfetched as this could happen. Just as Elizabeth had said before, *Keep this little bit of information locked away to only yourself.*

If Detective Young wouldn't help, the only other person I knew I could talk to was the very person who would tell me to mind my own business.

"Elizabeth, I need to talk to you."

CHAPTER 93

Cooper joined Captain Johnson at Dr. Santiago's medical examination room to go over the details of the latest victims.

"Tell me, Doc," Captain Johnson said to his friend and colleague as they looked around at the tables of bodies. "Are Mark and Margaret Hudson more of the Carbon Monoxide Killers' victims, or do we have a copycat?"

"All the evidence I see is that these two individuals were killed in the same fashion as the others. The same form of chloroform; no other wounds or signs of an attack or struggle; just like the other victims." Dr. Santiago stopped as he went over to the body of Mitchell Ebley, the park ranger who had been beaten to death. "Now this is something different," he commented, lowering the sheet from the decedent's head and exposing the gruesome execution.

"That is very different from the other victims," Cooper expressed in shock. It took all he had not to throw up on Johnson's shoes.

"This does not fit the murders of the other victims, but it appears that Mitchell Ebley probably came upon the Hudsons and was viciously attacked. Or..." he stopped in contemplation.

"Or what?" Johnson asked.

"Or you could have something worse. You could have a couple of killers that are getting bored and trying something new. Or you could have a new accomplice that doesn't follow the rules established during the previous kills."

"I never thought of a new accomplice. It would fit because they used a new setting for getting their targets last night," Johnson said in dismay. He saw the killers' profile flip upside down or even break up into a thousand-piece puzzle.

"Is there any DNA on Mr. Ebley?" Cooper asked, stepping closer to the bloody mass that used to be a solid and uncrushed head.

"Only his," Dr. Santiago replied sadly. "I did find a few strands of hair, but it was artificial from a wig of some type. There were no fingerprints; no other sweat or blood from anyone else that I have found. Once again, these people have carefully planned their kills down to the most minuscule detail. I don't know what else I can tell you."

"Thank you, doc," Johnson concluded as he and Cooper exited Dr. Santiago's office with the victims' medical examination files. "This keeps getting worse, Cooper. Go back to Young and look over the video footage from last night. These killers can't keep outsmarting us. We have to find their Achilles' heel, and we have to find it fast."

Cooper got back to the station to find Young still on desk duty, likely as punishment for his fiasco from the previous night. "So, have you found anything?"

"Nope. Nothing new," Young groaned as he twirled around in his swiveled chair. Cooper grabbed a seat next to his to look over the subway station video footage.

"There's got to be something here."

CHAPTER 94

"You did what?" Elizabeth asked, shocked at my morning rescues. "If I was that kid's mother, I would have smacked you for barging in."

"I saved the kid's life for heaven's sake!" I countered with disbelieving laughter.

"True, but how do you know if someone else wasn't going to save him?"

"They didn't in my dream," I answered coolly, trekking north across Washington D.C. "Okay, moving on," I sidestepped the conversation to focus on the main reason for my call. "What do you think of me telling Wint?"

"Tell Wint?" she asked, scoffing at the notion. I was unsure if it was from my question or her attitude from my previous events of the day.

"Those psychos are going to kill again tonight, and the cops won't listen to me."

"Solo, I love, well, maybe not love, but I respect the idea of you trying to change the outcome of the dreams. But have you ever considered that you are playing God?" she asked solemnly. "You are changing the events of the future for what you believe are the best results. What if you're wrong?"

"How is letting that little boy die the best result?" I spit out with venomous rage.

"Who called whom, Solo?" she fired back. "I'm not the one who called you to catch up on your heroic tales! You called me for my opinion, did you not?"

"But..." I tried to interject, but her speech wasn't finished.

"But what? Why are you getting so bent out of shape when I pose a question? I'm not saying that you are wrong. I don't know what is right or what is wrong. All I'm doing is playing a little devil's advocate," she said, finally stopping her tirade with a more friendly manner.

"You are your sister's sister."

"Bite your tongue, you little--" she said before I interrupted.

"Now. Now. Don't say anything you may regret later."

"Twerp!" she laughed. "I'll keep it G-rated for your virgin ears."

I listened to Elizabeth state her case about merely watching from a safe distance and not getting caught up with the idea of saving everyone as the lovely, fluffy clouds invaded my attention. "Not everyone can be saved, and to be honest, not everyone needs to be."

"Ouch! Survival of the fittest? Has Jeremiah converted you to his way of thinking?"

"Newsflash, darling, your churchy faith of loving one another ended in the fifties."

"Why does church have such a stigma?"

"Because it's run by people," she stated bluntly and honestly. "Whenever there is something great out there, we dive all in and junk it up with our baggage and drama. Look at the rainforest, deserts, arctic tundra. This is really nice, but you know what would make it better? A five-star resort. Just us running toward it with a bulldozer and dollar signs in our eyes."

"I could see you being one of the investors in one of those resorts. Heck, I could see you driving the bulldozer. How did we get onto the rainforests?" I asked, laughing as I turned off the highway and started cruising down a country back road aligned with trees and woodland creatures.

"I don't remember, but I've got to get off. I have to get ready for tonight."

"Big plans?" I asked as I watched a deer stroll across the road and dart into a wooded area.

"Going out with Jeremiah."

"Have fun. And Elizabeth," I stopped, not sure of what I wanted to say. "Thanks for listening."

"Not that it's going to do any good. I know you're still going to do what you want to do."

"Now, that was rude."

"I am Veronica's sister. What else would you expect?" she said with a chuckle, ending the call.

It had been a long week with many highs and many lows. Looking back, I wouldn't have changed anything. A family was enjoying a Saturday afternoon together with their finances intact. A young boy who enjoyed his hotdog could become a criminal or he could be the next great biochemist. Life was all about decisions. Sometimes we made right ones and other times the wrong ones, but life didn't end with the wrong decisions. It only caused another outcome. We could either move on from bad choices without a second glance or try to fix them.

I was a fixer.

CHAPTER 95

She sat in Sunny's Salon, mind-numbingly flipping through the latest edition of *People* magazine, trying to pass the time as the hairdresser cut her gorgeous curls that she'd sported since she was little.

"Are you sure about this, girl?" the spiky-haired stylist asked as she combed her fingers through the velvety brunette locks. "Once you cut it, there is no going back."

"I'm sure," she said glancing up exasperatedly with a look that would have caused a normal person to take a step back. But not Sunny. She was a pro with attitude. That was how she made a name for herself.

"Some people would hesitate or cringe at losing this beautiful head of hair," Sunny said as the metal blades swooshed musically with each cut. A foot of curls fell to the ground like fragile leaves.

"I'm not most people," she stated coolly, going back to her article about George Clooney. She eyed the room, listening to the different conversations among the various ladies from the twenty-year-old ranting about being stood up on her blind date the previous night to the retired grandmas planning their nightly canasta game. Her ears perked up like a huntsman hearing the crush of autumn leaves by a pair of hooves.

"What's going on with this city?" a woman asked. She glanced up from her magazine to look into the mirror to see who posed this interesting question. The questioner was a fifty-year-old blonde, resembling Emma Thompson. She was speaking to another woman, also in her mid-fifties who hadn't aged quite as well with her graying locks.

"I know. Makes me a little nervous to walk the streets at night anymore," she commented as the Emma Thompson look-alike nodded in agreement.

"Well, I don't think you need to worry about that. It seems like they are poaching the subways for their victims. Can you see us riding the subways?"

"Oh, my," the older woman chuckled. "I haven't ridden a subway in quite some time. Herbert would frown if I ever dared to mention us taking a ride on that again. I can see him saying, 'Now Rosie, I didn't become senator so you can ride that blasted subway like a commoner.'"

"So romantic," the blonde giggled feverishly. "Does he really talk like that?"

"Only when a camera or a reporter is around."

"What do you think?" Sunny asked as she spun her customer in all directions to see all sides of her creation. "I think the pixie cut works on you."

She reached back feeling the shortness of her hair recalling how just moments earlier it had draped over her shoulders and down her back. "Can you cut a little more off?"

"More?"

"Yes, I need a little more off," she said pursing her lips as she reached for a different magazine. She didn't feel like reading *Women's Home Journal*, so she closed her eyes and envisioned what the night was going to behold. She didn't know how she was going to look with the bald cap on, or how her brother was going to respond to this change in roles. And she didn't care. They needed to spice up their routine a little more. "Honey, you can put the scissors down. Use the trimmer."

"Are you sure?" Sunny asked, but by the expression on her customer's face, she didn't need an answer.

She closed her eyes and listened to the humming sound. It was a sweet, hypnotic rhythm that caused her to drift away on a lake of villainess relaxation. A childish smile emerged as she allowed her mind to replay her murderous week.

"How's it look now?" Sunny asked revealing a buzzed cut.

Here eyes opened with a hint of playfulness. "Yes. Oh, yes. This will work very nicely." Reaching down to her purse to get cash to pay for her new hairdo, she smiled wickedly at the sight of the blood-stained hammer. She paid Sunny, giving her a nice tip for a job well done.

As she walked through the salon, she thought about how those women had no clue who they were sitting next to. She stopped by the two ladies on whom she was eavesdropping and secretly wished that Rosie could get her blasted husband to ride the subway tonight. It would have been the ride of their lives, or at least the last one. "You need to be careful, ladies. You never know who the crazies are these days."

CHAPTER 96

The squad room was quiet as Cooper replayed the video footage compiled by the IT department. The video showed the Greenbelt Station and a part of the journey to the Greenbelt Park before the killers had started traveling roads with limited or no surveillance cameras.

"See anything?" Johnson asked, standing behind Cooper while they both looked at Young's computer.

"Well, it's more what I'm not seeing."

"What is that?"

"We picked up Charlie Kitchens this morning at the Hilton. He said that the car stopped and gave him the room key."

"Yeah, so?" Johnson inquired, not seeing the correlation.

Cooper rewound the footage of when the killers were leaving the Greenbelt Station parking lot, slowing down at the place where the car stopped beside a pedestrian. "What's that?"

"Yeah, they stopped and handed Charlie Kitchens something. But look how he is walking," Cooper pointed as he noticed a slight hobble as he came close to the vehicle.

"Is he limping?" Johnson asked, leaning closer to the computer screen. "Replay that again and try to zoom in closer."

Cooper clicked around on the keyboard until he zoomed in as close as he could without the image getting too blurry to see. "Dear lord," Cooper said as he replayed the video. He watched the vehicle pull away as the man limped down the street to an empty bench to rest his feet. "What if?" he started to say, looking up at Johnson whose thoughts were in unison with his.

"Quick! Pull up the data on Charlie Kitchens. See if he's in the system."

Cooper quickly started typing, searching for Charlie Kitchens while Young waltzed back into the room, staring at his phone. "You're not going to believe what Dakota did today," he said, stopping when he saw Johnson standing by his desk. He quickly shut down his Instagram on his phone.

"I don't care," Johnson remarked. "Get me Charlie Kitchens' contact information that you had him fill out this morning. We need to check on that guy."

The computer was processing Cooper's request as Young searched through the paperwork on his desk for the sheet containing Charlie's personal information. "Sir, I found nine Charlie Kitchens in our database, but the closest ones to his age were fifteen and thirty-two."

"Young! Find that form yet?"

"Got it!" he exclaimed, uncovering the paper that Charlie had filled out earlier that morning with all his information.

"Call him!" Johnson ordered as Young quickly dialed.

"Yes, this is Detective Young. Is Charlie Kitchens available? Oh, it is? I'm sorry." He hung up, looking closely at the phone number. "They said they don't know a Charlie Kitchens."

"Try it again," Johnson demanded as he paced around the small linoleum tiled area.

"Hello, this is Detective Young," he stopped and once again apologized for the wrong number. "Cooper, look at this. You try it. Maybe I'm seeing a number wrong."

Cooper looked down at the neatly written numbers, almost as legible as a typewriter's font. He dialed the number and listened to the phone ringing. An elderly woman picked up.

"Hello?"

"Good afternoon. This is Officer Cooper. Is Charlie Kitchens available?"

"Son, I told the other cop twice that I don't know of any Charlie."

"I am so sorry for bothering you. Have a good…" he started to say, then stopped. "Can I ask you a few questions before I let you go? It's really important."

"Sure. I'm not doing anything."

"Do you know of any skinny, nice looking, mid-twenty-year-olds with brownish or black hair?"

"Dear, I see all kinds of people in my building."

"Where do you live?"

"Franklin Park Apartments," she answered.

"On Springhill Drive?"

"Yes."

"Thank you for your help, ma'am. You have a good evening."

"You too. I hope you find who you are looking for," she said.

"Me too," Cooper said, sighing as he hung up. "Young, get a facial recognition of Charlie Kitchens. I'm calling this in. Someone needs to get over to Franklin Park Apartments now!"

CHAPTER 97

"Do you, Gerald, take this woman, Christina, to be your lawfully wedded wife? To have and to hold; in sickness and in heath; in good times and bad; for richer or poorer; keeping yourself solely unto her for as long as you both shall live?" the minister asked as the harpist gently played in the background. The music filled the whole church with its heavenly sounds that commingled with the faint aroma of roses and vanilla.

"I do," Gerald answered warmly, squeezing his bride's hands in front of all their friends and family, and me.

"Do you, Christina, take this man, Gerald, to be your lawfully wedded husband? To have and to hold; in sickness and in heath; in good times and bad; for richer or poorer; keeping yourself solely unto him for as long as you both shall live?"

"I do," Christina said, softly crying as Gerald's steady hand reached over to tenderly wipe the tear away.

I sat in the back of the church on a hard wooden pew that had been handcrafted more than a century earlier. I sat away from the friends and family section. The ceremony was filled with love, but I was more mesmerized by the stained-glass windows and crystal chandeliers than I was with the stereotypical vows and Pachelbel's *Canon in D Major*. Old churches had so much charm and an air of reverence that seemed to get displaced in the hustle and bustle of the Facebook age.

The ceremony ended with a tasteful kiss between the new husband and wife as the wedding party marched down the aisle. Gerald gave me a big thumbs-up as he passed by, quickly turning to whisper something in his new wife's ear. Maybe it was a heartfelt "I love you," but I presumed it was a quick retelling of the afternoon's events and how I miraculously found him walking the lonely road. Without me, the wedding would not have happened.

"Solo, I didn't know you knew Jerry and Christy," Jeremiah said as he walked down the aisle with Elizabeth on his arm. The two made a strikingly handsome couple. He was decked out in a formal tuxedo and flamboyant teal and polka dot bowtie. She wore a stunning strapless evening gown that matched his tie.

"Funny story, actually," I said as I looked over at Elizabeth who shook her head in amusement.

"Well, you can tell us all about it during the reception," Jeremiah commented as he grabbed my arm to join their dinner party. "You're staying, aren't you?"

"I believe I am," I said, smiling as we headed outside to the large white party tents in the church yard. Strings of white Christmas lights hung around the ceilings, and each table was covered with the finest china and silver. There were large centerpieces of roses and baby's breath encircling towering candles in various heights. After a few minutes inside, I forgot this was a makeshift reception hall.

"So, why were you driving all the way over there?" Jeremiah asked, as he and Elizabeth sipped their champagne.

"Just an afternoon drive," I answered with a clever wink to Elizabeth. "I guess it was fortunate for Jerry that I was driving by. He could have missed his wedding."

"And good thing that you did because Christy would have been devastated," Jeremiah remarked. "She is a tad bit spoiled. She's my dear cousin, but rotten to the core. Jerry is a good balance for her."

"Interesting how things just line themselves up," I commented as I turned to Elizabeth with a boastful smile. "I mean, if I hadn't shown up, who knows what would have happened?"

"Yes, very," she said, gingerly smiling. "Funny. It's as if you knew," she said with a laugh, "just like in Jeremiah's book."

"Yes, Jeremiah, how is your book coming along?" I asked, dodging Elizabeth's remark.

"It's coming along. I may want to bend your ear on it if you have any free time."

"My ear? Why me?" I asked, choking as I nibbled one of the hors d'oeuvres. I gave Elizabeth the evil eye for telling my secret. "I would think you would rather talk to Elizabeth."

"Elizabeth? Why? She's not a theology student."

"He probably meant to get a woman's perspective," she quickly added, aiming a menacing gaze in my direction. "Because you know what they say, Solo, a woman is always right. Right?"

CHAPTER 98

Young's computer flashed mug shots and driver's license photos from the department's database like a strobe light in a dance club. Cooper watched from behind as Charlie Kitchens' facial features were being quickly compared to that of everyone in the D.C. metro area. Amazing how a software could detect drooping eyelids and high cheek bones and find an individual with a 99% accuracy.

The officers who went to Franklin Park Apartments showed every resident Charlie Kitchens' photograph, but none of them recognized him. One elderly tenant said he looked similar to a kid that used to live in the building years prior, but it could have been anyone. She couldn't recall the name of the kid or the parents, just that the child didn't stay there long.

"This could take all night," Young said with a moan as he downed his lukewarm coffee and a handful of honey roasted peanuts.

"Do you have somewhere else to be?"

"Actually, I'm supposed to meet Allison between her newscasts. I'm thinking of popping the question," he grinned pulling out the little black box from his pocket. He showed Cooper the sparkling diamond as if they were best buds.

"Are you sure about this?" Cooper remarked, eyeing the diamond that would cause anyone woman to scream yes. "Wow! That is some rock!"

"Thanks, but what do you mean, am I sure?"

"Come on. Once you put that ring on her finger, all the games you play with Dakota and your other women are going to have to stop."

"Who says?" he asked, smiling and stuffing the box back into his coat pocket. "I bet Dakota won't mind being my work toy. It's all in good fun," he said laughing. He waited for Cooper to give him a congratulatory high-five. "Come on, Cooper. What she doesn't know won't hurt her. And it's about time I have someone to come home to each night."

"Whatever."

The next half hour was awkward and slowly trickled by like an hourglass of digital photos. Young tried to catch peanuts in his mouth as Cooper watched the computer screen like someone working an algebra problem.

"Oh. My. God."

"What?" Young asked as a flying peanut slid down his shirt. "Got something?"

"Meet Alexei Lechkov," Cooper said, jumping up and pumping his fists into the air as a mug shot of Charlie Kitchens' true identity glowed on the screen. "And this guy has a fairly long rap sheet."

"Attempted burglary, trespassing, vandalism, disorderly conduct," Young read aloud. "But nothing real bad. Nothing like murdering a dozen people."

"Print that out. Then do a search for that name to see if we can get his sister."

The printer spit out a few pages of Alexei's history. He was born in Sterling, Virginia, on February 3, 1993, but the rest of his information was stamped confidential until he reached the age eighteen. That was when it listed his crimes like a resume. "Why does it say 'Confidential' during his childhood?"

"There are no other Lechkovs in this area," Young noted as he spun his chair around to look at Alexei's report. "I wonder…" he said as he spun his chair back to his computer and opened another database to search.

Cooper watched in disbelief as Young carved a steady path through the foster care database. He searched for any mention of the name Lechkov in the last thirty years. "Well, here's something interesting. In 1998, Dimitri Lechkov was tried and found guilty of the death of his wife, Anne Samples Lechkov. She took two bullets to the head."

"Alexei was only five then."

"Their two children, Jenika and Alexei, were sent to Anne Samples' parents' home where they lived for three months until their grandparents were killed in an apparent revenge killing for testifying against Dimitri."

"Man, that is rough. How old was the girl?"

Young shook his head at the string of tragedies the young kids faced. "She was about nine. Since they had no other living relatives in the United States, they were entered into the foster care system. It appears that Alexei hopped around in the system all over the metro area until he was eighteen when the system kicked him out."

"What about the girl? Do you have anything on her?"

"No. It seems like she just disappeared shortly after she entered the foster care system. She might have been one of the lucky ones who got adopted. With her past, she probably received a new name, wanting a clean slate, so I'm not sure I will be able to track her down without knowing her name or the names of her adoptive parents."

"Hey, but we know who he is now, Alexei Lechkov," Cooper said, beaming. "I wonder if either one of them has visited their father in prison. Can you find out where he is?"

"Well, they might be visiting him, but it's not in prison," Young replied pessimistically. "He was killed in prison in 2000."

The printer spit out the image of Jenika as a young girl with her short dirty blonde hair and cheerful dimples. She looked so innocent and delicate like a matryoshka doll. But as Cooper held the picture, he knew that she wasn't innocent anymore.

CHAPTER 99

"Are you sure about this? We never rehearsed it this way before." He tried to straighten the blond chin-length wig he was wearing for the first time. "This is itchy," he said, scratching his head as she laughed without compassion, handing him a pair of fake glasses.

"Now you know what I have been dealing with," she giggled, sliding her bald cap over her new, extra short style. "You never commented on my new hair."

"Looks shorter than mine."

"Hey bud," she poked her long pointy finger into his chest. "I did it for you."

"I know. I know," he said relenting as his eyes sunk down to the ground as a subway train came howling through the station. "You're always beautiful to me," he shouted over the shrieking metal brakes.

"Oh, thanks bubby. Now help me with this cap. Is it covering all of my hair?"

He stopped scratching his head to help her. He walked around examining her from all directions. "Looks pretty convincing, but you can use a little makeup under your eyes to look a little sicker."

"Got it," she said, pulling out some white and gray powder. She quickly applied her makeup, covering her rosy cheeks then tying a silk scarf around her head to play the part of a cancer patient. "How do I look now?" she asked, pouting her lips with a depressed, defeated look in her eyes.

"Perfect, sis."

"You're not so bad yourself with that blond wig. You may want to wear it more often. You could actually get a date if you wanted one."

"Oh, I could get one if I wanted one," he said with a grin. "Remember what I did for money in New York? I never had anyone complain."

"Alexei, don't ever mention that to me again," she barked solemnly at him, reaching over to give her little brother a hug. "I don't want to picture you doing things like that. I should have been there for you. I should have protected you more."

"You did all that you could. It was them that didn't protect me," he snarled.

"Yes, it was them. Let's do this for them!" she whispered evilly as she pecked both of her brother's cheeks with a loving kiss. "Let's go kill some grandparents."

"I hope you're right about doing it so early today," Alexei commented as he looked at his watch and noted it was only 5:56 p.m.

"I told you. We had to make some changes tonight. They will expect us to come at our normal time, so let's throw them off kilter."

"I know, but will there be anyone on the subways for us to get this early?"

"Kiddo, don't worry about that. Washington, D.C. is preparing for some presidential dinner tonight with foreign dignitaries from all over the world. Many of the tourist attractions are closing early, and the roads are already being blocked and barricaded. Any normal old tourists will probably be heading for their hotel early tonight."

"Why are you so smart?"

She smiled as they started to leave the darkened hideaway with high hopes and expectations for the night. "Now don't forget. You're leading me tonight."

"Uh huh," he nodded, wrapping his arm around her back. "Come on, the train is coming. We have to hurry up or we'll be late." He looked around the station and saw countless gray-headed couples standing along the platform. They were waiting patiently, despite their swollen and tired feet. "Wow. We will have some prime picking tonight."

"What did I tell you?"

CHAPTER 100

The squad room was full of bustling cops ready to hit the street for the capture of the Carbon Monoxide Killers. Captain Johnson commanded the room like a drill sergeant, demanding the officers' attention as he gave orders for the night. "The majority of you will be monitoring the Yellow Line Stations and parking areas. This appears to be their chosen line. We have security guards at all of the stations on the lookout for Alexei Lechkov and his sister. Be careful! These two are brutal killers. They are willing to do anything, no matter who gets in their way."

He looked at Young, who sat like a spoiled child on Christmas who didn't get what he wanted, strumming his fingers on his keyboard. "Why don't you stay here tonight and man the phones in case anyone calls in with a tip?"

"Yes sir," Young said, moping as if getting picked last in gym class. It was a feeling Young had never known. "Why do I need to? Only crazies call in with tips," he muttered under his breath as Johnson walked away.

"What did you say?" Cooper asked, getting his gun from his desk drawer and stuffing it in his holster.

"Nothing," Young answered, grabbing his phone to text his girlfriend the bad news about dinner. He quickly realized that he would be alone tonight. *Come down to the station around 9?* he texted, smiling when she instantly responded with a thumbs-up.

Cooper and his partners for the night, Knightly and White, headed to the Greenbelt Station. Cooper had personally requested this station based upon his belief that the killers would use it as their target, just like they'd used Huntington for their first three.

Knightly recommended that one of them ride the yellow line up to Greenbelt. They figuratively drew straws with a game of evens and odds. White was the odd man out. He walked down to the yellow line as Cooper and Knightly drove to the station.

As he pulled into the parking lot, Knightly scanned the dwindling vehicles, staring in shock at how close the Greenbelt Metro Drive was located to the parking lot. "They attacked the last couple right here. Just think of how many cars passed by while they were dousing them with gas."

"Eerie, since it's so quiet and peaceful now."

"Yeah, that was probably what they thought too, just before they were attacked."

Cooper parked the squad car before splitting up to monitor the station. "I will go up to the subway station," Cooper said, "and you can keep watch down here."

"Fine by me. And before you tackle someone, make sure they are the killers," Knightly laughed as he strolled away from Cooper and started his first journey around the parking lot.

CHAPTER 101

She looked out the window of the yellow line subway train as it passed over the Potomac River, watching the moon's reflection dance upon the choppy waves caused by a few late-night boats. This was new territory for her, and she was hoping that her brother would rise to the challenge. She was the one who usually gave the signals and befriended their victims, but now it was his turn to play the role of caregiver.

She leaned her head on his strong shoulder, a shoulder that she had forgotten when they were split up after their grandparents' deaths. "I have a secret to tell you," she whispered in his ear as his eyes perked up. He still kept watch for any possible targets that may have boarded the subway car. "Grandma and Grandpa weren't murdered by Dad's enemies," she said softly as if telling him a bedtime story. "I shot them."

His head jerked to the side, staring into her sickly eyes as if trying to get a glimpse into her soul. "Are you serious?" he choked, shocked at the idea of his nine-year-old sister shooting them in their heads.

"I had to," she whispered defensively. "They were talking bad about Papa, and I couldn't stand them saying those horrible things about him. He didn't kill Mama. He didn't. He told me that he didn't, and he wouldn't lie to me."

"You killed them?" his voice quivered like a string on a violin.

"I did it for us. I did it for you."

"For me?" His warm exterior quickly vanished as his shoulder that exuded affection a moment earlier now was mere bone and muscles.

"Alexei." She snuggled into his arm like a puppy trying to get warmth from its mother, but it was no use. He didn't feel like giving any care, and she felt the discord. She rose from his arm and stared distantly out the window. It fogged when her warm breath collided with the frigid glass. She thought about wiping it away but decided not to. She didn't want to look out the window anyway. All she wanted was the closeness of her brother to return.

He looked over at his sister, angry and confused. He knew that she had been trying to protect him, but her act of bravery led to a lifetime of separation. "Because of you, they split us up," he stated calmly, delivering the words like daggers to her heart.

A sea of tears began to fill her eyes. Don't you cry. Don't you cry, she told herself since she didn't have time to fix her makeup. She also didn't want her little brother to look down on her for showing such stereotypically female emotions.

Controlling her tears, she wiped her wet eyes. "I didn't know they were going to do that."

"Because of you I never had a good home life. Because of you I never had a place where I felt safe. At least you got adopted. I still don't have anyone."

"I don't have anyone anymore either," she said, consoling him. "Except for you."

"What?"

"They died last year, a few months after we met up again."

"Why didn't you tell me?" he asked as his frigidness started to melt. He reached his arm around his sister's shoulder. "I would have…" he started to say, but she just shook her head.

"It's just the two of us again. And this time…" she stopped to watch an aging couple step onto the subway car. A smile landed on her face, causing him to turn his gaze toward what she was seeing. "Nothing is going to separate us. We good?"

"Yep, we're good," he said sighing. He was still hurt and wounded from the secret that was just unleashed, but he knew in his gut, her intentions were pure. The gruesome murder of his supposed caring grandparents had been intended as a heroic act of twisted love.

CHAPTER 102

"You don't say," Alexei laughed to the retired couple from some oil-drilling Texas town where everyone apparently said 'howdy' while tipping their cowboy hats. "Those are some nice boots," he commented pointing down to Texas "T-bone" Ted Appleton's snakeskin Stetsons. He stared at them in admiration, holding back the urge to feel the smooth scales of the creature that, when alive, had the power to kill with its fangs. His sister sat with her eyes closed, listening to how well he was doing. She wore a proud smile under her surgical mask.

"Thank you, son. Betty here gave them to me on our 25th wedding anniversary," he said with a western twang that smelled of horseback riding and hog tying.

"And what did he get you, ma'am?" Alexei gushed.

"Well, only this little ring," she said smiling, showing off a rock that would cause the Vanderbilts to take a second glance.

"Geez Louise, is that thing heavy? Did you see that, sis?" he said gently touching her side to start showcase her declining health.

"Hmm?" she opened her sleepy eyes. "Very nice. Very nice indeed."

"Your scarf is very lovely," Betty commented warmly. "I love the color of it. It goes so well with your eyes. So pretty."

"Thank you," she answered weakly.

"You okay?" Alexei asked, rubbing her back and neck like a skilled masseuse.

"I'll be fine. I'm just tired."

"Well, our stop is coming up," Alexei noted as he watched Ted feel around in his pockets for his car keys. The subway car glided into the last stop on the yellow line, Huntington Station, their home away from home. They knew where all the security cameras were and how to move their head so no clear images could be seen. "We're here."

"Help me up," she said, standing on wobbly legs that gave way, causing Alexei to catch her before she landed on the train's filthy floor.

"Here, let me help you," Ted bent down, helping Alexei with the sick woman.

"Why thank you, sir. Thank you," Alexei said.

"No worries, son. Betty had a fight with it a decade ago. You can do it, missy. You just have to fight. Betty here is a fighter."

"That's good to know," she commented. "Very good to know."

The four of them went down the elevator as Ted and Alexei stood on either side, making sure that the swaying movement of the old machine didn't throw off her balance. "I think I got it," she said as she tried to step off the elevator. Her foot caught in the uneven surface.

"Argh!" she screamed, falling forward dramatically as her arms waved like a newborn bird trying to take flight.

"Sis!"

No matter how fast they reacted, it wasn't fast enough. "You okay?" Ted asked as she laid sprawled on the ground. A couple of security guards rushed to their aid.

"I'm just...I'm just a little, a little startled," she jabbered. "I don't know what happened."

"You need to fix this!" Betty yelled at the guards, pointing at the tripping hazard.

"We will! We'll get it fixed," one of the guards said in horror, fearful of another lawsuit under his watch. "Are you going to be okay?"

"I should be," she said as Ted and Alexei helped her to her feet. "I don't think I can make it," she whispered to Alexei, loud enough for Ted and Betty to hear.

"We'll get you where you need to go," Ted said chivalrously. He came forward as Betty grinned proudly from behind.

The four of them walked to the nearby garage, the same one where Ted had parked. Alexei thought his sister drew a little too much attention to herself, especially when she fell off the elevator in front of the security guards. He wanted to slap her for tripping, but he controlled his anger. He knew that smacking a sick woman wouldn't look right. Now he wondered how his sister was going to get them into Ted's vehicle. He didn't doubt though. He knew she would make it happen. She already got them past the guards.

"I can't make it up to the top. It's too many stairs," she whined as if taking her cue from the director.

"Well, you stay down here with Betty, and we will pick you up," Ted offered.

"No, I can't make Betty stay here with her. It's dangerous in garages. Have you seen the news?"

"Son, we're lifetime members of the NRA."

"So, you're packing?" Alexei asked.

"We both are," Betty chimed in, patting her purse.

Alexei didn't know how to respond. He hoped that he'd figure something out soon because he knew another train would be coming shortly. The longer it took, the more witnesses would be arriving.

"Going up?" Ted asked as he started to climb the stairs.

"Right behind you," he answered, shrugging his shoulders at his sister whose bulging eyes were telling him that this was not going as planned.

"Hurry back," she choked out before both men were out of sight.

CHAPTER 103

"I'm so sorry about this," Alexei said for the fifth time. "I cannot believe I forgot where I parked. We must have parked in the other garage. Are you sure you don't mind driving us around?"

"Just as long as we get back to our hotel in time to watch the Longhorns," Ted laughed.

"It shouldn't take long," his sister said, lightly coughing as she rode in the front seat of the luxurious Cadillac Escalade. "I thought we were in the other parking garage, but I'm usually wrong."

"Never doubt a woman's intuition," Betty slouched as she clutched her purse in her lap, looking at Ted in the rearview mirror with cautious eyes.

Ted knew what those eyes were telling him, and he was heeding the warning. He pulled out of the first garage, watching the sick woman in the passenger seat as much as he was the road. She didn't appear to be able to do any harm, but looks could be deceiving. He pulled into the adjacent parking garage and started to quickly circle to the top.

"My throat is dry. Can I get something to drink?"

"I'm sorry, but we don't allow liquids in the car," Betty said quickly.

"Oh, I'm sorry," she commented with a crackling voice.

Ted rounded another floor as Alexei started to get nervous. "You okay up there? You're not getting car sick, are you?"

"I'll be fine, but I am feeling warm. Can you give me a wet wipe?"

"I've got one," Betty said pulling one out of her purse and handing up the lemon-scented napkin as Ted reached the top of the garage.

"Where's your car?" Ted asked pulling along the sparse selection of vehicles.

"It's that blue Mitsubishi over there," Alexei said, pointing to the group of vehicles in the far right corner.

"Oh, no, is this lemon?" his sister gagged.

"Yes. Why, what's wrong?" Betty asked as the frail woman started hyperventilating.

"She's allergic to lemons! Stop the car, Ted!" Alexei shouted as the car came to a sudden stop. Alexei flung open the door and ran around to his sister's side. "I can't find your inhaler. Is it in your purse?"

"I...I...don't...I...don't..." she breathed heavily in and out trying to catch her fragile breath.

"She needs to lie down," Alexei shouted as he helped his sister out of the car to lie on the concrete.

"I'm so sorry, dear. I didn't know. I didn't know," Betty cried as she threw her purse in the backseat, getting out of the car to help. "Ted, park the car."

"Breathe, sis. Breathe. You can do this," he said. He noticed Betty had left her purse in the backseat. He winked as he placed the oxygen mask over her face. She winked back. "This should work," he smiled under his surgical mask, shrugging his shoulders to

383

Betty. "Will you watch her? I need to see if I can find her EpiPen in my satchel."

Showtime.

He returned to his seat, pretending to scramble frantically for the lifesaving medicine. He waited for the lovely sound of the front door opening and Ted huffing to get out. "Found it!" Alexei shouted as he reached from behind Ted, covering his face with the chloroform wipes. Ted was strong, so Alexei did a quick jab into his kidneys, causing him to huff in pain and inhale more of the toxic fumes.

"Ted?" Betty yelled. "I thought you were coming."

"He's a little busy," the sister hissed wickedly as she plunged her oxygen mask over Betty's face. She flipped the switch to let the chloroform flood out of the clear tubes into her lungs.

"Hel--" Betty tried to scream. But it was too late as her villain held her mouth closed with tightly clenched hands. Betty's eyes quickly closed to a peaceful rest.

CHAPTER 104

The drive from Huntington Station to Little Falls Park was fairly quiet. Alexei hummed lightly to fill the void as he drove inconspicuously away from any traffic cameras he had memorized over the last year. He couldn't get the idea of his big sister shooting his grandparents to death out of his head. But he couldn't hold that resentment against her. In her young mind, she'd believed she was doing the right thing.

He'd never blamed her for his childhood, until tonight. He wished he could take back what he'd said like a regretful suicide victim one millisecond before death, but once the words were spoken, there was no amount of alcohol to erase that memory. He rubbed his head as if trying to wipe the jaded childhood memories out of sight. He glanced in his rearview mirror wondering why he was always thinking of what was behind him; he should be focusing on what potentially lie ahead. He needed to sweep the broken pieces of his youth under the proverbial rug of fate and use it as a mat instead of a scrapbook.

He looked over at his sister, still wearing the designer scarf she got at Bloomingdales during a weekend getaway to New York City. He couldn't help but remember when they reconnected.

He'd been surrounded by a galley of criminals, charged mostly with petty crimes. Their punishments were mainly a slap on the wrist and a swift reprimanding finger. Even though she had aged almost twenty years and grown thirty inches, her eyes were memorable. They were still as lucid as they had been when she was nine.

He'd watched through the bulletproof glass as she'd walked by. She had spoken to a few of the other inmates and caught his eyes but had not recognized him. He'd felt hurt. How could they have been so close at such a tragic time in their lives, yet be unrecognizable now that they were separated by a few inches. To her it might as well have been the Berlin Wall in 1982. He'd caught her looking his direction. He'd considered smiling, but his face wouldn't remove the stone cold features.

"Jenika," he'd said through the mouth holes in the glass as she walked by. She'd shaken her head no.

"You have me confused," she'd said as she returned to her seat with a set of files in her lap. She stood up when someone said an unfamiliar name. His heart had sunk. He could have sworn that was Jenika. However, in his life, he had learned that he was wrong much of the time. Looking up from a file, his file, she stared at him with a mixture of confused intrigue. She'd shaken her head, as if telling herself that it was illogical before she returned her attention to the file. Then she had looked up again to watch the young adult with interrogating eyes.

"Alexei Lechkov?" she'd asked as she approached the transparent barrier, touching the glass with her trembling hands.

"Yes."

"Who was your father?"

He'd stood with shackled hands and legs to whisper the answer through the glass. "Our father's name was Dimitri."

Whenever he felt alone, he would always go back to that memory of when he reconnected with his long-lost sister. It may not have been a Hallmark moment, but in his mixed-up shambled life, it was a tearjerker.

"Almost there," he commented to his sister, grabbing her shoulder as she reached her right hand up to pat his. "Little Falls Park," he read as he entered the desolate woodland park with hidden trails and dog walking paths along the winding road that had sporadic picnic sites along the route.

"I don't recall coming here before," she said, looking out the window, watching the bare tree limbs pass. "What is the plan for leaving here?"

"I hid your bike on the southern part of the Dalecarlia Reservoir. I put a tracking device on it for you to find."

"Lovely night for a bike ride," she said, basking in the glow of the autumn moon.

"I thought you would like that."

They parked the Escalade in the darkened parking lot, hidden behind a shelter house with various picnic tables and charcoal grills. They quickly maneuvered Ted and Betty to the front seat. Alexei then attached the garden hose with heavy duty duct tape to the exhaust before funneling it through the driver's side window. His sister went through the victims' belongings, pulling out the MetroCards, hotel key cards, and a little wad of cash for her brother. She also did a quick check for any possible evidence they may have left behind.

"Ready?" she asked as she reached through the vehicle to turn on the ignition.

"I guess so," he commented sadly, running his gloved hand down the side of the sleek midnight black exterior. "You should get one of these."

"Me? A Cadillac?" she laughed, starting the SUV. "Do I look like a retirement village junkie?"

"You can afford it. It sure drove nice."

"Maybe if you're extra special I will get one. And I will let you drive it."

"Really?" his voice rose to a shrill squeal as he controlled himself from skipping around the parking lot like a schoolgirl.

"Really. You deserve it."

CHAPTER 105

The cool air smelled crisp and clean as she walked through the woods. She inhaled the pure goodness, hoping her nagging regrets of the night would escape with each exhale. They didn't. She couldn't get the badgering voice out of her head, telling her that she shouldn't have told Alexei the truth about their grandparents. He hadn't known the truth before tonight, and he was just fine. She wondered why she'd suddenly felt the need to come clean.

She didn't have an answer.

"It was time," she tried to tell herself as she trekked through the wooded trail. She held her tracking device in her hand, watching the computerized neon green glow direct her southwest, as if she were looking for water using one of those witchdoctor miracle sticks. "He had a right to know the truth."

"Didn't he?" she asked herself. The doubt continued to slosh around in her churning stomach, which was ready to relinquish its contents at any minute. "Stop it!" she told herself. She didn't need to leave any DNA evidence. The cops may not be slick enough to connect the dots of her supper contents on the poison oak to the new murders, but she didn't want to give them any chances. She swallowed hard, pressing down the urge as her device blinked rapidly, leading her to her bike.

She took a few more steps forward to the figurative X on the map and saw a large bush with a few prickly thorns. Shining her flashlight behind the shrub, she spotted a large mound of rotting brown leaves. She carefully squeezed through the stabbing bush and kicked the leaves around, catching the feel of a rubber tire. She cleaned off her bike and brushed all the leaves away as she heard a loud scream from the distance.

She stood still to listen. She thought maybe it was just a wood creature howling in the night, or a bird screeching to the moon. Then suddenly, she heard the scream again. She could tell that a woman was screaming something, but it was muffled.

"Betty!" she thought as she jumped on her bike, quickly peddling down the path that she'd just quietly hiked. Slowly walking in the dark watching for tree roots and limbs was one thing, but a mad dash on a bicycle was another. She felt the roots that she couldn't see as the bike seat jammed into her bottom, causing her to groan. But she couldn't stop. She had to finish Betty before the woman finished her.

The trail was winding with the gravel rocks flying like confetti from her speeding tires. She didn't care about being quiet. As she whizzed by at a breakneck speed, the falling rocks collided back onto the path, and the rushing wind rustled the nearby trees and bushes. She had one thing on her mind and one thing only.

Her legs were numb to the ruthless workout as a surge of adrenaline coursed through her veins, keeping her body in check and her energy at full throttle. She knew that she could collapse after everything was taken care of, but until then, her body was an afterthought. She was fit since she was an avid biker who cycled all over Washington D.C.'s trails and bike paths, but this was different. Instead of trying to beat a clock or a competitor, she was trying to beat something entirely different. It wasn't just a finish line she was trying to get to; it was the spectators at the finish point.

She saw a break in the trees about a hundred yards ahead. Even though there weren't any lights except for the flashlight she held in her mouth, her vision was starting to grow accustomed to the night. She peddled harder knowing that it was a straight away and she was nearing the end of the frantic chase. As she grew closer, she strained her ears to hear something, but all she could make out was the sound of her own heart pounding against the wall of her chest.

The trees parted and her bike hopped up on the pavement of the parking lot. She quickly stopped, pain shooting through her legs and what felt like a gaping whole in her chest.

The SUV was gone.

Betty was gone.

They were screwed.

CHAPTER 106

"Wake up, Teddy. Wake up!" Betty screamed, slapping Ted's face as she sped with the windows down running through a stop sign on her way to the nearest hospital, Sibley Memorial Hospital, just a few minutes from the park exit down Dalecarlia Parkway. She thought she could hear some gargled breathing but couldn't make out if that was his breathing or just her hopeful imagination.

People looking at her would think that she was delicate with her diamond rings and pendants, but all her relatives and friends knew her as Betty Sue, the Texas Bull Riding Champion from 1984 to 1991. She may look gentle and feminine but being raised with eight older brothers knocked those qualities out of her with the first sucker punch.

"Come on, Teddy!" she prayed as she listened to the GPS countdown the yards to the hospital's entrance. She could barely see the sign through her tear-drenched eyes as she skidded around the parking lot, taking hard lefts and rights to get to the emergency room entrance. She held down the horn, hoping to announce their entrance to the welcoming arms of the medical staff. It worked.

A couple of nurses taking an unhealthy smoke break by the entrance saw the SUV race through the parking lot and rushed in to get anyone who could help. By the time Betty was at the ER entrance, there were three people wearing scrubs ready to take her and Ted.

"What happened?" one of the nurses asked as she flicked her cigarette to the ground while two people got Ted out of the passenger's seat and onto the gurney.

"Those...those...killers!" Betty screamed as she ran around the vehicle to hold Ted's lifeless hand.

"Ma'am, ma'am," the nurse yelled as she got a wheelchair from the lobby area. "Sit down and tell me what happened. They will take care of him. Did you say killers?"

"I have to stay with Ted," she said, coughing out the remaining fumes of carbon monoxide in her lungs. She limped beside the rushing gurney as the EMTs started checking for Ted's pulse.

"He's got a pulse, but it's faint," one of them said.

"You have to stay back," the nurse demanded, grabbing Betty's hand and causing her to stumble and lose her balance. Betty fell onto the newly waxed floor that smelled of bleach and lilac as the nurse quickly helped her into the wheelchair. "Who did this?"

"Those young killers!" she cried, raising her head to watch the EMTs sprint to an open room to begin their life-saving procedures.

"What happened to you?" the nurse asked again, standing in front of Betty to get her attention.

"We were on the subway and this young couple needed a ride to find their car. So Ted and I gave them a lift. I thought something was up with them. So when they attacked us, I pretended to get knocked out when they covered my face with some mask. I held my breath for as long as I could, but I still think some of the stuff got in me, because I passed out while they were driving. When I came to, I noticed that they had taken us to some park, and our SUV was filling with toxic fumes. They were trying to kill us!"

"Call the cops!" the nurse in pink scrubs yelled as she started to check Betty's vitals. "We need to get you checked out as well."

"I'll be fine. Just take care of Teddy," she moaned as she leaned her head back, stifling a cry before she passed out.

CHAPTER 107

"Breaking news! Breaking news," Brock Michaels, a television newscaster announced in a solemn tone. He was sitting at his news desk as the Channel 9 logo was plastered on the screens behind him. "There have been two fatalities tonight related to the Carbon Monoxide Killers. At 7:32 tonight, a police officer, whose identity has not been released, was killed at the Huntington Metro Station by the apparent Carbon Monoxide Killers. The tragic murder occurred in front of hundreds of passengers fleeing the scene as the lone police officer tried to detain the suspects. The suspects fled the scene after attacking and killing a woman. Her identity also has not been released. The suspects escaped in the victim's white 2008 Toyota Camry. Be aware that these suspects are armed and dangerous.

"The suspects are twenty-six-year-old, Alexei Lechkov, and his presumed sister, whose identity has not been confirmed. If anyone has any information on their whereabouts, please contact the Metropolitan Police Department of the District of Columbia. Once again, this is breaking news, and we will keep you posted on the events as new details come. Stay safe," Michaels commented, bowing his head in sympathy as the camera froze on his profile. The screen faded to the Emergency Broadcast Warning with multicolored stripes and a high-pitched buzzing sound, causing anyone with delicate ears to cover them in agony.

The warning signal grew fainter as the screen faded to black and a bell started to chime. Dong. Dong. Dong. Dong. Dong. Dong. Dong. Dong. Dong. Dong. Dong. Dong. Heavy breathing filled the darkness muffled by the sounds of vehicles zooming nearby. A bright light shone in the darkness. Nothing was visible except a narrow platform where a person was standing. The light was quickly coming closer as a horn blew from the distance. A splashing sound was heard from below as the man screamed into the light, "I can't swim!" The horn intensified as the oncoming light shone brighter and closer, as if staring into the sun. "Argh!" the man screamed as he moved out of the way of the threatening light. "Help me!" he screamed. He looked up at his hands which were clinging onto a metal railing. He could hear a loud clanking noise. He looked down in horror, seeing his legs dangle over the choppy Potomac River. "Help me!"

The nearby vehicles continued to pass, oblivious to the stranded man. The train grew silent with the distance as it carried on its journey to the next Metro station.

"Someone please help me!"

"I can't swim," he groaned as his fingers started to slide off the railing until the last fingertip touched the cold metal bar.

Splash.

I woke up in a heart-pounding sweat. I reached over to my journal and saw it was only 11:02 p.m. I was shocked at the early time, but after such a long day, I'd crashed in bed shortly after I returned home from Jerry and Christy's wedding reception. I started frantically writing all the details of my dreams. I didn't know what dream was worse, knowing that the Carbon Monoxide Killers were still on the loose for another night of murderous mayhem or coming face to face with my worst fear. Water.

I couldn't swim either.

CHAPTER 108

The moon was stunning as Knightly paced through the labyrinth of Honda Accords and Ford Fusions in the Greenbelt Station parking lot. His partners for the night, Cooper and White, were guarding the actual station. At least they had each other's company, Knightly thought, as he counted stars and played the alphabet game with license plates.

Knightly watched anxiously like an eager puppy for his master to come home from work as his friends left their guarding station and started walking his way. "Why so quiet tonight?" White yelled across the parking lot.

"What do you mean?" Knightly asked, walking toward them, following the light of the streetlamps.

"We've been trying to get you all night, but all we heard was whistling and humming," Cooper stated.

"I heard you say a few sounds here and there too," White commented.

"What are you talking about?" Knightly questioned, looking down at his two-way radio, noticing that the volume was turned down. "Really?" he shouted agitatedly as White and Cooper burst out laughing. "I was so bored down here."

"We know," White said, chuckling as he mimicked Knightly's whistling abilities.

"I thought you were ticked off or something. I mean, White kept asking how you were doing, but you never answered."

"Why didn't you come down and make sure?"

"Well, we could see you sometimes kicking the rocks, so we knew you were alive," Cooper answered.

"And we could still hear you, 'A B C,'" White recited like a grade school child.

"Cooper! Calling Cooper!" Young interrupted through the two-way radio.

"Cooper here."

"There's been another attack tonight. Head down to Sibley Memorial Hospital."

"Sibley?" Cooper asked confused.

"Yeah, Sibley," Young's voice crackled through the airwaves like a log on fire. "They're not dead, yet."

"Yet?"

"The man isn't in good condition, so you may want to get down there before things get worse. Who knows how the wife will react if they lose him?"

"We're on it!" Cooper exclaimed as the three of them ran to the police cruiser. "Where did this happen?"

"The attack?" Young coughed, tasting his growing dread as he recalled the phone call from earlier in the day. He was starting to see that he could have stopped this attack. He was feeling guilt and remorse knowing he could have ended their tyranny once and for all.

"Yes, which station did they use?"

"Huntington, Cooper. They used Huntington."

CHAPTER 109

Sibley Memorial Hospital admitted Betty to Room 342, quickly hooking her up to IVs to pump some fluids into her. Her room didn't have the typical bed, but a pressurized oxygen chamber that resembled a space age tube that could teleport someone in a matter of seconds. She laid in the glass coffin-like container, wrapped snuggly in a white cotton blanket as her nurse stood beside the casing to take her vitals. Betty's hands were folded neatly, resting on her nauseated belly. She breathed deeply, causing her body to rise and then fall with the exhale.

"How's Ted?" she asked the young nurse who was inputting the data onto her iPad. She took note of any fluctuations in Betty's breathing.

"Betty, you need to rest. You need to focus on getting yourself well first, and then you can worry about your husband."

"Honey, you're not married, are you?"

"No, not yet."

"Well, when you have been married for forty years, then you can tell me to focus on myself and not worry about my husband. We've been together so long that he is a part of me."

"I just meant..." the nurse started before Betty waved her off, telling her that it was okay. She knew that she was young, and hopefully one day she would know what true love felt like.

The nurse agreed as someone knocked on the door.

"Mrs. Appleton?" Cooper asked as he walked into the room that looked straight out of a science fiction movie. Betty opened her sleepy eyes to acknowledge his appearance. "I am Winston Cooper with the Washington D.C. P.D. Can I ask you a few questions?"

"Officer, she needs her rest," the nurse spoke up, blocking Cooper from taking another step into the room.

"I understand, but this is important. She is the first one who has survived an attack, and I need to talk to her ASAP."

"It's okay. I'll be okay," Betty choked as she watched the young officer come into the light. "Well, aren't you a pleasant sight?" she said, grinning warmly. "I always enjoyed seeing Ted in his Army uniform. Always made him so handsome. What lady doesn't enjoy the company of a man in uniform? Isn't that right?" she asked the young nurse, whose cheeks flushed a rosy pigmentation.

"Shhh. Betty, you need to save your oxygen. Short sentences."

"You're too kind, ma'am," Cooper said, smiling as he scooted a chair to her cosmic bedside as the nurse left.

"Now, what do you want to know?" Betty asked matter-of-factly, wiggling her stiffening body into her warm blanket.

"You better follow the nurse's orders, or she may be mean to you."

"Honey, she wouldn't last a day in Texas," Betty laughed as he joined in.

"Did you know your attackers?"

"No."

"Were they a young man and woman?"

"Yes, they said they were siblings."

"Good. Can you describe her to me? Did she have any distinguishing mark? Any tattoos or moles? Anything uncommon about her?"

"I'm sorry. I can't think of anything."

"That's okay, Mrs. Appleton. Did you scratch her? Did you get any DNA?"

"No, I was shocked when she got me."

Cooper looked out the door as Betty continued to stare at the ceiling. He watched a surgeon walk up to Betty's nurse and say something. It must not have been good news from the expression on the nurse's face. She covered her mouth in shock, and Cooper knew that his questioning was about to be over. His mind flooded with questions that he wanted answered.

"Did they say anything important?" he sputtered as the surgeon walked into the room, eyeing Cooper as if annoyed that he was in his seat.

"They said something about tomorrow being their last day until next year."

"Officer Cooper," the surgeon said. "Can you give me and Mrs. Appleton a moment?"

"Yes, but before I go, do you know of anything else?"

"Officer Cooper, please leave." The surgeon walked Cooper out before closing the door. Cooper knew that wasn't a good sign. He stood outside the door, saying a quick prayer for Mrs. Appleton as a heartbroken wail echoed through the silent halls.

"Poor woman," the nurse said, walking by Cooper and shaking her head in remorse. "Her husband passed away in surgery twenty minutes ago."

CHAPTER 110

The drive home from Sibley Memorial Hospital was lonely as Cooper couldn't shake the nagging memory of Betty's machine gun style sobs. He didn't want to bother her with any more questions for the night, so decided to leave her in her grief. He knew that tomorrow wouldn't be any easier, but the shock would hopefully have passed.

Cooper revved his BMW X6, gunning down Nebraska Avenue without hindrance. He was upset that they had killed again, and he was more furious at not being much closer to finding them. What caused his blood to boil was that they dropped their victims off in Little Falls Park, which was basically next door to his neighborhood. It was getting too close for comfort.

He knew that Veronica was safe since all the victims had been tourists of retirement age, but it didn't cause his fears or anxiety to subside. He turned into his neighborhood glowing with carved jack-o'-lanterns that aligned the covered porches with their weakening flickering flames. He prayed that when the children roamed the streets next week going door to door to trick or treat, they could enjoy the childish holiday in ultimate freedom.

Cooper pulled into the garage. As he turned off the ignition, he considered what the night was going to hold. He still had a knot in his stomach with the way he and Veronica had been handling their marriage.

They were playing married but not actually living married. He knew that he could be the bigger man and tell his wife that he loved her with all of his heart, that there was nothing that would stop that. He knew that this period in their life would pass. Every marriage had growing pains and seasons of pruning, an era of frigidness. Whatever period they were going through, he wanted it to conclude.

"Veronica!" he shouted as he walked into the kitchen hoping to find his loving wife waiting up for him by the fireplace in the living room. He didn't hear anything as he roamed through the house. "Veronica!" he shouted again, but just like before, there was no response.

He dialed her number and waited while it went straight to voicemail. "Veronica, I love you. We need to talk," he considered saying. But when the time came to leave the message all he could say was, "Veronica, well, I'm home. Where are you?"

He threw the phone on the kitchen counter, disgusted that she'd left without notice. He buried his head in the refrigerator and tried to find anything to fill the void, whether it be chicken or pasta. He found a container of leftovers from the dinner she'd made for her father the night before. He didn't even consider nuking it in the microwave, didn't care that the potatoes and beef Wellington were cold. He didn't know if he could feel the warmth even if it was heated.

When he closed the door, he saw a note: "Staying with Jenny."

"Good," he thought. "Maybe she can talk some sense into my wife."

Sunday

CHAPTER 111

"Hey, Wint. What's wrong?" I asked with a yawn, glancing over at my clock to see that only three hours had passed since I woke up the first time.

"Hey buddy," he said in a chipper tone to hide his fragility. "Nothing's wrong. I just wanted to check up on ya," he lied.

"Liar."

"What? Can't a friend just call and see how you're doing?"

"At 2 a.m.?" I refuted, sitting up in bed to get comfortable. I knew Wint better than most, and he wasn't one to divulge or appear weak. He was going to require some gentle nudging. "Spill it!" It was hard to be gentle at 2 a.m.

"I'm fine. It's just this case, you know? The Carbon Monoxide Killers."

"Yeah, I heard about those. Any closer to catching them?" I asked, wondering why the stupid cops hadn't listened to me. I'd told them this morning where the killers were going to be. Why hadn't they just listened? Probably because they thought I was crazy.

"We know who the guy is, but we can't find him. He keeps moving around like a vagabond."

"Vagabond," I said laughing. "Such a strange word. Did Verny teach you that?" Wint didn't respond, and I knew that it wasn't the case that had prompted this phone call. It was something much more personal. "So, what about his partner? Know who she is?"

"We have grainy photos that we have run through the facial recognition software, but they're no good. No matches."

"What? *CSI* can always catch their killers in thirty minutes."

"It doesn't work that way," Wint said laughing because he needed it. "DNA isn't as easily found like on TV shows. It's much harder to find than shining a black light. And then when you do find something you think is important, it's usually nothing. Then the crime labs get upset for running countless tests on a cat hair when they had other cases they could have been working on."

"So, what you're telling me is that Hollywood lies to get a more exciting plot line? No!"

"Why do I even talk to you?"

"Because no one else would have answered the phone at 2 am. You're my best friend, but I'm just a friend out of convenience." I laughed uncontrollably as I started my best Wint voice impression: "I can't call my married friends because their wives are either going to get mad about calling so late or they're going to get furious thinking that it's their mistresses calling at this ungodly hour."

"Solo, I don't sound like that."

"Yes, you do," I remarked still in my deep bravado.

"Whatever," Wint said, getting up from the couch to walk around the quiet house in his boxers and t-shirt. He had a sudden desire to see a golden retriever run down the long halls. "How does the name Silas sound for a dog?"

"A dog? Verny won't let you get a dog. Unless you get one of those girly toy show dogs to primp and pamper and carry in one of those fancy Gucci bags with a bow on her head." I readjusted my pillow that had started to slide down the headboard. "And she wouldn't call the dog Silas. It would be more like Sprinkles or Twinkles. I guess if you got a pug she could name it Wrinkles, but I don't see that happening."

"You are on it tonight," he smiled, standing in the light of the refrigerator and grabbing the chocolate milk to take a quick gulp.

"I'm on it every night," I commented before deciding to press the issue. "So, what's Verny doing?"

Once again, silence.

"Man, I know you heard me. What's going on with you two?"

"We're fine."

"Liar," I remarked insensitively. Sometimes the only way to get to the bottom was to punch the elevator buttons, and I was going to keep pushing his. "Wint, quit being a macho, macho man and tell me."

"Everything is fine. She is just away from home tonight, spending the night with a friend. I told her that I was going to be working late, so she made other plans. Everything is just fine. As well as it can be."

"Shut up! Just shut up! Why are you lying to me?"

"I'm not lying. We're good."

"Wint, you are a horrible liar. You always lose at poker because I know your tell. And your tell is overcompensating."

"So, that's how you always know when I'm bluffing?" he asked, making a mental note for the next poker night.

"You also change the subject," I spit out with a smile that I believed he heard in my tone. "So, what's really wrong? Are you two in trouble?" I sincerely wondered how I was going to help him save his marriage when I was the one who had begged him not to marry her in the first place.

"Maybe you were right," he said sounding depressed. I mentally saw him leaning against the kitchen wall, sinking to the ground.

"Stop that! Wint! Stop that! You love her, right?"

"Well…" he answered unconfidently.

"Wint, you fell in love with Verny the way she was, right?"

"Yeah, but…" he started before I interrupted.

"From what I'm seeing, she is still the same as she was ten years ago. Isn't she?"

"But I thought…"

"You thought what?"

"I thought we would have grown together."

"Bud, you both have grown, but from what I am seeing, she grew how she wanted, and you grew how she wanted. There wasn't any compromise. There's not much Wint in Winston Cooper."

"Man, oh man. What should I do?" he asked timidly hoping for a quick fix answer.

"What do you think you should do?"

"If I knew, I wouldn't be asking you."

"I think you know what you need to do."

CHAPTER 112

She cried while biking home in disappointment and bleakness after seeing that they had made a terrible, terrible mistake. They were rehearsed. They were planned. They were good at what they did, but they had never planned on this happening. She retraced the events of the night, trying to see the decaying link in their well-oiled chain. As far as she could see, the only person she could blame was herself.

She was the one who'd gassed Betty. She was the one who'd assumed that she was out. She was the one on whom all the burden and failure lie. In the midst of gloom and despair, people say that one can either sink deeper into the darkness or rise from the ashes in a state of renewal. She didn't want to be like everyone else. She wanted to be the exception. Her period of self-examination became one of self-declaration. She knew she had to clean up her mess, and there was only one way to do it.

After an hour of stalking Facebook for Betty Appleton of Texas, she learned all she needed to know to carry out her plan. She knew her favorite foods, her family history. She even knew her favorite authors and antidotes. In order to carry out her devious plan, she was going to have to morph into Jackie Sue Williams, Betty's redheaded niece living in Philadelphia who was about her same age and shape, give or take a few pounds.

She watched a few home videos of last December where Jackie Sue wished her family a Merry Christmas and grumbled about not being in Texas for the holiday because she couldn't afford the flight on her paralegal's salary. She started to mimic the video to get her voice to the same high western pitch as she curled her wig to match Jackie Sue's wavy style before going to bed.

After waking up early, she made a few phone calls and located Betty in Sibley Memorial Hospital. She went shopping like it was black Friday and purchased all of Betty's get-well basket treats at the local convenience store before heading back to her apartment to clean off her prints. She got a bouquet of sunflowers, Betty's favorite, and a few large get-well balloons. She then took a taxi to give the presents to the patient.

As she walked through the quiet hospital halls before seven in the morning, her heels clicked against the hard sterilized floor. She spoke loudly on her cell phone, annoying the patients and medical staff with her flamboyant attitude. She had learned in her psychological research that if she could not sneak in, she should do the opposite. She journeyed through the mazelike halls reviewing her plan.

It was similar to what she had accomplished about a year earlier with her adopted parents – first, her mother and then her father a few weeks later. She marked it as a declaration of payback, a revenge killing for not adopting her brother twenty years earlier. However, to the coroners it had looked like it was just

413

their time to go. She eventually found Betty's room with a strong, young, handsome police officer standing guard. Even in these moments, she couldn't pass by some good eye candy.

"Is this Betty Appleton's room? I'm her niece Jackie Sue Williams," she said in her recently learned accent.

"Let me see if she is able to see you," he said. She heard his muffled voice behind the heavy door before he returned. "She says it's okay."

She walked into the darkened room while the police guard watched from the open door. "Aunt Betty!" she squealed as she saw her inside the glass chamber. "How are you doing? It's me, Jackie."

"Jackie, you didn't have to come visit," Betty replied, staying in her prone position since the glass chamber didn't allow her to sit up.

"Well, Mom called me this morning and told me the news about you and Uncle Ted. Poor Uncle Ted," she cried.

"I know. I know."

"Well, I brought you some goodies," she said waving her bag at Betty's eye level and scanning the room for any cameras. "Where to put this?" she asked as she found the lone camera in the corner of the room. "Let me put it over here," she said, placing the get-well sack with the half dozen large helium-filled balloons directly under the camera. The balloons rose to the ceiling, blocking the camera from seeing anything but the colorful encouragements.

"I brought you your favorite cookies," she said pulling out her package of Oreos. "Mom said to get you the latest John Grisham book, so I have that for you as well."

"Dear, you shouldn't have. Sit down, sit down. Come closer so I can see you. I don't have my glasses, so all I can see is your beautiful hair. I've always loved your hair."

"Thank you, Aunt Betty, but I have more goodies for you," she said as she grabbed something out of the bag and clutched it in her hand. "Do you need anything?"

"No dear," she said appreciatively. A lone tear rolled down her wrinkly cheeks.

"Aunt Betty, don't cry or I am going to start crying," she stammered as she wiped her eyes and pulled a chair close to the IVs and other medical equipment. "Is this man keeping you good company?" she asked, pointing at the police guard at the door.

"Me and Carl have gotten quite close in this short time."

"I told your aunt that she needed to rest, but she wouldn't. She just kept trying to talk to me. I kept telling her to rest and just breathe. The doctor told you to stop talking three hours ago," he smiled from the door as he continued to poke his head in and out of the door like clockwork.

She watched the guard, taking note of how long he would look out in the hall as Betty continued to talk about her new friend. He was as constant as the guards at the Tomb of the Unknown Soldier. Every five minutes, he would step out of the room and do a quick scan of the hallway, checking for possible threats. The scan took twenty-one seconds each time. She waited twenty-five minutes before she started to make her move.

Betty was prying into Jackie's relationship status which she answered kindly with, "Still single."

"So, Carl, are you seeing anyone? She's single," Betty started, trying to play matchmaker with her last few breaths.

"Aunt Betty, you're going to scare him," she said, smiling shyly as she gave him an awkward smile that would terrify any man after first meeting a woman.

He chuckled kindly and shook his head no as he started to walk out of the room for his quick scan.

She pulled out her syringe with only oxygen in its tube and plunged the needle into the IV. "Jackie, sit down," Betty said, straining her neck to see what she was doing.

"Crazy old bat! Say hi to Ted," she hissed, a wicked smile dancing across her face as she watched the air bubble flow through the IV.

"What did you say?" she asked with horror on her face.

"Oh nothing, Aunt Betty. What's wrong?" she asked, calmly sitting down in the chair beside the incubation container. She could hear Carl's footsteps inching closer to the doorway. She smiled warmly to Carl who returned the friendly, and only friendly, grin when Betty screamed out in pain.

"What? What's going on?" she screamed looking toward Carl who shouted down the hall for the nurses. The heart monitor beeping changed to a high-pitched solid note. "She's flatlining!"

"Code blue! Code blue!" a nurse shouted through the intercom as another opened the glass chamber, watching anxiously as the container slowly parted.

"We're losing her!" one of the nurses yelled as a team of scrubs huddled around the dying woman.

"Aunt Betty!" she shouted as she rushed to Carl's side for a compassionate hug. "What happened?"

CHAPTER 113

Sunday mornings were for only a few things in my mind -- a quick jog, followed by a couple of Dunkin Donuts, a relaxing shower, and then off to church. The ride to church was filled with various phone calls: my time of the week to catch up on family.

I called my mom who asked first and foremost about my love life, just like in every phone conversation before. I thought about brushing it off, but this time it was different; I actually had something to tell.

"Praise Jesus!" she wailed like it was the miracle of the Red Sea.

"Mom, it's not impossible for me to get a date."

"In the last few years it has been. I was starting to think you were going to theology school to become a priest. At least that's what I was telling my friends with grandkids. Do you know how hard it is on me?"

Apparently, my relationship status affected my mother's social standings more than my own. How dare I do this to her? I silently laughed at her melodrama.

"Really? A priest?"

"Well, people were talking about you," she said, her voice changing to a tone one heard around the rumor mill of my mother's card playing table.

"Well, let them talk. I'm used to it."

"But, they were saying..." she started as I interrupted her.

"Anyway, how are things in Florida? Dad still playing golf?"

"Oh honey, your dad quit playing golf a few months ago. He just drives his golf cart around the condo now. It's pretty comical. It's like a biker gang for retired men."

We talked about the normal things – work, life, whether I was eating right, all the concerns that mothers had for their favorite son. I had brothers, but I always knew I was her favorite. Maybe it was because I called her, whereas my brothers always said they were too busy. We ended our conversation with the usual 'I love you's', and then I dialed the police. Again.

"I have some information on the Carbon Monoxide Killers," I spit out, hoping that the person I spoke with was going to take my tidbit of information with some importance.

"Homicide." The voice sounded familiar, but I was horrible with voices on the phone. To be safe, I decided to disguise my own voice again.

"Um, yes, I have something on the Carbon Monoxide Killers."

"What do you have?"

"They are going to kill at Huntington Station tonight at 7:30," I declared as if my life depended on it.

"How did you hear about this?"

"Let's just say that I have a reliable source."

"Sir, what source do you have?"

"A killer told me."

"Sir, sir, what is the killer's name?"

"Alexei Lechkov," I answered recalling the name from the future broadcast.

"And you are confident that it is Huntington Station at 7:30 tonight?"

"A hundred percent."

"Can I have your number, so I can call you back if we need more information?" he asked, but I quickly hung up. I looked down at my phone realizing that they could trace my call. Stupid, Solo. Stupid!

CHAPTER 114

"I am so ready for a day off!" Young said groaning as he walked through the squad room. He threw his car keys on his desk and his empty coffee cup in the trash.

"Late night?" Cooper asked as he stared at the notes about the Carbon Monoxide Killer. He started writing some new information that he'd just received.

"Well, a little! She said yes!" he shouted walking over to Cooper's desk for some congratulations.

"Congrats, man," Cooper said in a friendly but unconvincing way as he gave Young a thumbs-up.

"Wow, that's all I get?" he moaned. "My life is about to change!"

"Change? Why?" Dakota asked, walking up and sporting a new hair style. Her blonde locks were turned to a reddish brown.

"Wow, your hair," Cooper responded in shock. "Nice!"

"What? She changed her hair color and you act like that. When I told you my news, you gave me a lame thumbs-up."

"What news?" Dakota asked turning her attention from Cooper to Young.

"I'm engaged."

"Oh," her eyes widened with a baffled expression. She quickly realized this wasn't the reaction Young wanted. "I mean, congratulations!" she spread her arms to give him a big hug. He picked her up and flung her around like she weighed ten pounds.

"Thanks, darling!" he said as he headed out of the squad room. "I have to go tell the chief my good news."

"How are you really doing?" Cooper asked, standing up to pat Dakota on the back.

"Why do men act like that?"

"Like what?"

"Players," she drawled with disgust.

"Not all men," he refuted gentlemanly.

"I know. I know. You're the exception."

Cooper noticed that he was standing awkwardly close to Dakota. He took a step back and commented once again on her hair. "It really is nice."

"Thanks. I guess I did it because I knew I needed a change. My fake blonde wasn't helping me with my love life. Just me, Ben, and Jerry every Saturday night."

"Dakota, you'll find someone, and when it happens, you will know. Can I ask you something?" he asked carefully.

"Sure, I'm an open book for attached men."

"Come on, really. Why did you become a cop?"

"Want the real reason?" she asked as she darted her eyes around the squad room, making sure that they were still alone before she exposed her heart. He nodded yes. "To meet a husband," she smiled. She quickly grimaced at how idiotic that must have sounded. "I know, not the best plan. But you've heard the saying that you got to go where they are to get one. I thought that since there weren't very many women in this field and I am pretty cute, I could find someone pretty quickly."

"You did this for a man? Going through the police academy and all that just for the goal of finding a husband? Oh, Dakota."

"I know, sad."

"No, not sad," he said quickly. "It's not easy going through the academy. You are a strong, beautiful woman. You can be anything you want to be. Do you even want to be here?"

She looked around the room then down the hall at where the operator's room was located. "I would prefer working in here than down there."

"Well, why don't you do something about it?"

"Everyone sees me as the ditzy blonde."

"News flash! You're not blonde anymore."

"But they will still…" she started pessimistically as Cooper quickly hushed her.

"You were bold enough to change your hair. Be bold enough to change your life as well. Once you find confidence in yourself, other people will see it in you as well."

"Maybe," she said, contemplating the idea of moving departments. "It would be a change, but I'm not sure what my family will think about me being a cop."

"Dakota, you're already a cop," he said smiling and nodding toward the badge she wore proudly on her chest. "It's just time to do what you want to do and not what you think other people want you do."

"I've got a lot of thinking to do."

"Yeah you do," he said returning to his desk. "Oh, and Dakota, I need a partner. Mine retired a few weeks ago, and they have been looking for his replacement."

She smiled as he watched the wheels in her head start spinning. "You're a good guy, Cooper. Really."

"I mean it, Dakota. I can put your name in the mix."

"Sure, why not?" she said pushing the door open to leave the squad room. Cooper picked up his cell phone to send Veronica a text. He started to type when he heard a cheerful scream from the hallway. Now he wished he could get Veronica to shout with glee as well. He sent the text, hoping that it would be the start of something good. That's when something in his notes caught his eye. It was a phone number that the operators had given him. For some strange reason, it seemed familiar.

"Cooper!" Johnson shouted as he entered the quiet squad room. "Where is everyone?"

CHAPTER 115

Jeremiah and Elizabeth walked into Henry's restaurant and Gloria hugged Elizabeth with great enthusiasm. Elizabeth glared at me as I sat at our table for three. Her look clearly said, "Who is this freakin' woman hugging me?"

"Interesting place," Jeremiah commented as he pulled out Elizabeth's seat for her. "Very homey."

"If you were groped at your home," she scoffed.

"Oh, come on, Elizabeth. Gloria is just a loving grandma type," I buffered as I sipped my super sweet tea.

"The TSA could learn a few things from her," she moaned as she readjusted her clothing.

I rolled my eyes at her dramatic expression.

"I've walked past this place," Jeremiah started as Elizabeth butted in.

"And see that, we should have kept walking."

"As I was saying," Jeremiah continued, scolding Elizabeth with a disapproving look, "I've walked past this place many times and considered coming in."

"And then you came to your senses when you saw the horrified looks on the faces of the diners."

"Seriously? How horrible was your childhood that you were never hugged or pinched by an annoying aunt?" I asked, laughing as I started passing around the menus.

"My family doesn't hug," she remarked.

"Surprising," I responded with a wide-eyed expression.

"Thank you for the menu, Solo, and thank you for introducing me to this charming establishment," Jeremiah said.

"Until I make a call to health services and say I saw some rat droppings in the kitchen," Elizabeth added.

"And we just came from church," Jeremiah said grinning. "Tsk-tsk."

I choked on the tea I was sipping, causing Elizabeth and Jeremiah to turn their attention to me and away from their little squabble. "You just came from church?"

"Why would that shock you so?" Jeremiah asked. "Shouldn't you be excited for a lost soul going to church? Can I get an amen? Or a hallelujah?"

"Amen!" Elizabeth said mockingly, with her hands flying in the air, the gesture more appropriate for a Jay-Z concert than a church service. Although, to be perfectly honest, she would be a fish out of water at a rap concert as well.

"You always keep me on my toes, Jeremiah. You would think I would be aware of that by now."

"Maybe you should take notes," he said with a wink as the waitress came by and took our orders. I brought to his attention that his snide comment might have been overheard by the waitress.

"She could possibly think that the remark was aimed toward her," I said.

His eyes widened, and he quickly resolved the situation by clarifying himself to the young waitress.

The waitress stared at Jeremiah in confusion. She stated that she wasn't listening and not to worry about it. Elizabeth and I busted up laughing at Jeremiah's humiliation.

"Well, I just wanted her to know the truth," he stated plainly as he quickly took his seat to deter any more attention from the rest of the diners. "I'll leave a nice tip."

"You do that. Money fixes everything," Elizabeth said, nodding facetiously as Jeremiah stuck out his tongue like a five-year-old.

"Children, stop that," I chimed in like a disapproving father. "Anyway, do you two go to church often?"

"I go fairly often, but Ms. Elizabeth here only goes on special occasions," Jeremiah jabbed her side. "Funny isn't it? The atheist goes more often than the supposed Christian."

"I go when I feel like I need to go," she said, smiling gingerly, "which seems to be only on days that involve holidays or baptisms. Strange how my calendar coincides like that."

"Very," I chuckled. "But you know, not to get too churchy, but it's good to go to get refueled for the coming week."

"My refueling place of choice is Starbucks or a spa, to be honest," Elizabeth retorted without an ounce of reservation. "A daily shot of espresso and I can take on the world."

"Where's your place?" I asked Jeremiah.

"I find a great amount of solace in the peaceful moments. Some may call it meditation, but just getting alone and out of the way of the hustle of the world can do wonders for one's psyche. So, to name a particular place, I don't have one. It changes from day to day."

"Since we are being so frank here," Elizabeth said as her eyes locked on mine, "do you still believe that visions and signs are a bunch of hoopla?"

Really? I thought. She's calling me out now?

"Yes, Solo. Since you have had a week to think, have your beliefs tilted one way or the other?" Jeremiah asked.

I weighed each answer on a scale, but my mind couldn't process the outcome of either one. Would he consider my faith weak for not believing in such revelations? Or would he consider me a faith hopper for switching my story in just a week.

"Well, I have really been thinking a lot about this subject this week," I said, eyeing Elizabeth patronizingly. "I started the week saying that I did not believe in people having these types of revelations because I didn't have any personal experience that could prove them to me. But then something happened Tuesday night," I said as Elizabeth's eyes widened in fearful accusations. She had a secret that she was willing to keep hidden, and based on the last week, she would do many things to keep this knowledge away from the public eye.

"What happened?" Jeremiah asked, leaning onto the table and into the conversation.

"I was made aware, by Elizabeth here, that I shouldn't be so set in my ways. Once I become stubborn and unbendable then should anything come that could shake my faith, I would break."

"Elizabeth, you said that? So wise, you are," Jeremiah said proudly with a soft applause.

"Well, I don't recall exactly what I said. But..." she started as I quickly picked up where she was heading.

"But you opened my eyes, Elizabeth. You really did. If my faith is at the center of my existence, and if I assume that everything I believe is right, then either I am as wise as God, or I am as foolish as the next man. You opened my eyes to my foolery. And for that, I thank you."

"So, has your opinion changed then?" Jeremiah asked, returning to the topic of his upcoming book.

"I don't know if I would say it changed, but maybe it evolved."

"A God-fearing man believing in evolution," Jeremiah said, laughing heartily. "Now you have opened my eyes to my foolery."

"Once I say without a doubt that God cannot use signs or dreams, I am basically telling God that he can't do something. So, I have come to realize that in my arrogance, I was belittling God's mysterious ways. So, yes, I believe God can use these mystical dreams or signs. I believe God can speak through visions or revelations. I believe God can use mere men, who are but mists in a rainstorm, to give some insight on what He wants them to do. Once I say that God can't do that, I am as faithless as…" I ended, not wanting to point fingers.

"As me?" Jeremiah concluded.

"Yes," I shrugged. "Sorry to sound so heartless in my analysis, but if you want my honest response, a lie isn't what you are going to get."

"And a lie isn't what I deserve," Jeremiah said with a nod. "Thank you, Solo, for your complete openness and honesty. I may not see the world as you see it, but I feel like I have a friendship with you that is open to all forms of future conversations and theoretical debates. If you are up for them."

"Bring 'em on," I said smiling.

Jeremiah's phone started to vibrate, and he quickly excused himself from the table.

"So, does Jeremiah always talk that way? So prim and proper?" I asked, laughing as he walked out of earshot.

"All the time," Elizabeth groaned.

"It's like my vocabulary changes when I talk to him. As though it doubles, and I consider mimicking a British accent or something," I said in astonishment.

"That's not saying much with the few words you do know. I bet that sign language chimp at the zoo has a more extensive vocabulary than you."

"Really? All he can say is food, banana, and thank you."

"Good job," she said, snickering. She snapped her finger for the waitress. "Can we get a cookie for this young man? He deserves a treat for learning the word banana this week."

"Hardy har har."

"You're too easy to poke fun at, Solo. But back to Jeremiah. Sometimes I just want to shake him and tell him to talk like a normal guy, but I don't think he would understand."

"Probably not. But he's a good guy."

"Yeah, I guess so. So, any heroic deeds today?" she asked, a bit condescendingly.

"Well, I gotta try to save a cop and a civilian from those Carbon Monoxide Killers that are on the loose. Then around midnight, I'm going to try to stop someone from jumping off one of the subway bridges into the Potomac River. So, I guess I do."

CHAPTER 116

The concrete structure of the Huntington Station appeared as an incoming subway train pulled into the station. Hundreds of passengers sprinted from the cars and ran down the stairs to exit and head home or out for a night on the town.

One uniformed police officer remained at the station, pacing back and forth. He kept watch as the train departed, signaling that another train should be returning in a matter of minutes. He periodically looked at his watch, checking the time as if knowing there was a countdown.

Suddenly, the rhythm of a heartbeat drowned out the other noises until all that was heard was its eerie music. Thump.

Thump.

Thump.

Another train slid into the Huntington Station as the police officer took his stance. He was looking for someone. He watched each passenger as they exited and then quickly made his way to examine each car compartment before the doors closed and the cars exited the station. Once again, as the train departed, he looked at his watch. His pounding heartbeat started to get faster.

He spoke something into his two-way radio. He looked disturbed a moment later, presumably from the response he received. When he looked up, he noticed a subway train coming forward. He glanced down at his watch. 7:29 p.m. The ticking of the second hand started to harmonize with the heartbeat.

The face of the watch remained like a hologram as the second hand proceeded to spin around the face. He watched the oncoming subway train. The sound of his heartbeat was thumping faster and faster. Thump, thump, thump, thump, thump.

He felt on his waist, checking for his gun. He turned the safety off as the train came to a stop. Passengers exited each car, causing a mad rush of chaos. He became entangled in a group of teenage girls holding hands. He shouted for them to get out of the way. They turned frantic and frightened. He could see a middle-aged couple helping another couple in medical masks get out of the train car.

The policeman shouted something as he lifted his gun. He pointed it at the two in the surgical masks, flipping between the man and the woman. They each continued to walk toward the cop unfazed.

The middle-aged couple broke free heading down the stairs, screaming. The police officer continued to shout at the two. They continued to move forward until they each stopped and raised their hands, showing that they were empty. The thumping heartbeat and ticking sound faded, and the conversation became audible.

"Officer Cooper, so nice to see you," the female voice said as she stood in front of the stairwell. Her partner stood a few feet closer to the subway car. "We won't hurt you if you let us go, but if you do try something, we can't guarantee your safety. Or Veronica's."

"Freeze! Don't move!"

"But Winston, you won't shoot me," the female voice said. The two continued to converse incoherently like their dialogue was in fast forward. She started to remove her mask, causing the police officer's face to drop in shock. "Now!"

She ducked from the bullet that he fired. Her partner jumped toward the policeman. He tried to change his stance, but Alexei was too quick. He tackled the policeman, causing his gun to slide across the cement floor. They wrestled with all their adrenaline-fueled strength. The policeman reached for his gun just as the woman picked it up, aiming it at his head. "What kind of flowers do you want us to put on your grave?" she asked before she fired.

"Wint!" I gasped as beads of sweat ran down my face. I looked over at my clock. 6:41 p.m. My afternoon nap had run a little long.

CHAPTER 117

Earlier in the day Cooper informed Captain Johnson of the telephone call he believed to be authentic. He asked to be one of the officers to go to Huntington Station. Johnson granted the request but told him to not get his hopes up, reminding him that tips were not always the most reliable source of information. Johnson then gave orders for the other officers for the evening.

"I'm going to ride the subway this time," Cooper stated to Knightly and White. "You meet me at Huntington Station by 7:15."

"Got it," Knightly said before they bumped fists and got into their squad cars.

Cooper headed to the Archives-Navy Memorial-Penn Quarter Metro Station, jumping on the yellow line subway as Huntington Station was its final destination. He glanced down at his watch and saw that it was 6:42 p.m. He should make it to Huntington Station by the time Knightly and White arrived. He prayed that the call this morning was correct and that he and his partners would stop these killers once and for all. He stood on the subway train, allowing some older folks a spot to sit and rest their feet. He noticed them and looked carefully, knowing that they fit the profile of the victims.

Looking around the train car, he wondered if the killers could already be heading toward Huntington Station. What if they are on this train? he thought as his heart started to pump. He grabbed onto the handrails hanging from the ceiling, trying not to trip over pairs of long legs in the walkway. He decided that instead of just waiting around for the killers, he would start investigating.

Cooper surveyed the train car, and when he believed that it was safe, he moved to the next one. With each stop, he exited the subway train, did a quick surveillance of the waiting station, and hopped back into the car before the train left.

At each station, his heart pumped a little more blood. He couldn't help wondering if each stop was the one they were going to get on. He looked down at his phone and noticed that he didn't have any reception. His phone was on its last leg anyway. He had forgotten to charge it last night, which he almost always did every night before he went to bed. Since he and Solo talked until 3 a.m., charging the phone was the least of his worries. When their conversation ended, he quickly fell asleep on the kitchen floor. He woke up with a tiled imprint on his forehead that took a little bit of scrubbing and hot water to erase.

The subway train came out from below ground, causing his phone to vibrate with a message. He pulled out his phone from his pocket as well as a piece of crumbled up paper. It was the phone number that the operator had given him this morning belonging to the person who called with the tip. He looked down at the number quizzically before stuffing it back into his pocket.

Two messages, he thought. He clicked on the first one when the subway darted back underground causing a loss of reception before he could hear the voicemail. He watched his cell battery signal flash, warning him that he didn't have much longer before his means of communication with the civilian world would end.

He continued the routine checks of the passengers, but no one appeared to fit the description of the killers. That was when a thought filled his mind. If this was the last night for their killing spree, would they do something different? What if they didn't even disguise themselves? The thought terrified him. What if any of these couples were the killers?

In the middle of this thought, he received another message notification. Cooper pulled out his phone and saw his service had three bars and his battery was down to two percent. He considered listening to the message but decided against it. It could wait. If it was incredibly important they would call the station, and he would be informed by the two-way radio.

CHAPTER 118

Alexei stood in the darkened tunnel of the Gallery Place Chinatown Metro Station – the same place they met each night before they changed identities for a few hours of role-playing excitement. His sister quickly walked into the blackness and put on the costume for the night. Once again, she was going to be playing the cancer-stricken woman.

"Last night," she commented before he interrupted.

"I know. It's sad," he replied. "I know we made a deal about doing this for only one week a year, but now that it's over, I don't want it to be."

"I know how you feel, but last night…" she started before he once again sidelined her.

"Last night was awesome! It was so spur-of-the-moment and exciting that I almost had a hard time falling asleep."

She smiled warmly at the sight of her little brother having the time of his life. She thought she needed to tell him about Betty, but again, divulging every secret didn't always do any good. She had learned that the hard way from last night's confession of murdering of their grandparents.

They hugged each other for good luck and proceeded toward the subway car. The electronic chime warned them that the doors would be closing. He hurried into the subway car and caught the door for his sick sister to enter as another gentleman's hand stretched out to help her in.

"Thank you, sir," Alexei said politely as his sister nodded in appreciation before collapsing onto an empty seat.

"You're very welcome," said the aged man with a platinum silver beard and buzzed haircut. His wife beside him smiled compassionately at the two behind their medical masks but didn't engage in any conversation.

She nudged her brother in his ribs to start the dialogue, but he looked over at her and winked. He wasn't ready to pick a victim. They still had a while to go before they would end up at Huntington Station, and he wanted to savor the last victims. He wanted them to be the cream of the crop. He wanted them to be fighters.

She leaned over and started whispering in her brother's ear, "This week has been the best week of my life."

"Mine too," he said, winking at her.

"I wish Dad could have seen us. He would have been so proud of us."

"I know. Can you tell me another story about him?"

"Sure," she answered as she laid her head on his shoulder. She recalled the time that they dressed up for Halloween. "All four of us were clowns. Mom made each of our costumes by hand and then Dad painted each of our faces with makeup. You were a little scared," she said with a chuckle as she bopped his nose with her finger.

"I'm still not that fond of them."

"Well, we went trick-or-treating around the neighborhood, and then we pigged out on all of the candy. We ate so much that we were sick the next day. I missed school and Dad stayed home with both of us. We laid around in the living room and watched television all day. I will never forget because when he heard Mom pull up, he made us go to our rooms and pretend like we had been in them all day. He was the best."

"Yeah. I wish I remembered him."

"Don't worry. There are plenty more stories to tell."

Happy birthday, Papa.

CHAPTER 119

"Wint! Wint! Pick up. This is urgent!" I shouted, leaving him another voicemail. I had already left him three, and I didn't see the need to keep calling since he wasn't picking up.

I went through my phone contacts and found Verny's number. I rolled my eyes in annoyance at the thought of talking to her, but drastic times called for drastic measures.

"Verny," I said before realizing that I'd called her by the wrong name. By her tone, I knew she was already annoyed with me.

"What, Solomon?"

"Have you talked with Wint lately? He's not answering his phone," I spewed my words as if a life depended on it – his.

"I haven't seen him today. We texted a little earlier, but that's all."

"Veronica, I need you to call him. Maybe he'll pick up for you. Tell him that he is in danger. Tell him to go left."

"You're not making any sense."

"I don't care if I'm not making sense. You have to tell him to go left!"

"He's working. What do you mean go left?"

"Just tell him!" I shouted as she picked up on the urgency.

"Okay, okay. I will text him to go left. You two have some weird bromance going on."

"It's not weird. I love him, Veronica. I love him like a brother, and I know you love him too! We may not get along; we may not even like each other, but I know that he loves you. I don't understand what he loves about you, but I know that he would do anything for you. Do you understand that? Do you see that he would do anything for you? Even if that meant changing everything he was so that you would love him."

"What right do you have telling me this?" she yelled.

"Because someone needs to fix you two, and I guess since Chelsea is gone," my voice caught as tears filled my eyes, "that leaves me. Chelsea loved both of you so much. She was like Wint. He can see past my flaws just as he can see past yours. That is how Chelsea was. She loved you, Veronica. She would tell me every time after we would leave dinner with you how awesome you were. How smart you were. How beautiful you were. How lucky Wint was to find you because, well, as hard as it is for me to say, you are pretty amazing."

Veronica listened without saying a word, causing the awkwardness between us to grow like an early morning autumn fog.

"Um, Veronica, you still there?"

"I'm here," she said, blowing her nose. "I never knew that about Chelsea. I never got to know her that well."

"She was pretty amazing herself. Not a day goes by that I do not think about her and miss her. I don't want you to go through what I have gone through," I said quickly, wondering if I said too much.

"Okay, so, I'm supposed to tell Wint or Winston," she started laughing. "Oh, Solomon, you got in my head. I'm supposed to tell him to go left."

"Yes! And do it now! His life depends on it!"

"What? His life?" she asked, but I had already hung up.

CHAPTER 120

She closed her eyes listening to the incoming and outgoing passengers and taking in all the senses of their last night. She looked around the train, taking mental photographs of her surroundings even down to the advertisements for women and the benefits of breastfeeding. She didn't know why that was worthy of an ad. There wasn't very much money being made off of mothers breastfeeding, unlike the profitable baby formula industry. She had stared at the ad long enough before deciding to just close her eyes and relax.

They were four stations away when she whispered to her brother, asking him if he found a worthy candidate yet. He said, "Not yet, but I will."

She trusted her brother, especially after his brilliant performance the previous night. She also trusted her gut instincts that he'd better hurry up and start a conversation before it was too late. They left Braddock Road Station and her senses heightened. She started shivering frantically and tapped his thigh with her fist.

"Are you okay?" he asked as she continued to shake uncontrollably.

"Is she going to be okay?" a woman in her forties asked. She was old enough to be a grandmother but still young enough to be feisty.

"I'm not sure. She had a treatment today, and she hasn't been herself."

"I'm, I'm…I'm okay," she said in a quivering voice as her head shook slightly. "I'm just cold."

He wrapped his arm around her, rubbing her shoulders trying to give her some of his warmth. "Better?"

"A little," she said as she continued to shiver. She closed her eyes and felt a little guilty for not believing in her brother's system.

"Thank you for asking by the way," he commented, beginning to work himself into a conversation with the middle-aged couple.

"Oh, I was just worried," she replied as she leaned over to not speak so loudly and annoy the other passengers. "I'm a nurse, so I wasn't too alarmed, but I knew something wasn't right. So, she had a treatment today?"

"Yes, they are getting rougher and rougher. The doctor said that would happen, but she only has a few more and then hopefully, fingers crossed."

"Here's to remission," she smiled, leaning back into her husband's arm who was looking out the window at the nighttime lights.

"So, you're a nurse?" Alexei asked as she leaned forward once again.

"Yes, I'm an RN."

"Where do you work?"

"I work at a pediatrician's office in Utah."

He nodded as he leaned back and smiled beneath his surgical mask knowing that he had found his match. He glanced past the nurse to examine her husband, who had a solid six-foot frame and appeared to be in good shape by the way his navy sweater accentuated his muscular chest.

"We have them in the bag," he whispered to his sister. She opened one of her eyes to see the new targets, noticing that their hair wasn't gray, but blonde, and the only wrinkles they had were laugh lines.

"Are you sure about them?"

"Yes. The good people from Utah are definitely going to help me with you. It's like their motto."

CHAPTER 121

Go left? Winston kept repeating the cryptic text message he read from Veronica before his cell phone battery died. What does that mean, he wondered. Is she saying that she's left? Did she leave me? He paced Huntington Station, waiting for the oncoming subway car as he looked at his watch. 7:19 p.m. His heart pumped inside his anxious chest as a tiny drop of sweat dripped past his hairline. This was what he had been waiting for. A solid tip that coincided with their profile of the killers' history.

He wasn't thinking of this as a career advancement as many people in his department would. He just wanted to end these criminals' careers. As the subway train came to a stop, his mind flashed back to all the video footage and photographs of the killers. He recalled the various types of disguises they had worn this week. Wigs were a simple camouflage, but when done properly, they could conceal the deadliest of secrets.

The doors parted as the herd of passengers escaped, running down the stairs to enjoy the rest of their Sunday night. He did a meticulous scan of the passengers, and none of them appeared to be the killers. There weren't any young-looking passengers following some sixty-year-olds. He quickly poked his head in each subway car but didn't see anyone that appeared to fit the description. A few passengers raced up the stairs, trying to make it onto the subway before the doors closed. As the train headed back towards Washington, D.C., Cooper looked down at his watch. 7:24 p.m.

"Knightly, White, where are you? Do you copy?" he asked into his two-way radio as he stood on the deserted platform station.

"We copy," Knight answered. "We got stopped by a wreck on the George Mason Memorial Bridge. We are on our way and should be there in about fifteen to twenty minutes. We called for backup to handle this wreck; no casualties."

"I don't have fifteen minutes. I need backup now!" Cooper yelled as his heart started to pound faster, pumping uncontrollably.

"Cooper, we have already called the Alexandria police to go to the station. They should be there. Keep your phone handy because this radio keeps cutting out."

"My phone's dead and there is no one else here except for me!" he yelled louder, hoping that his message got through. It didn't. They didn't answer. "Knightly? White? Do you copy?" A growing sense of fear started taking over his courage as he glanced down the track to see the light of an oncoming subway car. His hands trembled as he glanced down at his watch. 7:29 p.m.

"You can do this, Wint. You can do this. You have been trained for this," he told himself as he took a couple of deep breaths, grabbed his holster, and turned the safety off. The screeching subway stopped at Huntington Station. A group of rowdy passengers rushed past him. He took a step back to give the riders easy access to the stairs and get in a spot where he could see as many train cars as possible.

He stepped forward and unknowingly got caught in a mob of bubblegum-popping, P!nk-singing teenage girls.

"Get out of my way!" he yelled, bumping and pushing free from the dozen arms. He caught sight of a couple of passengers wearing surgical masks.

"Whatever," one of the girls shouted with attitude as the rest screamed in fear. They followed the remainder of the fleeting passengers down the stairs.

"Alexei!"

CHAPTER 122

"Alexei!" Cooper shouted in the most robust voice he could muster. He was trying to squash his fear, hoping that a surge of bravery would take over. He raised his gun and took aim at the possible killers, shifting his aim between the two as they eyed one another.

"Freeze!" he shouted. They didn't stop. Instead, they slowly edged away from the train, moving in Cooper's direction. He was standing twenty feet away in the middle of the platform station, ten feet in front of the stairs that headed down to the subway entrance.

The forgotten Utah couple hollered as they ran down the stairs, hand in hand to escape, realizing how close they were to something horrible.

"You're caught! Just give up!" Cooper shouted as he continued to take aim. Alexei and his sister took another step before raising their hands in unbelievable surrender.

"Officer Cooper, so nice to see you," she said cheerfully as if meeting him for the first time. From the way his name rolled off her tongue, he had a strange feeling they had met before. "We won't hurt you if you let us go," she said childishly. "But if you do try something, we can't guarantee your safety," she said, her voice changing to a growl with her immediate threat. "Or Veronica's."

Cooper's heart sank. It was one thing to threaten him, but to threaten his innocent wife, that was reprehensible. "Freeze! Don't move!"

Alexei looked over at his sister, allowing her to control the conversation. He took another step forward, staying on the side nearest the subway. She was standing closer to the stairwell.

It was time.

CHAPTER 123

I could hear the commotion ahead. My heart pumped from the mad dash from the parking garage as I hopped over the ticket counter and hoped that one of the security guards would chase after me to stop me. They didn't. They just continued to work on their crossword puzzle.

I ran up the stairs, taking two or three at a time. I felt the burn in my legs, but it couldn't compare to the pain I would feel if my best bud was killed. As I neared the top, my stomping subsided, becoming more like the quiet steps of a leopard, stalking its prey. I could see Wint taking his stance as my head reached the top. I hunched down, waving from behind the female killer to try to get Wint's attention.

"But Winston, you won't shoot me," the familiar female voice said as I started pointing over to the other man.

"Go left!" I mouthed, but I couldn't tell if he saw.

Wint continued to take aim at the woman as she reached up to remove her surgical mask. "Now, now, now, Winston. Where are your manners? Is this how you treat a friend?"

"You are no friend to me!" he yelled as Alexei took another step forward, inching himself closer to Wint.

"But Now, now, now, Winston, we are friends," she said soothingly, slowly stroking the medical mask and letting the emotions of Winston's last stand intoxicate her.

"You're caught! Just give up!" Wint shouted again, watching Alexei from the corner of his eye.

"Now, now, now, Winston, is that any way to talk to us?" she asked kindly as her voice changed. "Your worst nightmares!"

"Go left!" I mouthed, but he didn't notice. All he could see were the two killers as they each took a step closer, cornering him. They knew he could only shoot one of them, and their dedication was until death.

"Stop! I will shoot!"

"Now, now, now, Winston, what have we done to you?" she growled as she twirled the dangling strings from her surgical mask. "What have we ever done to you?" she asked sympathetically, her voice taking a dramatic, sinister twist. "Your wedding was beautiful."

"Go left!" I mouthed again, watching this tragedy slowly play out.

"Backup is on the way! Just surrender!"

"Surrender?" Alexei laughed sarcastically. "Why would we ever surrender? The fun is just beginning."

"Go left!" I mouthed, knowing I wasn't going to be able to wait much longer.

"There's no way out of this alive if you don't surrender!"

"Now, now..." she started as I interrupted.

"Now!" I shouted.

CHAPTER 124

The woman turned around frantically as I caught her off guard. I hurled myself up the stairs and pounced on her like a linebacker smacking her onto the hard cement and knocking the wind out of her lungs.

"Argh!" Alexei screamed, launching his body like a rocket. But Wint went left and aimed. His trigger finger was faster.

"No!" she screamed hearing the gun fire again and again. Alexei's body flinched with each bullet entering his chest. "Alexei!"

Blood spewed from the two holes near his heart. His legs wobbled, causing his body to crumble like a puppet as he heaved in a couple of last dying breaths.

"Jenika!" he moaned, reaching out his trembling hand towards her flattened body for one last tender moment before the harsh, cold reality of death.

"I love you!" she cried, wiggling her arm free from my grasp, inching her fingers toward his.

"I don't think so!" Wint shouted. He ran forward in his black combat boots, stepping on each of their fragile hands, crunching their bones without a second thought. "Your victims couldn't hold hands when you killed them, could they?"

"I, I love…" Alexei started as his head fell onto the concrete like dead weight. His eyes were wide open, but the life in them was gone.

"No!" she cried, watching the ocean of his blood tide closer to her. "No! Alexei!"

Cooper bent down, checking Alexei's pulse. There wasn't one. He lay lifeless on the subway platform as I continued to hold Jenika down. She looked into his tranquil eyes whispering something unrecognizable, "Lutshe pozdno, chem nikogda."

"What did you say?" I asked, but she just responded with a haunting laugh.

Cooper got out his handcuffs and helped me up. I pressed my foot in Jenika's back to keep her down. He gave me a quizzical expression of confusion and joyful relief as he tightly shackled her hands behind her back. She winced in pain.

"Get up!" he commanded as a few sirens filled the distance. I helped Wint get her on her feet when I noticed her surgical mask covered half her face. Something about her eyes and cheek looked familiar. I reached up and lowered the mask to her neck as my heart plummeted.

"Jenny?"

CHAPTER 125

"But why?" I asked, trembling. My throat clenched as if I was one of her victims straining for oxygen. Wint Mirandized her while my chest heaved. I saw the platform station spin, wondering if I had been a puppet in her grand façade. A tearful smirk appeared on her grieving face.

"You have no idea what I've been through," she stated calmly, as if flipping a switch from sadness to professional attorney, ignoring her dead brother five feet away.

"What was so horrible that you had to do this?" I questioned, wondering if I was overstepping my bounds in the criminal system. By the expression on Wint's face, I wasn't.

"Do what?" she asked in bewilderment. "We were on our way to a costume party. It is Halloween next week."

"The jig is up, and you can stop lying. We have you for all the murders," Wint said as a herd of Alexandria police officers came rushing up the stairs to offer assistance and start taping off the crime scene.

"What murders?" she asked naively, fluttering her false eyelashes. "Oh, you mean those, what were you calling them, Carbon Monoxide Killers? You think we were doing those? Hilarious!" she said laughing hysterically as she turned her attention to her brother's body now being photographed by the crime scene unit. "If anyone is a murderer," she began in a psychotic scream, "It's you, Winston! You just killed my innocent brother! Innocent! You're going to pay for this!"

"Well, you can have your day in court," Wint growled as he grabbed her elbow and escorted her to a police cruiser to take her down for booking.

"Believe me, I will!" she cunningly hissed. "So strong you are, Wint. I now see what Veronica saw in you. Sorry to tell you," she whispered in his ear, "it's over. She told me last night when she came to my apartment crying." I listened, following in disbelief how the kind, warm-hearted girl I had lunch with was actually a cold-hearted killer with so little reverence for life. "But you know, hypothetically speaking, if I was one of those supposed killers, I would have one regret. I should have killed her in her sleep last night. It would have been so easy. I could have easily slit her wrists and placed her in the bathtub claiming it was the suicide of a depressed, newly-separated wife."

"Shut up!" I screamed from behind as Wint stayed emotionless. He did not let her attempted insults get through his bulletproof heart.

"But you know, I am somewhat glad I didn't slice her up like a piece of deli meat last night. If I am who you believe me to be. She was gone early this morning when I was running a few errands. Oh, I know. Maybe she went to work to draw up her divorce papers," she said, winking playfully. "Sweet, isn't it? To draw up your own divorce papers. I mean, she made her own pre-nup, so you're getting nothing. Better find a part time job, cop. Now, you will have to endure the humiliation and lengthy process of a divorce," she said, smiling, continuing her final game and playing it out until he would break.

It was all I could do to keep from stretching my leg in front of hers, tripping her and watching her unprotected body roll down the concrete stairs. What I wouldn't give to watch her head strike each stair until she ended up bloody and bruised, begging for death.

"I've had many clients say that a divorce is more painful than death. Because even though the marriage had died, their ex was like a ghost that would never go away. I hope Veronica takes you for everything you have. But you don't have anything, do you? It's all Veronica's already. She probably even paid for the underwear you have on right now. You're a boxers man, right? What a sweet sight that will be when she strips you of everything. You've always been a nice piece of eye candy. You can learn a few things from him, Solomon."

Wint remained calm through Jenny's rants and verbal daggers. But once my name was mentioned, his resolve vanished. "If you say anything, and I mean anything, about the woman I love or my best friend, so help me, you will never make it to a court room."

"Oh! Did I strike a nerve?" she asked, squealing like a damsel in distress. "But what caused this outburst?" she asked as if digging deep into Wint's mind. She had transitioned into a psychologist persona as if connecting the dots of what made Wint who he was. "Now I see why you and Veronica are on such shaky ground," she said, humming as if she found the smoking gun and was taking a mental note of her discovery. "Who do you love more, Veronica or Solomon? When you're alone, who do you think about more?"

"Oh, please just shut up! You are psycho!" I shouted.

"Mmmm," she said, smiling as she walked down the remaining stairs. "Is that why you're still single Solo? Is that why your friend here had to set you up with me? To keep you close? To play this charade or secret life? Does Veronica know? I can't wait to tell her."

"There's nothing to tell," I started before Wint looked behind shaking his head to stop the conversation.

"Don't even let this piece of trash get to you, brother."

The three of us walked toward the police cars as she kept talking wildly about anything that she presumed would get under our skin. White and Knightly pulled up in awe that Officer Cooper had single-handedly taken down the Carbon Monoxide Killers. "Take her to the station," Wint commanded as he threw her into the backseat. She pressed her lips against the car window, blowing Wint a sloppy wet kiss and rolling her eyes at me in disgust.

"They're boyfriends, you know," she announced to White and Knightly as if breaking a news story that was going to shake the entire force.

"Shut up," White demanded. They were all used to the ploys of criminal minds.

As Knightly and White drove away, she turned around in the backseat and eyed us seductively. It was as if she was saying that the game had just begun. I watched as the red and blue lights disappeared around the corner and waited for the sirens to dissipate into the night.

"You okay?" I asked, clasping his shoulder encouragingly. "You did it!"

His smoldering expression eased into a boyish grin, as if he'd just hit the game-winning homerun. "I just have one question," he asked as he reached into his pocket and pulled out a piece of paper with a phone number on it. He tossed it into the nearby trashcan. "Can I borrow your phone? I have a call I need to make."

CHAPTER 126

I gave my statement to the police, then watched from the bus stop bench as Wint paced around the parking lot, talking to Verny. His conversation was heated. Then it appeared as though a cold front passed through. Finally, the moonlight lit a smile on his dimpled face. He continued to walk under the light poles as a few more police cars and the coroner van arrived on the scene.

Wint got off the phone and headed my way with a new strut in his walk. "So, I think I need to thank you," he said as he took a seat trying to hand me my phone.

"Keep it. You may need it later."

He finally resigned the fight and stuffed my fully charged phone in his pocket. "Veronica told me what you said to her tonight," he answered, staring at the passing motorists that were totally unaware that the world was going to sleep a little safer tonight.

I looked over at him and then at the road he was watching. "Huh?" I didn't know what he was talking about. Was he speaking of my romantic advice or the elusive tip?

"I don't know what you said, but whatever it was, you got through to her."

"Oh, it really was nothing. Just looking out for my boy," I said.

"Well," he started before his voice began to choke. I had known Wint since we both wore Spiderman underwear, and he had never been one to show his emotions.

"It's all good," I said, patting his back like a coach.

He shook his head as a smile stretched across his face. "You've always had my back," he stopped. "Even when I didn't know you were watching out for me."

"No biggie."

"Solo, what I'm trying to say…" He stopped again, taking a deep breath as he looked into my eyes. I knew what he was going to say, but the words didn't need to be spoken. True friends always know.

"Sorry for setting me up with a serial killer?" I said, changing the mood with a brotherly smile.

"Exactly what I was going to say," he said, laughing. We watched the coroner's gurney slide Alexei's bagged body into the back of the van.

"It's been a day," I said feeling strange that less than an hour earlier that young man was alive and baiting his next victim. I couldn't stop thinking about how quickly life could change. A swerving car could either save a life or take it. A prescription bottle could either bring healing or an overdose. A single word could either bring forgiveness or division. A bullet could either bring protection or a death sentence.

"It sure has," he said standing up and looking up at the Huntington Station platform. He knew he needed to return to the scene to be questioned and give his gun and statement. "I have to get back up there."

"Duty calls."

We started to walk away from the bench. He was heading toward the station as I turned to go toward the garage. "Speaking of calls, I had the most interesting phone call this morning. Someone called in a tip and told me that all of this was going down here tonight at 7:30. Funny, isn't it?" he said, shrugging his shoulders as he continued to walk. "Wish I could say thank you to that guy. He saved my life."

"Isn't that what an anonymous tip line is for?"

"Yeah, I guess you're right."

I walked down the sidewalk between the two garages. I had a feeling that I was being followed. I turned around and saw that I was alone, but Wint stood watching from the distance as he spoke to another officer.

CHAPTER 127

It was a quiet drive home as I turned down the radio to reflect on the events of the week. It was hard to believe that last week at this time, I was sleeping peacefully with the occasional nightmare of falling off a cliff or other dreams that didn't make sense. If my coming week was like the one I'd just had, it was going to be another interesting seven days.

I reclined on the couch and flipped on the eleven o'clock news as Brock Michaels started the newscast with a live police news conference. Chief Grant Randolph stood at the lectern and commended the metropolitan police officers along with the surrounding area police units that had worked tirelessly to capture the Carbon Monoxide Killers. "This has been a devastating week, but it is over now." I proudly watched as Wint stood with a few other police behind Chief Randolph, but his name was never mentioned.

"What?" I yelled at the television as if an umpire had missed the strike that was clearly over the plate.

Chief Randolph stood in his formal police uniform. His graying hair had turned a shade whiter from the events of this week. "We received a tip this morning from an unknown caller with information about tonight's events. Because of that single heroic act, we have ended the threat of the Carbon Monoxide Killers who have been running loose for a week. So to that solo hero I just want to say thank you and there is a $50,000 reward for assisting in capturing these killers. If anyone has any information on who this person is, please contact our office."

The camera panned out as the live reporter in her crimson pantsuit started questioning Chief Randolph. Her hands trembled as she held the microphone. I didn't care about his comments or thoughts when I saw a blonde woman run across the stage and jump in Wint's arms. It looked like he and Verny would be making up nicely tonight.

CHAPTER 128

12:03 a.m. flashed in blue neon numbers as the sound of a passing subway train filled the silence. Heavy breathing and screaming broke through the clanking metal. "Help me!" the man's voice screamed at the top of his lungs as he looked over at a bridge of passing cars. The image of the George Mason Memorial Bridge was a few hundred yards away. He watched as the passing cars revved their engines. He looked up to see his hands gripping the metal bar; his wristwatch still displayed its digital blue numbers. 12:05 a.m. "Help me!" he shouted. It was no use. There was no one around. His legs dangled as the light from the bridge reflected the waves of the historic Potomac River. What he wouldn't give to see George Washington, or anyone, crossing the river right then.

"Help me!" he screamed, swinging his legs, trying to get enough momentum to fasten his legs to the metal ledge above the bridge so he could climb up. His body moved like a pendulum, but no matter how close he got, he was never close enough. "Help me!" His scream became a moan, a frightened plea. Glancing over at the bridge, he saw people singing in their cars at midnight, trying to stay awake. His Timex watch showed 12:08 a.m. He had only been hanging for a couple of minutes, but he didn't have a good grip on the bar, so his fingers were sliding.

"I can't swim!" he cried as his fingers slipped all the way off and he rushed toward the frigid waters.

There was no sign of life preservers or boats as he collided with his worst nightmare. "Help!" he tried to yell as water filled his mouth. His body tried to fight the current, but when it was coming from all sides, it was useless. He wiggled and tossed his flailing arms, kicking his legs desperately to keep his head above the waves, but it was too much.

He slid under the surface as his watch read 12:09 a.m. He reached his arms up to the moon that shone brightly, hoping his head would float miraculously to the top where he could just get another breath to continue this battle. He didn't. His lungs started to burn from the lack of oxygen, and it was all he could do to not scream in agony. He let out a ghostly whimper as a flood of water barged through his open mouth. He floated peacefully in his last few seconds of life as the Timex blue numbers blinked violently at 12:11 a.m.

Elizabeth woke up from her dream and looked at the alarm clock on her nightstand which said 11:29 p.m. Reaching over she found her journal under her lamp and started to write on the first blank page.

Man dies at 12:11 a.m. from drowning in the Potomac River around the George Mason Memorial Bridge. She recalled that he was dangling from under the subway bridge, so she crossed out George Mason Memorial Bridge and wrote subway bridge. She closed her journal to go back to sleep when a feeling of conviction swarmed her being like a cold wet blanket. She closed her eyes to fall back to sleep when the clock's numbers kept shining in her head. She had seen those numbers recently. That electronic neon blue middle-school styled watch.

"Solo!"

CHAPTER 129

"Solo, where are you?" Elizabeth spit out, rolling out of bed in the flannel pajamas she would deny ever wearing.

"Elizabeth?" a different voice asked, confused.

"Wait! Who's this?" she asked, looking at her phone to check the time. It was still 11:31 p.m.

"This is Winston. My phone died so Solo gave me his to use."

"Oh crap!" she muttered, quickly throwing on a pair of yoga pants and a sweatshirt.

"Elizabeth! What's wrong?"

"It's Solo. I think he's in serious trouble. I have to go find him."

"Where?" Wint asked. He was driving home with Veronica in the passenger seat and slammed on his brakes in the middle of traffic. The sudden move caused the cars behind him to honk their horns and flip him off.

"It's one of the subway bridges over the Potomac!" she exclaimed, not caring if Wint started asking questions about how she knew this. She didn't care if the whole world knew.

"Okay! We're just leaving the press conference," he said, gunning the engine. "We are on our way!"

"Meet you there!" She jumped in her car, praying that she would hit every green light. She watched as the clock reminded her that each and every minute was precious. If she didn't get there by 12:05 a.m., her new and baffling friend was going to die. She recounted the various news reports that she assumed Solo had his hands in this week, and a stabbing pain went into her gut. If she had not ever wished for him to know how she felt, he would not have been put in this situation. She saw the chain of dominos and realized she was the one who placed the first one.

"You can do this! You can do this!" she muttered to herself as she ran through a stop sign knowing that traffic should be pretty dismal this late on a Sunday night. And if she did get pulled over, they were going to have to follow her. That just meant more people to help with the rescue.

CHAPTER 130

I had always wondered how walking on the tracks of the subway line felt, but tonight wasn't the night I wanted to come face to face with that bucket list entry. After I parked my car on a side road near the river, I climbed up to the subway track, violating all the warnings and restrictions that were plastered on the railings.

My watch told me it was 11:45 p.m. Plenty of time to find the man and save him. I started walking across the subway bridge, staying on the metal platform beside the tracks that I presumed was used for maintenance. I shone my convenience store flashlight up the track, but the light quickly faded into the darkness, a mere thirty feet ahead of me. "Blasted cheap flashlight," I thought as I continued walking.

Before long, I had covered almost the entire length of the bridge, making my way toward downtown D.C. "That's odd," I said, scratching my head. I glanced down at my watch and saw that it was 11:58 p.m.

"Hello? Anyone out here?" I yelled, looking down at the waves beneath my feet. The blue river always looked so friendly in the daylight, but right then, it was as scary as the Carbon Monoxide Killers. I turned to start walking back toward the Virginia state line. I glanced over at the cars flying by on the nearby bridges. I had never realized how many people honked, even at midnight. I looked over and couldn't see any reason for the noise. There wasn't any traffic or wrecks; it was just a distraught driver, making a fool of himself most likely.

After a couple of minutes of frantically searching for this mysterious man, I felt a trembling in my legs. It wasn't that cold, but my legs were shivering. "Come on, man!" I yelled as I continued to walk back. I made it to the halfway point of the bridge. "Come on! Where are you?"

Suddenly, a light from behind shone brighter than any flashlight I could buy. It was more luminous than the moon or a passing car. The bridge started to shake violently, like an earthquake, so I grabbed the metal bar to steady my stance as I fearfully turned around. A subway train was heading in my direction, and I was dead center on the bridge. No matter how quickly I ran, I knew I could not outrun a subway in the dark.

"Run, Solo!" a female voice screamed ahead of me. "Run!"

I finally realized the truth of my dream. I was the man! I was the one who needed rescuing. I was the one about to die.

CHAPTER 131

My legs were running as fast as they could, but I could sense the light getting closer. I felt like I was jumping, but it was just the tracks shaking in every direction. The engineers who designed this bridge did so with the intention of a subway train attached to the tracks being the only thing on the bridge.

I'd always been told that when I run, to never look back. Keep my eyes forward. Wise words, yet I had to look back. I had to see where I was in relation to the train that was blaring its horn at me.

It was twenty feet behind me, but I was still a quarter's length away from dry land. I didn't think I was going to make it when the inevitable happened. I tripped.

"Solo!" a woman who looked like Elizabeth screamed as my foot caught in one of the metal brackets. My fast speed became a tumbling Superman jump. I grabbed hold of the metal guardrails to pull me away from the deadly tracks, but the force of the impact and the tremors shaking the bridge were too much for my clumsy body. I felt my legs flying overhead as I flipped over the railing.

"Argh!" I screamed as the railing vanished from my sight. I felt the hard metal in my tight grasp, but I knew my grip wasn't going to hold for long, especially with my stress-induced sweating hands. "Help me! Help me!" I felt the subway train overhead, shaking the bridge like it was a rag doll, and I was just a minor afterthought.

"Help me! I can't swim!" I screamed, kicking and flailing my legs wildly as I felt my fingers dance on the metal railing. "No, please!" I begged, pleading for God to save me. I couldn't help but wonder, Is this my time? Will this be my last request on earth? Is this my last prayer?

"Please, God! Help me! I don't want to die!"

My life flashed before my eyes. I saw the happy moments of my childhood with my brothers and Wint. The bloody noses, the sprained ankles, the playful jabs. I quickly realized that almost all my happy moments involved some painful experiences, but I guessed the saying was true, that what didn't kill us only made us stronger.

Quickly, Chelsea came into the forefront of my memories. Our wedding day that wasn't at all magical, even though I was marrying the woman of my dreams. I wouldn't have cared if a tornado tore through the church. The sound of her laugh could bring warmth in the chilliest of situations and filled my ears like a symphony. The way her hair flipped when a gust of wind blew past always caused my heart to beat a little faster. Her beauty was timeless, and my heart stopped when her life ended.

I looked down at the water and realized that a few years earlier I could probably have fallen into the crashing waves and let the frigid liquid engulf me. But now I had a reason to live. I had a mission. These dreams, these visions, they were not a curse.

They were a gift.
I just had to survive.

CHAPTER 132

I looked up at my hands, clinging onto the metal pole and saw my grip slide down slightly. The subway train overhead eventually passed, but its quaking had already done its damage. I looked underneath my tennis shoes and saw the clapping waves a mere twenty feet below. The black abyss scared the life out of me.

"Please!" I begged. "Help me!" My fingers slid until only a few tips touched the cold silver pole.

"We're coming, Solo! Hang on!" Elizabeth shouted, causing a wave of hope to spring up, but my body weighed it down.

I looked up and saw the moon. It was beautiful, appearing heavenly. I wondered if this was the last image I'd see before I met my Maker. I started to yell that I was falling when I felt a pair of warm hands wrap around my wrist. They tried to hoist me up.

"We got you, man! We got you!" Wint said, smiling as he looked down into my tear-filled eyes. I tried to remain calm, but on the inside, I was bawling like a baby. They were heaving me up when I felt something slip from underneath. I turned my head down to see my flashlight flipping like an Olympic diver. It caused a small splash when it hit the water.

"What?" Elizabeth teased gently as she caught sight of my wet eyes. "Thankful?"

I thought for a split second. Yes, I was much more than thankful, and they all knew it. I just didn't know what I was more thankful for. Thankful for life, thankful for them, or thankful for the life that I had with them? By the expression on each of their faces, I knew they were feeling the same self-worth at that moment. We had each saved one another this week, in one way or another. I wiped my tear away. "I just bought that flashlight."

CHAPTER 133

The four of us walked back to our parked cars lining the deserted gravel path. Elizabeth and Wint helped to give me some stability before the next subway train passed.

"Just because you saved my life tonight doesn't mean I had to return the favor that quickly," Wint said, laughing as he gave me a brotherly hug. He handed me back my phone. "Love ya, man."

I didn't respond. My nerves were so on edge that I didn't know what to say, but Wint knew I loved him. We were more than just friends. We had a brotherly bond so the word love didn't need to be said. Although he said it far more often than me.

"Don't you ever scare us like that again, Solo!" Verny scolded like a caring mother. It was a tone that I had never heard her use toward me. I finally caught a peek of what Wint always saw in her. Her passion, when used for good, was very alluring.

"I promise," I said, raising a boy scout gesture realizing that it wasn't just her tone but something else in her language that startled me. "Did you just call me Solo?"

"Slip of the tongue," she said, smiling. I could see a faint tear in her eye before she wiped it away. "Allergies are messing with me tonight."

"Well, I won't tell anyone, Veronica," I responded. "No one would believe me."

"It'll be our little secret," she whispered in my ear before she gave me a warm peck on the cheek.

"If you ever want to tell me anything, Solo…" Wint started as he looked over at Elizabeth without finishing his thought. He was pretty sure we each got the point. "Come on," he said grabbing Veronica's hand. "It's time to go home." They each waved as they got into their BMW. Elizabeth and I stood beside our cars looking at Washington's skyline.

"It's unbelievable, isn't it?" she started.

"Yeah, it is a pretty sight."

"Not that, you moron," she laughed. "This! This here tonight."

"Yeah, pretty unbelievable," I agreed as I breathed deeply with relief. "No one would believe us."

We leaned on the trunk of my car in silence for a few minutes. I finally asked the question that had been nagging at my heart from the first time I heard her scream my name minutes earlier. "Why did you come?" I remembered she didn't feel that it was her responsibility to do anything with her dreams.

"Something in my gut told me I needed to do something."

"Your gut?"

"What, did you expect some Jeremiah-type answer?"

"I don't know. I just wondered what changed, that's all."

The breeze was cool, and she rubbed her arms for warmth. Sitting on a cold trunk wasn't making her any warmer. "You."

"Me? Why me?"

"Do I really have to say it?" she asked, rolling her eyes as she took a breath. "Because you showed me that one person can make a difference."

"Really? Was that hard to say? One person can make a difference?"

"You're pressing my buttons, Solomon," she growled as she looked away to try to find one of the common constellations.

"Now you're calling me Solomon. This must be hard for you," I said, laughing at how guarded she kept herself. "It's okay to say something nice to someone. It's not gonna kill you or make you less of a person. I mean, Veronica kissed me tonight."

"Don't compare me to her," she retorted with a sassy head bob. "Fine," she huffed as she stood on the edge of regret. "Want a kind word? Here it goes, but I'm only saying it once. Without you, Solo, who knows what the world would be like? You're selfless. You don't meet very many people like that."

"Wint's pretty selfless," I added quickly.

"Yeah, but I'm pretty sure you had something to do with that as well."

"Me? Wint's the all-star. I'm the nobody."

"I'm not so sure about that. You have something special. I've never met anyone else like me before. You're already better than me and you've only had these dreams for a few days."

I stammered, feeling uncomfortable with this dialogue centered on me. I jumped up from the trunk, dangling my car keys. "I better be heading home. I've got a busy week."

She agreed as she opened her car door with a faint yawn. "I was sleeping peacefully tonight before the dream I had of you. And then that happened and messed up my REM cycle. I hope you can live with yourself."

"Whatever, Miss Priss! What have you got to do tomorrow? Volunteer for just a few hours at the school?" She smiled at the comment as I returned a friendly wink. "And you know I wasn't fishing for a compliment. I was just trying to…"

"Yeah, yeah, yeah, I know. Selfless Solo." She got into her car about to shut it as she quickly spit out, "Oh, and by the way, I think you are getting these dreams because of me. 'Night."

I stood surprised as I watched her drive toward the ramp to get back on the bridge to head to D.C. I didn't understand how it was her fault, but if getting these dreams saved my best friend's life, I would take them as a gift from God.

CHAPTER 134

"You're coming over, right? Veronica wanted to make sure," Wint asked as I threw my textbook on the kitchen table. It landed beside an opened envelope.

"Yes, I will be there. Six, right?"

"See you then."

I got off the phone, catching my reflection in the oven's glass. I hoped that my appearance would be approved. Even though Veronica had softened up, she still had some of her high standards that I had to try to adhere to. The key word was *try*. I turned to leave when the opened envelope caught my attention. I opened it and reread the letter that was sent from the City Department of the District of Columbia.

Dear Mr. Davis,

It has come to our attention that you played a crucial part in the capturing of Alexei Lechkov and Jennifer Ascot. We will protect your wishes to remain anonymous, but we are pleased to reward you with a small token of our appreciation. Thank you for your service to our community.

Sincerely,

Mayor William Ernst

I picked up the check again feeling the indigo blue ink of $50,000. I didn't know what I should do. I didn't feel like I deserved the check. I definitely didn't ask for it, but I knew that if I didn't cash it, I would be hounded by a few people. I stuffed the check back in the envelope making a mental note to take it to the bank sometime this week to deposit it into the same account that held Chelsea's life insurance money. I took another look at the check and smiled at the good fortune I had, not in wealth, but in life. It wasn't every day I got a check made payable to Solomon "Solo" Davis.

A text appeared on my phone. *You still meeting me later at the corner of Constitution and Louisiana around 10:30?*

If last week was interesting, this week was getting close to topping it. After almost a lifetime of watching on the sidelines, that night on the bridge opened Elizabeth's eyes to the gift that she had but wasn't using.

I'll be there, partner, I replied as I smiled, realizing what I had been missing in the last few years of my lonely existence. It was funny, really. It took a near-death experience to open my eyes at how fragile and important life was. If I had not ever been given the gift of dreaming my own potential death, I may not have ever started living life to my full potential.

No matter how chaotic the last two weeks had been, I wouldn't have changed a thing. I may have had a little more stress and pressure, but I also had a few more shoulders to lean on during those times.

Elizabeth was turning into a sister I never had, or even knew I wanted. She could put me in my place with a snap of her finger. Chelsea would have liked her too.

ADDITIONAL BOOKS

Mystery and Suspense

Solomon's Dreams 2 – Preying for Revenge
Solomon's Dreams 3 – The Price of Freedom

Intertwined

Bethany, Mississippi, is a quaint, step-back-in-time type of town, where its only protection is the symbolic white picket fences. But even small communities have big secrets. Even the perfect family. And their white picket fences can't protect them from the tragedies that lurk around the corner.

When a mysterious stranger saves a young girl from drowning in a secluded river, the question rises is he trustworthy or not? Where did he come from? Why does he keep hanging around the twelve-year-old girl he saved?

This tight-knit community is connected by more than their zip code. Their lives and secrets are woven into a tapestry of heartache and pain. As life unravels, there is a common thread that holds them all together. It's their decision to grab onto it or let it choke them.

What other secrets are they hiding?
Are any worth killing or dying for?

Inspirational

Dream Chases: A Journey of Faith

We all have a dream
We all have a purpose
It's time to use your dream to fulfill your purpose

We were created to dream, but so often we lose the childlike innocence of dreaming of things to come. This book is a compelling reminder that God has an incredible purpose for everyone's life. The Bible is filled with stories of people following their dreams — walking to freedom through a sea, defeating giants with mere pebbles, or watching loved ones be healed. These people dreamed big dreams, but not from their own imagination or merit. No, God ordained these great men and women of faith to chase their dreams, just as He still does today. In this captivating book, mystery and inspirational author, Eric Suddoth engages dreamers to begin a journey they were destined to walk.

First steps are always scary, but we are on this journey together. It's time to be Dream Chasers.

Unsung

Within these pages is a deeply intimate work of praise-filled poems, heartfelt prayers, reflections on hard lessons learned and hopeful reminders of God's infinite love and mercy. Each of these writings may not have been intended to become a song, but somehow found themselves, sometimes years later, sung behind my piano or guitar. The majority of these songs have only been sung from the safe confines of my home. Until recently, I believed these writings were just cherished moments between me and God. That is until now.

This book is decades in the making.

A book I never intended to publish.

Come and prayerfully meditate over these words. I pray that this book will bring a blessing to you and that God will sing over you as He originally sung them over me.

www.ingramcontent.com/pod-product-compliance
Lightning Source LLC
Chambersburg PA
CBHW031212050726
47495CB00017B/243